Books of Merit

The Glass Harmonica

ALSO BY RUSSELL WANGERSKY

The Hour of Bad Decisions
Burning Down the House

THE
GLASS
HARMONICA

RUSSELL WANGERSKY

THOMAS ALLEN PUBLISHERS

TORONTO

Library and Archives Canada Cataloguing in Publication

Wangersky, Russell, 1962–
The glass harmonica : a novel / Russell Wangersky.

ISBN 978-0-88762-524-4

I. Title.

PS8645.A5333G53 2010   C813'.6   C2009-907219-X

Editor: Janice Zawerbny
Jacket design: Bill Douglas
Jacket image: istockphoto

Published by Thomas Allen Publishers,
a division of Thomas Allen & Son Limited,
145 Front Street East, Suite 209,
Toronto, Ontario M5A 1E3 Canada

www.thomas-allen.com

The publisher gratefully acknowledges the support of
The Ontario Arts Council for its publishing program.

We acknowledge the support of the Canada Council for the Arts, which
last year invested $20.1 million in writing and publishing throughout Canada.

We acknowledge the Government of Ontario through the
Ontario Media Development Corporation's Ontario Book Initiative.

We acknowledge the financial support of the Government
of Canada through the Book Publishing Industry Development
Program (BPIDP) for our publishing activities.

10 11 12 13 14 15   5 4 3 2 1

Printed and bound in Canada

For Leslie . . . finally.

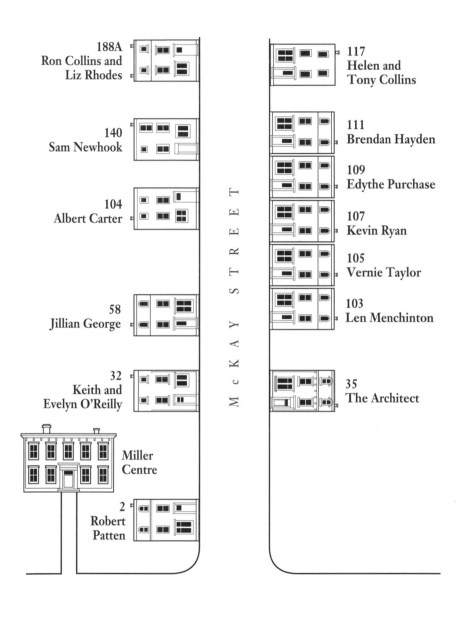

188A
Ron Collins and
Liz Rhodes

140
Sam Newhook

104
Albert Carter

58
Jillian George

32
Keith and
Evelyn O'Reilly

Miller
Centre

2
Robert
Patten

M c K A Y S T R E E T

117
Helen and
Tony Collins

111
Brendan Hayden

109
Edythe Purchase

107
Kevin Ryan

105
Vernie Taylor

103
Len Menchinton

35
The Architect

The Glass Harmonica

32
McKay Street

KEITH O'REILLY

FEBRUARY 11, 2006

MOST PEOPLE just don't know how to look—and if they do know how to look, they don't know how to remember. They get stuff stuck up there in their heads and forget about it back there, just wasting it. They can't see things and keep them handy. Me, I do both. I can close my eyes and tell you every single thing there is to see here: six margarine tubs with nails, five of them yellow and one white from the time I bought the wrong kind. I won't forget that in a hurry. They're all above the workbench on a narrow shelf I built, set up high enough so there's space underneath.

The white tub, that's ring nails for drywall. They don't even use ring nails anymore, they use drywall screws and cordless drills instead. It's faster, and a better job—but if you've got to tack in just a little piece, like getting in at pipes under a sink or something, ring nails work just fine. I can tell you about the space heater, out here in the add-on next to the house, because there's no heat out here otherwise, and about the radio I got, an old-fashioned brown one with a light behind the big

1

circular dial. I don't really listen to it as much as let it play on in the background.

It's the only part of the house that's really mine, one small piece of McKay Street that belongs to me, to Keith O'Reilly. Just one small piece of McKay Street where nobody else goes. Even Evelyn doesn't come out here anymore—forty years we've been married, and we've found a way to circle around each other without crashing into ourselves. I heard her tell a friend once that we wouldn't like the moon much either if it kept swooping in and almost smacking into the earth. That's Evelyn in a nutshell: sometimes, it makes more sense talking to the cat.

I built the add-on myself, did the framing-up and the roof and the clapboard on a long weekend at the end of August almost thirty years ago now, eye on the street in case there was a city inspector driving around or something. Made crooks of us all, the city has. The weekend comes and I can see all the neighbours loading up as if they were smugglers, hauling in all kinds of construction contraband. Sheetrock and big heavy boxes of spackling mud, and every now and then even bathtubs and toilets. Two-by-fours and two-by-sixes going in basement doors, and you'd swear the whole neighbourhood was owned by the guys who showed up in their battered vans and pickups, lugging saws and extension cords into every house on the street. Gypsy contractors, we used to say, but you can't get away with that anymore—said it a few years ago when the Roses were over, and Evelyn's mouth got so big and round you'd swear her nose was going to fall right down in the hole. Then, just like that, she sealed it up into that tight line and the corners of her eyes came right down. After, when we were putting away dishes, she told me you don't say "gypsy" now, but I don't see what the big deal is.

Like I said, I didn't need a contractor, as much as I need everyone to just mind their own business. Whole workshop is only about four feet wide, and it runs the length of the house all the way to the back wall. I've got an old door on the front cut in half, so I can lock the bottom and swing the top open in summer, lets the air in without letting neighbours get too familiar, if you know what I mean. Got a big vise on the end of the bench, and a spot to pile the empty beer cases—Evelyn doesn't like them in the house, and I can usually sneak a few more than she knows when I'm out here in the summer. No phone, though— probably should have had a phone, but then it's just going to ring and everything, someone trying to sell me insurance or make me get a new credit card or something.

Summertime, it's dark inside and the air's a little cooler, and no one really sees me back there in the shadows unless they know I'm there already. Not like down the street. There's a guy down there, Brendan Hayden, sits in the front bedroom upstairs with his computer lighting the whole place up like he was a lighthouse, all alone and guiding in the ships. He doesn't get it—can't see himself, I guess. That's the difference—the difference between being and seeing. When it's dark, I've got a scrap of cloth up there for a curtain, just enough of a scrim to let me have some privacy. Tourists walk by and I get scraps of their conversations: "It's so beautiful, the houses so close together and so colourful," and "I can imagine living here, can't you?" even though they don't know a damn thing about the sloppy nastiness of St. John's in March.

Runners go by, mostly in the evenings, and I feel sorry for the young guys, pounding along out there even though they're gonna get old anyway, and I can watch the women's asses—back out of sight, you can stare all you want. And sometimes I work on projects—I took the whole ball valve assembly apart on the toilet when it used to run all the time, and I packed the spaces in the shed with insulation and put up vapour barrier. I'll do the last of the drywall too, when I get around to it. The full sheets are heavy, especially for a seventy-year-old retired dockworker, and I'm not as steady on my feet as I once was. Built a thing once so that Evelyn could press a button and a little light would come on out on the workbench to let me know if it was suppertime or she just needed me in the house and I was lost in whatever I was doing out there. Should have thought about that a bit more—it's like building a leash for yourself—but at the time, it beat having her come out to find me whenever she wanted something.

3

Mostly, I nurse a beer or two and tinker away, taking stuff apart and piecing it back together, working my way through the day, waiting for the kid with the newspaper and the mailman, even though there isn't much mail. Pension cheques, the electric bill, the occasional letter— everything you'd expect, but still I get a little jolt when I hear the lid drop back down after the postman goes by the door. Used to be around ten in the morning, but now it's not until after noon, and I'm not sure if they changed the route around or if we just have a lazy mailman. Guy's got a face on him like an old boot, makes me wish I had a dog just so the thing could bark loud inside the door and give him a start.

It's easier to work in the summertime: there's always a reason to pry the lid off the trim paint and see if it's set up solid yet, and I can get at the sides of the house to the outside plug, set up the ladder for the eavestroughs and things like that.

February, it's harder. Lots of things I should have done—lots of things Evelyn always wants done—but I leave stuff too long, and once there's snow in the air, there's a bunch of things that can't get done and just stare you in the face until May. Trim around the door that's primed, not painted, and no one would be able to see it from the street, but Evelyn can tell just from the difference in the shine—the primer flat white, the rest of the door frame semigloss—and I can imagine the look she'd get on her face if she noticed.

In February, sometimes you just make work for yourself. One day, I'd taken out a couple of big ice cream tubs full of stuff—you know, the extra screws and nuts and bolts and nails you end up with, scattered bits of metal and pieces of electrical gear, the screws that once held the washer in the crate it was delivered in, the latch and the hinges from the old gate, that kind of stuff—and I was sorting it out, figuring which pieces should go into each of the smaller tubs and boxes. There's a secret pleasure in it, really, like I'm the only one who knows the code. It's a bunch of junk, but I recognize the old brass pressure valve I took off the water heater when the tank blew ten years ago and Evelyn found a big puddle reaching out across the flat of the kitchen linoleum, and the knobs from the first television we ever bought. I thought they might come in handy somewhere. There are three or four of those fragile mercury switches from thermostats, the little glass containers where you tip 'em and the mercury flows over and completes the circuit. Holding them in my hands, I could almost smell the furnace coming on. Didn't feel right about throwing them out, and I saw a movie once where terrorists used them to trigger bombs. They should be wrapped in paper towel and put in a hard-sided box so nothing can shift and crush them like eggshells.

That's the kind of work that's good in February, when the days are short and it's bitter outside anyways. Pick up the right scrap of something and it can send you back to a summer years before, the way picking up a can of fungicide, that bitter dry-bones poisonous smell, reminds you of rose bushes.

The heater was cranked right up behind me, and I could feel the heat of it on the backs of my legs, the fan battering the hot air against me. After I got the heater, I read on the box that it had to be "two feet away from any combustible surface." But two feet away really means one foot and someone just covering their ass. Two feet away from me and I wouldn't even be able to feel it, not the way you should feel heat right into your bones, and an old guy deserves a little comfort wherever he can find it.

When I started sorting, it was still light and it wasn't snowing yet, the sky that kind of slate grey that says the bad weather's already looming over you but it doesn't have the guts to just get on with it already. Weatherman had said there'd be snow, a fair amount of snow, and you could tell it by the traffic, by the way it had thinned right out, no one driving unless they really had to. Soon there'd be snow all over and you'd hear the taxis coming, spinning on their bad bald tires, engines revving too high with frustrated feet on the pedal.

I'd pile the bits in groups of similar parts, pick out the screws and nails and put them in their proper places, find the occasional unfamiliar scrap and dig around in my brain trying to figure out what it was and where it had come from. I'm not one of those people who goes around to yard sales and buys up tubs of other people's scrap—

no, all of this was my own, so every piece had its own little history.

I don't know how long I was sitting like that when I realized all at once how foolish it would look from outside, an old man sorting useless scraps of metal and staring off into space like someone's reached in and shut his brain off completely. And the day had gone away into night, and the snow had come straight down the road in a wave, the wind trying each door on both sides of the street as it passed.

Even in the darkness the snow still has shape, whorls and columns and devils that build and fall away, and I lifted a corner of the small curtain on the window so I could watch the sheets and eddies of snow and try to decide if they're just passing squalls or the kind of snow that will fall all night, packing in tight against the front door. The kind I'd end up having to shovel, wondering each time if now was the time when my heart was going to simply pick up and just stop.

Across at 35 McKay, where the architect lives, there was a small foreign car—it's almost always foreign cars now—parked on the side of the road, its engine running, exhaust white, the headlights catching handfuls of blowing snow. There was someone in the front seat, but not the driver: the driver was out of the car and up at the front door, right in the architect's face. Strange guy, the architect, a nice-enough fella but sort of distant, as if he wasn't really talking to you as much as he was making fun of you back there inside his head.

Then, all at once, the driver from the car was hitting the architect, over and over, hitting him like some kind of crazy man, short, sharp, accurate punches. Hard punches, too. I've thrown one or two punches like that myself, so I could imagine the jarring force of them, the way, when you connect with your fist, it travels all the way up to your elbow like an electric shock.

And the architect—I wish his name would come to me—wasn't swinging back at all, in fact he was barely getting his hands up in front of him as the other guy whaled away, and as soon as that, the architect was down in the snow and the other guy had picked up a snow shovel from next to the door. And watching it was sort of strange, like watching television or something, especially when the shovel blade broke off the handle and flew out into the street, more like a prop than a shovel. Then just the handle, up and down, but fast. I reached for the doorknob then, but my hand stopped before it closed around the metal— in fact, before it even touched the knob—so that it was half clutching at air.

And then the other guy was heading back for his car, and I ducked down because he was looking back towards our house, scanning the whole neighbourhood, and just before I got down below the edge of the window frame I saw it was the pizza guy, that Collins kid, I don't know his first name but I knew his father, lived down the street before he got fired from the city.

Maybe I should have done something before then, but a seventy-year-old man against some crazy young guy with a shovel? Besides, it was all over before I would have been able to get across the street anyway, and it was pretty obvious that the guy had to be dead. Not my job to get involved, two guys got a problem with each other—but no one wants to be left knocked out on the ground in a blizzard, either. You gotta deal with your problems, and you take care of your own—that's the way it's supposed to work. And then Evelyn was flicking the light on and off behind me like it must be bedtime, and you can tell that she's angry or pissed off or she's been calling for a while and I just didn't notice, because there's barely a second between each flash. Blink-blink, blink-blink, over and over again.

I knew, if I went in and told her, Evelyn would want me to call the cops. I know she would—but I don't like talking to the cops and I never have. I worry that they might have questions about why a guy would spend so much time looking out the door at his neighbours. No one wants to get a reputation as a busybody, after all. In my head, I could hear the way she'd keep at me about it, and I knew she wouldn't let go. But I also knew I'd end up telling her sometime anyway, because what else are you going to do?

I called them from the kitchen, but the truth is that the police hardly took me seriously, and it seemed like fifteen minutes or more before a police car nosed its way quietly through the snow. By then, the snow was coming down hard, and I could barely see the guy on the ground, just a hump in the snow like someone's put their garbage out the night before and now the garbage truck driver's never going to be able to find it. Snow coming down so fast that everything is new again right away. The cop got out and looked around for a minute, tried the front door at 35 and opened it, sticking his head in the door, slow and nonchalant, and I thought I was going to have to go over and show him where the guy was. But then he poked away in the snow next to the door and started talking on his radio right sharp. Then, in a big rush, there were cops all over, and two of them, plainclothes guys with big hands and sharp questions, came over to talk to me.

I took them back to my workshop, to show them where I was looking from and what I could see, and besides, why have the cops getting Evelyn all worked up and everything? She wouldn't have seen anything anyway—I could see the light from the television in the living room when I was on the phone, and once she's sunk deep into the TV, there's not much that's going to get her attention short of another world war.

The cops wanted to know a lot of stuff, like the make of the car and what the guy was wearing, but they just sort of stopped when I said, "It's the Collins kid from Superior Pizza," and after that it was like they weren't even taking notes anymore. It was almost as if they were deflated or something, as if they were working up to solve a case that turned out to be all too easy in the end.

After the cops walked back across the street, I went into the house to tell her, ready for her to think that I did the right thing, but also that I could have done it a little quicker. They'd got the lights all set up at 35 McKay like it was a movie set or something, so bright that the edges of the window ledges on the front of the house were casting sharp shadows as dark as smudges of soot. Grown men down on their hands and knees, sifting through the snow like kids playing in the sandbox, with their cars shunted in next to the curb even though we're on a snow route and there's not supposed to be any parking there anyway. Cops make their own rules when they want to. It's supposed to be a tow-away zone—not that they'll be towed away—and the plows will end up making a mess of the whole street because of it.

Evelyn was in her chair in the living room, like always. Bob Barker and *The Price Is Right* is her favourite, and she was watching it on the Edmonton station. Thank God for cable.

I can't stand that show, but she's been watching since before Barker's hair turned white, and she's settled away in there like she always is, her chair almost square in front of the television, the sound up on bust. The world's not right now, not with *Price Is Right* on all hours of the day and night. With the different time zones, you could be watching the afternoon soaps right up until you go to bed, and watching them all over again the moment you got up. It's just not the way it's supposed to be, that's all I can say.

She didn't even hear me come in, and I could see the white hair on the back of her head, the hair on the top lit by the changing colours of the television, and her hand still flicking the switch back and forth, back and forth, and I knew that out in the shed it must look like some kind of carnival show, only the one light left in the place and it keeps going on and off, on and off, like a ringing phone that no one ever picks up. And all at once I think back to the shed, of how I must have been silhouetted there, that flashing light drawing attention the way flashing lights always do. A bald, bent old man, caught in the act of lifting up a corner of a curtain like some nosy spinster aunt. And I realized that the Collins kid probably should have known that I could see him out there.

Evelyn's legs aren't as strong as they were—sometimes her knees just buckle and she goes down in slow motion, her housecoat out all around her like the petals of a flower, her muscles trying to take the weight and just fading away. So I help her up and down the hall, like to the bathroom or the bedroom—the house is all on one level, at least there's that, and I think like I always do that we're like the blind leading the blind.

Except she's not blind at all, she can see as well as anyone. She just can't speak is all, and hasn't since the stroke—I imagine the words are all in there, piling up on themselves like people at a dance club trying desperately to get away from a fire through a locked exit door. Doctors say she's deaf in one ear, too, but I'm darned if I can tell how they figured that out, because she's always angled her head at you when you're talking, like a parrot trying to figure out what two words will make its owner hand it a cracker.

And I don't know why, but I feel guilty. I think it's because I always thought it would be me—I'm the one with the bad habits, the one who drank more, who didn't even give up smoking until the doctor and Evelyn got together and gave me an ultimatum seven or eight years ago. Still, she's the one who needs the shoulder to lean on going up to bed, and now that I'm thinking about cigarettes again, I remember the pack I've still got tucked away out in the shed for when I just gotta have one, when it feels like my skin is just going to crawl right off me, and I wonder what it is I think I'm saving my health for now, anyway.

The cops told me they'd pick up the Collins kid, so I've got nothing to worry about even if he did see me. At the same time, I can't help but hope he has a little while out there, still on the run. I picture him running, looking back over his shoulder, mouth open, sucking in big gulps of air, young and strong and fast and alive. Out on the run while he can still run. I don't know why I even think about it.

Later, in our bedroom, lying on my back, I can see through a small gap in the curtains that the snow is coming down again, gentle and light and orange in the street lights, falling the way that snow's always supposed to fall. The room is quiet, and everything—the pictures, the plants, the few little pieces of jewellery I've been able to afford to give her over the years—is in the right place, each one in the place where Evelyn decided it should go.

And there is no 35 McKay Street, there's just this room and the ticking heaters and the way things are supposed to be.

And Evelyn's rolled over on her side, back on to me.

I can put a hand between her shoulder blades, her lying there, and she shifts back against me and I know she's the same Evelyn she's always been. You can look at her and not realize it, but like I've always said, people look at a lot of things and then don't remember anything about them either.

Eventually, her breathing goes long and even, with the familiar hint of a half snore that's been bothering me for more years than I can count, and I know she's asleep.

Then, I can sleep too.

35
McKay Street

RON COLLINS

FEBRUARY 11, 2006

HOURS EARLIER, when the snow hadn't really started in earnest yet, Ron Collins watched the tall girl kicking the other one in front of the Supreme Court—kicking the one who was down on the ground shrieking, the swear words carrying easily through the closed windows of the car.

"I get up, I'll fucking pound ya," the one on the ground was yelling. "I'll show ya, ya fucking skank."

He watched, half interested, half bored—but the pizzas were getting cold. So Ron reached down to put the Tercel into gear, and Liz reached across from the passenger seat and held his arm just above the wrist, stopping him. "No," she said, her voice strangely eager, almost breathless.

It was almost fully dark by then, the big stone court building looming over the girls and throwing long, inky shadows. The snow was coming down in thin scrims in front of the street lights, softening all the angles, smoothing lines.

It wasn't softening the sight of the two fighting girls. Across from them, two teenaged boys were sitting on a low wall next to the courthouse steps, watching too. Probably the boyfriends, Ron thought, although neither of the two was doing anything to break up the fight. He had been startled at how wild the two girls had been when it started, hands and feet going, both of them beyond caring how it looked. The one in the long coat had gotten tangled up and had fallen flat on her back before the kicking started. But Ron knew he couldn't stay, no matter how much Liz wanted him to. The car didn't like idling, not on cold nights. The beaten-up Toyota was running rough and threatening to stall already. Then there'd be the trouble of getting it started again, the pizzas would be cold, and Louis would be right in his face, telling him, "There are plenty of people looking for work in this city," and his favourite, "I can replace you just like this," followed by a snap of his flour-covered fingers.

Before they'd stopped at the courthouse traffic lights, Liz had been drawing happy faces on the condensation on the side window. The car heater seemed to have a mind of its own, and most of the time the air coming out of the vents was as cold and damp as if it had come straight in off the harbour. Ron watched her out of the corner of his eye, trying to remember the next address without opening the pizza bag and letting any of the heat out, trying hard not to be conspicuous as he looked across at her. Liz was beautiful, he thought. Beautiful in a strange way, really, a narrow face with a thin, small nose and overfull lips, at the same time with a pronounced underbite that could make her look feral and somehow slightly dangerous. She had never mastered wearing her feelings on the inside instead of bare across her face, and Ron knew there were a thousand things right there that would tell him how she felt, long before she ever got around to telling him in words.

Like the way it was all right when she was drawing happy faces. If she got bored enough, the happy faces would turn their lips down, sad at first, then angry-looking, and he knew from experience if she started drawing handguns or round-looking spaceships—jagged space rays shooting outwards from their noses—there wouldn't be any chance that later he'd get to slip his hands inside the tight top of her jeans. If she got bored enough, she'd turn inwards first, and then start lashing out. How she couldn't believe how stupid he was, how she couldn't believe she'd ended up stuck with someone like him, that she'd wound up tooling around through the cold of a St. John's winter in a junky pizza delivery car.

It was worse because it was February, and the snow was always coming, lashing down for a few minutes in angry little warning flurries that disappeared as soon as they arrived, whipping out of side streets in curling, tight bursts. Always waiting to just rush down on you out of any one of a row of leaden-grey days. It was February, right in the guts of winter, he thought. Not enough had gone by, and there was still so much to come—the inevitable March wet, the April snowstorms, the heavy, sticky spring snow that packed tight like concrete under the car. No, Ron thought, February was the worst of it, when you're tired of it already and there's not even one scrap of light at the end of the tunnel.

It had been all right in the summertime.

They'd been going out seriously for a few months then after a couple of years of on-and-off, and it had all been a laugh, driving all hours of the warm nights with the windows down. Summer, when, if you were lucky, the last order on the run was a four a.m. house party where nobody minded if a pair of strangers stayed on and partied too.

Once, he and Liz had fucked on a bath mat in someone's huge bathroom, the door locked, bladder-swollen beer drinkers on the other side trying the doorknob again and again. Inside, both of their heads kept banging against the side of the bathtub, and they couldn't stop laughing. Later, they'd turned down slices of the same pizza they'd delivered, having lost their appetite watching Louis sweating over the pizza an hour earlier, hard at work with almost his whole upper body over the outspread dough. And when they'd left, they'd both talked about the bathroom, the taps, the huge hot tub—the way the bathroom alone was big enough to cover half of their entire apartment.

Even coming home after daybreak wasn't bad, the heat having fallen away, so that they could wake up in the middle of the afternoon, still twined around each other like tree roots. He could remember falling asleep with the liquid burble of the robins loud in the brightening dark, the sky shifting up from black into a rich, deep and promising blue.

But the winter was harder, working all the time with the headlights on, a whole shift of unremitting night. One headlight had blown in the third week of January and there wasn't enough money to buy a replacement, so that driving the car was like driving with one eye closed. The colder it got, the more Liz sank into her seat and the door on her side of the car, wrapping her arms around her chest. Ron kept telling her that she could stay home in the apartment, but she wouldn't. "We'll get turned all around," she said, arms moving, hands pulled back into the sleeves of her sweater. "I'll be sleeping nights, you'll be sleeping days, and pretty soon it will only be breakfast, dinner and sleep. And what's the point of that?"

It made sense—he had to admit it. But she looked wretched in the car, especially in the big snowstorms. Ron loved the big snowstorms, when everyone was wishing they'd bought that expensive four-wheel drive, when cars were being abandoned on the crosstown arterial by drivers with shit for brains. In whiteouts and deep fresh snow, he loved how the Tercel kept chewing its way along, the tires as bald as they could be, the car moving only because he knew it so well, because he could feel the wheels starting to slip and knew when to hit the gas and when to back off. Delivering pizzas to the stormbound, to houses with buried cars and new snow tires and not two ounces of common sense to rub together. It was as if he were shouting out at the windows that he didn't need their money, that he could get by just fine without it.

Snowy nights, and the sky would turn matte orange and flat with the reflected glow of the street lights. The streets would lie empty and quiet, and even if it was cold, he'd run with the windows down sometimes to clear the condensation, looking for the blue flickering reflection of the snowplow flashers rumbling up the side streets, trying to hook up with a city plow going in the same direction. It made Ron feel like he should have one hand out the window, waving to the passersby struggling through the snowbanks on foot. Like he was the featured attraction in a parade. It wasn't the same for Liz: often he'd come back with the tip money and find her sound asleep against the door like some hypothermia victim on the very edge of icy death. He always wanted to shake her awake, just to be sure she was all right, but also so she wouldn't miss the way they were suddenly the centre of it all. Instead, he'd slide the car into gear gently and try to get it going and back into the middle of the street without the tires slipping, so the car wouldn't lurch or buck and wake her up.

35 McKay Street—the architect—must have been looking out of his window, Ron thought. Big blue house, clapboard, all tricked out with multicoloured trim. Ron hadn't even touched the doorbell when the door started to open. That's when people usually yell at you, saying you're late, Ron knew. And he thought, like he'd been thinking all night, that he shouldn't have stopped to watch the fighting girls at the court, because the lectures just weren't worth it. But it turned out the guy was just eager.

"Gotta pay you in coin," he said. "All I've got. It's twenty-one dollars, right? Here's twenty-six." He had both hands full of loose change, quarters and dollars all tumbled in together, like he was daring Ron to stop and count them.

"Pizza delivery guys and taxi drivers, we all like change," Ron said, and he could feel himself grinning for no reason. It made him angry, wondering if 35 McKay was looking at his teeth. Ron could feel his lips tightening, pulling closed again—he wanted to tell the guy that they had met before, wanted to ask him, "Don't you remember me? Don't you remember?" but he didn't.

35 McKay was grinning back, with his own two rows of even white teeth. Ron thought he could feel Liz's eyes on his back, and he wondered if she was comparing the two of them somehow. Ron knew he was taller and fitter: 35 McKay was a dumpy soft guy with a big gut and an expensive-looking haircut. 35 McKay smiled too fucking much, too.

Ron could feel the muscles tensing in his arms. He shook his head, trying to clear his thoughts. It felt like it was too late to still be on the road, and it was altogether too cold. Maybe it was the fight they'd seen earlier that had him all shaken up—the strange sense there was about it, out in the open and with no one moving a muscle to stop the girls from hurting each other. Or maybe it was just something like an exhaust leak in the back of the Tercel—maybe that was what was making his head feel the size of a watermelon.

He went back to the car and reached over to Liz's window without stopping to count the money, knocked on the glass with two knuckles. Liz rolled the window down and he handed her the change. Her hands were white and cold-looking when he dropped the loose change into them, but she didn't drop even one coin. He liked that—she was always ready, ready for anything.

But suddenly there was something he didn't like: perhaps it was the way she was looking past him, her eyes level with his hip. Maybe she likes this end of McKay Street, he thought. The expensive end. Maybe she liked something about number 35, about the solid, warm yellow light that hung on the dark blue clapboard next to the glass front door, about the long, warm yellow hallway stretching back. He could hardly imagine what it would be like in there. But Liz could. He saw she had found a distant, almost sleepy smile as he walked around the front of the car to climb back in. He turned towards her as he closed his door, and he noticed her hips were just settling back into the seat. Pulling away from the curb, he threw the car too quickly into gear and the back wheels dug down and hit asphalt. And then Liz brought up one white hand and wiped all the condensation away from the side window with one quick sweep, happy faces and all, and she turned in her seat and looked back towards the house until they took the next corner.

The pizza shop was hot and damp and spare: Louis had never bothered to put anything up on the walls, because there were only the three small red tables, and nobody ever sat at them unless they were waiting for takeout or buying a single slice. Down-in-the-mouth guys looking for a little warmth, the big pizza oven's heat going right into their cores until Louis pointed at the No Loitering sign and yelled at them to "shift their ass."

Ron dumped the change onto the counter, spread it out. And it was not twenty-six at all—eighteen dollars, no tip, in fact three dollars short for the pizza in the first place.

"That's money you'll make up," Louis shouted from the other side of the counter. Louis was a big man, all in white, and he had patches of flour on his forearms and his face. Ron knew from experience that the flour gathered anywhere Louis sweated. Winter or summer, Ron knew, Louis sweated—only more in summer.

"You'll make it up, 'cause he shorted you, not me," Louis said, shrugging, and he turned to put another pizza into the big oven. "Mebbe now you learn to count." The heat roiled out of the open door of the oven in a wave.

But Ron had already turned his back, was already on his way out the door.

The Tercel fishtailed in the snow, going downhill too fast. Liz was huddled tight against her door, as if forced there, a tight dark bundle of winter jacket, not talking. He could only see the back of her head, the fine hair above her collar, hair he knew was impossibly soft to the touch. He didn't reach across to feel it.

And then he was banging on the door of 35 McKay. That pretty glass door, he thought, that door with the frosted design over part of the glass. And there were still lights on in the back of the house: he could see a sliver of kitchen down the long hallway, a white coffee maker, and he could see someone coming towards him, backlit and black against the kitchen lights. And he could feel himself winding up tight like a spring, so that his hands—bundled almost without thinking into fists—felt oddly heavy hanging down by his sides.

"You stiffed me, smartass." Ron said it as soon as the other man opened the door. "Twenty-six dollars, you said. Like there was enough there, like there was a five-dollar tip in there."

"There was twenty-six dollars," 35 McKay said, looking puzzled.

"There was, was there?" Ron knew he was smiling now, not caring about his teeth, a wild, broad grin as the architect dug himself in deeper. "Think I can't count, do you." He said it flat, so that it wasn't a question, so that there wasn't any sort of possible answer.

But 35 McKay tried anyway. "Of course you can count . . ." he started, his voice falling, calming, trying to mollify. He stepped out though the door, but Ron wasn't waiting anymore. He grabbed the man by his shoulders and pushed him hard back against the clapboard.

"I'll get you fired," 35 McKay said, trying to twist out of Ron's hands.

"Like I care about that," Ron said. "Like I'm not almost fired every night." He wasn't letting go, and the snow had started to fall more heavily, coiling around and flattening sounds. Ron was thumping the man softly, rhythmically, against the front of his own house. A car came down the street, cautious, its headlights probing out ahead. But the car didn't slow down, just kept going on its way.

In the Tercel, Liz was keeping a circle of glass carefully clear with the sleeve of her jacket. 35 McKay pointed over Ron's shoulder. "Her," he said, still trying to squirm out of Ron's grip. "Maybe your girlfriend took it," he said, looking over Ron's shoulder at Liz's face, round and white and indistinct behind the glass.

The man's voice was high now and shrill, because 35 McKay Street was obviously frightened. And for a moment a thin shadow of a memory ran through Ron's head: he was walking around the front of the car, looking through the windshield as Liz arched her hips upwards from the seat, straightening her body as if she had been pushing something into her front pocket. Ron had seen her hips lift like that a hundred times before, angling naked towards his own. The two images flicked back and forth in his mind—in the car, then Liz at home, smiling languidly, lifting her hips so he could slide off her underwear. It was confusing, and complicated. But it didn't matter.

"Just because you've got money doesn't mean you gotta right to steal more from me," Ron said, and then he hit the man in the side of the face with his fist—and the man sagged immediately, so it was like there was no satisfaction in it at all. Ron found himself holding the man up like a big sack of flour with his left arm while he kept hitting with his right, sometimes in the stomach, more often in the face, until finally the man fell right out of his grip.

Ron was breathing heavily by then, and the wind was rolling fast up the street, pushing loose snow in front of it so the lead edge of each gust looked like a wave reaching in over the cobble of a long, flat, empty beach. He still had one arm pulled back, ready to hit the man again if he even started to move. Ron looked back towards the car, and there was a happy face in the small circle that Liz had wiped clean of condensation. It was Liz's face. She was smiling, and, Ron thought, her teeth looked sharp—sharp like a weasel or a fox. Like she could bite— like she would bite and enjoy it, too. He could see the tip of her tongue darting out at the corner of her mouth, licking her lips. Two small round circles fogged the glass in front of her nostrils and faded, then fogged again.

There was a shovel next to the door, aluminum, painted dark red with a silver-coloured edge where the metal had worked through from scraping against the pavement. He picked the shovel up and started to hit the fallen man with it, over and over again, until the wooden handle broke and the blade of the shovel skittered off across the pavement and into the street. But Ron didn't stop, still swinging with the shovel handle. Hitting the man again and again, the man's skin splitting like a peach, blood breaking through. Then the shovel handle falling out of his hands as he turned and went back to the car.

After they pulled away, Liz grabbed Ron's right hand and pushed it between her legs, the muscles of her thighs tight. She held his hand pinned there, so that the Tercel whined high in second gear because he couldn't shift, the back end of the car swinging wildly. If I move my hand, Ron thought, I might even be able to feel the stolen change. But he kept his hand right where it was, looking in the mirror to see if anyone else was coming out through their doors, if there was anyone running to help or to try to catch the licence plate number. Ron couldn't remember if the light over the licence plate on the back of the Tercel was still broken. It probably was. But Ron didn't see anyone at all.

Behind them, the snow caught in the fallen man's eyelashes first. It caught in his eyelashes, so gently that the flakes could have been winked away with a single flutter of his eyelids. They melted when they landed on skin. For a while.

More snow fell, and the wind stacked the snowflakes gently against the front of the house.

As the back end of the car swung again, Ron thought about his parents, about what they'd say when he got caught and they found out. What his mom would say. His dad.

But his father didn't have the right to say anything, did he?

Tony fucking jailbird Collins wouldn't have the right to say anything to him at all.

117
McKay Street

TONY COLLINS

MAY 2, 2005

ALMOST a full year before that snowstorm, they had caught Tony with the back of his truck full of plywood. In the cab, Tony Collins kicked himself, because he knew—because he'd known all along—this was going to happen. That it was just a matter of time, a once-too-often-tried gamble, his own sort of Russian roulette.

Ten full sheets of three-quarter-inch, good-one-side, lying flat and heavy in the back and covered up with bags of garbage, and he'd already gotten a price for them, because he was going to sell them for cash on Warbury Street to a guy who was putting up framing to fix the foundation of his house. The gatehouse was the last thing between him and the money.

He tried to talk his way out of it at first, tried telling the guys in the gatehouse that he'd bought the plywood and just had it in the truck with him ahead of time when he'd come in for his shift, but then they shook their heads and walked around to show him where they'd marked every sheet, just a little black stripe across one corner with black Magic Marker, and then they held him at the gate, waiting for the police.

Every now and then, the guys in the gatehouse had looked straight across at him, their mouths turned down at the corners like they were having a hard time believing it, like it was the kind of expression they thought they were supposed to have.

In the truck, Tony could only sit and look down at the cracked blue plastic of the dashboard, reaching across with one finger and picking away at a spot where the plastic had blistered and split from sun and age.

He thought for a moment, just for one fleeting moment, about stomping on the gas pedal and running straight through the thin wooden arm of the gate, smashing through the alternating yellow and black stripes like they weren't even there. But they knew him anyway, so it wouldn't have made any difference, it would have just meant that the police would have come to his house, the front wheels of their cruiser crackling as they rolled up onto the loose gravel of the drive-way, and how stupid would that be? Making them come and find him, come and hunt him down, on the run for ten lousy sheets of plywood?

And even then Tony knew it wasn't as simple as the plywood. Because there was a zero-tolerance policy at the depot for stealing, a policy written right into the contract now in lawyer's language, so it was twenty-three years of driving plow in the winter, dump truck in the summer, all of it down the drain, and Helen was going to kill him, he thought, even if he really was doing it all for her.

When the police came, they'd be all set to write it all up in simple police shorthand. *Anthony David Collins, 54, of 177 McKay Street. Long-time employee of the City of St. John's, caught red-handed stealing city property*—he could see it like it was already written in the paper, just a couple of sentences, and the paper would be going into mailboxes all the way down the street.

It was the kind of case that would barely get a ripple of interest on the court docket, the courthouse regulars all gravitating towards the graphic testimony of sexual assaults or the gruesome violence of the occasional St. John's murder, almost always family members killing family members, or a fight that had started between friends in a kitchen. Once in a long while, stranger killing stranger.

Just the same, Tony knew it was the kind of case that marked the complete end of the way life used to be. The police report wouldn't explain anything, Tony thought, even if every single word on it was perfectly true. It wouldn't even begin to explain.

It wouldn't explain how Helen's dad, Mike Mirren, had left his only daughter 117 McKay when he died, that the house had been all paid off and Mike had been proud of that, but that now, almost inexplicably, it was carrying eighty thousand dollars in a mortgage in Helen's name, a mortgage that was pretty close to as much as the place was worth.

It wouldn't explain why Tony was running just as fast as he possibly could, every single day, and that there were only so many places money could come from before you wound up looking at stupid last resorts, at bad decisions made good by desperation.

At first, he'd taken every scrap of overtime he could get, driving the big green dump all night long for snow removal, up the sharp hills and then down again to the harbour to dump the snow from the blowers so the tide could carry it away, and then he'd fallen asleep one night and put the front end of the truck, with the big square rack for the plow, right through some guy's fence on the low side of Empire Avenue. It was a good thing the curbs were high there or, sound asleep behind the wheel, he would have gone into the guy's living room, Tony thought.

Two o'clock in the morning, and he had to stand outside and listen to the guy who owned the house screaming at him about his damned fence until the supervisor got there, the front end of Tony's truck stuck through the splintered pressure-treated lumber like a big green beetle eating a meal of sticks. The top of the fence, Tony noticed, cut in gingerbread curves, too fucking cute by half.

The supervisor, Ted Greenaway, slid out from behind the steering wheel of his pickup like his big belly had been greased, a huge round man who wobbled, balanced on two too-slender pins of legs. And Greenaway had spent years driving just like Tony, but they all knew he'd been looking for a supervisor's job all along, that he'd been looking for the little green pickup of his own for years, and that he'd sucked up to anyone he could until he finally got there.

Ted smoothed it over with the homeowner, told him "it was clear it was the driver's fault" and that the city's insurance adjuster would be by in the morning, and that accidents happen but "you wouldn't want us to just stop clearing the snow, now, would ya?" because Ted was good at that kind of thing, the words pouring out of him like it was some kind of heavy syrup, made thicker by the cold.

Ted had motioned at him to back the big truck out of the yard, and the last thing Tony saw as he pulled away from the curb was Ted shaking his head, as if he'd been asked to discipline a particularly unruly child.

Management had looked real hard at Tony's hours then, and cut him back sharply when they realized he was well up over seventy-five hours some weeks, and if he had been driving transport truck, he knew they would have pulled his logbook at some inspection station and written him up for not taking the time to get enough sleep. And that pissed him off even more because, he thought, rules just don't understand.

"Things are getting so expensive," Helen told him when his paycheques came and went. "The prices just keep going up. I don't know how we're going to keep up if the union doesn't get you guys a raise this year."

Even with the cut in hours, Tony drove most nights that winter, the metal scrape of the snowplow blade often leaking into his dreams while he slept restlessly through the light of the days, the curtains never able to hold back all the light. He liked the nights, especially liked the early mornings when the colour was just leaking into the horizon in a blue so pale it looked almost like grey. Then, as dawn got closer, Tony would see the big upturned bowl of the sky brightening, and even when he saw occasional faces drawn to windows by the sound of the heavy plow, it was still like he was the only real person alive, cutting through the fresh and trackless snow on the only necessary errand in the world.

Out under so much sky, the truck seemed to get smaller and smaller, a tiny creature depending on the brute strength of its back legs to push ahead through the snow. It was the best time to forget everything else, a time when it seemed as though the only world that truly existed was framed by the inside of the cab of the truck, when time itself was measured not in hours but by the metronome of the snow-shrouded parked cars the plow passed along either side of the road, by the corners you cut wide, swinging down empty side streets and flinging the heavy, curling wave of snow and slush up onto the curb.

The universe was self-contained and well drawn then, complete and completely under control, Tony thinking of himself as being as regular a cog as the tiny gear he imagined turning every single second hand on every single clock in the entire world. And that tick gently tocking ahead specifically under his hands.

It was, he was sure, just about the only thing that was under control.

On evenings when he wasn't working—evenings that were few and far between—he'd sometimes go down to the bar with Helen, one block over and three blocks down to a quiet downstairs pub with a single pool table and a dartboard that no one ever used, even though the light over it was carefully angled to throw the yellow and black wedges of the board into high relief.

The regulars all knew her there—sometimes Tony thought they might know her better than he did. It occurred to him that she was a regular at the bar herself, and for a single flashing moment he envied her that, envied her the ability to have a particular place where she clearly fit. Tony was keenly aware that he didn't fit, no matter what he did: he could watch hockey on the big bar television, drink a pint of beer and make small talk, but it was always like the people on either side of him tolerated his presence and his attempts at conversation, but little more. He felt strangely angular away from the big smooth steering wheel, square peg and round hole, so he said little and watched more, his eyes catching the ranks of bottles along the bar, the soccer towels they'd found somewhere and hung from the ceiling, the long row of draft beer taps.

But Helen?

She'd come in with him and then shift her weight sideways onto the stool closest to the pool table, call out to the bartender and wave, and she'd drink club soda, just club soda, and play the machines, the bright lights playing off her face and making strange-coloured, two-toned shadows, like clouds moving quickly through the shafts of sun lighting her face.

As she concentrated, it gave Tony a chance to just stare, and he was overtaken by a simple confusion, as he always was, staring at her: how had they even ended up married? But that too was only half of it. A bigger piece was the question of why she'd ever agreed to have him.

Even now, in her early fifties, Helen was a strikingly beautiful woman, high, sharp cheekbones still, wild, curly hair more restrained than brushed, and comfortably able to smile in a way that just made her face lapse straight into beauty. Tony wondered if, as a teenager, she had practised that smile in front of a mirror, perfecting just how much of her teeth to show, letting her eyes widen slightly at the same time in a distracting, alluring way that almost always made you fall straight in, even if you sensed all along that her expression just might be a deliberately planned and even mercenary trick.

But he had asked her to marry him, and she had improbably said yes, both of them barely into their twenties, and they'd managed all of it up until now: one child, a boy who got into more trouble than seemed possible, then that same boy moving away, and finally the sudden death of her father, Mike, of a heart attack, right at the top of the stairs beside the bathroom.

It seemed to Tony, although he'd never said it out loud, that Mike had gotten up from his chair in the living room all of a sudden and decided to head straight up towards heaven, or wherever it was he went, making the choice to slip right out of his body exactly at the point where he ran out of stairs and could climb no higher inside his skin.

Perhaps it was the expression on the dead man's face that made Tony think that was what had happened, because he'd been in the kitchen when he heard the thump of the old man falling, and had run up the stairs and turned his body over in the narrow hallway. When he did, Mike Mirren didn't look surprised or frightened or in pain or anything like that, not like any of the clichés Tony had been led to expect. Mike Mirren's mouth had been set in a straight, purposeful line, turned up slightly in the corners, as if he were setting out on a particularly involved task that might, in the end, turn out to be almost enjoyable. Like he had his eyes fixed on something in the distance that was on the very edge of out of sight, something both curious and perhaps a little funny.

Tony and Helen had managed to get past that, he thought, had gotten used to their son Ron quitting school right after grade ten and running around with a girl they hated, a girl named Liz who Tony imagined, for some reason, had a thread of vicious running right straight through her. He didn't trust Liz and he didn't really know why, but whenever he saw her, Tony caught himself watching her, watching her hands, trying to figure out just what it was she was up to.

Fact was, he thought, he and Helen had made it to a point where the days were ticking past themselves in an almost-constant comfortable state. They didn't even have to talk, because almost every single thing between them had been said at least a dozen times already. Even the arguments were old and familiar, less argument than stage play, both of them anticipating the other's next line.

Until the morning when Tony had been home and awake when the mailbox banged shut outside and he'd gone out to get the mail. And it had only been a couple of furniture flyers and one lone envelope with the electric bill. Helen always paid the bills, but Tony opened it simply out of curiosity instead of leaving it on the counter. And it was three months overdue by then, and there was a cut-off notice attached, the cut-off part printed in bright red.

Tony got a lot of stares from people the next day when he wheeled the big green city tandem dump truck into customer parking at the power company, filling two parking spots. He paid the entire overdue bill with cash, watching carefully as the woman behind the counter stamped the face of the bill with her date stamp and then initialled the payment. Watching until he was sure she had entered the payment into the computer in front of her.

He didn't mention to Helen that he'd paid the bill, but looking at her that night in the living room, he felt as if twin weights were conspiring to pull each side of his face downwards and that there was absolutely nothing he could do about it.

That was only the first late bill. He started catching others when he could, overdue accounts threading their way into the mailbox, where he would quietly pay them too, with any cash he could gather up. He'd take a quick swing down McKay Street on the days he knew she was out, just long enough to climb down from the idling truck, rifle through the mail in the mailbox and climb back into the driver's seat again. But he didn't tell Helen, not even when he intercepted a bank statement showing the cash advances on their joint chequing account, and the size of the numbers took his breath away.

And more.

He hadn't even known that they had a line of credit, nor that it was already all spent by the time he discovered its existence. He just knew that it was in her hands, and that whatever it was, he wouldn't be able to ask. He also knew then that it didn't matter how many hours of overtime he managed to work. And he knew that he would have to find other ways to put money together.

First, it was a circular saw from the equipment locker, one of the battered old saws that travelled all over the city rolling around loose in the backs of different city trucks. Surprisingly, it didn't feel like he was crossing any sort of line by taking it: it didn't feel like anything at all, except simple, plain necessity—it was there, and he needed it. Tony noticed the saw in the open metal locker when he came off shift, and simply tossed it into the thin space behind the front seat of his pickup. He didn't think about it, really.

The guys on the gate were supposed to give personal vehicles a going-over for city supplies on the way out of the yard, but Tony knew they rarely came out of the gatehouse when it was raining. That morning, his old wipers could barely keep up, smearing back and forth across the windshield glass, and the guard on duty had just waved him through, newspaper up in front of him. But Tony checked the rear-view mirror for blocks anyway, looking over and over again to see if a police car was pulling up behind him. When he thought about it later, it was the first and only time that he ever felt as if he had done anything even remotely wrong.

Soon he began to think that, in some ways, it was all their fault, because they really should have caught him then—because he was careless and impulsive, and because it was the very first time. And if he'd thought they would check the truck, he wouldn't have been able to do it at all.

But they didn't, and he did.

When he got home, Tony slammed the door behind him in the driveway and left the saw in the unlocked truck, and almost wished that someone from the neighbourhood would come along and take it. But no one did, and he got thirty dollars for the battered saw from a neighbour after he peeled off the inventory sticker and wire-brushed the city ID number away.

It was like he'd crossed a line he hadn't even really known he was crossing.

And each time, it got a little simpler. When he thought about it, he thought about the mechanics—not the stealing itself but how to do it. Pressure-treated lumber, steel-toed boots, power tools—he took all of it, and more. He learned things as he went, like the obvious fact that the newer a thing was, the easier it was to sell. Other things too—like the larger something was, the harder it was for anyone to believe it was actually stolen.

Once, at four in the morning with the guy in the gatehouse sound asleep, Tony had gotten out through the gate with one of the big-wheeled jackhammer compressors, right out in the open and hitched to the back of his pickup. He sold it to a guy who spray-painted it grey and sold it right away again as surplus, no questions asked, in another part of the province, and that was eight hundred dollars in quick cash, even if the compressor was worth thousands.

That time, Tony had been sweating driving away from the depot, sweating because it was just so obvious, and for the next three days he'd kept expecting one of the supervisors to call him up to the office "for a chat." But no one noticed, at least not right away.

The street-repair program hadn't started for the spring season, and it was three weeks before the police even came to look into the theft, and when they did, they interviewed everyone on shift, including Tony. He feigned a kind of uninterested nonchalance, and it was almost as if that nonchalance rubbed right off on the two police detectives who came and sat and did interviews in the lunchroom.

They looked bored the whole time they talked to him, one of the officers, a tall guy named Ballard, fiddling with his coffee cup as he worked his way down the same list of questions they wound up asking everyone. The two policemen gave off an air like they felt they were being asked to investigate something that was far beneath them, like being asked to chase graffiti artists instead of busting up drug rings.

The police ended up being more interested in Wally Norman than anyone else, because it turned out that Wally had a record that no one knew anything about, some scheme from his twenties where he and his buddies used to go out to the airport and just grab random baggage off the luggage carousels and head for the door. If someone came up and stopped them, saying, "Hey, that's my suitcase," they'd just hand it back and say, "Sorry, I've got one that looks just like it."

But Wally and his friends had tried the scheme once too often and been spotted by security, because guys in their twenties just weren't flying every week. While all of Wally's friends had gotten away, he'd been tackled by a wiry old commissionaire as he tried to get to the car, and was pinned on the rain-wet pavement out next to the crosswalks until the police arrived. The commissionaire's glasses had been broken in the struggle, so the police tagged Wally with an assault charge too.

"Guy thought he was back in World War Two or somethin', 'stead of stoppin' someone stealin' fuckin' suitcases," Wally said matter-of-factly, like it was a hockey game they'd all been talking about, a sloppy outlet pass or bad penalty killing. "Like he was catchin' a bank robber or sump-thin."

When they finished their interviews and got ready to leave, the police stopped for a moment in the lunchroom to tell Wally in front of everyone else that they would be keeping an eye on him. And Wally shrugged, a big, slow, over-exaggerated shrug that telegraphed "Who gives a shit?" as clearly as if he had said it out loud, right there and then.

As soon as the police left, Wally told the guys that they'd taken the suitcases more as a game than anything else, because "most of the time it was just old clothes 'n shit, 'n half the time we'd just flick 'em out the door onto the highway anyway. Big old suitcases, spinning off into the ditch. Burstin' open. Ya should've seen it." But he didn't seem to regret any of it, not even the idea that the police were now looking at him as a suspect. "You make a choice and jest go from there," he said, and went to get more coffee.

Tony sat with his drink at the bar and stared across at where Helen was sitting, and it seemed to him that he was suddenly aware that he was hearing something urgent being spoken in a different language, a language that he didn't fully understand but that he needed to hear.

He was sure that everything important was happening right there in front of him, right then, if only he could figure out what all the various pieces meant, and how they all fit together. Like a chain with one important link missing. He looked around the room, trying to see if there was a secret code written on the walls or hovering over any of the five people up at the bar, huddled close together as if they were freezing cold. Looking for the switch that was just waiting to be thrown.

And Helen's purse was open, the lights from the lottery machine playing across the front of her blouse again so that it seemed as if her clothes were magically changing colours, flicking from one shade to another.

With her hands barely moving, she was threading twenties into the thin slot in the front of the machine, over and over again without even looking, a motion so practised that it seemed to take no effort whatsoever, that it seemed to take neither aim nor concentration. It looked for all the world as if she was just holding her hand in front of the machine while the money magically disappeared from her grasp, and she didn't even look away from Tony as the money simply vanished.

He noticed the expression in her eyes didn't change when she turned to look at him—in fact, her eyes didn't move at all, her gaze holding his in one simple and straight line. And the whole time, he could feel her eyes on his face, staring straight across at him, and when he looked up and back at her, she smiled that familiar smile, her eyes widening just enough. And Tony fell hard, just like he always did.

He fell, but he also knew.

Two days later, he got the keys for a city backhoe from the sign-out locker and two hard men from downtown did all the rest without him, driving the piece of heavy equipment straight out through a chain-link fence without stopping and onto a low-rider flatbed already parked just outside on the street. And even though it must have taken them more than a few minutes to chain the backhoe down, no one admitted to seeing anything. And there was money in a plain white envelope in the mailbox when he got home, his name on the front in pencil in block letters, as if it could just as easily be erased and replaced by someone else's.

That same week, he managed a mitre saw and a set of air chisels, and that was despite the fact the city had hired a private firm to beef up security, and there were strange new serious faces in the lunch-room and strolling through the equipment yard at odd times.

Once they caught him with the plywood, Tony was pretty sure that they would want to blame him for everything. Would want to play the familiar old "one bad apple" game and declare the problem solved, even if there was city equipment in garages and basements all over the place. They just didn't have enough proof—so Tony knew they'd go to the wall for ten sheets of plywood instead.

Wally Norman took him aside and quietly said he understood, and by way of condolence admitted that he had four of the city's five-ton hydraulic screw jacks in his own garage if anyone ever took it into their heads to come looking. "Ya haven't done nothing that anyone else here hasn't done," Wally said, smacking a hand down between Tony's shoulder blades, but Tony didn't get any particular comfort from the admission.

"I still can't believe it, Tony," Helen said quietly while they were sitting together in the small, overheated courtroom, waiting for his case to come up. It had already been a month without pay, a month when, "suspended pending," he hadn't driven a truck or been up early enough in the day to see the wonder of the darkness fading into blue. He wasn't even allowed on city property, and at home, the money had dried up completely, bills now lying unopened on the counter because they were questions that Tony and Helen couldn't begin to answer.

"I just can't believe it, that you were stealing. What were you think-ing, anyway? And what do you think my father would have said about this?" Helen said. "You always said you wanted him to think well of you." And something about that whole speech rang funny, even though Tony couldn't put his finger on exactly what it was.

And she'd been saying that for a month, saying it ever since the court date had been set. He didn't feel like starting what would have become unstoppable finger pointing, hadn't once mentioned the gam-bling machines, didn't even bother putting words together into some-thing that might seem like an explanation.

What was he thinking? Her words stuck in his head and nagged at him like a splinter until the moment when he figured it out. When Tony suddenly realized that none of it was about thinking, really. That it was actually a whole bunch of different things, layered in on top of one another. That it was about reacting, about watching and picking up unspoken cues. And he thought that, perhaps, if he'd laid it all out for his father-in-law, Mike Mirren might have understood completely, and smiled, and talked to him for a few minutes about all the things it turns out you really don't have any choice in after all. And he would have gone back to being dead then, still smiling faintly.

Eventually, it was Tony's turn, the whole courtroom waiting and quiet, and there really wasn't much left to say. And the prosecution lawyer stood up and said they wanted to add extra charges, that since his arrest they'd found the backhoe and the compressor too, and they had three witnesses they wanted to bring forward, and they were talking about charging him as "a career criminal." Tony smiled a bit when he heard the words, hearing them differently and deciding that it was exactly true, that a career was what had been stolen after all.

So Tony stood up, leaning over for a moment so his lips were by Helen's ear, and over her shoulder he could see Ted Greenaway taking important notes in a small notebook for the city's disciplinary hearing, his arms resting across his large stomach as he wrote, face carefully pulled into a frown.

"I love you, Helen." Tony said it simply, like that should explain everything. As if those few words made sense of all the rest.

Then, when he was asked by the judge, Tony found three more simple words. And they explained everything, and yet only a tiny part, too.

"Guilty, your honour."

It was simple, just like that, and Tony knew exquisitely, exactly, what was slipping away right then, knowing the words Greenaway would be writing so carefully in his notebook.

That nights and snowplows and wonder were gone, like a chapter slapped closed in a book for good.

Guilty, Tony thought, guilty like everyone. And stuffed full of things he knew and didn't dare let out.

32
McKay Street

BART DOLIMONT

JANUARY 3, 1991

FOURTEEN YEARS before Tony's sentencing and there was another thief on McKay Street:

I could write the book on this stuff, Bart Dolimont thinks. *How to Steal and Get Away With It.* It would be a bestseller, too—not bad for a nineteen-year-old with no high school, he says to himself.

He is outside on the sidewalk, walking towards the O'Reilly house, steps away from the short walk to the front door, taking in every piece of information he can from the dark windows.

Don't stop and stare at the house, he thinks. Don't look around to see if anyone's watching. If they are, if they aren't, I'm back-on to them, and they'll know little more than my height. Looking around will just draw attention. People don't look at you if you're confident, if you look like you belong. It turns you into the expected instead of the unexpected, and their eyes wash over you and go on to something else, catching on nothing.

You go straight up to the front door like you belong there, arm straight out, palm the doorknob and give it a steady, even turn. If the door's locked, relax your hand enough to let it slide around the door-knob. Turn around, walk away.

There are plenty of houses in the neighbourhood where people don't lock their doors, or forget to lock them some nights. Or just don't push them all the way closed before they go to bed. Plenty of places where a ground-floor window's open, and all you have to do is cut away the screen and climb in, look around, take the first few things that are worth grabbing and head out on your way.

Doors are easier, though. If it's unlocked, walk straight in. If there's someone there, you can always say you were coming in to tell them their door was open and you were wondering if they were all right. If you hear something, just leave. If you can lock the door behind you as you go, even better. Walk away down the street. Don't run, even if they start yelling.

Inside the O'Reillys', and Bart stopping to listen. No dog—knew that already, he thinks. That's a good thing.

I can hear Mister snoring away in the back like a freight train, he thinks. He's fifty if he's a day, but works down to the dockyard, so he might be tougher than he looks, ready to mix it up if he wakes up.

Let your eyes adjust to the light—no rushing. It's all about nerve. Wait for the walls to slowly swim into view from the darkness, wait until you can see the shapes of the picture frames against the lighter walls, even if you can't make out the pictures themselves. Take your time, don't rush into unfamiliar geography. Always take your time.

No pushing into chairs or knocking over lights. Slow, hands and feet in short arcs. Hit the high-percentage places. Purse on the counter. Wallet in the pants pocket in the bedroom. Move slow but deliberate.

Best thing is to take stuff that won't be missed right away. Little things. Don't get greedy, eventually there's always lots, even if it's not here tonight. Find a purse with eighty dollars, take forty. Chances are they'll be too busy blaming each other to even think there's been a break-in.

Sometimes, with big stuff like cameras, stuff you can carry that's valuable, you just take the whole lot of it and hope you can wait out the heat. Or else have someone who's interested ahead of time.

Old coins? See fifty, take ten. Make it so it's hard for anyone to put their finger on when something went missing—that can be important later, when someone like a cop is asking you questions.

Bart moving down the hall, setting his feet down gently, wary of creaks in the floor.

People are creatures of habit, yes they are, he thinks.

Sock drawers: there's stuff in there that no one's even thinking of—at least, they don't look for it every day. A few days' grace before anyone notices anything, and when it's gone, they start by looking for someone familiar to blame. Interesting treasures in there sometimes. Old watches, sometimes old bills—but don't even think of trying to unload them right away at a coin shop or something; this is just too small a town. Wait for the buyers who come in once or twice a year, the guys who set up at the hotel and buy the full-page ads in the paper. They'll rip you off on price, thinking you're some small-town rube who doesn't know what you've got in your own hands, but it doesn't matter that they're always shorting you—they don't know that you got it for free, and they'll be moving out of town long before anyone says, "Hey, wait a minute." They're not in a big rush to have the cops around their inventory either.

So everybody wins—you just win more than anybody else, and nobody knows any better, either.

Bart sees the long lumps of Keith and Evelyn in bed under the blankets, neither of them moving, both breathing with great long breaths, sleeping soundly.

Don't rush, pull the drawers open slow, stop if you feel them start to bind at the edges like they might squeak—just leave 'em. Search by touch, fingers like electric current. The lump of the wallet in a pair of pants on a chair—don't lift 'em, the tang on the belt might fall and ring like a single chime. Wallet out of the pocket if you can, leave it if you can't—take two of the twenties, slide the wallet back.

Lots of things to remember—like the fact that older people don't like banks, so sometimes there's big money. But it's not always easy to find. These guys, not that old. Some people like to wake the real old-sters up and threaten 'em, get them to give up whatever they're hiding, but not my style, Bart thinks, can't stand the idea of seeing that look in someone's eyes. Plus it can go bad sometimes, some old guy up out of the bed ready to fight, and people get hurt that way. It's not always the old people that get hurt, either.

Back to the dresser, sweep your eyes across the top, looking out of the corners of your eyes, the edges of your vision often better in the dark.

Jewellery boxes—don't even open 'em unless you're sure. Some of them are music boxes, and weigh the risks: in this neighbourhood, chances are the jewellery is cheap stuff, not worth the risk of trying to sell it.

Better to move quick, already a bit of a score here in the bedroom, move on, always take the fewest chances you can.

Take tools if you get the chance—they're always getting misplaced anyway, and they're easy to turn for cash, even at a yard sale. Bart remembers selling a set of rabbitting bits once at a yard sale, right back to the guy he'd stolen them from.

"Lost a bunch just like these," the guy says. "Chances are I'll probably find them the minute I get these ones back home."

"Always seems to happen that way," Bart answers, folding twenty dollars and sliding it down into his front jeans pocket.

Back through the kitchen now and out towards the back—careful, though, because there's the kid's room somewhere, and kids are unpredictable. Sleep through anything, or wake up at the drop of a hat. Don't even try the door—not worth the chance. Not likely to be anything in there anyway.

Through the kitchen door and into the workshop, and Bart looks around, takes the drill bits, a glass cutter, takes another couple of bills from a glass jar on a shelf there in the light from the street light, the orange triangle running down on the floor to a square of loose dry-wall by the heater.

Old-timer's trick, Bart thinks.

Easy and slow, his eyes working real good to pick it out.

No one ever learns, Bart's thinking, moving over towards it, letting his fingers slide along the edges. Like no one's ever done this before.

Probably a couple of pornos back there, he thinks, or maybe a flask. Maybe the mad money he doesn't want her to know he has, and if it's gone, he's not even going to be able to complain about it.

Shifting the small square, jiggling it out of place, it moves easily enough, someone's done this a few times before, Bart thinks. The drywall no longer crisp on the edges, it's been pushed in and taken out so often. Behind it, there's pink fibreglass insulation, the nasty stuff that gets into your skin and itches like the devil, Bart thinks, and it's all tufted in and under the edges of the wall, so it's not like he has to pull it out and look behind it too.

Then he sees there's a little hollow in the insulation at the bottom, and tucked into it, a small, dark purse, and Bart thinks, Now this is interesting, I'll just be taking this and we'll have a little look inside later, won't we?

Not a bad little haul at all, he's thinking, at least sixty dollars now with the purse and the wallet and some tools, and no one's going to be the wiser, at least not at first.

And just then, someone else comes in the front door, not even trying to be quiet, the door slamming back into place behind him, and it's got to be a him because the guy's just moving so goddamn big, Bart thinks, and Bart's looking for a place to hide that just plain isn't there.

A big guy finding you in a house is bad.

Calling the cops on you is bad enough, but big guys finding you can end very badly, because they're either scared or angry, and either way they tend to overdo it, even if you're not fighting back at all.

Bart doesn't know Glenn Coughlin, but it's Glenn heading to the fridge for a beer because he's run out, his feet heavy and clomping across the kitchen. So Bart takes advantage of the noise to slip over and slide the little half door open, heads out and under and across the yard, and he doesn't start breathing again until he's hopped over the fence and is back on the sidewalk. Puts the purse safe inside his jacket, zips it up, wonders what makes it so important that it's got its own special hidey-hole.

Remembers that he's left the drywall out of place, the hole open. Much too late to be going back now, he thinks.

Maybe it'll be a few days before anyone notices anything wrong. Maybe longer. Maybe not.

Keeps walking.

And no one shouts.

Back at home, and he's got the purse out on his bed, and there's nothing there worth anything at all, just really old ID for a teenaged girl with a familiar-sounding name, and Bart Dolimont can't remember just where he's heard that name before, and he sure doesn't recognize the face on the student ID card.

But wait.

Then he does.

This is an ace in the hole, Bart thinks. Just something to keep in hand, something that might be useful someday. And he wonders: how did this guy get a missing girl's purse?

This might be something I'd have to be paid to forget, Bart thinks.

32
McKay Street

VINCENT O'REILLY

JANUARY 5, 1991

TWO DAYS LATER, and no one even knew Bart had been in the O'Reillys' house. Glenn Coughlin, standing in the front doorway, said, "Gonna be just like your dad, aren'tcha?" and he smiled when he said it.

Nine years old and serious, Vincent O'Reilly stood in the front hall, his arms straight down by his sides as his mother knelt in front of him, doing up the buttons on his coat. Big Glenn Coughlin from the dock-yard, standing just outside the door on the front steps, the door wide open, two paper cups of coffee steaming in his hands. Across the street, Coughlin's fourteen-year-old truck was idling next to the curb, exhaust pillowing out into the early morning air in short, uneven chuffs.

Fine snow was coming down out of a clear blue sky, almost magically, the individual shards of broken flakes caught glistening in the hard white winter sunlight as they fell. Vincent looked over his own shoulder and stared at the vibrating exhaust pipe, at the ancient dark green truck with the rust holes in the quarter panels and the distinctive light green outline of flames drawn along the sides, the stencilled outline now coming apart with age. It was topped with the ratty white camper back that Glenn had bought somewhere on the cheap, a camper top obviously designed for a different truck and slightly too large for the pickup's back. It perched, more than fit, on the truck's box. Vincent had often heard his father say, "Glenn doesn't care what anyone thinks about how something looks, as long as it does its job."

Keith O'Reilly and Glenn would load up the truck in the fall to hunt moose, cases of beer tucked inside the back, against the tailgate, then take a whole weekend and come back smelling of dirt and cigarette smoke and stale beer. "Went up to the cabin on the Northeast," Keith would say when they got back, but if they were ever successful on their hunting trips, Vincent hadn't seen any sign of it. They never brought a moose home, head on the roof of the pickup, and rabbits never made their way into stew. Vincent knew his dad came back from the weekends almost deflated, and in its own way that was a good thing, like pressure letting go before it was too much to contain. He came back rumpled, Vincent thought, and smelling somehow like overripe plums, as if he'd gone bad a little out there in the country, something spoiled taking root somewhere around his neck and shoulders and breath. He also came back with something Vincent would only be able to describe later as blunted menace, an important slowing of unreasonable anger: whatever else there was in the small house, there was an undercurrent that if things didn't go Vincent's father's way, there could easily be serious trouble. It wasn't something Vincent could put his finger on. It was simply there—and Glenn Coughlin was right in the middle of it.

"Keith's on his way now, Glenn," Evelyn O'Reilly said, looking back into the house over her shoulder, hearing her husband's footsteps. Vincent looked at the man he was always told to call Mr. Coughlin and wondered what it was that he didn't understand about the man.

Glenn Coughlin, Vincent had realized, was the only person who walked into the O'Reilly house whenever he wanted to. Glenn didn't ring the doorbell, he didn't knock—he just parked his truck, hitched his pants, strode up the sidewalk, put his hand on the knob and walked right in like he owned the place, as if he had every right to be there.

Like it was his own house. He actually lived ten blocks over, on Bond Street, in a small, detached two-storey house with white vinyl siding and new windows that were so small the house looked as if it had been designed as a fort with narrow gun emplacements instead of real windows. Vincent had never been inside, had never done anything more than drive by the place, and it sometimes seemed to him that he could say the same thing about Glenn. Coughlin spent more time at their house than he spent anywhere else.

It might be five in the morning or nine at night, but Glenn almost always had two cups of coffee with him in a takeout tray, one for himself, the other for Vincent's dad. Glenn even called Vincent's mother Ev, and no one did that, not even Vincent's father. But nobody seemed to mind Glenn doing anything—at least, no one said anything if they did. And it didn't stop there. Glenn could walk back into the workshop and grab tools—the precious chainsaw that no one else touched, the Vise-Grips, anything—and walk right straight out of the house again, and Vincent's father wouldn't get angry, wouldn't do anything but laugh that hollow little laugh that seemed completely connected to Glenn Coughlin and absolutely no one else. More than once Vincent had heard his father pleading with Glenn to return one tool or another, his father caught in the middle of a project that needed something that had gone missing. Other times Vincent had gotten up in the middle of the night, everyone else asleep, only to find Glenn in the kitchen, silhouetted by the light from the fridge as he searched for something to eat. "Hi bud," Glenn would say, his mouth half full, leftovers in his hands and sometimes on the side of his face.

Glenn worked in the dockyard with Vincent's dad. They'd gone to school together from boyhood, Glenn always the bigger of the two, always willing to step in when Keith was in trouble with someone else—Keith, small and ready to fight but always outweighed, Glenn slower to action but always ready to turn on whoever was tormenting the smaller boy and settle matters with quick, heavy fists.

They'd finished high school together, sporting identical low-average marks, started work at the dockyard together, and stayed together on the same shifts for years, Glenn backing up Keith with his size, Keith talking Glenn out of corners, like the time Glenn decided he was going to beat up a supervisor—a supervisor who was later fired when his locker somehow ended up full of gear stolen from the skipper's cabin on a provincial ferry that was in the yard for a refit.

Keith would move to sandblasting for a change, then Glenn would catch up, moving over to the same crew within a week or so, like an old couple who argued publicly but really couldn't stand being away from each other. They had stayed on the paint crew for all of three weeks before deciding that they hated painting more than anything they'd ever done, and both promised they would never, ever go back. They had top welding tickets, and either one of them could fire up the big D9 Caterpillar bulldozer and use it to haul a ship up onto the synchro-lift, black raw diesel smoke belching from the short stack on the tractor as it hauled the ship along, the tractor in the lowest possible gear. Both men had enough seniority to bump just about anyone else off a job, and they weren't afraid to use it, either. Keith always led: every time Keith tried something new, it was like Glenn decided he wanted to try it too, and it seemed they would leapfrog around the yard into any job they wanted to. "Ya gotta like the union, Keith," Glenn said, and he said it often, especially when the shop steward was in earshot, and then Glenn would wink.

It was quiet in the front hall where the three of them were waiting, and then Vincent's father was coming down the hallway towards them fast, his arms in tight next to his sides, hands up high so that it looked like he was racing down the narrow hallway towards a fight. He had his coat on already, hands pushed angrily down through the sleeves so that, inside, the sleeves of his sweater were pulled up in bunches on his forearms. It didn't matter: five minutes after they got to work, every-one would be in the dark blue insulated coveralls and steel-toed work-boots anyway, hard hats perched on their heads like yellow cherries on sundaes, the dockyard logo on a rectangular patch right in the middle of their backs like they were small blue billboards swarming all over the latest ship.

"Come on then, Vincent, time to get going," Keith O'Reilly said gruffly, as if Vincent had been the one holding them all up.

Vincent didn't say anything, knew better than to say anything, but he picked up his bookbag quickly, accepting a kiss on the cheek from his mother as he turned for the door.

"The three men, all heading out together for their shifts, hey, Vincy?" Glenn said, laughing.

Glenn was always laughing, Vincent thought, even when there wasn't anything funny to be laughing about. Vincent swung his school bag up over his shoulder, walking between the two men as they crossed the street. Vincent looked both ways, just the way he had been told, before he stepped off the curb. He noticed that Glenn didn't bother, as if a car hadn't been made yet that would dare to hit him.

On the other side of the truck, Vincent's father held the passenger door open, stood there as if trying to make up his mind, and then climbed into the cab of the truck himself, sliding into the middle of the bench seat next to Coughlin.

"You take the outside, Vincent. You're going to be getting out first anyway."

"First in, last out, just like the contract says, hey, Keith?" Glenn said, slipping the truck into gear and pulling it away from the curb. As they drove, Vincent looked out the window and into the side mirror. It was starred and broken, several shards simply gone, as if someone had driven a fist into it as Glenn had pulled away. The truck mirror had always been like that. Vincent liked looking in it, liked looking at the way the different pieces broke up the view behind the truck, so that every single shard showed the world in a slightly different way, each one highlighting its own particular facet of the things they passed. His father noticed him staring at the mirror.

"Why don't you get that damned thing fixed, Glenn? Been broken forever," Keith said. "Don't know how this thing passes inspection anyway."

"Don't need it, do I? Besides, a new one's close on sixty dollars," Glenn said. Then he laughed again, a dry little shallow laugh, like he was making a point. "Some people can get around just fine without it, and without hitting stuff."

Vincent's father crossed his arms stiffly across his chest at that, glowered, and didn't say anything else.

"Lighten up, would ya?" Glenn said.

They drove in silence for a few minutes down the snow tunnel that was McKay Street. The city plows had been out overnight, turning big curved berms of slush and snow up against the sides of the parked cars on the road, the corridor so precise that it seemed like they were on a private road, a road built just for them. Vincent was watching the sun play off the rounded slush, the backwards curve made by the plow's blade now hardening into ice. He watched the way one line of bright sun seemed to run along ahead of the truck on the freezing bank, the reflection never getting any closer to them nor any farther away, the way the light made longer points on the top and bottom, so it was like they were following some simple, always-moving schoolbook drawing of the Star of Bethlehem.

"Foreman said we can work inside on the trawler if we want, or we can go back to the paint crew in the tanker. It's our pick," Keith said. There were only two vessels in the yard, nothing else waiting or even scheduled to come in, and most of the short-timers had already been put on layoff for the rest of the winter. Keith had been complaining for a week about the two ships, wishing the yard was empty and that the whole crew could be on layoff for a little while. "Hate winter," he'd mutter.

"We can be freezing cold outside, or inside in the warm and the whole day stinkin' of paint. That's pretty slim pickings," Glenn said.

Vincent thought that the pair of words sounded just the way Glenn always talked—"slim pickings"—just a couple of sudden words that didn't seem to mean anything at all on their own but that fit him perfectly. "Slim pickings"—"Fat chance"—"No way." Not "No damn way" or "No fucking way" either—and Vincent had heard both of those before, from his father and from other men at the yard—but just "No way," and the way Mr. Coughlin said it, it sounded far more serious than anyone else could make it sound.

Glenn stopped the truck at the four-way stop and then turned onto Bond Street, passing the house he never seemed to be in, a narrow trench dug through the snow towards the front door like he felt the digging was hardly worth the effort. The back wheels of the truck slipped because the snow had melted and then frozen again overnight where it had run out in a long tongue just past the crosswalk.

The sky was flat white and still, all the blue bled out of it by winter and the latitude, the sunlight thin and distant and struggling to throw down any heat at all.

Vincent looked up at his father out of the corner of his eye. It looked like his father was going to say something else, but then it was like Glenn could read his mind. He gave a small shake of his head, raising both his eyebrows at once.

Glenn Coughlin, Vincent decided, had eyebrows that were far more bushy than any he had ever seen.

They drove in silence for a few more minutes, the streets still relatively empty, Coughlin taking the corners wide and fast, his side of the truck often in the other lane. When they met another vehicle, it was the other car or truck that acquiesced and coughed up the right-of-way. Glenn had no compunctions about sitting in the street, nose to nose with someone else and at a dead stop, until the other driver changed his mind and let Glenn go on.

Then the pickup was in front of the school. It was an old school, a big, two-storey brick building with too-large windows, and there were scores of other children spinning up the sidewalk towards the front door like busy ants. Down among narrow streets of row houses, each house seemed to be disgorging more kids onto the streets every moment, the narrow sidewalks blocked with snow, and every child was producing his or her own tiny engine-like plume of steam as they moved in masses along the curb.

Vincent opened the truck's door, and as he did, Coughlin reached across in front of Keith and ruffled Vincent's hair. "Work hard," he said. "Do your best. Get good grades. You'll probably end up down on the dock with us anyway, though."

And no, I won't, Vincent thought even then. Vincent liked geography best of all, because it was the study of everywhere else. A study that made McKay Street, and even St. John's, the smallest possible speck.

Glenn took his hand away by giving the boy's head a sudden little shove and then a sharp, harsh knock with two of his knuckles, as if suggesting any sort of kindness was a passing thing.

"See ya, Vincent," his father said quietly.

"See ya, Dad."

Coughlin put the truck back into gear and was pulling away from the curb before the door was fully closed. Halfway down the block, the truck's horn gave a forlorn little toot, as if remembering something it had forgotten, but Vincent's hand was already on the big brass door handle to the school, and he barely bothered to look at the truck as it vanished downhill towards the harbour.

The tide of children surged and pushed their way in through the heavy door to the school, jostling all around him and carrying him in through the door like he was a chip of wood suspended in a current, the direction he was going to travel already decided upon by everyone else.

188A
McKay Street

RON COLLINS

FEBRUARY 18, 2006

L IZ TOLD RON she was leaving their apartment the first time he managed to reach her on the prison pay phone. It was only a week after he'd been arrested, and it was as though every single thing about her had changed.

"I'm not really supposed to even talk to you, right?" she said, her voice tinny and distant through the earpiece of the phone, and he could imagine she was winding her right index finger in her hair while she said it. "I'm a witness."

She said it like it was an important job she'd been individually selected to do, as if the term had a special and particular weight, like it was "I'm a doctor" or "I'm an engineer." He remembered the way her voice sounded as she said it, remembered that tone and pitch for days.

The phone was pressed against his ear and he could feel the hard plastic circle of it against his skin, even though everything else around him had reduced in the same instant to a circle of grey, sparkling fog. Behind him, the voices of the other inmates were bouncing off the blue-painted walls in the long hallway, high and harsh, sharp and metallic and constantly in motion, but to Ronnie it seemed as if they were simply fading out of earshot with the impact of what she was saying.

"If I see you or talk to you or anything, you can be charged again. So it's for your own good, really, you not calling here anymore. Your mom's coming to get your stuff and she'll put it in the basement. And I had to sell the car, but I sent your parents half."

Liz kept talking, but suddenly he wasn't listening, and instead was hopelessly picturing her naked in front of the refrigerator in their apartment, drinking orange juice straight out of the carton so fast that he could hear the sound of her swallowing, the liquid rushing down her throat urgently, like it was needed in some kind of immediate and elemental way.

And then he remembered the way she would close the fridge door and turn towards him, legs apart, one hand on her hip, not the least bit shy, wiping her lips with her other forearm. He wondered if that whole memory was at risk, if he was now the only one who remembered it, and, if something happened to him, whether all of that reality would simply be gone.

When he hung up the phone, he figured that, out of the two of them, he was the only one close to crying.

The guards were slamming the doors back on the range, getting everybody out of their cells at once, forcing them out to exercise for an hour in the prison yard, where the only thing you could see up over the walls was the plastic shopping bags caught in the razor wire and the top of a building that had once been a nurses' residence. Sometimes the guards took that opportunity to turn a few of the cells upside down, searching for contraband or homemade weapons, so that prisoners would come back and find the only place they had that was even close to home turned over like soil in the rows of a field of harvested potatoes.

The guards had a small house just outside the walls where they would throw parties on the weekends. Everyone inside thought that the guards went out of their way to be as loud as they could, just so the inmates could hear them having a good time, the guards rubbing in that they could do exactly what they wanted and the people on the inside of the walls couldn't.

Other than the searches and the noise, the penitentiary, an ancient grey stone complex squatting at Forest Road, wasn't at all like Ron had thought it would be: it wasn't like television, he hadn't been beaten up or threatened. There weren't gangs or much in the way of hard drugs, beyond abused prescriptions. Nor were there assaults by burly men in the showers or hissed warnings from guys thick with inky, smudged prison tattoos. Most of the time, Ron was just bored silly, spending every single day in his cell, waiting to hear from anyone, the days ticking by metered only by the small bit of sky outside the reinforced-glass window of his cell and the endless routine of every day.

The jail was regularly overcrowded, but all that meant at first was that he sometimes shared his cell with an overweight convicted drunk driver serving his conditional sentence on weekends. "New guys with serious charges, we like to inch them into the regular population," one guard told him, a rumpled old guy who walked down the range as if every shift was his last before retirement. Most of the guards didn't speak to Ron unless they were telling him where to go or what to do, short, sharp sentences that involved the guards either pointing or flexing the muscles in their arms.

Ron wondered what the drunk driver had done to earn a spot in a cell with a murderer. It must have been something good, he thought. Maybe the guy was mouthy on the first day in: whatever else the guards were, they certainly didn't have short memories. You piss them off, Ron thought, and every other prisoner in for a weekend sentence would sign the book and be let out because the prison was full—and you'd find yourself at the end of a hall next to someone high on smuggled meds who spent the whole night bouncing off the inside of his cell like he was a rubber ball or something.

Ron found it funny that the pudgy little drunk driver wouldn't look at him, even when Ron tried to force him to talk. The guy just made himself as small and nondescript as he could on his bunk for almost every moment he spent in the cell.

Too many nights watching *The Sopranos* or *The Godfather*, Ron thought. Too many movies.

Sometimes he'd hear the drunk driver crying at night, and he couldn't imagine how the guy could spend so much time feeling sorry for himself. One night the guy said something like, "Someone like me's not supposed to be in here," and Ron found the whole idea so funny that he almost laughed out loud. He'd already learned that, if you listen to them talk, everyone in jail is innocent.

"You and me both, buddy," Ron had said, but his cellmate only looked carefully at the wall and pretended not to hear. Ron understood looking at the walls: they were heavily coated in thick blue paint, but get close enough and you could find spots where earlier prisoners had scratched messages right into the cinder block, carefully etched reminders scribed with unbent paper clips. *Fight Back*, a message near Ron's head said, but the leg on the *a* was thin and filled with paint, so Ron read it as *Fight Bock* and spent the nights imagining Bock and getting ready to fight him.

A couple of days after he talked to her on the phone, at a bail hearing that his lawyer told him was just a formality—"No way they're letting you out," the lawyer had said, and closed his briefcase like a door slamming—Ron had seen Liz leaving the courtroom with one of the cops, a lanky fellow named Ballard who'd been one of the guys in the room when they had first questioned him. Ballard had thick dark hair and a bushy moustache and, when he occasionally used it, a deep, flat voice where the lack of inflection made it sound like the police officer didn't believe anything, not even his own words. His questions didn't sound like they had question marks.

Ron wasn't sure if Ballard was an investigating officer or just a supervisor. He seemed to be there whenever they brought Ron into the interview room, a coil notebook open in front of him on the table in the back of the small room. Ballard only took a few notes, and Ron couldn't remember seeing the officer blink or look away. He had a big square head that was almost set right into his shoulders, his neck practically invisible. Sometimes he'd step into a gap in the questioning and throw out one flat, expressionless sentence, and Ron was never sure whether he was supposed to answer it or just accept it. Other times Ballard would get up for no apparent reason and leave the interview room. And every time, a few minutes after he did, the interview would end, the other two police officers would turn off the video camera on its tripod, and it would be back down to the police cells to wait for the prison van to make its trundling tour around the city, picking prisoners up from the police station, the lock-up and the courts.

At Ron's bail hearing, Ballard sat in the back of the court, not saying a word, his eyes flat and gathering. Ballard and Liz weren't even sitting together—that didn't mean anything, Ron thought—and Ballard's face hadn't changed when Liz said her piece from the witness box.

And, Ron thought, what a piece that had been.

Liz had somehow made herself look even smaller up there on the stand, made her voice tremble like she was afraid, stopping and looking down a lot. At first it was short answers, only a few words at a time, the Crown chiding her along like he was trying to pull the story out of her piece by piece. For Ron, it was like watching an accomplished actor on stage. He almost believed he was listening to a completely different person than the Liz he knew.

Once, she even built a shuddering, almost full-stop sigh right into the middle of a sentence, and Ron knew every single man in the room— even the judge—was somehow leaning towards her, ready to protect her if something suddenly happened. Like they could rip their shirts right open and the big Superman *S* would be there on their chests, Ron thought. Every one of them like John Wayne in an old movie, waiting to say, "Need a hand, little lady?" while knocking him down and putting a few boots in for good measure.

He wanted to jump up then, jump up and shout that Liz wasn't really like that at all, that she was just saying whatever they wanted her to say, but his lawyer seemed to realize what was about to happen and looked across at him, shaking his head, the motion keeping Ron in his chair. It was good advice. Whenever Ron moved the least little bit in the prisoner's box, it was like the air in the courtroom changed, the sheriff's officers leaning in slightly towards him. They looked almost as if they were swelling up inside their white shirts, getting ready for trouble, and everyone in the room, from the lawyers to the clerks, seemed to react to their cue.

It was like magic, he thought: every single thing Liz said was true, yet when you took it all together, none of it was. It was like things had all been taken out of order and then rearranged to reach a different and specific conclusion, and when Liz was finished talking, Ron sat in the prisoner's box for a moment, stunned, not completely sure whether or not he was supposed to applaud.

Then, when it was Ron's turn on the stand, briefly, his words turned to ashes before he could get them out properly. The judge was looking down at the desk in front of him. He didn't seem to notice Ron was speaking, and immediately refused bail, banging his gavel once before standing up in a swirl of black robe and red sash. He left the court without speaking another word.

It was when he was getting his handcuffs put back on that Ron was suddenly completely certain that Liz was involved with Ballard, that at least one other person in the courtroom probably now knew all about orange juice and faked shyness and sharp, savage teeth.

Ron knew Liz. He just knew.

He knew the truth from the way she kept cutting in close next to Ballard, knew at once that she was keeping an orbit too small and pro-scribed to be anything but deliberately gravitational. Her hands didn't actually touch the police officer, but at the same time she came care-fully close, close enough that, watching, Ron could remember the del-icate thrill of those hands, a feeling on his skin that involved both warmth and something like a gentle, constant vibration.

The door closed behind them while the sheriff's officers were pulling him down out of the prisoner's box.

He could imagine the sound of her panting in Ballard's arms, and tried hard to shake the sound from his head while the sheriff's officers pulled him back to the holding cells and the other inmates waiting for the van to haul them back to the prison. He cut up his knuckles by pounding his cuffed hands slowly and repeatedly against the cinder-block walls, blood appearing in stripes on the paint until the other inmates started yelling, afraid of what might happen if he hurt himself seriously. Then the sheriff's officers came in and knocked him down, cuffing his hands behind his back instead. They left him lying face down on the floor of the big cell, unable to stand or sit until court ended for the day and the van finally came. The other men in the holding cell stepped around him and over him, staying away from his head as if he were a big sleeping dog that might wake up and all of a sudden decide to swing its head around and bite whatever it could reach.

Back in the prison, days later, when Ron finally had a visitor, when he was called up to the small room and sat down at the empty table and was told "No contact, hands or feet," it turned out to be someone from a different range in the prison, someone from general population.

His father.

"Called in a couple of favours," Tony said, shrugging. He was sitting across from Ron, the room so narrow his knees were almost touching Ron's legs despite the rules. The guard against the wall, watching. "Lots of people get their start working with the city—firefighters, guards, cops, everyone."

And then Tony sat silently across from him in the blue-painted room as Ron tried—and failed—to find the right words.

"It wasn't . . . I didn't mean to . . . It was like it was all out of my hands the whole time," he said. "I was there, and I was doing it, and it was like there was no deciding at all. Like there was nothing I could do to stop it, even if I'd wanted to."

Then Ron stared hard across at his father, a challenging expression on his face, daring his father to say anything. Instead, he was startled to see Tony looking straight back into his eyes, with something close to a half smile that seemed to be sad, resigned and understanding all at the same time, as if nothing he had said had been news to Tony at all.

Ron was suddenly overwhelmed by his father's familiar smell and the look on his face, and it was like he was five years old all over again, holding on tight and trusting his father to make it all stop.

"Can you fix it, Dad?"

Ron couldn't believe at first that he was even saying the words, but he couldn't believe he was crying, either. This won't happen again, he thought, willing the tears to stop, feeling them running hot down his face.

Ron could see Tony shaking his head.

"There are some things you can't just fix," Tony said. "Believe me."

107
McKay Street

KEVIN RYAN

JULY 14, 2006

FEBRUARY had turned to summer when Kevin Ryan first saw the yellow rubber gloves. His first impression, there in the dark, though, was neither that they were yellow nor that they were rubber.

The gloves stood out under the dark blue sky and the orange of the street lights as if they were brilliant white and perfectly smooth: for an instant they seemed almost disembodied, floating there in the air, because the rest of the old woman's clothing was so dark. She was bent unnaturally, as if her waist was too high, so that she seemed more like a moving pile of clothes than like a person.

He saw her from a distance, while he was walking home from a downtown bar, one too many beers in him, unable to resist it when the bartender spoke to him, even if it was only to ask, "Another?" He was walking slowly, revelling in the sheer absence of people on the street. Except for the headlights of occasional cars sweeping over him, he felt wonderfully, perfectly alone. Except for her.

She had a rake, and she was reaching along the gutter, raking the soaking wet and blackened leaves towards her feet. "You've got the red car," she said carefully.

Kevin Ryan nodded, and then, realizing that he'd be hard to see in the darkness, answered "Yes" as well.

"I've seen you," she said. "Seen you leaving. You're up for work early in the morning."

"Pretty much," Kevin said.

"Here," the woman said, handing him the rake. "You get them. I can't reach that far."

The handle of the rake was wet and slick with black fragments of rotten leaves. As Kevin started to rake up the overwintered and oily-wet mess, he saw the woman bend down and start to pick up wet handfuls of them, stuffing them into a garbage bag. He thought the only real word he could use to describe her was *thick*. Every part of her he could see was stout, so that it seemed as if every joint bent only with the application of a steady and determined force. As she moved up and down, back and forth from the gutter, he got small glimpses of her face in the glow from the street light: snapshots, he thought, or perhaps single frames of a movie. The light caught her only in flashes—the tip of her tongue in the corner of her mouth, overlong eyelashes around black, bead-like eyes surrounded by leathery wrinkles—so that it seemed as if she were a collection of constituent bits, more a collage than a face.

"There are two girls living in your basement," she said, her face at that point partially turned away from him, the words careful and distinct.

"Yes. Heather and Claire."

"They're too loud late at night," the woman said, turning back, her mouth small and disapproving as it shaped the words.

"And they sleep all day."

The woman hefted the garbage bag up onto her shoulder with obvious effort, then pushed it up over the gate blocking the narrow lane between the houses, ignoring the thump as it fell. Kevin had cleaned the narrow space out several times before, a gap between the two houses barely the width of his shoulders. Once, he'd found a discarded fisherman's sweater, once a clear glass beer bottle, another time one lone and soaking black man's glove, its fingers bunched into a hollow, useless fist.

The woman rocked slightly, put a hand against the side of the house as if she might suddenly topple over. Kevin took a step forwards to help and put out a hand, but the woman moved, unexpectedly nimbly, backwards and away from him, two small, quick steps for every single one of his.

"Be careful," the woman said, stopping in her open door as if frozen, looking hard at him, a foot extended without even looking down to hold the ginger cat back from coming out through the opening. The front door right there on the sidewalk, two straightforward steps to the inside. He wasn't sure at first if she was talking to him or about him. Then, "Someone could grab them."

"What?"

"Grab them. Those girls. Chase them. Grab them. Take them. It happens. I've seen it before. One day they're here, and the next they're gone. You hear the car doors, then the tires. And no one wants to say anything, but you can see it on their faces, what they've done."

She stepped backwards and slammed the door.

Kevin heard the bolt slide across, saw the front of the house lit suddenly by the headlights of a passing taxi turning the corner, the briefest moment of the lights, like a flashbulb going off to capture the moment for posterity.

He found out later that her name was Edythe Purchase because of mixed-up mail. Edythe Purchase, and he guessed that she had worked for the phone company: her name on what he imagined were pension statements, looking at the return addresses on the envelopes. Three of them, bundled in with his mail on the front, a thick postal rubber band wrapped around all of it. He dropped her letters into her mailbox on his way to the car one morning, and felt her eyes on him with every step without even seeing her. She opened her door before he could get behind the wheel.

"I saw it," she hissed, and for a moment he thought she meant she had seen him dropping the mail into her box. "I saw it with my own two eyes, but people never believe me. Get far enough from the door and they'll see you. Might decide to take one of yours next."

"But where would they take them?" Kevin looked over the woman's shoulder, looking for someone else, anyone else, in the narrow hallway. All he saw was the narrow staircase over her left shoulder, balusters climbing upwards, and, in the shadows, another cat, yellow-eyed and baleful.

"I don't know. Maybe to be sex slaves. Maybe to be strippers in Montreal." An undertone then, the words half a single breath breathed out. Mrs. Purchase fixed her eyes on him, coal-black and as expressionless as glass. "A few days in the papers, that's all. That's what you get. Then everybody forgets, everybody moves on to something else. You can't convince them to do anything." She looked hard at him, daring him to disagree. "You think you know better, but you don't."

Then the door whispered shut.

A week passed, and Kevin was up early, a cup of coffee in his hand, shivered awake by the rasp of the starlings calling in the tree branches, the racket compounded by the unexpectedly complicated effort of trying to figure out what the sound of the birds actually was.

Outside, on the back deck, he could look across a range of yards—out over the back to the small triangle where a woman kept her two cats on leashes, off to the right where a riot of raspberry canes was spreading faster every spring, and then over to the other side and into Mrs. Purchase's tidy yard, where the grass stayed as short as if it had been a misplaced golf green. Mrs. Purchase's yard, where the rows of tulips faltered only when the legion of geraniums started their scarlet and sharp-smelling march in clay pots brought out from somewhere deep inside the house. A yard where, even this early, Mrs. Purchase was already outside, working among the perennials.

He called out to her, "Hello, Mrs. Purchase," the words thrown out like a rope over the shoulder-high, rust-red fence that circled his yard.

She was out beyond the fence, patrolling the yard with a watering can, dressed in a cream-coloured dress with small burgundy flowers speckled over it. Kevin knew she had to have heard him, and though he even caught her eyes flicking over him, she gave no sign of recognition. Above her, the maple leaves on all the trees, his and hers, had been reduced to leaf skeletons, chewed away by an unexpected summer army of black, hungry caterpillars. At night, the small black pellets of their droppings rattled down steadily on the remaining shreds of leaves, sounding for all the world like a constant and artificial rain.

Sometimes, she watered plants in the individual terracotta pots—and sometimes, the water arced out of the neck of the watering can straight onto the ground, as if she was watering a flowerpot that only she could see, as if someone had snuck in moments ahead of her and stolen the pots before the curve of silver drops of water could land.

Later that same evening, when the light was starting to fail and the ragged clouds had all put on pink edging, he saw her again out in her yard, Kevin looking down from the windows up high in his bedroom, and for a moment, in the fading light, he was convinced that she was dancing, circling the grass with a broom in her hands as a partner. Until he saw the cat, the nasty black and white cat with the green eyes, the cat with the red fabric collar and the single silver bell. It was a cat that Kevin knew well: it was the cat that came up on the deck and resolutely sprayed Kevin's back door, its tail high and eyes blank as it looked over its shoulder, as if it knew exactly what it was doing and didn't care if Kevin saw it.

Mrs. Purchase got close to the cat, over and over again, close enough to swing the broom, and every time, the cat moved a few feet away from her, often without even seeming to look at the woman as she swung.

Kevin opened the window a crack and heard the late robins, their songs roiling out of the maples like syrup. And he heard Mrs. Purchase—small, breathless sentences, sentences bursting out of her, sentences that got shorter and sharper with every hurried stride.

"Don't know who sent you," he heard her say, puffing hard by then. "But I recognize you. Lookin' in the window at me. Bold as brass." Her sentences came in little gasps, as if she had to take the time to swallow hard between forcing out each one. It made the short sentences sound round and perfectly formed, like a kind of ordered poetry.

"Remember my husband Frank?" she said harshly to the cat.

"He'd still have the restaurant.

"If it wasn't for you bastards.

"He was always on time.

"Always had the money.

"But you always wanted more."

And she swung again, hard, the broom coming closer than it had any time before. The robins had all stopped singing by then, as if they had gotten involved in the chase and had decided to stop and watch.

"I saw Keith take 'er. In the truck.

"I know I did.

"But the police didn't want to hear about it.

"Didn't want to listen.

"Said I'd complained too many times before.

"Thanked me very much.

"Ignored everything I said.

"Sent me on my way.

"But I still know it was him that did it."

Mrs. Purchase swung the broom again and the cat moved away with studied nonchalance, more interested in a stumbling long-legged crane fly, which the cat snagged out of the air with one paw.

It was suddenly cold for a summer evening, the air coming in around the edge of the window in a quickening wave, and there was a hint of woodsmoke in it—hardwood, maybe birch—as if someone in the neighbourhood had shivered once too often in a chilly living room and had decided it was finally time to go ahead and set a fire in the fireplace.

That night, late, Kevin woke up, the sheets around him soaked with sweat. The green numbers of the clock stared at him, well after three a.m. He hated being alone in the big bed, but he was: Cathy was in Ottawa, at yet another conference dedicated to making the world decidedly unsafe for anyone who would dare to try to cheat an insurance company. Cathy, who was away far more often than she was home, high enough up in the insurance company hierarchy that even the insurance frauds of a whole province weren't enough to hold her interest.

He loved his wife, but he knew how calculatingly cold she was too, how quickly she could unravel the most elaborate of compensation lies. She was the worst kind of nightmare for claimants: she was the dry, unforgiving voice on the telephone that everyone must dread hearing, a voice that could make even the legitimately disabled doubt the pith and substance of their injuries. One call and you would already be on the defensive, listening to Cathy's carefully probing words, the way she tested every single sentence you uttered, like a climber checks his ropes, because his life depends on them. Kevin knew how the claimants felt: even telling the complete truth to Cathy, her eyes fixed on him, could leave him shifting in his socks, his eyes moving away as if trying to escape a lie that he hadn't even started telling yet.

Downstairs, the girls should be asleep, he thought. But he didn't really know anymore. They kept uneven, unframed hours, the girls did, both on the edge of nineteen now, his daughter Heather and her best friend, and sometimes it would be five or six o'clock in the morning before he half heard the door close behind them and he could let himself finally fall off into a complete sleep. By then, hours of sleep had been wasted already, wasted in tossing and rolling, sliding an arm under the pillow and pulling it out again, listening for the dry hiss of the water pipes that would tell him they had to be home, because someone had flushed a toilet or cracked open a faucet somewhere else in the house.

They'd worked out a simple code he could depend on if he was really worried: if the girls were home and sleeping, the door into their basement room would be closed; if they were out, they'd leave the door ajar. It was an agreement that was never formally made, never even talked about, only assumed—but it worked through complete constancy. To check, he didn't even have to turn the lights on—just make his way down the long staircase in the black midnight, make the turn to the top of the basement stairs, bend at the waist and look.

This time he went farther, just to be completely sure.

Downstairs, the door was open; peering inside, he saw the bed-clothes thrown back, the lights off, and knew that neither of the girls was home. And Kevin knew the simplest thing to do was just to try to suspend his worry and go back to sleep. To hope, maybe trust, that they would be back in the morning, and then they actually would be—exhausted, staggering, maybe even hungover—but safely home and then down the stairs to bed.

But in the darkness of the stairs, climbing up, he couldn't help hearing Mrs. Purchase's words again.

"Might take one of yours next."

That's foolish, he thought. Just another night out—they didn't even have the car. At least, he didn't think they had the car.

They're together, walking back from somewhere, he thought. Probably getting coffee at one of the all-night places, winding down from dancing and poker-faced with exhaustion.

"Might take one of yours next. Sex slaves. Montreal."

He could only imagine trying to explain it all to Cathy.

"But they're supposed to be in college," she'd say.

Cathy was big on the order of things, on personal responsibility and making sure that responsibility was imposed if it wasn't properly assumed. He could hear the words already. "But you know it's a week-night. They're barely nineteen. What were you thinking? How did it all get this far?" Then, as if prompted by Mrs. Purchase: "Don't you know what strip clubs are like?"

And to make matters worse, he'd have to admit to her that he did, that he'd been to the clubs, to see the peelers, as the guys at work called them, especially when he was on the road alone in Toronto or Montreal. There would be no way to lie, no way that he could keep his eyes from dodging, and he knew she'd catch it at once.

He remembered the clubs too well. The anonymity of them—no one to suddenly walk up and say, "Hey Kevin, whatcha doin' here?" as if that wasn't immediately obvious.

In the big clubs, it seemed like there were hundreds of them. Maybe it was the lights and mirrors, but it was like being surrounded by young, soft bodies with powdery skin that was so smooth and fine that it seemed to trap the dim light. It was hard to imagine anyone's skin could ever be that taut, he'd think. That taut, that perfect, and that smooth. And it was easy to imagine, easy to believe, that some of them were fifteen or sixteen, depending on shabby and smudged fake driver's licences to get them in the door and onto the ratty stage. Easy enough to imagine them getting off buses in the downtown of some big city, fresh from Quispamsis or Gaspereaux or Canso, with eager little faces, still soft and unformed, keen only to get away from whatever sort of hell they believed themselves to be in.

After a couple of weeks, they all had the same bored eyes, the same indifferent way of studying the ceiling tiles. The road from independence to resignation was a short one, Kevin thought. He'd pay them for lap dances and then talk instead, and he knew that it meant they'd single him out to each other as unusual and strange—perhaps even dangerous.

The clubs were never good places to be singled out as different. It was better just to pay for the overpriced beer and blend in.

Once, Kevin spent an hour talking to an Eastern European girl with ungodly huge breasts, uneven teeth and a lisp, until she sized him up and dismissed him gently. "You go home now," she said, putting the twenty dollars he handed her into the small purse that all the girls carried—no room for pockets, dancing nude—and snapping the clasp shut. "You go home to wife and kids." She put a cold hand on his cheek for a moment then, and he saw a row of thin white scars on the inside of her wrist.

In the cab, he tried to forget everything about her. It worked, for a while, except that her voice and the inside of her left wrist kept swimming back into his memory unbidden. And he wondered just what it was that she was going home to, seeing the thin white parallel lines like empty sheet music, waiting for their defining notes.

Out on the street in front of Kevin's empty house, he heard the engine of a heavy truck rev up, heard the bite of the tires on the pavement as the driver popped the clutch. From the sound of the tires, Kevin could imagine that he was watching the back of the truck fishtail slightly from side to side, the bright red gems of the tail lights shrinking to small glass beads as the truck pulled quickly away.

A strange and wandering thought struck him: Can you really tell anything from tail lights? Could you look at them and get some kind of idea of at least the model of the car that was driving away from you? In a moment of stress, could you even remember what those two small red lights looked like?

Kevin sat down heavily on the couch in the living room, wearing a bathrobe over a T-shirt and his underwear. Occasionally a car would whisk by outside, and the headlights would sweep across the ceiling above the level of the curtains. The room would light up for a moment, and then it would be even darker than it had been before.

There was, he noticed, a fraction of a second as a car was passing when you could watch the shadows of individual pieces of furniture move across the wall, as if the furniture had decided to rise on its heels and creep across the room, tugging at the curtains for a quick look outside.

He waited, wondering just where the girls were.

There was no way to reach them, and no real way to explain why he was even worried. No one to consult, no one to ask, no one to call.

And later, there'd be no way to explain to Cathy, either. He was pretty sure that the girls took advantage when she was away, that perhaps Heather realized how they could make him melt by just reminding him of those few short years when she had been a toddler. He would flash back to that if she gave him just the right hint of a familiar smile. He wasn't sure that she knew she was doing it, but he suspected. "Can I take the car?" sounding no more significant coming from her than "Can I have another cookie?" and really, he'd think, why not?

Why not, when her eyes were so simple and innocent, her skin perfectly smooth and magically soft, without even a single scar?

The "why not" wouldn't sink in until much later, when all of a sudden he'd feel both ashamed and angry, sullenly wondering whether he'd just been played by a calculating, sharp-eyed stranger hiding inside the girl he once thought he'd always know.

With that, he got up and pulled the curtain open, looking outside to see if the car was there, and of course, it wasn't.

It wasn't, and the space where he had parked it earlier that evening looked as naked as if whoever had driven away had peeled up a patch of asphalt and taken it with them in the trunk as well.

There were moths circling in the glow of the street lights, hapless and confused, an amateur Aeroflot always on the near edge of a mid-air collision. And he was caught again on the knife-edge of trust and terror. Heather would be furious if she knew his fears, if she guessed that he was questioning whether she knew how to take care of herself. And yet, if something was wrong, he'd be losing valuable, irreplaceable time.

Heather with a rectangle of silver duct tape across her mouth, her arms pinned behind her back, caught between two faceless men on the bench seat of a speeding pickup truck.

Heather and Claire being thrown around in the pitch black of the trunk of a car, the trunk lid closing over their struggling bodies.

He heard a car stereo, loud enough that the Doppler of its bass shook warnings in the window glass of houses it hadn't even gotten to yet.

And then Kevin woke up, still on the couch, and it was daylight.

Outside, he could hear people shouting—two voices measured, the third high and frightened. He went outside without even stopping to put on his shoes, realizing it only when he felt the rough prickle of the concrete on the bottoms of his feet.

Mrs. Purchase was half in and half out of a small Toyota, the car muscled in tight to the curb, close enough that he noticed that the side walls of its tires were scuffed black from contact with the cement.

Both her hands were still outside the car, turned backwards and with the fingers splayed flat against the roof so the couple holding her couldn't close the back door of the car without closing it on her hands.

"Come on, Mom," the woman was saying. "Come on. We're just going to look. You don't have to stay—we just want to see if you'll like the place. They have gardens, too. You'll see."

Mrs. Purchase batted ineffectually at the woman's hands with one of her own, not relinquishing her grip with the other hand, and Kevin thought of the powdery wings of a moth batting uselessly at the hot glass of the street light.

The woman who was holding Mrs. Purchase's wrists was someone whom Kevin could not remember having seen before.

"I don't know you," Mrs. Purchase was saying quietly, urgently. "I don't know you."

She looked up as Kevin let the screen door slam behind him, walking towards the trio. Mrs. Purchase's pupils pulled into sharp focus as she recognized him.

"I told you," Mrs. Purchase hissed plaintively at Kevin, her eyes wide. "I told you what can happen. You just don't know. I saw her in the front seat. I did. I told them. I told them years and years ago. And I never saw her again."

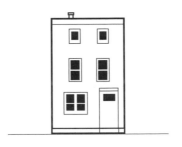

104
McKay Street

ALBERT CARTER

NOVEMBER 15, 2002

THE LETTER was on the kitchen table, the envelope beside it. Three and a half years before Mrs. Purchase told Kevin about the girl, Albert Carter had already written it all down. But what he'd seen was buried, lost, mixed in with everything else. Carter picked the letter up, meaning to fold it and seal it in the envelope. He picked it up over and over again, but always put it back down on the table again, the pages still smooth, the typed letters sharply black against the white paper.

He had crossed out some words, filled in others, but he tried to keep it as neat as he could, the changes between the lines in fine, careful script, black ink, the letters in each word looping up so that every letter was at exactly the same height, as if they'd been written between two ruled lines. The Jesuits, Albert thought grimly, they'd done their job with him. They'd been perfectionists about everything. Disciplined— severe even—not like the way things were now.

He spread the letter out flat on the kitchen table, the morning light streaming in behind him from the small yard, and started to read it again.

To the Right Honourable Prime Minister and to the Justice Minister of Canada:

First of all, in this case I am not the Instigator. I am not the cause. That is for certain.

As Prime Minister, and as Justice Minister, you should both know that. You should both understand that clearly. I am not to blame, I am just a citizen of this country like anyone else, and I have the right to have the quiet enjoyment of my property, even if lying, instigating Chris Wheeler doesn't seem to think so.

I should say first of all that I have lived at 104 McKay Street for 47 years now, and during that time I have been no trouble to anyone. There is not one living person who would have said that I was any problem at all, not even the least bit of a nuisance.

Live and let live, that is my personal motto, and it always has been.

At least, until lying Chris Wheeler moved here with his blue Nissan Sentra—Newfoundland and Labrador licence RPN 3L3—and his huge car stereo, on which he plays loud music at night, and since his lying, instigating friends started spending so much time here, disturbing the peace with their foul behaviour.

McKay Street in St. John's, Newfoundland, is a good street. It is a quiet street, not a street where you expect to hear loud music all the time. It is part of a neighbourhood that's been full of families for years, a downtown neighbourhood that was busy when driving was a luxury. Most of us are older now, and if anyone is to blame, it should be the City, because they gave Peter Kavanaugh permission to subdivide his house into two apartments and then move, lock, stock and barrel, out of town, leaving his property in the hands of a succession of tenants, none of whom could really be trusted.

Leaving all of his troubles behind for the rest of us.

Leaving us with lying Chris Wheeler.

Lying Chris Wheeler, he is the worst tenant Peter Kavanaugh has had yet, the worst, laziest, most deceitful tenant yet, and Chris Wheeler has told so many people lies about me now that I swear I cannot go anywhere without people staring at me, and Heaven only knows what they are thinking.

Even my friends look at me differently now, people who have known me for years and who should know better. People for whom I have never had a bad word, people I have gone out of my way to help. But instigator Chris Wheeler, he has dragged my name through the dirt, and I am sure he is the reason why everything has changed.

I know there are those who will say that you shouldn't listen to me, who will whisper, who will write their anonymous letters and say that you should ignore someone who has had a conviction registered against them already for disturbing the peace.

Even the police might have something to say about me, might say "Listen, Prime Minister, we remember that man." But they are not the only ones who remember things.

Let me say that I remember them, Constable Peter Wright, badge number 432, and Constable Reg Dunne, badge number 881, and I remember that they didn't even listen to my complaints, not even when my cat was killed and they wrote the things I said down in their black notebooks and then closed them up and forgot the whole thing.

And later their fellow officers listened to the likes of lying Chris Wheeler and his lying skeet friends Roger McInnes and Rory Andrews and that quiet one, Alma Jones, the police listened to them when they said that they were just playing music and I came out for no reason, carrying a shovel and swearing and waving my fist, and that then I broke some of their beer bottles next to Wheeler's precious car.

The judge went further than the police, said it was "beyond a reasonable doubt" that I had struck lying Wheeler's car with my shovel, because all three of his friends stuck to their made-up lying story, and the judge even ordered me—*me*—to pay Wheeler. Pay him for paint for his car—when I am the one whose rights were being abused, and are still abused on a regular basis.

I thought the judge would have some sympathy for what was happening to me, because he looked as though he was just about my age—there on high and all fancy in his black robe, but able to understand the sorts of things people our age have to deal with, his face perched up above his robe like a shrivelled old angry apple, but I was wrong and he didn't understand at all.

He probably lives in a big house in the east end somewhere, with a huge garden where he can work way up in the back and never even hear the street noise, let alone have to deal with the likes of Wheeler. I imagine he never has to deal with neighbours at all, beyond a little chat if they meet putting the garbage out by the curb. And his neighbours are hardly likely to slink over to his fence and pitch their trash into his yard when he's eating a fine dinner and listening to classical music.

And I have a restraining order now, an order that says I can't go near Chris Wheeler, but it certainly doesn't mean he can't come near me.

I understand that justice isn't perfect, and I understand that the police don't care if someone climbs up over my fence or just throws their garbage into my yard from the laneway out back, and I understand that the police have better things to do than to come promptly when someone, some ordinary citizen like myself, makes a complaint about someone doing something as simple as vandalizing a flower garden.

But I don't break beer bottles or swear or shout people down, I don't sneer and call anyone "old man" and tell them to "get away and stay on the other side of the street where you belong." And I have certainly never called anyone a "fucking old busybody," even though plenty of things like that have been said to me.

I am much more reasonable than that because I understand the Charter of Rights and Freedoms, because I have read it completely. And I understand the Bible and turning the other cheek, and believe me, I have done that a good few times as well.

But the instigators know that it was four people saying one thing and me saying something else, even if my word is good and theirs are worthless, and that the courts understand four against one better than they understand the truth sometimes.

I have paid my taxes my entire life, and I have a copy of each of my tax returns to prove it, and they are stored upstairs, chronologically and in brown envelopes, should anyone doubt my word and want to come see them.

I have paid my taxes completely and in a timely fashion, and I should remind you, with all due respect, that you both work for me just as much as you work for instigating Chris Wheeler, even if his lying words seem to mean more than my honest ones.

I may have talked to him with the shovel in my hand, certainly I may have done that, but I don't remember doing it. It certainly would have been a mistake in judgment to cross the street with a shovel, but they are young and strong, and an old man can be frightened too.

Because they have tormented me for years, carefully and deliberately, and anyone can lose their temper once in a while.

Everyone should have the ability to enjoy some quality of life in their home, a home they have bought and paid for with sweat and hard labour.

Since the police seem unwilling to investigate, I can tell you that I have watched lying Chris Wheeler and his friends from my upstairs windows, and I have kept careful track of their movements, both in the night and the day. I have thorough records, thorough and diligent and timely and exact.

My watch no longer keeps the best time, but every afternoon I listen to your National Research Council time signal, and I reset my watch even if it is only a few seconds out. Not much escapes me when I am on watch: I write down anything unusual and it stays with me for years—for example, I can remember all the way back to when I saw Keith O'Reilly driving Glenn Coughlin's green truck with a strange girl sitting next to him, both of them lit up under the street light like that. I didn't see the licence plate to be absolutely certain, but I don't think there's another truck like that one. It was years and years ago, but I don't forget.

Things like that stay in my mind, when things show up where they shouldn't be, things that don't fit. And if I wanted to, I could go back and find the exact day, even the time. I am sure it is in one of the notebooks. I recognized her—that girl who went missing. She had been ringing doorbells, probably begging for change. As if people on this street were made of money or something. I looked down at her from the window upstairs, but I didn't open the door.

And I kept a record. I am thorough about things like that.

But I am especially thorough about Wheeler and his friends. I have notebooks full of their hours and their activities, and if they claim to be looking for work, their unemployment insurance should be cut off immediately, because they are never doing anything for the summer months except sitting on lying Wheeler's steps, staring at the young girls in the neighbourhood and drinking beer.

Dominion beer, in red and yellow cases, and they just twist the caps off and throw them out on the street. And twelve beer rarely lasts for more than an afternoon, and at least once a week they have enough empties to put them in the trunk of Wheeler's car and cash them in for more. When I can sneak the window open, I can sometimes catch a few words of them speaking, and I record those too, in case they might turn out to have some value.

"Chris, you bastard, I can't believe you took the last one, when I bought it, too."

"The skank you were with last night was the ugliest one I've ever seen you with."

"Roger, you said you cracked Alma, but you never."

(I think they were talking about giving Alma Jones drugs then—she is only tiny and young, just a stick of a thing, and I'm sure as impressionable as anyone else that age, willing to do whatever it takes to be accepted.)

I should mention that they appear to be using drugs, and they are probably selling them too. To the young ones, to teens like Ronnie Collins, to the Haydens and Chaulks who buzz around there like anxious busy little flies.

I am not sure, but it seems to me that lying Chris Wheeler has far too many visitors, and I am sure that there is some kind of exchange that takes place there, hand to hand, and there would be proof of it in my notebooks, careful records, if only my eyes were better and I could make out what they were doing when they got in close.

I have seen him talking to children, children who could hardly be more than eight or nine years old, children who are just bicycling by those steps, and who knows what sorts of crimes Wheeler is doing with such innocents, and what kind of behaviour he and his slovenly friends are inciting.

When I am at the grocery store or if I have to go to the pharmacy, I know that Wheeler or one of his cronies is likely to come into the yard behind my house, walking down the laneway and coming through my gate as easily as if they actually owned the place.

I know that they saw the sunflowers back there on one of their thieving explorations, probably coming into the yard to peer into the two windows in the kitchen to see if there was anything inside worth stealing. A waste of time, that errand, because I am on a pension and have little that would interest them.

But I did have sunflowers.

I had sunflowers all along the back fence, such beautiful sunflowers, and the spring is so cold here that when they were just seedlings, a single strand of green growing up with two unformed and hesitant-looking leaves on the top, I would go out on the cool spring evenings and put styrofoam coffee cups over each one, an individual insulating cover to protect them from the frost, and every morning I would go out again and lift those small shelters so the sun could reach them.

The sunflowers that escaped the slugs grew taller and taller, and when their big green buds finally opened and turned upwards, I could look down from my bedroom on the back of the house and see those cheerful nodding faces up against the sun, and they were the kind of thing that can lift your heart when everything else conspires against you.

I had such dreams for those flowers, that in the fall when their flower heads browned and tilted down, the city chickadees would come and hang upside-down from them and pluck out the seeds, one by one. The chickadees don't eat them all at once—when I've left seeds out for the birds, I've found them tucked away in torn-up spider's nests under the lip of the clapboard along the back of the house, carefully saved for winter.

But the chickadees didn't come, the chickadees won't ever come, because on the 17th of August, while I was getting my prescriptions filled—I have four regular prescriptions, all properly given on my doctor's advice, a diuretic and a heart drug and two for blood pressure—lying Chris Wheeler and his friends came into my yard and ripped all of my sunflowers out by the roots, and they must have run around the yard swinging them at each other, because when I got home, the sunflowers were strewn all around the yard and the stalks of the flowers were so battered that they were limp like old green rope. And the sight was so shocking that I sat down in my yard, I sat down right there in my yard, and it was all I could do to keep from crying. I know my hands were in front of my face, because I remember seeing it all through the frame of my fingers. And wouldn't Chris Wheeler have liked to have seen that?

They must have watched me come home from the store from where they were sitting on Wheeler's steps, their eyes following me the whole way, and I think I knew that something was different about their reactions. I knew something was different about the way they were looking at me, even before I went out back and found the flowers.

I am sure they heard me yelling, but I was not swearing—no, I was not swearing. I was angry, and I was yelling, but I was yelling about the Charter of Rights, and I'm sure I need not tell you about this, but it was Section Seven, and I will copy it down for you, just so that you know for sure that I know what I am talking about—that "everyone has a right to life, liberty and security of the person and the right not to be deprived thereof except in accordance with the principles of fundamental justice."

And that is really all I am asking you to protect for me—my life and liberty, and my faith in fundamental justice.

Because I do not think it is just that I should be persecuted by lying Chris Wheeler, that I should have to be on my guard all the time, that the security of my person should be at risk while the likes of Chris Wheeler get to make decisions about what the quality of my life will be like.

When I looked out the window at them that afternoon, that 17th day of August, I could see from their smug faces that they thought they were pretty smart, just as smart as they must have thought they were in April when they put cold chicken bones and chips and gravy into my mailbox, just to see if they could get me in trouble again, just to see if they could make me come after them.

When I found the chicken bones, I stayed calm, but I carefully looked around to see if I could see anyone watching me, looking to see my reaction.

Wheeler's car was across the road, but there was no one in it.

I am sure they were watching from inside, from Wheeler's basement apartment with the small windows, standing there like they were watching a movie or something. I could not see them, but I had to be careful not to be caught staring—that's all I need, for them to know that they were getting to me. When you deal with bullies for long enough, you know how a sign of weakness will set them off.

Cocks of the walk, they are, and it seems there is nothing that anyone can do about it.

Daring me to do something, and the restraining order was barely restraining anything. I can tell you more serious things, tell you about how they killed my cat Marble, a sweeter cat you will never have seen.

I was in the front room upstairs, the small room with the desk where I keep all my papers, and I couldn't help it—my hands were bunched tight in fists and I was even shaking. But when you've already got a restraining order against you, well, it's never that far from your mind that it doesn't take long for the police to show up and pull your hands behind your back for the handcuffs, even if they can never seem to find the right address when it is me who is calling them.

They do not like me here because I came from a different part of the city, because I bought this house cheap before anyone else had a chance to, and I freely admit that, but we live in a capitalist country, and it is my choice to invest my capital in the ways that I see fit.

I shouldn't have to live like this. And I shouldn't always have to expect worse, just waiting for whatever it is they choose to do next. I am not stupid, and I can see the weaknesses in my own house.

There is a small window at ground level in the front of my foundation, and what used to be a coal door, boarded over now with old wood. On the back of the house, there is only the door and the kitchen windows, and I barricade the door at night so they can't get in.

It's darker back there, but I imagine they will wait until I am sleeping, until everyone on the street is sleeping, and then force their way in through the scuttle into the basement. Both the scuttle and the window are on the street, so I can hardly reinforce them without being seen—and if I'm seen, I know they will only change their plans.

For two weeks, I collected jars and broke the glass with my hammer, carefully, the bottles lying on their sides on newspaper I'd spread on the counter in the kitchen. I carried the shards downstairs still wrapped in the paper, and I could feel the sharp edges grinding against themselves inside the paper, and I filled the concrete valley under the coal lid with them— five trips in all, and even in the gloom of the basement, the glass shards looked wickedly sharp. Lying there, it looked as if they were just waiting to bite, like hungry teeth.

If Chris Wheeler's friends come in that way, they will get a fine surprise.

They might still come through the window, but it is very small—I hope I will hear them coming, even if they wrap something in soft cloth and use it to smash the two small panes of glass.

I have to confess, I did one or two other things to be sure that they can't surprise me. Either way they get into the basement, they will still have to come up the basement stairs. So I have cut the stringers under the treads right at the top near the door. I've cut them very carefully, and I even swept up the sawdust so that they wouldn't have any kind of warning at all.

I've cut a few other beams as well, in spots they wouldn't suspect but in places that I circle around carefully, so there are places where the floor is not at all like it should be.

It took me a long time, because my hands get stiff and sore very quickly working the saw. The stair risers were only spruce, but they are very dry, and they feel as hard as stone. If nothing else, I should be able to hear them, the stairs falling in under their weight.

And I trust that men in your position will not share these personal confidences, not if as officers of the Crown you serve all Canadians, instead of just serving the Chris Wheelers of this country.

Because Wheeler is not without cunning, and given any warning at all, he will no doubt search out another path, one of less resistance.

I will certainly call the police when I am sure I hear them down there, but by the time they get here, I'm sure that lying Chris Wheeler and his friends will be far away again, probably sitting on those steps and trying not to burst out laughing. And if Wheeler and his fellows do find a way up here, I will be in no shape to even answer the front door before the good officers shrug and stroll back down to their police cruisers, because there's coffee to be bought and doughnuts to be eaten.

You should now realize full well my circumstances, not only because of this letter but because you can certainly read up on all the complaints I've filed, complaints that no one has seen fit to do anything about.

Because you and your people have chosen to believe lying Chris Wheeler and his dangerous-driving friends, friends who say that all this clear torment is just practical jokes and paranoia and nothing more.

But if I put my bike down by my back gate, unlocked and leaning on the fence, and then I lie on the kitchen table in front of the window with the shotgun and the window just slightly open, well, if someone tries to steal my bike, then I am only defending my property, and I am well within my rights to do so.

The shotgun is easily as old as I am, bought for rabbits when I was young enough to get out of the city, when I was strong enough that no one would dare to mess with my property while I was gone to the country. It may be old, but it is regularly cleaned, its barrel still blue with gun oil, and even though it is single-shot and bolt-action, I know I could load at least a second shot before anyone made the distance from the gate to the back of the house.

I have a new box of slug ammunition, it could knock down a moose, not that your new federal legislation made it any easier for me—an honest and law-abiding citizen—to buy those shells. And even though the gun kicks hard, I think I would get off a few shots, at least two, even though it would take days for the cordite smell of the gunpowder to completely clear from the kitchen.

So when that gate opens, I will only be defending myself, even if lying instigator Chris Wheeler or one of his friends is only planning to steal my bike as some sort of joke or something, a joke I can no longer find in the least bit funny.

Because a person can only be asked to put up with so much, and I have certainly been more than fair and reasonable over the years that lying Chris Wheeler has made my life a living hell.

At least I am man enough to ensure that I can protect my own property, and well read enough to understand that the law makes some distinction for those who are pressed to the very limit of their endurance, suffering abuse the justice system is, for some reason, not willing to address.

Honourable sirs, I know that you will understand my circumstances and the torment that has driven me to this. I realize you may interpret my concerns about the state of justice in this country as meaning that I do not believe you have properly done the jobs you have sworn to do. If you feel that way, then so be it.

I, good sirs, am no lawyer, but I am an honest man and a taxpayer, and I rest my case.

With every best wish,
Albert Carter
104 McKay Street

Albert signed the letter carefully and then addressed the envelope, wondering for a moment when his handwriting had gotten so uneven and what the Prime Minister would think of that.

32
McKay Street

VINCENT O'REILLY

MAY 13, 2002

SOMETIMES Vincent felt the uncontrollable eagerness under his skin as clearly as if he was at the starting line in a race, just waiting for the gun to fire. Every part of him straining forwards, pushing, waiting to explode out of the blocks. And at the same time, he was always left with the feeling that the gun would never fire. He knew nothing good would come of waiting.

Twenty-one years old, and Vincent spent every night anticipating the morning and every morning, waiting for something to finally happen.

And every morning, it felt like he was having the same conversation.

"Why do you have to go? And where do you think you're going to be, anyway?" his mother would ask. Hearing the questions never failed to almost completely empty his mind. The answers that looked so simple in his room, while he was staring up at the same ceiling he had always known, sounded both complicated and hollow in the daylight, and after explaining them a few times he almost couldn't force the words out anymore.

It was simple, if anyone was willing to really listen. Here was a trap, and the only way to spring it was to find a place somewhere away.

"I'll find something, Mom. I'll find something every bit as good as I'm going to find here." Vincent imagined that he said the words with his chin pushed out, as if he were the one picking the fight every time.

"But you're not even looking for a job here."

There was a desperate, reaching tone to her voice, a high note at the end, that rattled around while the early spring sunshine was belting in through the window and lighting the table and the toast. Vincent's father was already up and gone to work, close enough to retirement that it seemed like he was trying even harder, turning it on because the finish line was almost in sight. Vincent had grown, but the world inside the house hadn't changed. Vincent was reasonably sure he was stronger than his father now, but there was no way that Keith O'Reilly would give up even an inch of the power he held in the house: his arms might not be as strong, but his voice was harder and sharper and louder, and he was more frustrated, his edicts on what would happen in the house, and when, even more hard-edged. And his mother just took it—that always surprised Vincent, because she had been the disciplinarian all through school. Sometimes a flash of frustration would light her face, but mostly she went along, even as Vincent bridled.

And Vincent couldn't explain that he didn't even want to look in this city, that the whole purpose was the getting away, that a job in St. John's would just be another anchor, another thing that would stretch out a sticky cable and fasten him tight in a place he no longer felt he should be. That each new string just made the spiderweb stronger, and that any job, anywhere else, would be preferable to being given even one more reason to stay.

Because staying now had a feeling like forever to it.

Vincent felt tied to the chains of the everyday, unable to reach for anything. How do you explain to your mother that when she makes toast for you every morning, it is like she is trying to keep you prisoner?

After he finished eating, Vincent left the house and walked down one shoulder of the city until he reached Forest Road. Past the penitentiary, along the edge of the lake, and then he turned off and headed up towards the bare knob of rock above Quidi Vidi village. There was no real path to the top of the rock, a dome that arched a hundred feet or more above the water with plenty of sheer rock on the sides, but there were breaks in the low spruce running up the sides of the hill, and occasional wide fans of washout where the angle of the incline had brought water down the hill fast enough to strip away the thin sepia clay. It was possible to climb up there, using occasional handholds and footholds of purplish puddingstone, a rock made out of some long-forgotten and petrified river bottom now tilted unnaturally up to the vertical by tectonics, the gritty sandstone packed full with a leaven of round stones like raisins in bread. Even though it had been warm, there were still thick pads of ice on the edges of the parts he was trying to climb, ice that was rounded and sweating with melt, but ice just the same.

Every now and then a breeze would blow across the sheltered snow and ice under the branches, and it would come out from under the edges of the trees like a low, cold breath on his skin, unsettling enough that he would look over his shoulder to make sure he was alone.

The higher he went, the more the ground cover thinned out, falling away to lower and lower bushes, stick-thin blueberry with the fat buds that would soon be leaves, rhodera with its waxy leaves browned from the winter but still smelling faintly of their August rush of faux eucalyptus. Without any cover, the ice vanished, leaving the flattened bushes behind it. There were yards of partridgeberry curled up in snow-flattened coils and wormed, complex patterns, and when Vincent finally reached the top of the hill, his breath regular and heavy, there was nothing left that was higher than ankle-deep, except for one low alder thicket and the grey shoulders of rock shrugging up through the ground. The tops of the rocks were white where the seagulls liked to stand, and there were small collections of bones—chicken scraps, the occasional T-bone—the gulls had brought up to the top so they could strip off remnants of meat without disturbance.

The sun was warm on Vincent's shoulders, and he was high enough up that the elevation entirely flattened out the waves on the sea below, the peaks and valleys of the rough water erased except for the pale scars of the whitecaps, and even they seemed to have no more depth than an eyebrow has on a face.

It was far enough along in the year that the sun felt like it had finally decided to start working seriously, and the water reflected chips of sunlight back at Vincent in bright semaphore. He had to shade his eyes while he watched a red and white Coast Guard vessel chew its way towards the harbour.

If he turned around, Vincent knew that he could point directly towards the house, back behind the low roll of Signal Hill, his arm straight and unerring as any compass even though he couldn't see a single patch of the flat roof. And when he thought about that, knowing exactly how something was—trusting where it was, maybe—without actually seeing it, Vincent thought it might be the perfect explanation for why he was sure he would have no choice but to leave.

But how do you explain to your mother that if you're able to point out the house where you grew up, you know you're too close to home?

111
McKay Street

BRENDAN HAYDEN

FEBRUARY 2, 2006

BY THE TIME four years had passed, Vincent had escaped the confines of his childhood home. Almost a block away, Brendan Hayden hadn't. The only distance Brendan found was on the Internet, and in his imagination.

Brendan hadn't thought that the Niagara River was going to wind up being so important, not when he'd never even seen it, not when it was thousands of miles away. The idea of Niagara Falls—the concept of it, that he knew.

Who wouldn't know about Niagara Falls, about the honeymooners, the strip of motels, about the ribbon of bright lights throwing themselves up against the sky along the photographed edge of the gorge? But this was something different, the way he felt about it now—this other Niagara River, the one he kept tripping over again and again, finding in report after report. He'd been ready for a lot of things, for the hard photos and the blunt descriptions, but the repeated references were what really jarred him, the idea of people going to the very same place just to hurl themselves over the edge and into the water.

Was it supposed to be somehow significant, or was it just that the height of the falls was so great that it could be expected to do the job completely?

As he read the shorthand notes, the words kept jumping out at him: several reports said "found near *Maid of the Mist* docking platform," others had "near the 'Whirlpool,' Niagara River" or "in the water intake channel for Sir Adam Beck Hydro Generating Station, Niagara River." It seemed to Brendan that the police must be just constantly pulling them in, and he couldn't help but imagine there was a whole grim-faced detail of police boatmen out there on the river, clad in blue rainsuits and carrying long, wicked boathooks, working the misty shoreline below the falls, pulling bodies in over the gunwales day after day after day. "Look, Joe, there's another one. Better haul him in too."

And Brendan resolved then that, no matter what happened, he'd never make a pilgrimage to that falls, not for a wedding or a honeymoon, and certainly not for a memorial service. Not to be part of a solemn group of besuited relatives flicking a hapless "In Memory" wreath out into the water just to watch it slowly drift away, perhaps following the same arc of current as the not-so-dearly departed, perhaps just pulling away towards those intakes all over again.

You're not supposed to just lose a brother, Brendan thought, the way he thought it three or four times every single day. At the same time, he couldn't help but think that losing Larry hadn't happened all at once, either. And even if you had lost a brother somehow, Brendan thought, you weren't supposed to repeatedly find yourself punching your way into a police website that tried to identify unnamed and unclaimed bodies.

You were especially not supposed to be hoping to find your brother in there among the unknown strangers.

It wasn't clear-cut and simple, it wasn't like Larry had gone out hunting one day and by the next he still hadn't come home and it was time to organize the search party. No, Larry had vanished slowly, like he was moving away, moving deliberately and carefully backwards one step at a time into heavy fog. Thinking about it, Brendan found he couldn't even put an exact day on when his brother suddenly slipped out of sight. He'd go and reappear, leaving St. John's but eventually calling from Toronto, for example. After Larry had turned up in Toronto, he'd had his own apartment for a while, and Brendan had even been up to see it once—a one-bedroom flat in a nondescript building next to a downtown park, remarkable only for the number of vagrants who stayed just inside the front door by the mailboxes, soaking up the warmth.

Later, there hadn't been an apartment, no telephone number for Brendan to call, but Larry had still sometimes kept in touch, calling collect every now and then from noisy pay phones just exactly when it seemed as if it had been too long since anyone had heard from him. The calls were far apart and short on detail. Sometimes, Larry would say that he was working. Calls from the fruit belt, where Larry had been picking peaches, and once or twice from job sites in Alberta. Most often, though, from Toronto, where Larry would be landscaping or picking up a couple of weeks' work on a construction site before inevitably being the one fired again.

Those calls, sometimes rambling, frightened Brendan, who wondered if someday it would be the police on the end of the line, asking if he was a family member and preparing to spill the details of some horrendous event that Larry had fallen into. But there was always a small snatch of the brother he knew just before the call ended, a gentle declination in Larry's voice, a switch to a softer, quieter, more familiar Larry: "Take care, Bren, and tell Mom not to worry." There was always just enough, still, of Larry in that distant voice to let Brendan wind back the alarm, to quiet the tremors that the phone calls always set off in his stomach.

Then even those scattered phone calls stopped, and Brendan could remember the exact night when he'd woken up from a dream where Larry had been one of those shadowy, dirty men you run into on Toronto street corners, asking for change and sleeping under the viaducts. It was like Larry had suddenly become detached from the known Earth, like he was floating in his own particular orbit without the need for any fixed waypoint on the ground.

After that, Brendan had waited enough time for his concern to feel legitimate, and then he called the Toronto police. They sounded professional, took details, age, height, hair colour, asked about distinguishing features like tattoos and scars, and then offered up the information that Larry Hayden hadn't been arrested for anything, but little more than that.

They'd asked if Larry had ever done anything like this before, taking off and not telling anyone, but Brendan kept that answer to himself. If he'd ever been missing, if he'd ever pulled up stakes and just disappeared. They'd asked if he'd ever been convicted of anything in Newfoundland, whether he might have fingerprints on file with the police, and Brendan had said no, even though it had been very close to a lie. Whether Larry had been married or divorced, whether there was anything obvious he might be running from.

It seemed to Brendan as if it was suddenly very important for the police to find a reason to not be concerned, as if they were looking for just enough information to feel comfortable dismissing Brendan's call and putting the whole thing safely on the back burner forever.

And Brendan thought about when Larry had left, about Constable Peter Wright and Constable Reg Dunne coming to the door, his mother bringing the police officers upstairs to Larry and Brendan's room, standing behind them when they started to ask the boys their questions, and how she had her arms folded across her chest, her mouth a thin, hard line.

They had never been a close family, even though they'd grown up right on top of each other, just two brothers and Brendan's parents in the two-storey row house. Brendan and Larry had shared a bedroom—front left bedroom at the top of the stairs, a ten-foot-by-ten-foot room pressed up tight against the Chaulks' next door, close enough that, if they were quiet and both lay on Brendan's bed, they could hear Laura Chaulk tearing careful, deliberate verbal strips off her husband in the bedroom.

But while they might have been closely packed into their room, Larry and Brendan weren't that close themselves: Brendan moved separately with a pack of neighbourhood kids, a gang ranging up and down McKay Street as if it was their own personal playground. Larry, meanwhile, seemed to haunt the edges, always around but never really part of anything.

Brendan and Ronnie Collins and the two Chaulk boys, Murray and Twig, could be carefully stealing mail from old Crazyman Carter's mailbox, and Brendan knew he would be able to turn around at any time and, if he was careful enough, find Larry lurking at the corner or next to a fence, half his face hidden, watching them. Or they'd be running around with Vincent O'Reilly, throwing crabapples from Mrs. Purchase's tree against the fronts of houses after it got dark, and Larry would somehow always know where they had been and what they had been doing.

Several times, Brendan remembered wishing that Larry would just die, that his brother would stop dogging his steps, peering at him all the time like some vagabond scrap of conscience, his eyes always hollow and staring, always looking as if there was something strange going on back there in his head, some strange calculation in which Brendan was being measured—and failing—every single time. The only benefit was that whatever calculation, whatever judgment, Larry was making was religiously private: everything went in, but nothing ever seemed to come out.

Yet.

Brendan at least had that fleeting safety, and the fear that it might change.

Everyone in the neighbourhood knew Larry and stayed out of his way, and everyone had something to say about how odd he was—as soon as they were certain he was out of earshot. They weren't always right about that. Larry could appear from between magazine racks just as Mrs. Butler was telling the drugstore clerk about seeing him down in the rose bush at the end of her yard. Or his head would pop up over the fence just as neighbours were discussing how long it would take before he did something weird enough to put him in the boys' home.

Larry would watch everything, big eyes sucking it all in, but it never seemed to slip back out of him. Everyone knew he was peculiar, but they didn't ever catch him at anything. He was just Larry—Larry who always knew too much.

Brendan knew that Larry had been around somewhere when Ronnie killed the cat, knew that Larry knew all about it, even if Brendan couldn't figure out exactly where his brother had been when it happened. There wasn't much room between Mr. Carter's house and the one next door, so Larry would have had to have been at one end or the other.

Brendan and the Chaulks had all watched, stunned into silence, as Ronnie had smashed the cat's head against the dark blue clapboard of the side of Mr. Carter's house, over and over again, long after the cat had stopped making any sound at all. The noise had been horrible: not really meowing at all, more a kind of unnatural screech that you'd imagine should have been coming from metal being scraped hard across metal.

Brendan felt the loose feeling in his stomach again just remembering the sound, and remembering, he knew, was only a fraction of what the noise had really been like. And Brendan couldn't help but think that Ronnie made it all look so easy, the short, hard swing, focused and simple, like throwing a baseball, and then precisely and deliberately repeated, as if it were a motion Ronnie was already well familiar with.

All four of them had been cutting through Mr. Carter's yard again, a quick heft up and over the fence with strong teenaged arms, and then a quick, quiet rush along the side of the yard until you got to the gap between Mr. Carter's and Mrs. Harris's next door. They'd often stop there and reach out to slam a fist against the side of the house, and then run before Mr. Carter could find his way to the door. They'd hear him swearing, hear his progress through the back of the house as if he was forcing his way through piles of rubbish, struggling to get to the door in time to catch them.

Every time, they'd start right at the back corner, running down between the houses, pushing at each other with their elbows to try to force their way out of the narrow opening ahead, each boy trying to be in the lead.

Except for that time.

That's when Ronnie had stopped to pet Mr. Carter's cat, not expecting it to arch its back in panic and swipe out a paw and rake its claws straight down the back of Ronnie's arm.

They hadn't expected Ronnie's reaction either, hadn't expected him to snap his arm out quick and grab the cat by its neck, his hand crushing into the fur.

Ronnie was breathing hard when he dropped the lifeless body onto the thin gravel strip next to the house, and Brendan remembered thinking it was like some great force had come along and sucked every single bit of air out of the space between the houses. There was no sound afterwards, except for Ronnie's breathing, all of the shapes in the darkness sharp-edged, like Brendan's eyes had learned a new and more effective way to focus.

"Little bastard scratched me bad," Ronnie said, twisting his arm so that he could look at the parallel stripes running down from the point of his elbow, parallel scratches that were barely bleeding.

Murray and Twig were already gone, fading out of sight the way they always seemed to be able to do, fast and so quiet that you could almost imagine they could make themselves disappear, moving together without a single spoken word to co-ordinate their actions. They hadn't made a sound, not even a whispered, "Jeez, Ronnie," before stepping backwards and running.

Then Ronnie had turned towards Brendan, and it was like his eyes had changed completely, as if they had slipped from one person to another in an instant. "It never happened, and you never saw nothing," Ronnie said, menacing and taking two steps so that his face was inches from Brendan's. Almost no light left in the failing evening, and the brightest parts of Ronnie were the whites of his staring eyes and his teeth, and it was an expression that stayed with Brendan for months.

But when the police came to the house, it was Larry they wanted to talk to—Larry, who hadn't been part of it at all—and Brendan remembered feeling a strange combination of relief and disgust: relief that he wasn't going to be questioned, disgust that Larry was wrongly going to get the blame. Again.

The first police officer, Constable Wright, had walked his mother back towards the landing of the stairs, talking to her. The other one, Reg Dunne, was from the neighbourhood, and he leaned in tight to Larry's face and said something fast and quiet that Brendan couldn't make out.

"What did he say?" Brendan asked his brother later.

Larry had shrugged. "He said they knew it was me, and that the weirdos always screw up eventually. That he'd be waiting to see me in the lock-up, and he said 'because your mommy's not always going to be around.' That they had a special way of dealing with people like me."

"You gonna tell?"

Larry shook his head, and when Brendan had reached up to turn off the light at the head of his bed, he could see Larry in profile lying on his back in bed, his eyes wide open and staring at the ceiling.

"You could just tell 'em," Brendan said in the darkness, the words coming out in a long, smooth slide like one exhaled breath. "Wasn't nothing you did. Was Ronnie. He's always getting into trouble anyways."

Brendan heard his brother move heavily, turning his shoulder down into the mattress, his face towards the wall now. "And what?" Larry said. "An' have Ronnie come after me instead?"

Brendan didn't have an answer for that, so he lay as still as he could and made himself breathe with long, steady breaths, faking sleep. His last thought before he did fall asleep was that he was sure Larry was still awake across from him, still awake and staring at the wall and as rigid as a board.

Larry would end up leaving St. John's three years later, nineteen years old and admitting nothing, but knowing that, after what happened to Jillian, there would be a lot more than a few questions and a threat.

So he just left.

No one ever said anything to his face, but Brendan knew there was a prevailing feeling in the neighbourhood of "good riddance," that Larry was different enough to make people uncomfortable and they were glad to see the back of him.

Brendan's father only talked about it once. "Nineteen means you can make your own mistakes and your own decisions," Terry Hayden said, his face in the newspaper the whole time, his cigarette smoking next to him in the ashtray as if helping to make the point. And then he had pushed his chair back and headed to the front door to see if Ted Cooper had come to pick him up for work yet.

Brendan's mother continued to change the sheets on Larry's bed every time she changed Brendan's, smoothing the blankets flat and squaring the pillow up at the top, but she always did it silently, like a task plucked from memory and done absolutely automatically. She didn't explain, didn't even speak, didn't change her expression, just pulled the fitted sheet on the bottom, shook the top sheet so that it billowed and fell into place, tucked in the blanket and squared the comforter. And then she left, the clean sheets she had taken off the bed held tight against her chest.

Sometimes, Brendan would stretch out on his brother's bed and imagine that the entire world could look different from there, imagine that he could look at everything with his brother's eyes. And then he'd try to think about what Larry's eyes were seeing, wherever he was.

And what Larry knew and remembered.

Brendan saw Mr. Carter's new cat nosing through the front curtains of the house a few months later, and he stared for a few moments at the animal's flat, impassive face behind the glass. The cat stared back, looking as unconcerned about Brendan as if it were looking out at a picture designed merely for its own distraction.

107
McKay Street

KEVIN RYAN

JULY 15, 2006

I**T WAS SIX MONTHS** before Brendan would finally give up on Larry.

Down the street, in his own way, Kevin Ryan was giving up too. He had walked to the house several times, and each time he hadn't managed to bring his hand up and knock. He knew she was there: he'd been watching from the upstairs window when her car had pulled up, and he had watched the top of her head travel around the back of the car, open the trunk and take out the flattened cardboard boxes, and then watched her as she headed for the door.

But when he finally did knock, it took a few minutes before she answered. When she did, Kevin noticed the sheen of sweat across her forehead, her red hair tied tightly back out of her face.

"Hi, I'm Kevin," he said.

"I know. From next door. I'm Mary," the woman said. She was only a slip of a woman, her wrist where she was holding the door thinner than a child's, but Kevin thought she made up for her size by being packed with obvious energy—like a small animal quivering with incipient motion even though she wasn't actually moving.

"I was just wondering about Mrs. Purchase," Kevin said. That wasn't completely true—what Kevin really had been wondering was whether he'd done the right thing at the right time. Whether he should have done something when Mary—because he recognized her now—and the other man were putting Mrs. Purchase in the car.

"I'm her daughter," Mary said. "Why don't you come in? I've got a lot to do, and I'd rather talk while I'm working, if that's okay."

Kevin stepped inside, closed the door. At the top of the stairs, he could barely make out the shape of a huge cat staring down at him. To his left was a small living room, and the only word he could think of was *overstuffed*. A fat grey sofa filled the space under the front window, with chairs on either side so close that their arms touched the sofa. A china cabinet with glass doors—china cups and saucers piled ten deep on the bottom shelf, the upper shelves filled with figurines so close together they looked like passengers on a rush-hour figurine subway. Every flat surface in the room—tables, the mantel—was covered with more knick-knacks, ancient, browning spider ferns reaching out over edges, their runners plunging all the way to the floor as if seeking some futile escape.

"What I was wondering is whether she's all right."

"Depends on what you mean by all right," Mary said dryly. "If you mean alive and pretty comfortable, sure. If you mean all right upstairs, that's something else again."

Mary walked into the kitchen and Kevin followed. He could see that she was taking things out of the kitchen cupboards and packing them up. The kitchen was just as overstuffed, as if a giant plant had taken root in the house and quickly outgrown its original pot. The counter was packed with utensils poking up out of containers, and a row of tubs labelled *Sugar* and *Flour* with masking tape covering the back half of the counters. Mary had one drawer open and was filling the box with a variety of strange and foreign kitchen equipment: what looked like a wire harp designed to slice eggs, a set of tongs with great wide curves. Mary caught him looking.

"Jam tongs," she said. "They're for lifting the bottles out of boiling water when you've sterilized them." She smiled. "Need anything? Help yourself. Lords knows she had enough of everything. When I did the bathroom and the hall closet, I found twenty-five pairs of tweezers and at least as many pairs of nail scissors. It's like, when she couldn't find something, she just went out and got more." Mary shook her head. "I've been taking stuff out of here for days, and I don't know where it's all going. My basement for now, a car trunk full of boxes at a time. Ever done this? Every time you throw something away, you feel like some kind of family traitor. But I don't see my brothers here, so they can put up with it. If they've got a problem, they can damn well come and do some of the work."

Kevin must have had a stricken expression on his face, because Mary looked at him and stopped, saying, "Sorry—you probably don't need my whole family history here. But it's so hard not to tell you when there's so much to do and so few hands to do it."

Mary looked around the room and at the boxes open on the floor. To Kevin, the boxes had an air of futility, as if things were being gathered up with no clear plan beyond simple motion—things put in boxes because something had to be done.

"It just never ends. I've got to get the place ready to sell in a couple of weeks, and I don't know how that's going to be possible," Mary said. "There's all the sorting of what to keep and what to get rid of, all of the things that were important to Mom and probably don't mean anything to anyone else.

"It's not like she'll know. It's not like Mom will be coming back here or anything. There's something serious wrong in her head, and there probably has been for a while. Alzheimer's, maybe, a tumour— they're trying to find out. Things that happened, she doesn't always remember too well. Things that didn't happen, well, she remembers them just fine. And she'll argue with you about them until she's blue in the face."

All of the cupboard doors were open, and for Kevin it was disturbingly like the old woman's diary was open there in front of him:

orange pekoe tea, oatmeal every morning, a more expensive brand of shortbread cookies that said "I'm an indulgence, but at your age you deserve it."

"I should have done this a long time ago. I should have come in and had a really hard look at this place before now. She could have killed you, you know."

"What?"

Mary picked up a wooden spatula from a container next to the stove. "Everything's fine, right? A little old lady just minding her own business," she said. "Wrong." She turned the spatula around so that Kevin could see the pattern of the stove burner charred deep into the back. "That's just the start. She had the fire department here ten times a month, but I bet they never saw the electric kettle that she tried to heat up on the back burner of the stove. The whole base of the kettle was melted into one big black mass on the burner. But she's complaining about the wires buzzing in the walls."

Kevin noticed that Mary wasn't packing as much as simply dropping things into the open boxes. He felt like he should help, like he should start pulling open drawers and emptying them. Like it would be all right to simply slide the drawers out and turn them over, dumping everything at once into boxes.

"I'm a nurse," Mary said. "I should have caught on to all of this a lot sooner. You're supposed to watch for things like 'acuity,' for whether patients seem disconnected from reality or their surroundings. But she's always been a little like that, and there was no point where I could say she clearly crossed the line. I've come to see her and found burners on and the smoke detector going off, and I'm sure now I wasn't the only one, but she's always been able to convince me that it was just a one-time accident." Mary smiled for a moment. "You just kind of figure she's safe in here, doing her own thing, getting by. Marking time. Like always. But I suppose you can only really do that for so long.

"You're lucky she wasn't a smoker, you know. You would have all been dead in your beds. She would have left lit smokes all over the place, a couple of puffs before putting them down and then forgetting about them completely. And you know that this whole row of houses has to be as dry as a bone, just looking for a spark."

Kevin looked around the small kitchen, at the dated cabinets with the brass knobs worn away to their silver cores, at the ancient stove and fridge. Mary caught his eye, and when she spoke again, her voice was softer.

"You can't really judge the place by the way things are now. She used to have a real pride in this house, but she's been on autopilot for years. It's like one morning she woke up and decided the world had changed—that nothing was fair anymore and that there wasn't a lot that she could trust."

"Was that when your father was kidnapped?" Kevin asked.

"Kidnapped. Yeah, right. Like I said, she has an interesting grasp on the way things are supposed to have happened. Truth is, she doesn't have much of a grasp on anything anymore."

"I could give you a hand," Kevin said. "I don't have much to do anyway. The girls are out somewhere and Cathy won't be back from Montreal for another five days at least. I've never minded a bit of hard work, and you shouldn't have to do this all alone."

When he said it, Mary held her face funny for a moment, and then her expression simply started to crumble. She had an egg beater in one hand, a steel potato masher in the other. She dropped them both into an open box with a clatter.

"She was just supposed to go on gardening. Just working in the yard quietly and not really hurting anyone," Mary said quietly. "She wasn't supposed to get sick or have to go into a home. She was supposed to be here for years yet."

And then Mary was crying in Kevin's arms and he couldn't even say how it had happened. Then, he was sure he heard a distinctive voice with an Eastern European accent, heard it as clearly as if the woman speaking the words were right there in the room: "You go home now— you go home to wife and kids."

He knew that it was the time to make excuses and a dignified exit. Except this time, Kevin stayed right where he was. He knew it must be how the big mistakes sometimes started.

But he stayed anyway.

32
McKay Street

KEITH O'REILLY

MARCH 15, 1980

TWENTY-SIX YEARS earlier, Keith O'Reilly was still in his forties. And desperate.

"It's in the paper."

Keith said the words simply, the two of them in the truck, heading down the steep hill at Leslie Street, and it was like the words had just emerged on his lips and had then accidentally fallen straight out into the air. The words hung, like they could get caught in the cold air in the cab and hover there, waiting for something to crash into them and break them into pieces.

Slush on the road, splashing up underneath the quarter panels on the truck, heavy and spattering. A clear day, the sun out, the temperature just the other side of melt, and the snowbanks were receding. It was still too early to start thinking about spring—too much disappointment in a St. John's March. There would be snow again, but it would at least be the heavy, wet, clinging spring snow, the kind that tires ride up over and press down into hard white ice, the kind that doesn't last as long with the wind turning warmer.

"Whatcha mean?"

"There's a story in the paper. Today. About the girl."

Glenn frowned, but his eyes didn't leave the road. Every time they passed a driveway, there was wet snow thrown out onto the road by someone clearing a large path to their door, and every time, Glenn's hands seemed to flex tighter on the steering wheel as the front wheels thunked through it. Then the back of the truck would shake over it as well.

"What'd it say?"

"That she came down here from Labrador, that she was working at the Dominion on the cash and then she didn't show up for work Thursday. And that now she's missing, and that no one's seen her. That she was nineteen years old, Glenn. Nineteen fucking years old."

Glenn still didn't look away from the road, but Keith could see his mouth working slowly, could see it in the muscles of his cheeks, more like Glenn was chewing over a thought than anything else.

"That's what they got? That she didn't show up for work? Doesn't seem like a hell of a lot."

"The police are asking if anyone saw her getting into a vehicle, so they've got something, don't they?" Keith said.

"That's the question they ask about anyone—and since no one's been saying anything, I guess so far nobody saw anything," Glenn said. He looked over at Keith: the other man was looking out the side window of the truck, fidgeting. Then Glenn said, "C'mon, Keith, think about it. After all, it's not like anyone's really going to be looking for her, is it? They'll go through the motions for a while, then more important things will come along. So stop worrying."

The truck eased down the long hill towards the harbour, slowed for the traffic lights and the sudden left turn, and when they got to the dockyard gates, Keith looked up, almost frightened by the sight of the huge fishing trawler looming down at them from up on the blocks, a big Latvian factory-freezer hunched up there and waiting for the workers to come back.

There was always an otherworldliness about the dockyard for Keith, the way the big ships were up on shore like they'd been tossed aground by massive waves that had themselves pulled back and disappeared, leaving everything behind them in the wrong place. The ships looked too tall and heavy to float properly, great slab-sided metal boxes that really should sink like stones, more like fortresses than vessels. Each one different, each one with its own particular problems, each one designed with a specific purpose by a marine engineer whom no one had ever heard of.

They'd had to bring the exterminators in on the Latvian ship first. The *Novlyov* had been crawling with armies of rats and roaches, and a whole shift of dockworkers had flat-out refused to go down below and start work on the propeller shaft until the rats were dealt with—the propeller shaft and its channel low down in the bottom of the boat, dark and greasy and the kind of place where the rats could hide by the dozens.

The propeller shaft had bent as the huge vessel had slowed enough to accidentally let its own trawl lines slide back over the prop, the trawl wires binding tight and twisting the shaft out of alignment. Even after the crew had managed to unwind the trawl cables from the propeller, the slight bend in the shaft had been enough to make the whole ship hum with an even, regular vibration every time its crew tried to bring it up to a reasonable speed. No speed, no trawling. And no trawling, no fish, so the captain had reluctantly made port to have the repairs dealt with.

Not without complaint, though. The captain had complained about the cost of the exterminators, and had complained even more when the yard foreman told him he'd have to take the whole crew off the vessel until the work was done. The exterminator's vent covers were coming off as Glenn drove towards the gate, the vessel's crew bunched up next to the tool shed with their bundles of clothes, waiting to go back on board. Some of them had found their way out to the city dump and had spent their time digging up and packing their pockets and clothes with dozens of cans of thrown-away tinned peaches, all of the cans well past their expiry dates and buried at the dump by a food wholesaler. Later, the peaches would be the cause of scores of cases of on-board diarrhea and, finally, the source of a better batch of homemade alcohol than anything the prisoners had been successfully making in the St. John's penitentiary.

Glenn stared at the exterminators beetling over the deck in their white suits, taking the plastic wrap off, dropping it over the sides of the ship like glassy parachutes, where it blew around on small gusts of wind while other members of the extermination crew tried to gather it up before it blew into the harbour and out of reach.

"Can't tell you how much that fumigation stuff stinks," Glenn said. "Gets in your nose and won't come out. Sour as anything. Like tin on your tongue, only worse. But at least it meant I had the place all to myself. Made me think when I was lighting the torch, though—make a spark and take the chance of blowing the decks right off." Then Glenn smiled, his mind moving quickly to other things. "Betcha they try the water trick. It looks like their style."

Occasionally, vessels from Soviet republics, short on hard currency, would have the crew sneak out in the middle of the night just before the vessel was to leave dry dock and fill the potable water tanks from the fire hydrants. It was free water, something they'd have to pay for once they were docked wharfside, and it often made the vessels so heavy the D9 pusher couldn't shove them out of the dry dock and back into the water. Then the foreman would complain about the weight and the captain would deny everything and there'd be a stalemate, the vessel building up day charges, all work stopped dead, until finally someone relented and drained enough of the water out of the tanks so that the ship could finally be shifted.

"If they only took half their tanks, we could just shove them out, no problem," Glenn said. "You'd know it if you were driving the dozer, you'd feel the weight of it and all, but no one would say nothing. But everybody's got to be greedy. Everyone's got to go whole hog, have more than their fair share, take two handfuls of everything every single time. That's life."

Keith didn't say anything for a moment.

When they reached the gatehouse, Glenn's green pickup was waved straight through. He pulled into the employee parking, stopping the truck. Glenn pulled the keys out of the ignition, tossed them up in the air and caught them again. Then he reached across with the keys in his open palm, held them in front of Keith and smiled wickedly.

"Want to borrow the truck?" he said. "Or have you gotten that out of your system by now?"

Keith didn't answer, and he made no effort to get out either, his arms still and heavy and hanging at his sides. "Where did you . . ." he started, but Glenn cut him off quickly.

"There's stuff you don't really want to know, so just don't ask," Glenn said. "There are a lot of places in a ship that get closed off and then never get opened up again, Keith. You know that. Means there are a heckuva lot of places where no one's ever going to look. A boat looks pretty little out there all alone on the ocean, but it's pretty damn big inside, full of nooks and crannies."

Keith still didn't move, his hands now in his lap, fingers moving against each other. "You gotta understand. It wasn't . . . She . . ." Keith said, and then stopped. "Bold as brass, she was. Right there on McKay. I just stopped to ask if she was looking for someone and she climbed right into the truck. Like she knew the game." He looked down at his hands. "We drove down here. I brought her under the overpass there where it's good and dark, backed in up behind the pillars. You know, out of the way where no one's going to see you. Things got carried away. I was telling her what I wanted and she just went crazy. I thought we had a deal, I thought we were going to do it right there, and then she said she wasn't like that, and she was trying to get out of the truck, and then she was out and running."

He stopped talking, looking down at his hands in his lap, looking at them as if they belonged to someone else. He turned his hands palms up, looking at the legacy of scars from cuts and marks that cut across the pads of his fingers and the heels of both his hands. Work scars.

Glenn shoved him with his shoulder, trying to get his attention. With that, Keith started talking all over again. "I just wanted to talk to her, to try and calm her down. I got past her and then put it in reverse, tried to cut her off just so we could talk. It's so fucking hard to see anything backing up with that big camper top on there, and I caught her with the bumper, drove the truck and her right up against a telephone pole. Didn't even feel it until I hit the pole, too. And it was over like that. I got out to see if there was anything I could do, but . . ." Keith's voice trailed off. "I was on Water Street then, lights on up and down the street, like there were people awake everywhere. I mean, anyone could have come out and they would have seen it all.

"You and your damned broken mirrors," he said. "You can't see anything in that piece of junk. It shouldn't even be on the road."

Glenn's voice went hard. "So you're saying it's my fault now? Somehow it's all my fault for not fixing a mirror I never use anyway? It's my fault, for lending you the truck when you asked me for it?"

Keith sighed heavily, slumped down against the door, the vinyl hard and slick in the cold. "No. That's not—"

But Glenn cut him off. "You call me, you tell me you've got a problem, and I come and help, no questions asked. Then there's a dead body in the back of my truck—a dead girl—and you're a mess, you can't even tell me what happened till now, and I take care of it for you. All of it. And it's my fault?"

"No, no," Keith said. "I didn't mean that. It's just that, well, someone's going to be asking questions, and eventually someone will say they saw something . . ."

"Well, if anyone asks about any of it—and they won't, you can be certain they won't—but if they do, you just say that you were with me," Glenn said. "And I'll tell them that we were together, that we were downtown having a couple of beers, and we walked back up to your place together. Simple as that. 'Truck in the driveway all night long, officer. Someone must be mistaken, officer.' And forget about it, Keith. You can just owe me. For all of it."

He got out of the truck and then he waved at Keith to come out as well. Keith didn't move.

"She'll just be gone, okay? There's nothing to even connect her to you. Not one single blessed thing."

Keith reached up, his arm incredibly tired, and opened the door. You don't know it all, he thought.

Glenn didn't know that in the rush to get out of the truck, the girl had left her small dark purse and wallet behind on the seat, that Keith hadn't found it until he had already rolled her body over the tailgate into the bed of the truck and climbed back inside the cab. Glenn also didn't know that the small purse was at Keith's house, buttoned up beneath the insulation and behind a small, square piece of wallboard near the heater, a piece of wallboard that was just waiting to be fastened in place with a handful of drywall nails. And Keith could only imagine what Glenn would think about that, if he knew.

They walked across the yard and into the low, corrugated steel building where the men changed and where the small lunchroom was, plastic chairs and hard-topped and chipped Formica tables that had been there for longer than any of the workers.

Keith and Glenn were standing in front of their lockers, the same dark green side-by-side steel lockers they'd had for years, shouldering themselves into their overalls, before Glenn spoke again. Keith would later remember every single word Glenn said, hearing the simple structure of the sentence, the intonation, and he would remember thinking that Glenn's words were too carefully precise to be accidental. That he was almost calculating in the way he set it all up.

"Your Evelyn, she's still quite the looker, isn't she?"

103
McKay Street

LEN MENCHINTON

AUGUST 12, 2005

IT'S ALL innocent enough, Len Menchinton thought. He was sitting outside on a sunny day, a full twenty-five years later. It's innocent enough, like watching girls on the street, as long as they don't catch you staring and get nervous or anything.

Innocent, because no one would get hurt, because no one really needs to know anything about it.

Most of all, not Ingrid. Because she would be hurt. Len was sure of that.

Ingrid would most certainly be hurt. But Ingrid was always hurt: Len thought she'd made a science of that long before he'd met her, that she had designed a way to hold her face that just made you think you had no choice but to do what she wanted, if for no other reason than to make that look go away. It had always been at the core of their relationship: he would do something, something unexpected, and her eyes would fill with that great disappointment, and Len would find himself falling all over the place to try to move things in reverse, to undo the damage, until finally she let it all wash from her face again like makeup coming off.

But this was different, this was something he felt he couldn't hope to escape. It started in May, when the first of the new leaves were coming out but the trees were still bare, still showing the neighbourhood through their branches in a way that would soon become impossible. It started with the laundry next door, hanging wet and embarrassed on the line for the very first time that season. Laundry: as simple as that. And he wouldn't have believed it if someone else had tried to convince him that it was true.

Len couldn't help thinking it was already an awkward time of year, a time when everyone seemed suddenly and sharply aware of the changes in their routines. The gardeners had already started in on the raw ground, but moving hunched over and with fast, darting motions, as if they always needed to be aware of the possibility of snipers and the probability of late and bitter snow. No broad garden hats and languid sweeps with the hedge trimmers here, Len thought. No teams of landscapers hired to put down easy soft-skinned annuals in even, regular rows that end up looking like fountains of floral plenty. No, this was emplacement gardening, digging foxholes and trenches and laying in the heavy work, turning compost and hauling fallen branches. Not for lightweights, not in a place where the weather seemed to delight in frustrating growth.

At the back of the yard, he saw a black and white cat with a red collar stepping carefully along the grass just inside the vertical grey palings of the fence, looking straight ahead with that kind of rapt concentration cats always find when they are homing in on prey, and it struck Len that the cat was learning the outdoors again for spring, just like he was.

It was the time when other people seemed to wear a constant look of mild surprise at the outdoors—a kind of blinking wonder that winter might be ending after all, a rediscovery that the world on the other side of the walls marvellously existed after the evil, cold wet of April. Nearby, at the rehab hospital, he had seen that they were even wheeling the patients out for a little bit of vitamin D, a few quiet minutes in the sunshine, Len thought, before heading back into the noise and echoes of the linoleum hallways—and what a tantalizing hell those few minutes outdoors must be.

Len liked to sit behind his house and look up the long, greening yard towards the back fence. It was a narrow yard, no more than fifteen feet wide at the widest point, but it was plenty long enough, three, maybe four times the length of the house, Len thought. He had an office administrator living on one side of him and a grocery store manager on the other. The office manager was Art Taylor and the grocery store guy went by the unfortunate name of Tinker. "That means I'm either the soldier or the spy," Len would joke to friends, even though he already knew which one he was.

Private investigator was what his card said, but what it didn't say was that he spent more than half his time trolling for shoplifters in chain stores, an unassuming-looking and small man with bright blue eyes, wearing the easy camouflage of a red-and-black-checked felt jacket.

He had developed a curious way of making himself seem almost invisible: people could stare straight at Len and then completely forget that they'd even seen someone, to the point that they'd swear they'd been the only ones in housewares or linens. And if they did manage to remember him somehow, they were almost always completely unable to describe him successfully. Asked what he looked like, they might approximate his height before stalling completely, unable even to pull up the colour of his hair. The trick, Len knew, was to always be looking away from them, and to never be spotted doing anything when anyone else was looking.

It was easy enough work, he thought, really just a matter of always keeping his eyes open, easy enough to keep both himself and Ingrid comfortable, the paycheques nibbling away at the mortgage every two weeks. The worst part was when there wasn't anyone stealing, the boring times when he spent his shift walking down the wide store aisles and fingering the fabric on men's pants he'd never buy, his eyes always set on "slightly distant" in case someone a few rows over was making off with underwear and bras.

And Len realized eventually that he liked the thieves better than the average shoppers. The thieves, at least, were interesting. He'd watched the shoppers long enough to develop a strange sort of disdain for them, an urge to always group them into two or three different types, like herd animals he was paid to look at over the fence and keep a constant eye on. There were the pilers, the pickers and the snubbers—they might as well have been the pigs and the chickens and the cows. The pilers with their perilously full carts, stuffed as if expecting the apocalypse; the pickers with one item, then another, then back to the first item again; and the snubbers, picking things up and tossing them down, bored and gum-chewing.

The thieves, now, they were different—they had a kind of purpose that set them apart, the need to grab and move and hope that no one was going to try to stop them. Sure, sometimes they'd try to run when Len put his hand on a shoulder and said, "Just a minute, please," but for the most part they gave that up as soon as he had them cornered.

Once or twice he'd known them to make it as far as the parking lot, but that was rare. When they'd been caught, they were almost always immediately resigned, willing to sit quietly in the small office with the single door, the single desk and the single steady-eyed video camera, waiting for the police. Often they'd empty out the stolen merchandise from their pockets themselves, telling Len they'd never have thought he was security, not even for a minute. Telling him they hadn't even seen him, even when he'd been standing right behind them.

And each had a particular method. They'd even start explaining it to him: how they'd managed to squeeze their way into several pairs of pants, all different sizes, in one of the small dressing rooms, and how they'd already lined someone up at one of the flea markets to help them unload the stolen jeans on the weekend. They'd talk, that's one thing he'd learned. They'd almost always talk if he just stayed quiet, digging themselves in deeper with every single moment that the tape just kept on rolling.

Sitting out on his deck, Len thought that was the single most important thing he'd ever learned from the shoplifters: there are things you always do wrong when you get caught. Don't start explaining—let the empty spots in the conversation stay the way they were, empty. It's hard, he thought. People hate a vacuum, hate the waiting, feeling like they are somehow required to fill up the conversational space between themselves and someone else.

But admit nothing. Resist the urge to starting digging your own grave.

He kept that thought in mind, even made it into one of his rules—rules of which there were really only two. The second rule was just as absolute, and in its own way just as simple. It doesn't matter what you're arrested for, it doesn't matter how ludicrous and impossible and stupid the charge might be—hire the best lawyer you can, right away. Whatever it turns out that the lawyer is going to cost, it will almost always prove to be worth it. Bad lawyers will dig you into a hole faster than you can dig the hole yourself, he thought.

And don't wait to call—no one's going to change his mind and just let you go. No one's going to listen to you, feel sorry for you and just open the door—"Go on, buddy, you caught a break this time, everyone makes mistakes."

Len couldn't believe how often people messed up the rules and called the first lawyer's phone number they came across. And he couldn't believe the way they always thought they'd be able to talk their way out of it. The police are just doing their job, Len wanted to tell the shoplifters every time, wanted to tell them before it was too late. It's just that their job is arresting people. Period.

From where he was sitting on his back deck, Len had a view up over the fence, and two yards over he could see Mrs. Purchase trundle out through her back door, down the grey-painted steps and into her yard. She was carrying a red plastic bucket, and Len knew that when she got to where she was going, she'd upend it, thump it down onto the grass and use it for a seat, her knees shot and her mind not that much better. May was almost the only time when he could see Mrs. Purchase clearly: there was a big silver maple in the back corner of the yard, and instead of just growing upwards in a big fan, it had spread out too, growing unexpected tufts of saplings up from the ground that all but blocked the neighbours' houses from view once the leaves came out.

He got a long-distance lecture over her fence from Mrs. Purchase about those maple shoots just about every year. "You should cut them back," she'd shout. "They'll drain the energy away from the main trunk." But Len could never get up his own energy enough to go back there with the brush hook and the saw. He didn't have the heart, either, the heart to go ahead and lop off all that hopeful, eager, questing life. He figured the tree had to know what it was all about, its natural impulse likely the best choice.

Instead, he watched the branches spread out every spring and summer, wondering at how the sticks seemed to be able to find every scrap of clear space to throw out their new leaves, filling in and grabbing every torn rag of sunlight. At how the tree could spread out underground and push up new growth like eager birthday candles, absolutely unaware that someone could be trundling along pushing a lawn mower, ready to cut everything right back to the quick. And how the tree would never learn about that, and keep sending the shoots up anyway.

Len waved to Mrs. Purchase as she stumped down her steps and she waved back, and he thought again that, every single year, she seemed a little more tentative. Age comes for all of us, he thought, stopping for a moment, remembering that he was not really that different from anyone else.

That was the other thing catching shoplifters had taught Len Menchinton, something else he thought about regularly: every single one of them thinks he's different, he knew, every single one thinks she's unique. They all think they can get away with stuff—believe that the bad things won't ever happen to them. Until they do. No one ever thought the store would prosecute—but the store *always* prosecuted. Charges every time: no excuses, no exceptions. How often had they sat there, right in front of him, their faces in their hands, snuffling, "This can't be happening to me." With Len across from them, his eyes rolling because he was thinking, It sure can be happening to you, and actually, it is.

He knew that. Knew that bad things are all pretty much inches away from everyone all the time, just inches away and waiting for the day when you take your eye off the ball. Robert Patten, he'd lived down McKay Street almost his whole life. The guy had been driving a company car when he hit a moose on the Trans-Canada Highway. No more walking, no company car either. It can happen, Len thought, and it will happen—so no use crying about it.

Then Len saw Vernie Taylor come out of her house next door— well, he heard her, anyway. That's what I would have to say if I were asked under oath, he thought. Not that I saw her, even though I knew at once that she was there. Judges are sticklers for precision, and you can gain a whole bunch of credibility just by correcting yourself before anyone else in the court gets a chance to.

The Taylors' house was on the left and just a little bit shallower than Len and Ingrid's, so that the Taylors' yard was deeper, even though it ended at the same fenceline down in the back. What he heard, instead of saw, was the Taylors' door slamming, and then the thud of something being dropped heavily on the porch.

That's correct, your Honour, Len thought, practising his testimony even on his day off. That's what I heard. A distinct, clear thump.

You have to be confident in court, he thought. Precise. Direct. Stick to the true parts, and always keep your sentences short. Let the silences hang there, unfilled—because the silences are just a trick to make you start talking.

Len didn't stand up, didn't want Vernie to catch him staring. There's a regular diplomacy to neighbours and nearly shared backyards, he knew, a diplomacy that suggests that an immediate reaction to a neighbour's presence is never expected or welcomed. You have to ease yourself in at the edges, so that you're noticed obliquely.

Then he heard the sharp metal screech of the wheel on the far end of the clothesline, and Len realized that Vernie was hanging out the wash. The wash, he thought, and felt it like a solid beat in his chest.

There seemed to be a set scale to her laundry, Len thought, the first few items creaking into view, the line moving with jerks and stops as each new piece of fabric was added. It was a diminishing scale, as if the first items to be hung were the largest and most difficult and each piece that followed was slightly more manageable. In Vernie's case, the first two things were bedsheets—looped over the top of the line and hanging down loose and wavering—and then a precise row of squared-off towels, clothespins in each corner and an extra one in the middle, to be sure. After that it was trousers, some facing towards Len, some away, the ones facing towards him with their flies open and the corners at the waist button hanging down, gaping, as if the jeans were trying to undress themselves from the line.

And still Len sat, watching the clothing move slowly out.

A row of tight knit tops—women's tops. And then a short line of women's underwear, all together, like a flock of small lingerie birds twittering brightly together.

Len couldn't help but think it was too early in the year for hanging out laundry. You'd have to be really keen for the smell of fresh air on your clothes, he thought, unless you were one of those crazies who went whole hog and put the stuff out in the middle of winter just to haul it back in stiff and half freeze-dried so you could throw it in the dryer anyway.

But that underwear, the colours and shapes and the simple fluttering drape of it—it gave him a quick trembling feeling in his chest, and he found he couldn't stop staring.

Len waited until he heard the Taylors' back door slam before he got up and went back inside.

Len woke up in the middle of the night, lost for a few moments before realizing that he was in his own upstairs room, and that Ingrid was sleeping quietly next to him. Len realized that he'd been dreaming about Vernie Taylor—not that he could picture her face in the dream, but he was sure it was about Vernie Taylor nonetheless. And that he'd had a wet dream, the first one he could remember in thirty years, since at least high school, and that he was soaking wet.

Embarrassed, he tried to get out of bed as quietly as he could, the front of his pyjama pants a sticky mess, while Ingrid mumbled and shifted slightly in her sleep next to him.

A day later and outside, and Len suddenly thought there is a point in spring where everything just leaps forward. One moment the grass is gradually shifting into green and the next there are dandelions, big and bold and staring, and they are like the starter's signal in a hundred-yard sprint: as soon as the gun sounds, everything is off and running. Biology just waiting to burst with that signal; all of it held back there, stymied, waiting for the moment for buds to burst and flowers to throw their lust outwards.

Sitting on the deck again, Len could suddenly see more flowers than he could possibly begin to name. There were some that he knew, some of the more obvious ones. The last of the tulips, shedding their petals now and leaving short-lived, deadheaded and obscene pistils. Buttercups and forget-me-nots, just illicit weeds waiting to be pulled up along garden edges but flowers nonetheless, and then the starting greenery of some of the more obvious flowers he knew names for, like bleeding heart and poppy.

There were others that he wished he could name, if only he had more experience with their appearance and smell and feel. It's funny how things can escape you when you haven't taken the time to look and touch, he thought. If I was a little bit more of a gardener, Len thought, I'd think about words like *foxglove* and *lupin* and a picture would jump into my head as quickly as if I thought about something familiar, like the feel of silk or denim. *Laburnum*—he'd heard the word before, thought it had a sound that bordered on the obscene.

Len could only see flashes of Mrs. Purchase working along her side of the fence now, little more than glimpses through camouflaging leaves that were now fully open.

Mrs. Purchase would know every flower here, he thought.

Mrs. Purchase would know everything.

Every now and then he'd see the silver flash of her gardening trowel driving down, as bright and fast-moving in the sun as if she were impaling something dangerous on the tip of a bayonet. Len could hear the blade sliding into the earth, the sharp scrape of it as it moved past small stones caught in the soil.

And then he heard something else. Vernie's door again, and then the familiar sound of the heavy laundry basket thumping down on the deck.

First into sight, it was dark blue coveralls, obviously belonging to Vernie's husband Reg, jerking into view. Then it was towels again, and pants, and then socks.

In its own way, it was almost like a striptease, he thought. We're just working our way down through layer after layer, and perhaps that's almost the point of it all.

Finally, gloriously, it was underwear again, first the spare utility of men's jockey shorts, then a breathtakingly brief line of plain women's underwear, white and cotton. Then several pairs of black panties, and finally a low-cut pair of wine red underwear, opaque and somehow shiny when they turned just the right way, and Len sat transfixed for a moment, watching the way the underwear seemed to move in the wind as if they were made of a sheet of solid material.

Maybe polyester, Len guessed, and the finger and thumb on his right hand were moving together as if of their own volition as he tried to imagine which one of the many fabrics he'd ever felt would feel like the touch of that pair of underwear. In his head Len was flitting through a dozen department stores, past scores of clothes racks providing cover for the inevitable shoplifters, rows of underwear there but somehow sterile because they weren't part of anyone yet. The feel of a hundred different pieces of fabric under his fingers, yet none of them that could possibly live up to the promise of these.

Len wished Ingrid had something like that last pair of underwear: something deep red and cut low across the hips, something saucy that you might catch just a glimpse of and realize that your wife was up to no good, that she was thinking about you every bit as much as you were thinking about her. Like a high school girlfriend sticking her tongue out at you, and then using one hand to undo the top button on her blouse while she sat across the classroom from you. The kind of thing, Len thought, that might make me want to slide my hands up under Ingrid's dress while she was standing at the sink.

And then he stopped again. Stopped, like always.

Because nothing as simple and easy as a new pair of underwear would ever make one little scrap of difference with Ingrid. You don't spend twenty years with someone, living with one set of marital rules, and ever expect that she will be able to turn on a dime and be anything other than exactly what she naturally is already, Len thought. You can't climb into bed one night and just announce that you want it all to be different, that this time you want all the lights left on, or that this time it will be fine to go at it right there in the hall by the stairs, the front door only a few scant feet away, only fogged glass between your nakedness and the street.

If that turns out to be my lot in life, even if I've made my bed and slept exactly, precisely, in it for going on twenty years now, Len thought, that doesn't mean I'll live my whole life without ever waking up in the middle of the night and wishing that something could be different. It was something he'd thought about before, something that he already knew was a dead end.

Like I could explain it to Ingrid, Len thought. Like I could explain it to anyone. Like I could even begin to tell anyone that my wife didn't want anything to do with me in bed anymore, and that every single rejection would make me feel like even more of a big fat slob than any mirror ever would.

On the line, Vernie's red panties waved back and forth, a scarlet and saucy flag.

Something, more a lack of motion than anything else, snapped Len out of his reverie and made him stare across the garden and across the Tinkers' yard as well.

The wind was shifting the leaves at the edge of the garden, but behind them Mrs. Purchase wasn't moving at all. Len could see her red bucket and flashes of her yellow shirt; he could even see the shiny silver of the trowel, held elbow-high. And he couldn't shake the feeling that, back there through the leaves, while he was watching Vernie's laundry, Mrs. Purchase was motionless, watching him. And Len knew all about watching.

He shook himself upright and headed around the side of the house, moving towards the door.

140
McKay Street

SAM NEWHOOK

JULY 21, 2003

THE SUN rose facing straight onto the upper side of McKay
Street, sunlit mornings bright and hard and hurting in your
eyes like thrown sand. It was two years before Mrs. Purchase
would catch Len staring at Vernie's laundry, but she was already watching everything.

Mornings were like snapped-open window shades, Sam Newhook
thought. The sun was already pouring in harsh through the small rectangle of his bathroom window, while he was absently scratching his
stomach, naked, his eyes half closed against light that seemed determined to bounce off every single tiled surface in the room and fly
straight into his face again. Heavy curtains, light curtains—it didn't
seem to matter. It was the kind of light that bled through the weave
and poked around the room in brilliant pinpricks, waking him far earlier than he wanted.

He wasn't sure if he was ever going to get used to mornings like
this, to the way the sun caromed off the flat sky and the sea at a slight
angle, so that it seemed to double itself, storming into the house

always at a full run, ignoring everything that tried to stand in its way. But at least the fog was gone. Sam wasn't absolutely sure which was worse, the glare or the grey, but even with his eyes still stinging, he was pretty sure it was the fog.

Sam hadn't had the house long, and was still repeating the simple mistakes over and over again: There was the short step down outside the bathroom, only an inch or so, but it jarred his back every time he stepped off it unexpectedly. One of the cupboard drawers in the kitchen seemed to roll closed faster than it should, jamming his fingers between it and the countertop. Even the sliding closet door upstairs—the one that skipped out of its track because it was square and the house, overall, wasn't. Anywhere. The way he pulled the sliding door hard across to open it made it jump out of its short railbed every single time.

He knew the missteps were a collection of things that he just hadn't experienced enough yet to have them built right into him, things he didn't know so well that they had become practised and ingrained. It was a new house, he thought, a new house built out of an old house and oddly filled with new sharp corners.

A new house to him, anyway.

Sam still had trouble keeping the address straight, kept giving out the number to his apartment to taxicab drivers instead, an apartment that was half the city away and in the wrong direction too, so that it was an expensive mistake any time he was drunk or wasn't carefully paying attention.

His new house was one of a trio of row houses that a developer had snapped up as a group and had then renovated throughout, knocking down walls and putting in new floors to label the places "open concept," plunking soaker tubs with jets in the upstairs bathrooms and pressure-treated patios out beyond glass doors that opened off the master bedrooms. The kind of places you advertise with a sturdy-looking hunk in a white bathrobe out on the deck with a steaming cup of coffee, master of everything he surveys. And that's exactly how you're supposed to feel in the model suite, Sam thought. And it worked fine for him.

It was like they'd found a realtor's checklist somewhere and followed it to the letter, a list of things that a young professional expected as a matter of right when picking out a house. There was only a thumbnail of lawn out back, the grass just recovering from the rough surgery of construction and coming up green in weedy patches, but the market was looking for dinner parties, not gardens or picnics.

Sam had put a bid in as soon as he looked at the place, and he hadn't realized until the lawyer searched the deed just how much the price had gone up between the time the developer had bought the places and when Sam's offer had been accepted on the renovated space. After he found how much the markup was, Sam felt a little like he'd been cheated, but the offer was signed by then and the lawyer suggested he should just try to make the best of it, that he was getting what he wanted anyway.

Just one surprise among many. It was a neighbourhood full of surprises.

There was a woman in his bedroom again, still sleeping, and he was pretty sure that, this time, her name was Jillian. He was completely sure it was Saturday morning, though, and there was no easy escape in having to head out to work. No way to just put on a shirt and tie, mutter a half-chagrined "Sorry, gotta go," and head straight away for the door, hoping she'd be gone when he got back.

By the time he was finished making the coffee, she was leaning on the door frame wearing black panties and a T-shirt. Bare feet, one small foot flat on the floor, the other tilted up against her opposite ankle.

She pointed at her chest. "Jillian," she said, bringing the third syllable up high, like a question mark.

"Yeah, I know."

"Just making sure."

She had curly light brown hair. Good legs. A small, sharp face with high cheekbones, her eyebrows getting all involved with the conversation whenever she spoke. Looking at her, Sam wished he had a more complete picture of the night before. Some of the evening was sharp enough—he remembered coming back from the bar, leaning on the front door messing with the keys, and the part where they were laughing in the living room about spilled Scotch and a glass knocked off the side table. And the part where elbows were getting caught coming out of shirts.

But there were important short gaps, and when he thought about it, he could remember nothing at all from the part just before sleep. Looking at her now, he wished he could remember a little more about that. And just how it was that they'd met, well, that was a little less than clear too.

Jillian was drinking her coffee quietly, staring at him over the top of her cup, probably making her eyes big like that on purpose, he thought. And the kitchen hovered around them, the perfect space it was supposed to be, all formal and poised and quiet, and Sam couldn't help but think that the room was equally ready for the comfort of pancakes or the easy show-off of eggs Benedict.

And that wasn't such a bad thing either.

At least she wasn't playing the know-it-all card with him, not yet, not nudging at him by repeating things he couldn't even remember saying to her, catching him out for forgetting lies he couldn't remember her telling him in the first place. The occupational hazard of meeting people when you've already got a few drinks in, living a night where things are running faster than you would normally let them.

"Nice place," she said, staring around the kitchen. "Nice to see when people take the time to do things right."

"Get what you pay for," he said, hoping she wouldn't ask exactly what it was that he had paid.

He had already started trying to figure out a strategy for getting her out of the house when he was pulling on his pants, but by the time he had really thought about it, she was already gone. Coffee-finished, clothes-on, kiss-on-the-cheek gone, saying only, "Gotta work," and "My number's on the fridge, if you want." She'd turned it all around, he smiled to himself, pulled the work thing on him before he'd done it to her first.

And how easy was that?

One broken glass, one of the good, expensive ones, but he was pretty sure a good fuck in return, judging by the torn-up bed—sheets strewn across the floor like they'd been involved in some kind of Olympic event—and even a telephone number on the fridge, he thought. He could throw the number away after his shower if he felt like it.

But he didn't.

He looked at the phone number for a moment when he came back downstairs, and even that impressed him—seven spare, unfamiliar digits and her name in a script that was only mildly looping and feminine. No circles or hearts over the *i*'s, he thought. Just *Jillian*, no last name, one sweep through across a sheet of notepaper in ink, her script even and steady and plain. Simple and straightforward. Like the number was something she was quite happy to share with him but, at the same time, it wouldn't be the end of the world if he crumpled it up and tossed it in the trash.

He left the note where it was.

His hair was still wet and the clock said it was still morning, so he went outside into the bluff, bitter snottiness of a Newfoundland June, looking one way and then the other before making the decision to head towards Duckworth Street.

Sam's house was the middle one of what was fast becoming an assembly line of rebuilt row houses, his a sharp rust red clapboard bracketed by similar houses in dark blue on one side, forest green on the other. Blue was two married lawyers both trying to make partner, the woman with a fine ass but neither of them ever home until the middle of the night. Forest green owned a downtown bar and Sam had already complained once about noise when the whole crew had come back there after closing to continue the fun. In their own way, they were an island of three small castaways in the middle of an ocean of McKay.

Looking at the buildings, Sam realized just how precise the developer had been. All three of the houses were bright enough colours to be trendy, to be almost leading-edge, but still cautious enough to be instantly saleable. Sam felt something like he imagined a fish might feel, just when the cautious-colours hook struck home. That caution, though, was something that clearly hadn't occurred to all of his other neighbours: there was a flame orange house on one corner, three storeys straight up like an escaping bonfire, and a brave attempt at purple down the street that had somehow fallen flat, as if the rich round grape that had looked so very good in the paint can hadn't survived the translation to the flat expanse of the clapboard.

But they were something of an exception. More and more houses in the neighbourhood had new doors, new windows, new flat paint on new clapboard, and Sam knew without even peering in the windows that there would be hardwood or laminate floors inside, that the tile work in the new bathrooms wouldn't have had a chance to mildew yet.

And the redone ones were spreading through the others like a virus. The older ones were more careworn, dressed out with eyelet curtains and sheers that were yellow with age or heavy smoking, and even though it was almost summer, there was still one with a plastic Santa out front, its face carefully punched in.

Father Concave Christmas, Sam thought, wondering how hard someone would have to swing his fist—and what kind of mood he would be in—to beat up Santa.

The more ragged of the older houses always seemed to have pairs of haughty, patchy cats staring out the front windows, or else small, angry dogs barking up close behind the front doors. The kind of dogs that seemed to sense you passing, that listened for the gritch of your shoes on the pavement so that they could go berserk on the other side of the heavy doors.

And the older houses were like a secret handshake, he thought, like their owners had a membership card in the unspoken language of the "we've-always-been-here-and-you-haven't."

It was as clear as a tide line on the beach, he thought, the difference between the old and the new. The old ones were being slowly shouldered out, the separation between the two sets of houses as clear to Sam as the water's edge.

Three doors down from the corner, there was a former rooming house where there had been a spectacular but short-lived fire. One of the addled residents had set up a hibachi in the front hall because it was raining and he didn't want to get wet cooking hot dogs. The box the barbecue came in said "Not for Indoor Use," but the man hadn't ever had the box, and he wouldn't have liked the lecturing tone of the warning—only an approximate translation from the Japanese—anyway.

The fire was like its own kind of natural selection, Sam thought as he walked by the burned-out house.

When the house had been burning, the neighbours all came out and watched the firefighters breaking out the windows and cutting holes in the roof, watched with that peculiarly serious formality that comes from knowing your house and all your possessions are only a couple of doors away if the wind comes up and the firefighters suddenly lose control. It's one thing to be vicariously concerned about someone else's life and possessions, Sam thought. It's something quite different to be concerned about your own.

The row houses along the street often shared walls, and sometimes they shared misfortunes as well. People were only as safe as their neighbours were careful, and sometimes only as safe as the fire-rated wallboard city inspectors forced on them during renovations.

The rooming-house residents were gone now, the shell of the house snapped up in a real fire sale, and its interior walls and ceilings were piling up in scraps in a big blue Dumpster in front of the house. A couple of months and someone new would be buying the place, unaware there'd even been a fire, the only hint a faint smell of wet charcoal when the fall rains really came and the humidity was stuck up somewhere in the range of instant migraine.

Bit by bit, the whole neighbourhood was changing, Sam thought, and in a year or two his place wouldn't be overpriced for the block, but instead an obvious, solid investment. The whole street would be different then, with only a handful of the stubborn old owners left, hanging on like bad teeth, and they'd hardly be able to afford to stay on—because if the city was good at anything, it was good at ensuring the municipal taxes would rise in perfect lockstep with the neighbours' house prices.

You could already tell who was who just by the cars, Sam thought, the difference between the dull-painted Reliants and Tercels and the newer Volkswagens, even the occasional Volvo.

There were still signs that this had once been a self-contained small neighbourhood, the kind of place that might have a name like Georgestown or Rabbittown, a traditional kind of name that would be loosely known by every single person who lived there, even if the neighbourhood's real boundaries were only clear to the inhabitants who lived within them.

There was still a small butcher shop on the corner, but it was losing ground fast, the hand-drawn poster-paint signs for pork chops and hot Italian sausages fading in the sunlit front window because they hadn't been changed in months. Sam had never even been inside, but he imagined a white-aproned butcher, like you'd see in a sandwich-meat commercial, maybe with a moustache, red stains on the front of the apron, a bulky, square man standing rigid behind a wall of chest-high, old-fashioned, white-enamelled, glass-fronted coolers.

There wasn't a bakery anymore, but there had been. Now it was just an empty plate glass window in the midst of another conversion. But there was a corner store at Prescott, just a shell of itself, totally dependent on the triple addiction to beer and smokes and lottery tickets, looking as broken down and fading as many of the customers who shuffled their way in.

Mornings are hard here, Sam thought, looking down the street. Two neckless beer bottles, dropped. The bottles' decapitated tops were still capped, lying jagged and right next to each other, their bottoms half inside a torn shopping bag.

There was a wet wool hat, slowly draining the rain it had harvested overnight onto the pavement, and a spot where someone had bent over and thrown up next to the curb. There had been pigeons working over the remains of the vomit until he got close to them and the biggest of the pigeons poked its head forwards once or twice, feinting like a small and cocky fat-necked boxer. Then all the birds stumbled and tripped into the air and away, wings clapping together, wing tips touching with a light feathery slap like they were right on the edge of overreaching themselves in the effort of escaping.

Then there was more broken glass on the street: patterns of fallen shards where car mirrors had been starred and smashed out by a rock or a passing fist. At least it was only mirrors, Sam thought. It was cheaper to fix side mirrors than to be replacing car windows, and there were certainly parts of town still where people sometimes took out a car window for something as simple as a handful of change in the cupholder or the briefcase in the back seat that you'd forgotten to bring in overnight.

Ahead of him, someone on the street had put their garbage out early, ignoring the schedule so that the dark green bags had slumped on the curb for days, and the bags had been torn into by cats or seagulls. There was some kind of plastic packaging pulled and tufted out through the holes like the bags were in the process of being disembowelled.

And that was just the bright morning leftovers. There were leftovers at night too.

There were still plenty of loud fights when there would be a police car left on the street, empty, its roof lights spinning and battering the houses with splashes of blue and white and red, while indoors a police officer would be standing between an angry couple, a referee up until the point where someone went too far, and then it would be a trip to the lock-up.

Screaming some nights, already one night clear enough that Sam could hear it from his bedroom. "Just fuck off and stay away from me, you bastard. Do you think I want whatever it is you caught from her?"

But that was surely changing, surely being shoved aside by the higher incomes and new people, he thought. It couldn't change fast enough for him, and he walked down McKay Street singling out houses in his head where he thought people should move, and the ones where they would be allowed to stay: 56 and 58 should go, 60 could stay, and 62 should just be torn down to the ground, the clapboard faded and hanging loose in places along the front, the windows already practically rotting. He felt like a judge at a dog show, scoring each house to decide best in class, and he went all the way down the street to the end before turning around, crossing the street and walking home, rating the houses on the other side as well.

Around six, back in his own kitchen, Sam had only a moment or two of misgiving before he took the number off the fridge and called. He looked around the kitchen while the phone rang on the other end, looked at the oak cupboards, running his hand along the granite countertop. The developer had done a good job, he thought. You can't say enough about good workmanship.

Then Jillian answered. It was a short conversation, mostly Sam saying, "So, do you want to go out?" before writing down the name of the bar she gave him almost immediately. Just down the hill, she said, the kind of place you fall into and just feel you'll never be out of place in again.

Outside that evening on his way to meet her, Sam decided the air was finally leaning towards summer evening, that it had a high kind of still and holding humidity, the thorough heat that makes sweat a clear disadvantage.

At least it's downhill, Sam thought, turning and heading for the harbour, where the light had already fled and the water was black glass, even though there was still some light left in the sky. There was a broken bottle on the pavement again, darker than the lengthening shadows, and he kicked some of it away from the curb and in next to the foundations of the nearby row houses.

Sam took long, overstretched, eager downhill steps, feeling the satisfying pull in his legs and hips, his eyes already up and looking out for the bar she had told him about. He walked by the place twice before he found it, just a small bolthole door off a narrow dark lane, the kind of place where precise directions aren't really that much help—but then again, once you'd been there, he thought, you would probably be able to find it in your sleep.

He was late, and she was already halfway through a vodka cooler in a clear bottle, and he watched her at the table, watched her drink a mouthful while he was still standing in the doorway, her neck long and smooth and perfectly angled, before he walked over and hung his jacket on a chair.

"Hi, Jillian, sorry," he said, looking up at the British beer signs tacked up on the walls and at the tarnished brass lights over the pool table. "Nice old place."

"You don't really know much about anything, do you?" she said, staring at him, and he stared back, startled.

Sam thought her voice sounded sharper than he had remembered, as though the length of the day had hardened her into a drier, more spare version of herself, cutting away convention and even politeness like it was unnecessary fabric.

"This is all new," she said. "The whole place. The pool table, everything. It came in the door looking old, but only because it was meant to. It's always been a bar, but not like this. Used to be just a dive. Now it's a fancy dive." She stopped, took another drink. "It didn't even used to be wood," she said, looking up at the walls. "Yellow paint, it was then." She had peeled the label off her cooler, her fingernails looking sharp and dangerous when she did. "And the beer used to be cheaper then, too. You can't just take things at face value. You gotta leave a little room for some experience, too."

Sam wasn't sure if she was lecturing him or if she was laughing at him, and he knew his face was tilting towards a sulk, that it was moving towards the sort of formal face he kept, always at the ready, for strangers.

"I've got . . ." he said, but the words came out woodenly, and he realized that, despite the night before, despite the sheets and the feel of her legs against his that he remembered all too well, they were still essentially unknown to each other. It was a depressing thought, draining, like starting a long and exhausting road race all over again.

She tilted her head, calculating, her eyes sharp and reading, obviously teasing him now. "How about a blow job in the men's room?" she said, and she said it loud, suddenly grinning, staring right at him, daring him to look away. And at least two faces turned towards them from the bar, one of them a lawyer whom Sam had done some business with.

The lawyer smiled. With that, Sam could feel the tension drain away between them like water down the drain.

At ten o'clock, a thin guitar player with sunken eyes and curly hair set up his equipment in a corner of stone wall by the front door, settled onto a stool, and after a few minutes put his guitar on a stand and walked over to the bar, ordering a beer.

"Another hour and he'll play," Jillian said. "That never changes. Tease you at ten, sing at eleven or twelve, done at three. It must be written down in the musician's handbook somewhere."

So for an hour they talked, and with each passing minute, each sentence back and forth, Sam could feel the comfortable familiarity between them coursing back.

When the guitar player did start playing, he was better than Sam expected, the man's long fingers drawing notes out as if surprising mice in corners, and Sam noticed that Jillian was drinking at the same rate he was, bottle for bottle, though she was drinking coolers compared to beers for him, so she had the edge on alcohol. She wasn't really showing it, though, her eyes fixed on his, as bright as birds. But he noticed that she would look away when the door to the bar opened, nodding slightly to people as they came in, and sometimes offering a short, open-handed wave.

"You're from this neighbourhood, then," Sam said.

"Born and bred." And this time it was like the last syllable spiralled slightly downwards. "Lived on McKay Street for my whole entire life. It was my grandmother's house, and then my father's. Plenty of us around here then, the whole neighbourhood full of kids. We all grew up together, same street, same school, same plans."

"Not me," Sam said.

"You think?" she said wryly. "I know that. I know your house, know it better than you do. I know it from when it was Mike Murphy's place, and from when his two girls were growing up. Alison was in my class, all the way to grade twelve. I played with dolls in that backyard, back when there were shrub roses all along the back fence."

Sam listened and Jillian talked, and sometimes he managed to tuck in an observation, but mostly it was like she was drawing a map for him, explaining more and more about the street and the people. About Mr. Carter, whom hardly anyone ever saw anymore and who seemed to be living on whatever food he could buy at the closest convenience store, about the people who had been arrested for theft and those who beat up their spouses, and all of it was connected to the street and yet was still unconnected to him. And Sam realized that when there were screaming fights at night, Jillian would be able to pick out who was fighting just by the sound of the voices and where the police cars were stopped, by something as simple as the angle of the flashing light bars on the roofs of the cars.

And for one wistful moment, he found himself wondering what it would be like to fit so well in a place, to have the comfortable feeling of knowing exactly where you belonged and exactly what it was you were supposed to be doing, dovetailing into everyone else's lives. As he listened, he thought that he and his two immediate neighbours were intruders, that no matter how long they lived there, they might never find a place in the curious fabric of the street.

And then the bar was closing and they found themselves out on the street, heading upwards, and to Sam's surprise they were even holding hands, their arms swinging back and forth in unison in a big arc. Heading back to his house, and he smiled and thought it wouldn't even be so bad if more Scotch glasses got broken. The night was close and humid by then, and up the street above them a group of teenagers were gathered at the edge of the street. Sam could see the bright tips of cigarettes as they got closer, but he wasn't paying attention, talking instead, eager for a chance to explain the things he saw in the neighbourhood.

"That butcher shop is—" Sam started.

"It's not a butcher shop," Jillian interrupted, like he'd missed a point she'd already tried to make. "It's Harringtons, okay? They've owned it for years, we call it Harringtons."

"Okay, Harringtons. It's not going to last much longer, and—"

"What do you mean? It's been there forever."

"I mean it's not going to last much longer." He was exasperated, thinking he was in danger of starting to lecture. But he also felt powerless to stop, feeling the words digging their own defensive trenches around an otherwise indefensible position. "I mean, it's obvious the place is going out of business, you just have to look at it." He could feel his face getting flushed.

Jillian, angry now: "Three generations at least. And maybe it looks like it's on its last legs, and maybe a bunch of other things around here are too, but it doesn't mean we have to come up behind it and give it a shove down the stairs, just to be sure it's really good and on its way."

They were closer to the corner now, and up ahead of them the group of teenagers had coalesced into two distinct and separate groups, facing each other. Sam felt Jillian's fingers tighten around his own, felt as much as heard her suddenly go quiet.

And two of the teenagers were pushing each other now, first one, then the other, harder, and then they had their fists up, too. One of the smaller teens staggered backwards into the low fence right on the corner, and as Sam watched, the boy turned and ripped one of the fence pickets free, holding it up over his shoulder, baseball-bat-high.

In the light from the street lamp, Sam could see the steel shine of nails.

There were lights on in some of the windows up and down the street, but it was like the houses were looking out and beyond whatever was going on in the street, not paying attention to it at all.

"Come on," Sam could hear the kid with the fence picket yelling. "Come on, you fucker. Let's see you come on now."

And it was like there was a discernible change in the air: one moment they had been loud and angry but like actors playing expected, formal parts, and the next they were all scrambling for weapons of their own. Other fence pickets came free. A bottle was picked up off the ground. What looked like a short length of copper pipe appeared in a hand, maybe grabbed from the rooming-house Dumpster. All of it held up high, twelve o'clock and serious, all of it meaning business.

Dangerous, this, Sam thought. A bunch of ramped-up teenaged kids with no idea how much damage they could really do to someone, kids who might think you could belt someone with a fence picket and that person would fall down and somehow later still be able to walk away. Kids old enough to feel rage and strong enough to do something about it, but not old enough to really understand consequence. Movie violence, but violence that would have real results.

And Jillian was tugging at his arm, pulling him around the corner and down onto McKay Street even though his body was still turned the other way, his face and shoulders still facing the teens while she pulled him almost backwards down the street, his legs feeling like they were working the wrong way.

"But I've got to do something," Sam said. "Someone's going to get hurt."

"Yeah, someone's going to get hurt all right," Jillian said, but she said it resignedly. "Someone always gets hurt. Sometimes badly. Sometimes enough to stay in the hospital for a while. And if you're not careful, it's going to be you."

Sam tried to pull out of her grasp, but she wouldn't let go.

"Look—I'm from here and you're not. And I'm telling you that what you want to do with this now is to just stay out of it," Jillian said, her voice suddenly flat, almost impersonal. "They won't even blink before they lay you out cold. Or worse. We should keep walking, let them sort it out themselves."

"I can call the cops," Sam said, deciding and pulling his phone out of his pocket.

"Suit yourself," Jillian said, letting go of his arm, "but make sure you know what street you're on so you can tell them the right place to go."

And that was the last thing she said.

When Sam opened the phone to dial, when he held it up next to his ear, the cellphone lit up the side of his face with a pool of light blue, and Jillian didn't so much vanish as she simply faded away from beside him, so softly that he didn't even feel the shift in the air as she disappeared.

Even as the 911 operator was answering at the other end of the line, the teens were all turning towards him, recognizing the blue glow, their arms spread, a semicircle, like an opening fan of playing cards. And instead of two groups, there was really only one, and everyone was looking straight at him. A big kid, his face hidden back in a hood, was coming towards him.

"Get 'im, Ronnie," someone else said.

"You're in the wrong place, mister," the kid they'd called Ronnie said. "The wrong place completely."

32
McKay Street

VINCENT O'REILLY

JUNE 5, 2006

THREE YEARS later, on a hot summer afternoon, Vincent O'Reilly was looking at inch-and-a-half bright-stainless finishing nails. There were maybe a hundred of them, rolling around loose in the bottom of a margarine tub. Years since I've been back here, he thought, and it's like not one single thing has changed.

The lip of the tub had been tightly sealed when he picked it up, as if the nails might spoil if they were exposed to the air. They whispered as they slid across the plastic, rolling back and forth, fetching up against each other in tight patterns, rolling in an order as precise as if they had always known exactly where they were going to end up.

There was stuff like that all over the workshop, he thought. Above the workbench there was the series of long cardboard Velveeta cheese boxes, the kind they hadn't made for years, still stacked up one on top of the other. There were enough cheese boxes there for Vincent to remember just how many grilled cheese sandwiches he'd eaten growing up, and each and every box had something about the contents written on it in black Magic Marker. His father's handwriting. Keith O'Reilly might be dead, but the writing looked alive, craggy and sharp and running up in unexpected peaks as if it had lost control of its temper travelling the rugged uphill grade.

In the corner there was still the old space heater, even though that hadn't worked since God knew when. And Christ, Vincent thought, there was enough crap in the place to fill the back of a pickup truck four times over, and there would still be more left to haul away. And all of it was precisely what he expected and, at the same time, none of it was even close to being the way he had thought it would be.

He'd heard what had happened in a curious kind of past tense, knowing the end of the story at the very beginning and then being told the rest over the phone by a police officer who sounded like he was reading from someone else's notes. The words came in bunches, in short, fractured sentences, as if the person who wrote them hadn't been able to keep up with the way they'd been spoken. The quiet man on the other end of the telephone sounded almost bored.

Vincent found out more from the neighbours when he got home.

A young woman from slightly down the road and across the street, hardly more than a girl, really, had seen Keith O'Reilly out in the small front yard early in the morning, stretched out and lying flat on his stomach in his dark blue overalls with the dockyard logo still centred directly between his shoulder blades. He'd been face down on the gravel path next to the wet grass, his arms stretched out in front of him as if he were attempting a shallow dive.

The girl told the police her name was Claire, that she couldn't decide if he'd just fallen down or if he had been lying there overnight, so she'd hurried over, hoping she'd wind up being wrong and embarrassed and that he was just working on something low down in the narrow front garden. She told them she realized quickly that she was too late to help, individual, unnecessary details spilling out of her like water and running right over the officers—like the fact there was a can of white gloss enamel open next to him on the walkway but that the brush in his hand had settled down into the dirt instead of finishing the bottom of the trim. Things that didn't mean anything but that pulled the story out of her in manageable order, so the officers listened and let their pencils hover in place until she got to the details that really mattered, at least as far as police reports were concerned: time, place and then time again.

When the paramedics got there and rolled him over, she said to the police, she couldn't help but notice that the first thing they did was to brush the loose gravel away from where it had stuck on his face. Much later, she told her sister the sight of the small, white, bloodless pockmarks where the gravel had lodged stayed with her for months. She told the police that the paramedics walked to the back of the ambulance to get the stretcher, and that they walked slowly. Somehow that said everything to Claire that she would need to know.

The police officer told Vincent they weren't really sure just when it was that his mother had died, just that she'd been in the chair and the television had been on when they'd gone in to tell her. It was as if she had just turned off, like a light bulb blowing, a bright and instantaneous flash going unnoticed in an otherwise empty room. The police officer didn't put it exactly like that, but that was the way it all held together in Vincent's head—his mother travelling from alive to dead in an instant, her filament failing with one last peaking spark.

Vincent managed to keep himself from asking the police officer whether *The Price Is Right* had still been on when they found her or if Bob Barker had finally left the building for good. But he had wanted to.

Out in the workshop on the side of the house, Vincent went back and forth next to the workbench, occasionally reaching out to touch individual, familiar things: the olive grey jacket that hung on a nail near the door to the kitchen; the big old radio that used to get warm to the touch when it was on for more than half an hour.

A pair of cotton gardening gloves that used to be white, crumpled together stiffly on the workbench, coated with spruce pitch and curled as if there were still hands there inside them. There was a case with a dozen beer bottles, Old Stock, most of them empty but three with their caps still in place, as if his father was saving them for later, as if he still had it in mind to come back and finish them off. Six cigarettes in a crumpled package, tucked up within reach on a shelf even though his father had told Vincent he'd given them up years before.

On the shelves, the scores of boxes with nuts and bolts, and one with more hooks and eyes than anyone would ever need. Vincent found himself taking the boxes down one at a time and opening them, and it was almost like Christmastime, because he wasn't fully sure what to expect inside—the notes on the front made perfect sense to only one person, and he wasn't there to explain it anymore.

Every now and then, Vincent held one of the boxes a few inches above the workbench and then let it drop, waiting for the sharp snap of it to see if his father's trick would work, to see if, as soon as he heard the sound, Vincent could be sure about what was inside the box as well.

Nails and screws were constants in the collection, like underwear and socks in a dresser drawer. They were ranged and regular in their different sizes, but there were also barrel fuses and black plastic fuse seats; big triangular barn-door hinges that looked as if they would be capable of holding whatever weight could be thrown their way; small coils of lead solder and copper wire, able to create a necessary connection between two very different points.

And after that, there were other, more esoteric pieces that defied all description. Like the four mercury switches, carefully taken out of thermostats somewhere and nested there in small wrapped bundles of Kleenex, like eggs. Lined up in a row, like the four of them were supposed to mean something. And Vincent couldn't help but think that, somewhere, there were four thermostats unable to contact their furnace, shells of themselves rendered mute and incapable of explaining what it was their personal duty to explain: that they were meant to topple over and complete the circuit with that familiar white-blue spark. Their sole purpose now forever unfulfilled.

Outside, the afternoon gave way to the beginnings of early evening, and Vincent was suddenly aware of the light changing above the tattered strip of cloth that acted as a curtain.

Faith hadn't come with him on the long, hopscotched flight from Victoria, talking to him instead about her job and how one of them had to keep some money coming in, explaining it all with her hands up busy around her face, waving the way they did when she was using them to try to distract you from the fact that she didn't really have a point.

He'd already been packing his clothes in the small bedroom by then, getting ready for the skip and jump of Victoria–Calgary–Toronto–Halifax–St. John's, the only flights available and none of them cheap. And he wondered distractedly just when in their relationship she'd started throwing her hands up like that, and whether it would ever be the kind of thing that eventually grated on you enough that you asked for your apartment key back. Feeling at the same time like, by even thinking it, he was betraying her right then. It was a feeling that rang with a ping as sharp as a penny dropped on sheet metal.

Because Faith, and even Victoria, had been a haven.

When Vincent had left St. John's in the first place, it hadn't been the kind of "don't want to leave but I have to work" thing everyone else talked about before going. It hadn't been that way for him at all. So many of them were people forced by economics to cut and run, to set down shallow roots somewhere else, but somewhere else they were always insisting could never be home. For Vincent, it had been a pell-mell flight to away, a desperate need to be anywhere else—at least to be far enough away that he couldn't feel either his mother's or his father's hand reach out and touch his shoulder. He knew that, for some people, family and friends were the kind of anchor that kept everything making sense. For him, they were the kind of anchor that felt like they were holding him down, his face completely underwater and drowning.

Back then, leaving was critical. It was a time when it was simpler being away, a time when, in fact, everything had been simpler. His parents were safe in the familiar walls of their home, close enough to be reached with an occasional long-distance telephone call, but far enough away that they couldn't look across McKay Street and see just what it was he was up to, and whom he was up to it with. They couldn't ask about Faith Monahan or question him carefully about "who her people are," nor would they know every sin that the entire Monahan family might have been responsible for, and feel they had to tell him those sins, too. Faith wouldn't have to go through that cat-and-mouse game that always ended with judge, jury and executioner.

He'd brought a girlfriend home once to meet them, a girl from the neighbourhood named Jillian George, only to be told after he'd come back from walking her home that "no one in that family has ever amounted to anything" and that he really should be setting his sights higher. And that, as his mother had put it, if they had to "grope each other like animals in an alleyway," they might have at least not done it up against the side of Mrs. Purchase's house where their behaviour would become a topic of conversation for the entire street.

Once Vincent was in Victoria, he knew they couldn't keep asking him every single morning what he thought he was going to make of his life, where he thought he would end up or why he hadn't wound up in a solid career. His mother said she didn't understand why he hadn't thought about staying in school and becoming an architect or a lawyer. His father said that even trying to get on full-time at the dockyard for a while would be better than just shifting from menial job to menial job.

"And I still know a few guys down there, even a supervisor or two," his father had said. "I can put in a word..."

But Vincent didn't want anyone putting in a word.

He just needed to put a safe distance between himself and anyone he knew—and he couldn't even explain why, any more than he could explain that meeting up with old high school buddies all over again held no more magic for him than meeting long-forgotten aunts and uncles. A recognized but distant face, a slight, emotionless connection, the politeness of near strangers—he didn't see the point.

He had started with a Victoria lawn company on the very first day he'd gotten to British Columbia, amazed that it was only May and everything was already in full bloom. Out in the amazing rich green, there were farmers paying workers minimum wage just to show up and pull the renegade daffodil bulbs from their fields, bulbs that just seemed to be waiting to branch out in every direction. It was all-day, bent-back work, but it was also out in the warm air and the occasional sun, the temperature and wind unthreatening in a way that seemed completely foreign to Vincent. He would look up and see big trees fountaining down green all around him, and it was like he'd woken up and found himself transported to a sort of tamed rainforest.

For Vincent's mother, bulbs had been something you had to steward through the winter, protecting them carefully in your garden so that they could poke up tentative in the spring, desperate and spindly, something you had to nurture instead of treat like a weed.

But in Victoria, it turned out, lots of things were different. Like Faith.

Faith worked in the lawn company's front office, and she'd filled in the forms for him when he had started work. She was small and quiet, with a face he could only describe as sweet at first. Sweet, because she said so little that you almost missed her in the office. She was always sitting when he saw her, her legs invisible under a steel desk that must have dated from the 1950s.

And invisibility was a state Faith would have understood completely—because she herself felt invisible. Everyone went by her as they came into the office, and everybody passed by her again on the way out, and except for the occasional cast-off words in her direction, she wasn't really sure if they were talking to her at all. It was, she thought, an extension of high school, where everything seemed to go by in front of her but without touching her. Not experiencing anything as much as constantly observing it from the outside. And then there was Vincent—Vincent who always talked to her, always looked right at her, straight into her eyes, and she thought it meant more than it did. Months after they became a couple, she had told him about that, and he had laughed.

"Everyone thinks Newfoundlanders are friendly because we look right at your eyes and always say something: 'How about the weather,' 'There's rain coming,' something like that," he said. "But it doesn't mean we like you—it really only means we're being polite."

But he did like her after all. Weeks went by and she had put up with his puns, when he called her Faith-full because she'd eaten a doughnut from the box in the office kitchenette, or Faith-less when she called in sick.

"You're one of the lucky ones," she told him bluntly after they spent their first night together. "People spend years hoping to someday have Faith."

Sometimes he felt he had done exactly that, that he had spent years hoping to have some faith, and he couldn't believe how seamless it all felt when they started spending nights, and then days, together in his small apartment.

"Faith, Hope, Charity, Chastity," he'd call out to her from the bedroom in the first few months when he was trying to get her to come back to bed, teasing that she was so slow that she probably should have been Chastity after all.

"How about we stick with Hope?" she'd call back, making coffee in the small kitchen. "Because at least then you'd have a Hope."

And they'd laugh and get coiled up in the sheets and fall asleep wound around each other until the sun finally woke them up, and they ended up being late for work together, too.

That had stayed with him for days—the thought about having a hope, maybe just for a clean, straightforward future—winding around in his head while he shovelled dark mulch and peat in and around flower beds.

That hope seemed far away back in St. John's. Roaming in his parents' bedroom, picking things up one at a time and setting them down as if he were trying to find something hidden among them, Vincent found the old jewellery box on top of the dresser, the one that played "Für Elise" when it was opened. As soon as the song started, it was painfully familiar because two of the small metal tangs had been broken off the tinny little harp for years, so the music played with two scattered missing notes, like the musician had broken off a crucial mental tooth and simply left a hole behind that you were supposed to fill in by yourself from memory.

When Vincent looked inside the box, there was the same jewellery that had always been there. Small-time, really, Vincent thought, but he could picture each piece around either his mother's arms or her neck, and he could imagine it too, in his father's blunt-fingered hands, big, stubby hands that turned the gold chains and bracelets over and over curiously, as if they were impossibly difficult to make and as if some clue about their manufacture was hidden away in them somewhere, a clue that was always on the side away from his touch.

A slim blue diary lay flat on the bottom, down underneath all of the jewellery, with a single rubber band wrapped tight around it, a pen tucked in neat under the garter of that band. Alone in the bedroom, Vincent kept looking over his shoulder, expecting to hear someone else moving around in the house, or at least something as simple as a dry, thrown-away cough. He felt like he'd get caught peeking into his mother's private belongings, even though there was no one left to catch him at anything. And then he wondered what was supposed to happen to old, mostly cheap jewellery when its owner dies, anyway. Maybe someone would want to buy it, he thought, but selling it seemed somehow disrespectful. At the same time, it wasn't the sort of thing he could see keeping: Faith wouldn't want it, and probably no one else would either. Away from where it belonged—and whom it belonged with—it was as if its value, its meaning, would be immediately diminished.

For a fleeting moment he thought about getting the round-nosed shovel from the workshop and digging a hole in the backyard, taking the jewellery out and burying it all so that it would either be lost forever or else be found by someone new someday, someone for whom it would be a preciously discovered and brand new treasure. Like the treasure it had been to his mother, he thought, every single time his father had come home and gruffly pushed another store-wrapped and -bowed box towards her.

Vincent bundled all of the jewellery up in a worn dishcloth from the hallway linen closet and stuffed it into a pocket of his suitcase, the gold chains all tangled into the bracelets, charms that had been like small totems catching at the pilled fabric of the cloth, thinking that Faith would know what to do with it. Then he stopped, took it out again and dumped all of it back into the jewellery box, covering the diary with chains and necklaces. His worry, not hers.

On top, the opal brooch that his mother had opened and looked at, and then she'd said, "Keith, don't you know that opals are bad luck?" There was the heavy, old-fashioned charm bracelet with no room left for new charms—each piece, now, with no one who knew its complete story.

"Für Elise" stopped with a snap, as it always had, the moment the jewellery box lid closed. Vincent put the box on the kitchen counter and walked through the door into the workshop, his decision made, looking for the shovel.

As he looked around the small workshop, the thought hit him: he was a homeowner, even if it was not the way he'd ever imagined it would happen. Whenever he thought about the house when he'd been in Victoria—and that hadn't been often, he had to admit—the house had his parents set firmly, irritatingly and constantly inside, like it was a clock and they were part of the necessary workings. After memorial services and funerals and everything else, he thought he should be able to get past that idea, that he should be able to see that thick line between life and death and recognize that things had changed. That the house went on without them, two-by-fours and plaster and glass and shingles and little else.

But despite all the ritual, he couldn't shake the lingering emotional belief that they were still there. And in some ways, he thought, maybe they still were.

Looking out the small, darkening window, Vincent saw a pair of runners scoot by on the road, their pace rhythmic and regular, and he thought absently that the shorter one—the one with blue stretch pants tight across her ass and the striped top—wasn't bad-looking, compact and nicely proportioned. Yes, he thought to himself, she wasn't bad-looking at all. And he wondered if his father would have agreed with that assessment. And that brought another thought.

Maybe he's still in the workshop somewhere, Vincent thought, tucked in under the boxes and watching from the shadows back behind the scraps of old tin flashing. Hiding behind the odd leftover rectangles of Gyproc, watching, silent, still intent on measuring everything I do. And maybe Mom's somewhere in the living room, caught in among the order of some parts of it and the disorder of others, he thought. Hers the last finger on the remote, his the last straightened curtain after it was pulled aside to stare at whatever was going on out on the street this time. Every single doily and blanket precisely ordered by their hands, placed in the spots where they wanted them to be.

He was the only one who really knew them, he thought, the Rosetta stone now of the O'Reillys, the only piece of the family with enough information left to know that his father sometimes grudgingly made waffles for his mother but that Evelyn only ever made Keith pancakes.

He had forgotten about the shovel, had walked right back through the house without even noticing, his feet knowing how to get around the island in the kitchen and through the crowded living room without his eyes even paying attention. Walking through the door of his old bedroom, he realized that the space still made perfect sense—that nothing had really changed there, old posters still on the walls, the bedcovers still placed the same way, a rank of pillows at the head. Four pillows, and he would shove three of them off the bed every single night and wonder why he couldn't just live with that one. The four pillows that his mother put back every single morning.

Vincent also knew, without a doubt, that if he waited until dark and stretched out under the same covers he'd always had, he could look up and out through the same side window and see the same old constant wedge of stars, the same familiar and expected cycle of the ordered heavens that he could remember seeing for a child's lifetime. He knew that the dusty, simple smell of the air in his closet would still unlock as many doors as it ever had, that it could make the clock spin backwards as if he were eleven all over again. He also knew, with absolute finality, that no matter how much he wanted them to, no matter how long he waited, no one would be coming in to wake him up and tell him to be ready in time for school.

That sadness didn't make stretching out on the bed and just waiting for morning any less attractive—and it didn't make it any less possible, in that racing-heart way of ideas that seem right in the very moment that you have them and then spend the next few days looking impossible.

After all, he thought, they probably needed landscapers in St. John's more than they ever would in Victoria, where growing things was so damn easy. Maybe the problem was that, in St. John's, they just didn't know how much they needed landscapers yet. But that thought needled too, at odds with every reason he had for leaving, the thought that, by dying, his parents had managed what they never could have while alive. And maybe, if he'd been able to separate himself from the emotion, Vincent might have said that dying had cut off all of his parents' sharp edges. It was an idea that had strange foreign purchase with him, that after spending so much time cutting the roots out from under himself, he might want to find those same severed roots all over again.

It was unsettling, the clinging attraction of it: the thought of being able to spot people he knew and then wave hello, of going up to people he couldn't wait to get a thousand miles away from just a few years before. At the same time, he had the unsettling feeling that going out and meeting those people would somehow be like holding magnets in either hand, moving them closer and closer together without knowing what the end result would be. Not knowing whether they would get close enough, opposites attracting, to pull each other together, or whether it would be a case of just close enough to feel the push of the two like poles, packed tight full of a similar charge, and so inevitably familiar that they ended up trying desperately to repel each other.

"So what do you say? Feel like moving out here and starting over in a brand new place?" Vincent kept his voice light on the phone, the familiar beige dial phone in the kitchen, trying to make it seem as though it didn't matter either way to him.

In his head he was racing around, at one point decided, and at the next completely panicked. Feeling that he was betraying Faith, and at the same time that he might be betraying himself. And on the other end of the phone, he heard Faith's voice catch and then stall, like the sound of a small airplane trundling through the sky towards you and then its engine stopping, the plane starting to fall away.

58
McKay Street

JILLIAN GEORGE

JULY 21, 2003

JILLIAN GEORGE ran, leaving Sam Newhook behind.
She ran fast and quietly, ran like someone who really knew how to run, no amateur here, her head down, hands coming up with every stride, looking straight ahead and never glancing behind. Her legs lashing forwards in the darkness, her feet coming down light on the pavement, wasting not one scrap of energy as they thrust her forwards.

She only had a few blocks to cover, but she thought she had left it too late. From a doorway by the butcher shop, she'd stopped to see how badly they were going to hurt him, whether the beating was going to go on until they'd killed him or whether they'd break it off if he was smart enough to just stop fighting back.

It was over fast enough for him to have a chance, she thought, so she took the opportunity to come out from cover and run, the street numbers unfolding as she went. She had a head start of well over a block when one of them saw her streaking away, but she had one clear disadvantage: as soon as they recognized her, they knew exactly where Jillian George was going.

And she knew them. Jillian knew all of the guys chasing her simply by their shapes and voices, knew their parents and their houses. She was even passing many of their houses as she ran. She knew all of them from school, but it was like she didn't know any of them at all. Later, she'd know that it was all wrong place, wrong time, that they had stumbled onto a situation where the voltage had already been cranked up, just waiting for a place to spark.

Jillian could hear them coming down the street fast and she felt completely alone, as if every house was empty, no one looking out at the noise as they passed. No time to bang on doors and wait for someone to come to the front of their house: no way to take the risk of stopping and waiting and having no one come. It was better to run and keep running. She counted down the street numbers as she went, knew they were getting closer behind her, and decided, close to her parents' house but not really close enough, that she wouldn't be able to get there before they caught up with her.

Instead, she cut down beside Albert Carter's, heading for the back laneway so that she would come up behind her own house and in through the back door. The back door was always unlocked, so there would be no fumbling with keys, just the quick rush through the door, turning and slamming it home. She knew the rules and so did they: once inside she'd be safe, and they'd all melt away like water. Chances were they'd never even mention it again, like it was something as simple as a game gone wrong once the sharp anger of the chase faded.

It was, she thought, her best chance.

Except that, at the back of his house, Mr. Carter had blocked off the gap between the houses. Blocked it off right before the lane, a new ragged fence just a couple of feet long there, built out of rough lumber. Even in the dark, half lit only by the street light out front, she could see the crazy pattern of shiny nails sticking out through the wood in all directions where Carter, no carpenter, had pounded them through, missing the fence stringers so that the wood had spines everywhere, like some armoured prehistoric beast. No way to climb over, not from that side, and there were already heavy feet coming down the gap behind her from the front of the house, and she knew there wasn't time to carefully climb the fence, no way to pick her way past the metal teeth.

So Jillian stopped and turned around.

It was dark, but she recognized a few of them. Ronnie Collins and Brendan Hayden. The Chaulks, out of breath and gasping for air, not used to running, especially Murray. Twig, as rangy as his nickname suggested, thin, long arms and legs, standing there as if he was waiting for instructions. Somewhere nearby, probably, Chris Wheeler too, or Larry Hayden—not participating, but always aware.

"Okay," Jillian said, her arms at her sides, hands in fists. "You caught me. So what now?"

Ronnie was out in front of the other teenagers, close enough that she could feel the warmth of him. Then she felt his hands on her wrists. A part of her was afraid, another part resigned, a voice saying let's just get this over with already. She wondered how Sam was, whether he was still out there bleeding, unconscious or worse.

"So you like it when they're from away, do you? Or is it just their money you like?" Ronnie said.

"Come on, Ron," Brendan said. "It's bad enough already. The cops are going to be here any minute."

"Shut up, Brendan. Get out to the front of the house and keep your eyes open. You saw what happened to that guy—you want to be next?" Ronnie turned halfway towards Brendan, still holding Jillian's wrists, but Brendan was moving back down towards the front of the house. "You'll have your turn."

High up on a fence on the other side of the laneway, right down at the back edge of the property line, Larry Hayden was perched on the top of a garden shed, his eyes narrow in the dark, looking over the fence at the group of people and already thinking about getting away. Through the back window of the house, he could see Albert Carter walking back and forth through the light, carrying tools. Larry could see Brendan at the front in the gap between the houses, the long, narrow gap lit by one lone street light out on McKay Street, the dark bunch of the other four people silhouetted against the street light, moving like cut-out characters but with their actions absolutely clear.

There wasn't any sound at all from between the houses. Off to his right, a dog barked a few sharp warning barks and then stopped. It was the kind of night when the air hangs still and wet, like sweaty clothing, and sounds seem to come from far away, cleanly divorced from their source.

No noise from between the houses still, but the motion of the cut-out shadows brutal and sharp.

2

McKay Street

ROBERT PATTEN

JUNE 30, 2006

THEY SAY you're not supposed to feel anything, but that's bullshit, because I could feel the whole damn thing, the moose still alive or dying or whatever and he was all the way inside the car with me then, kicking around through the back of my seat, flopping my head around like a fish in there, and I kept wanting to yell, "Fuck you, just hold fuckin' still and we'll do something about this," and I'm sure that was when most of the damage was done.

And there was plenty of damage done. But I'm getting ahead of myself here.

There's a big curve on the Trans-Canada Highway down near the Avondale access road, see, just a big curve like so many others, and it's tailor-made for moose down there, high ground looking out over a couple of ponds and a big long stretch of flooded bog. I'd even been in there trout fishing a couple of times, down where the beavers had it all blocked, all the hardwood cut out and dragged into the water and the beavers even starting in on the softwoods because they'd finished up everything else already.

The woods were so full of moose sign when I'd been in there fishing—crap and footprints and everything else all over the place—so much sign that you couldn't help but keep looking around just in case there was a bull moose standing right there behind you, thinking that he was lonely and you were available.

It's tight spruce and fir in there, with the occasional big lonely birch left, but just a solid wall of fat grey trunks and fallen snags all over the place, windfalls mostly, rough terrain to cross because there's peat bog-holes all around. And when you're not scrambling over a snag, you're toppling headfirst into something else with one of your feet up to the knee in soft bog.

The moose are on the move in the mornings and evenings, because they feed in the valleys and they like to rest up on high ground. Out near the highway there, it was moose trails all over the place, they just shrug their way through any small trees, their routes meandering through the woods in all directions, big oval prints pounded right down into anything soft, clear as a bell, like they were left there deliberately.

And I was on my own in the car coming back from Clarenville, the Doe Hills already well behind me and the sunset out behind me too, and up there I had the long shadow of the car cast out in front like unexpected company on all the downhill stretches, daring me to try to catch it. Every single thing all around was lit up with the orange of the sinking sun, and I was thinking that it was a Friday night and I'd be able to get back into town in an hour or so, the road wide open and dry, all the traffic coming the other way, people pouring out of the city for the Easter long weekend. Me in a white rig with potato-chip company logos all over the outside, Robert Patten, a manufacturer's agent for a snack food company. We used to kid around at the warehouse that if there was salt all over the outside and you could eat it and it was downright unhealthy, we were probably responsible for selling it to you.

And by Avondale, it was all of a sudden cutting down towards full dark, just at the point when there's really a difference between high beams and low beams on the pavement out in front of you, and I was rocketing down a long, swinging curve to the left, knowing the road so well that I was already getting set for the big pullback in the other direction under the access bridge, caught between the guardrails that kept the cars from going off the road and down into the culvert.

And he came up out of a little dirt road there on the right, right where campers sometimes set up on the edge of a pond, little more than a widening in the brook, really, and he came up fast through the one small gap in the guardrail.

As quick as that.

A big moose, a big slab-sided, fast-moving bull moose, fifteen hundred pounds of solid animal, and he was on his way across the highway before I even had a chance to think more about it than, "There you are." Then, "Of course you are," the brakes already right to the floor, because where the heck else would he be going, and where else would a moose be more likely to be?

And all the planning—what a waste of time that turned out to be.

I mean, you can't be on the highway in Newfoundland all the time and not expect to see plenty of moose, not expect to eventually have to make a split-second decision about what to do. You have to plan and prepare and wonder, especially when you've come up on the wreckage of a few moose–car collisions, the kind of wreckage that you'd expect from a car hitting a block of meat that weighs more than a ton.

The experts say aim for their backsides, because moose move forwards at different speeds but don't ever back up. Aim at their backsides and then you're supposed to be guaranteed at most a glancing blow, one that makes sure they won't be coming through the windshield or flipping up and landing on your roof. A huge stupid animal standing on four thin stick-like legs, just waiting to topple onto your car roof and fold it down onto you in a great big bowl.

And I'd seen plenty of moose through the years, even nicked a yearling male with my passenger-side mirror once, and I'd had close calls where they barrelled up out of the ditch and onto the pavement with no notice whatsoever. But never as close as this one.

In the end, I didn't get a chance to try to decide where I wanted to hit my moose. At 120 kilometres per hour, there wasn't really time for that kind of decision.

No decision at all, really. I just hit him.

One moment, no moose, the next, all moose, and all over me.

I was driving the best and newest of the three little company SUVs, the only one with working four-wheel drive for snow, because at thirty-five, believe it or not, I was the senior guy by then. In sales, you're always moving on to the better commission and no one ever holds it against you. That's just business. As it was, the level of my hood was right above knee level for a moose.

And really, that's what you don't want.

I saw brown fur in the headlights, and immediately after I hit him, he was past the headlights and into the windshield and then I didn't see anything at all.

My brother Tony is a mechanic, and when I went in to see him at lunch one day, he showed me a van he was working on, an auction purchase by the garage owner after it hit a moose, the animal coming right in through the windshield. Just a little project for Tony to fix up in his down time, so the owner could sell it off in the classifieds later without ever bothering to mention that it had been an insurance write-off. A nice sideline for the ethically challenged.

Inside, there were tufts of torn-off moose fur on every projecting point: on the knobs for the windows, on the stump of the rear-view mirror, on every single seat belt mount from front to back. On the headrests.

My brother told me that particular moose had finally stopped moving when it fetched up solid on the inside of the hatchback at the very back of the van, after it smeared its way over every single seat for the entire length of the vehicle. That the wildlife officers had opened the back of the van and the dead moose had fallen straight out onto the pavement, like someone had brought along a big meaty suitcase they hadn't secured very carefully.

The RCMP officer who came in to see me at the hospital said I'd been in "a trademark moose/vehicle accident," and he slapped his black notebook closed when he said it, like he was disciplining an inattentive student. "Nothing you could have done about it probably. Just bad luck."

Small consolation, that. Especially with the way he left the "probably" just hanging out there, like there was always the chance it was all my fault after all.

The moose slid straight across the hood when I hit him, breaking in through the windshield with his back and then sliding right over me into the back seat. Make yourself comfortable, Mr. Moose. Make sure your seat belt's on—mine was, and that didn't make anything any easier.

The moose was panicked and dying and trying to get away, and it started kicking out wildly, its hooves tearing out the ceiling of the van, tearing into the seats. The police officer showed me pictures of it, sure I'd be interested. The hoofs were tearing into me—into my back and neck, while I was safely pinned in place by my seat belt and all the bent metal.

And three other cars stopped right after the accident, even before the police got there, but the drivers couldn't even get near me until the moose was finally dead and not jerking around anymore.

They needed a tow truck. Not just for my car, but to haul the moose carcass back away from me, and I could smell blood and shit and blown-apart moose guts for most of the time I was awake. I was slipping back and forth between consciousness and unconsciousness. Luckily, the consciousness part didn't continue when they were taking the car apart to get me out.

I woke up later in the hospital, not even sure at first how I got there, and by the time I'd really figured it out, really started to remember things and join them up with the scraps that people were telling me, they'd shifted me out of what they call "acute care" and into the much more slow-motion kind of thing, long-term care, the kind of place where the doctors come by every week or so to measure your incremental progress instead of coming in every day to check how you're doing. You work real hard, gain an inch here and there, and they write it down in your file and nod a lot.

They tell me there's six months ahead of me in a wheelchair anyway, best-case scenario, and I can't shake the clear feeling that I'm just some poor slug who met a moose on his way back in from Clarenville, the latest unlucky one of the collection of unlucky they're more than used to seeing in here. This is the last refuge for the winners of the losers' lottery, accidents and strokes and the whizz-bang aneurysm patients who started off with a massive headache because a vein let go up there in their head somewhere, and now they can't pull up their pants. We're all in here, dribbling and moaning on cue.

In here: *here* is a rehabilitation hospital called the Miller Centre, where some people come to try to recover and others come simply to give up and wait for the regular small thrill of a tepid dinner and fresh linen. It's a place for the terminals and the slow-movers—the slow-movers being the ones who recover but who are recovering nowhere near as fast as they'd like to.

Luckily, I think they've got me classed as one of the slow-recovering ones. They keep telling me it's going to be a real long time, and they're pragmatists about it. Like, "You're going to be here long enough that pretty much everyone's going to stop visiting you. So, you should get ready for that." It comes out like they have a program, and the very first item on the agenda is making sure I don't think I'm just going to get up and walk out of here any time soon. Tamp down the expectations good and hard, it's better for everyone later if no one's expecting anything good.

It's tough-love kind of stuff, and fair enough for them. I mean, how many people are they supposed to put up with, sitting around and just blubbering away instead of getting down to business? It would drive me mental to have to put up with that, the blubbering. But the slow progress is driving me mental anyway. Some of my day is spent in rehab, but the rest is just plain waiting—holding the television-channel changer buttons down while it cycles through channels I don't want to watch, or else being pushed from spot to spot so that the scenery changes but your perspective doesn't. Three and a half feet high always, upper body fixed in a brace, wheels out on both sides of me. Roommates who are stroke victims with blank looks on their faces, so that you look at them and think, "Who knows what's going on inside that melon?"

The staff are evil enough here in rehab that, as soon as they could, they arranged a blanket over my knees and lugged me out into the cold of May-month, so that I could see beyond a hospital room, and see all the other stuff I'd been trying to forget that I was missing. I think of them all back there at the desk, coffee breaks all around because the crips are out for their little look at what they've lost and what they should be trying extra-hard to get back. Like the sun on your face, the first of the spring leaves coming out, that rain-metal smell of the spring air. They were wheeling me out and then just stopping wherever they liked, like I was due for my regular three-quarters of an hour of sun, or like they were practising their parallel parking so they could get it right for another patient who really counted.

Always parking us in the same place, for the same small collection of minutes every single sunny day.

And they never, ever, ask if this is where I want to be.

They don't know that I'm looking straight across at the flat black roof of the house where I grew up, right down there at the corner of McKay Street, number 2. It used to be a kind of ochre-red. I don't think it is anymore, but I mostly see the roof from here. And what a small town this really is: after they'd been bringing me outside for two weeks, I found one of my fellow sun worshippers is Evelyn O'Reilly, and she's lived at 32 McKay Street for just about forever. Except this is just a husk of her, her mouth all caved in like they took all of her teeth away and she can't remember how her mouth is supposed to work.

Mr. O'Reilly keeps coming in to see her, and he recognized me. "Keith," he says sharply, sticking out his hand at me and just letting it hang there, like I'm supposed to reach up from my swaddling and grab it, and since I don't, he's confused about what the next step is supposed to be. His name stuck out in the air too, final, like it always has to have a period on the end of it, big and black and obvious. There's a lot of him like that—stuck out in the air, like he's always known exactly what it is he was supposed to be doing, but now that's all shot to hell and none of the pieces make sense anymore. He's always moving her chair to keep her in the sun every time the shade moves across her, like kindness in overdrive, caught up in doing every little thing right because the big ones are so far out of his control. And there's something about his mouth too, something wobbly, like he's trying to find words that aren't there anymore, as if he's moving his tongue around in there and finding spots where molars are suddenly missing and he doesn't know what to do about it.

My mom knew Mrs. O'Reilly, but she always said she wasn't easy to get to know well, that she had a way about her, "like she was always thinking of something way up over my head," my mother used to say. I think Mrs. O'Reilly seemed that way to everyone—like she was slightly higher in the air than everyone else. My mother and her would see each other on the mornings when the city was picking up the garbage, each of them out to the curb with that same last bag, the stuff their husbands could never catch on to getting. With Mom, it was always the trash can in the bathroom; it was like Dad had a blind spot, could never figure out there might be trash in there too. And it was like Keith O'Reilly had the same disease.

The first thing Evelyn said to me at the hospital was, "I was going to be a teacher." She said it as clear as that, too, clear as glass.

The only other thing she said was once when Keith O'Reilly was there and he picked her hand up off her lap, and she pulled her lips right back from her teeth and said, "Don't ever touch me again, Glenn," and it sounded nasty, like when a strange dog curls its lips right back when you reach down to pat it. Keith dropped her hand like it was burning hot.

"I didn't have a choice. Maybe I should've . . ." Keith said, the words running out of him quick and trailing off at the end like they lost all their pressure, just hanging there like a balloon low on air, and then he didn't say anything else. She didn't move. There was no sign that she heard him at all. I watched him leave soon after, and I remember that he just looked small, like a few inches had come out of the middle of him somewhere.

The way she said, "I was going to be a teacher"—that stuck with me. She said it with the sentence rising at the end like she regretted it. Except I knew she had never been a teacher, had never been anything at all other than Mr. O'Reilly's wife and Vince's mom. Vince who got away—it's strange, but that was the way I always thought about him. Everybody on the street fixed in place, like this was where we came from and this is where we were meant to stay, but Vince had found a way to jump on a plane and not even get dragged back by the phantom homesickness that's really a kind of sideways slip in confidence.

I didn't—I didn't get away, that is—but there it is; to each his own, everyone's different, even if they plunk us all down in a wheelchair eventually and treat every one of us like we were absolutely, precisely identical. We all want plastic bowls of vegetable soup, and we all want those soft little balls of barley with their stiff little spines hiding in there. Fuck, I hate barley.

We're like checkers, we are, all lined up somewhere while the people who play the game are back there getting themselves coffee and Danishes and complaining about how tough they've all got it, humping us out of bed day after day while they've still got two good arms and two good feet and they get to walk around without even thinking about how much we'd like to be doing exactly that. What I wouldn't give to be able to be changing some old-timer's diaper right about now.

It's the same row of us every day, and most of the time the only ones I recognize are Evelyn and a guy who was my roommate for a couple of weeks before surgery. Something happened in the operation: sorry, drew your ticket and, guess what, you lose again. Something went wrong and it didn't fix anything. He's in pain all the time now, so he's got his own room where the constant moaning can't get on anyone else's nerves. Even the nurses can't handle it, they're always slapping his door shut and keeping their faces down at the desk.

They never take us out when it rains, because I guess we might melt in the rain like the Wicked Witch of the West or something, or else because we're not really supposed to know that it ever rains, because we're just too damned fragile to be able to take anything like that on top of everything else we've got to deal with.

But I'm a lot less fragile than anyone thinks. I'm pretty sure that, by now, I can put up with anything.

Anything but him, anyways.

The problem is that, when they've got me outside, I keep seeing him. There he is again, every single day, boiling around the corner on his springy, stringy legs.

Him: he's some fifty-year-old bastard in flippy little dark blue running shorts and a tight T-shirt, bald as an egg in front, and where he's not bald, his hair is shaved down into a perfectly formed grey fuzz. He waves to us every single time he goes by, the same condescending little half wave, like, "Sorry you're so wrecked up, but look, I'm not," or maybe, "Sorry, you pathetic potted plant, but at least you've got someone to turn you around towards the sun."

It wasn't so bad at first, because he's just such a strange-looking guy that you could almost laugh out loud. Long shanks on him, that kind of stretched-out, extra-long build, long, flat muscles and businesslike tendons as fat as rope in the backs of his legs holding the whole assembly together. And he runs with a stride that has something like a little hop at the end of it, like there's an instant in the middle of his step where nothing at all is even touching the ground, like he is defying gravity. "Look, I'm doing all this running and I've still got energy to spare, more energy than you'll ever have again."

And that was the start of it. Like I don't know all about energy.

When they get me propped up between the goddamn parallel bars, I'm like some kind of crip Olympian, I'm sweating like a racehorse after even the first couple of steps, just trying to get my legs out in front of me one at a time, and it's the hardest work I've ever done in my life. And Mr. Runner-man doesn't have someone half a room away all the time barking at him, "Keep it up, keep it up, Robert, that's good."

And I keep hammering away, the sweat pouring down off me in streams, stinging my eyes because I can't let go of the bars to wipe it away without running the risk of falling flat on my helpless ass. "Good boy, Robert. Good boy. Keep it up, you're doing great."

Yeah, doing great: all of point two on a scale of one to ten.

I don't even know the guy's name. And fuck, I hate seeing him. I hate seeing him more than any other single thing alive.

109
McKay Street

EDYTHE PURCHASE

JULY 15, 2006

EDYTHE PURCHASE remembered the outside of her house best, remembered it brightly, precisely, like she had simply willed herself never to forget it. White siding, small sliding windows, the number in black on the right-hand side of the door. Even the little glowing orange eye of the doorbell.

She practised every day, remembering it as if she were in the process of focusing her eyes and staring right at it, trying to draw it up sharp in front of her and fix it in her memory with glue. They can't take that away, she thought. They can't take that away, even if the law seemed to let them take everything else.

Edythe knew she would remember the inside of the house better if she'd had the chance, if she'd even guessed for a moment that they were coming. I could have used my eyes like a camera, she thought, just like I did outside, *snap, snap,* so that it was all safe and locked away in my head perfectly. She'd done the outside of the house while they were trying to put her in the car, and she was proud of that, proud of remembering to take a crucial few moments and get a clear, solid image.

Inside, she could remember the living room and the kitchen, but not as well as she would have liked: she couldn't open the drawers, and her only memory of the backyard was with it always in bloom, as if winter never ever came. She tried hard not to think about the other parts, about being loaded into the car and taken away like a sack of potatoes, the woman in the car calling her Mom and telling the doctors that it couldn't go on the way it had been going.

"She's calling the power company ten or fifteen times a day now," the woman had said while Edythe looked around the room—a waiting room, she decided, or an examining room, and there was a man in a white coat, all dressed up like a doctor, although you couldn't be too sure. People can pick any getup they like, Edythe knew, passing themselves off as anything at all. That's why you have to be careful at the door, she thought. Just close it quickly—or don't even answer it at all.

She looked at the man in the white coat again. Anyone can nod and take notes on a clipboard, she thought. You don't need a medical degree for that.

"She tells them that there's a problem with the electricity, and they have to come, even if they're sure it's going to be nothing." The woman stopped talking, looked at Edythe and then leaned in close to the man in the coat. As if I'm hard of hearing, Edythe thought, and I most certainly am not. "The power company guys have taken to pretending they've found something and tell her it was a good thing she called. Otherwise she just keeps calling them back, over and over, all night long, saying the problem's come back and they have to check it out all over again. And then, if that doesn't work or if they don't come fast enough, she calls the fire department." The woman shook her head. "That's only part of it. She's told the police everything under the sun, they don't believe a word she says anymore. The police say they'd charge her except that it's not really her fault, the way she is."

What is she talking about? Edythe thought. Where there's smoke, there's fire, and that's why you need the fire department. You don't just wait to die there in your bed. But Edythe didn't say anything out loud, and the man in the white coat wasn't paying attention to her anyway.

Edythe hated it when people did that: when they talked about you and all around you, and if they ever got around to speaking to you at all, they either yelled or treated you like you were a complete simpleton. And you call the power company when there are electrical problems—you're supposed to, she thought. They have advertisements on the television telling you to do just that, for God's sake. And when you hear buzzing and crackling sounds in the wires, there are obviously serious problems. There is such a thing as a short circuit. They are the kinds of things that start electrical fires and burn you to death in your sleep. Not a day goes by, Edythe thought, when you don't hear about a fire somewhere in the city started by an electrical problem. Old houses, old neighbours.

"She doesn't remember my name or Bob's, or Dennis, and she looks at us like we're total strangers," the woman said.

"Tests first," the doctor said to the woman while he wrote in a file. Edythe noticed how the heavy paint was bubbling up at the tops of the walls, as if there had been a leak that had been painted over instead of being fixed. A large poster of a man on one wall, stripped away to his arteries and veins. A blood pressure cuff hanging from a box on a wall. One of those lights for looking in ears. So it's an examining room after all, she thought. Or it's supposed to look that way.

"We'll put her in semi-private," the white-coated man said, "get an MRI and some other diagnostics and see where we go from there."

They made her sit in a wheelchair and they took away her shoes, then another person she'd never seen before wheeled her to an elevator. The trip led to a room with three beds, two of them occupied. Edythe saw the room number, 437, and tried to save it up in her head where all the other numbers were. Too many numbers over seventy-five years: they jostled up there in awkward, overlapping quarters.

"Arnold. You have to get Arnold," the woman closest to the door said as the nurse wheeled Edythe into the hospital room.

Edythe didn't like the way the other woman stared at her, the way she kept her eyes wide open and big and staring straight at her.

"Find Arnold," the wizened woman said again, and Edythe could imagine the woman's hands clawing at her sleeve. Those gnarled, veiny hands, held up high in front of the woman's chest. Edythe didn't like looking at them, but had a hard time looking away.

Edythe didn't like the smell either. It smelled like soiled babies and old milk, and there was lots of noise. Machines beeping. Loud radiators. Someone calling out from down the hallway, the words muffled, indistinct and clearly urgent.

The nurse saw Edythe paying attention. "Don't worry about him, we'll close that door." She stopped at the bed next to the window. "You're here. You're 437B, if anyone asks."

Facing Edythe, an older woman sat as still as a statue, a length of tubing tucked up under her nose like some sort of clear plastic moustache. The woman stared at Edythe, her face impassive.

"Your roommates are Mrs. Tinden and Mrs. Walters," the nurse said. "Mrs. Tinden shares the washroom with you, because she can still get around. Mrs. Walters stays put, and if she tries to get up, you can press your button and call the nurses' station. We don't want Mrs. Walters trying to get up." We? Edythe thought.

The nurse came around to the front of the wheelchair and helped Edythe up and onto the bed. I don't need any help, Edythe thought as the nurse pressed gently on Edythe's shoulders, turning her and then lifting her legs up onto the bed. Edythe was looking out the window at the parking lot, at the standing cast-iron radiator, the thick institutional paint. There were tall curtains on rails, curtains that could be pulled around her bed to offer some privacy.

"I don't want to be here," she said to the nurse. "I want to be home."

The nurse was pulling thick sheets over Edythe's legs and didn't seem to be paying attention.

I'd leave if I could, Edythe thought. But they had taken her purse, her keys, her shoes and her clothes. She had kept her socks, but they had made her change into a suit of loose blue hospital clothes, too large for her frame.

"Make yourself comfortable," the nurse said. "The doctor will be in later to tell you about the schedule for the tests."

Mrs. Tinden was the goggle-eyed woman.

Mrs. Walters sat quietly, hoses hissing.

Were they here against their will too? Edythe thought. Maybe one of them was there to keep an eye on her neighbours, Edythe thought. What was it they called it on television? A plant? Maybe she shouldn't say anything at all—and for a little while, she didn't. But Edythe had never been in a place that was so noisy and yet so empty, that so needed to be filled up with words. The other women stared, and the silence tugged at Edythe. Down the hall, there was the sound of someone crying quietly.

"Men are all pigs," Edythe said. "But you two don't need me to tell you that. Get to be women of our age and you already know."

"Arnold?" Mrs. Tinden said quietly.

The other woman, propped up in a sitting position, just stared, her oxygen whistling softly.

"Len Menchinton?" Edythe said—and then the words were falling out of her in a rush, and she felt like she had to slow them down somehow to keep them from rolling right over each other. "He's a pig. For certain. Disgusting."

The other women were silent—but they were paying careful attention, an audience open to whatever was coming next.

"You should have seen what I saw, with his hands all over her underwear. Ronnie Collins? Just an animal. Keith O'Reilly? I hardly know where to start."

Mrs. Purchase looked at the women, one at a time. Looked straight at each one of them. Started talking again.

"You know what they're like. They preen and walk around like they're the cocks of the walk. So full of themselves and talking down to you so you'd never guess they were up to anything at all. Never guess that they've each got their dirty little secrets, that they are so ready to just roll around like dogs if you let them.

"I told Ingrid Menchinton about Len. I did. I had to. And I was right to, because you shouldn't be made a fool of, shouldn't be walking around with everybody quite able to see what is going on and you in the dark, everyone laughing at you. And it didn't do any good, you know. She's still with him—I see them in the big window in their kitchen, laughing, necking like teenagers, his hands right up there under her shirt. Some women just have no self-respect at all. I did right telling her, though, even if I was the one that got told off for it."

Edythe paused, caught her breath, looked out the window. Even if it was only the fourth floor, the room was pretty high up, she thought, the hospital up the way it was, cut into the side of the hill. You could see for miles. She turned back to the two women, giving each one a careful stare before starting again.

"I should have told Evelyn too, whatever the consequences," Edythe said. "I regret that still, for sure. To this day. But I tried to tell the police, and you know, you can't even trust them, they're in it for themselves. Like everyone.

"My husband Frank trusted people, trusted anyone who came in the door, and look what that got him. Now, he was a good man. You might have heard of him—no one could ever say a bad word. He ran a restaurant on Water Street called the Doryman. Got in trouble with the wrong people, he did. Bought St. Pierre liquor, French liquor, no tax stamps or anything, they told him everyone was doing it and no one would ever get caught. And him so innocent. One stupid mistake and then they were into him, made him pay protection money. Black-mail."

Neither of the women moved. Both of them stared.

Edythe, suddenly uncomfortable, found herself picking at the lint pills on the flannel sheet. The sheet said *Property of Eastern Health* on it in big blue lettering. There were scores of pilling lumps on the fabric. Every time she stopped talking, the room was quiet again. Only the hissing of the hoses.

"He told me about it. Told me they were threatening him, that they beat up Mike, one of the cooks, and broke his arm. Frank said he had to pay more and more, every week some new demand, and that they wouldn't listen to anything. I told him he should stand up to them. That it was a matter of principle. But he wouldn't. Because of me. He just kept paying. We were almost bankrupt, but he wouldn't go to the police. Told me they said they would hurt me if anyone said anything to the police."

Edythe looked at Mrs. Tinden out of the corner of her eye. The woman hadn't moved, her hands still up tight in front of her chest. But she was staring at Edythe, wide-eyed.

"One night, after closing, he just didn't come home. Maybe they wanted more money than he had for them, maybe he finally decided he wouldn't pay anymore. I don't know. He never told me that he was going to do anything different, but he must have. I didn't believe it at first. He was their gravy train, their easy money. But they took him. Maybe they were trying to make a point to other businessmen downtown. I don't know. I never heard another word, and the police didn't do a thing, just told me there were no signs of disturbance in the restaurant and that people sometimes just decide to disappear. But they were taking the case seriously—that's what they told me every time I called. They were taking the case seriously.

"Someone must have got to them too. They get people. Sometimes people are just gone. There are people you don't cross. You don't cross the mob, for sure, I can tell you that. And you don't stand up to them either. Not if you want to walk away in one piece."

Edythe paused and lowered her voice. She could see that both of the women were following her with their eyes, no other reaction.

"You don't know how evil people can be. You don't know until you see it with your own eyes. Ordinary people. Even people on your own street, people you run into every day." Edythe smoothed the sheet across her lap, looked up again. "I knew it years ago," she said primly. "I knew the truth of it."

This was it, she thought. The big secret, the one no one ever wanted to listen to—but neither Mrs. Walters nor Mrs. Tinden was moving. Maybe they wouldn't leave, Edythe thought. Maybe they couldn't. Edythe felt the truth in her chest like she had swallowed a whole egg, big and round and just wanting to come back out. In a movie, she thought, the music would swell up now, dramatic, so everyone would know it was an important moment.

"I saw it all through the window. I saw Keith O'Reilly stop that truck, her just walking on the sidewalk, minding her own business, him calling out to her, 'Get over here now, slut!' nasty like that, and then he was getting out of the truck, coming around the side where she was."

Edythe felt flushed then, knew there was colour rising in her cheeks. It always did when she thought about Keith O'Reilly and that poor, innocent girl.

"He practically stuffed that girl into the truck. Grabbed her arm. Wouldn't let go. And a hand over her mouth so she couldn't scream or anything. He must have had it fixed so she couldn't get the door open again. The lock jammed so she couldn't pull it up. Her fingers scratching away useless on the inside of the glass. When he got in the cab, he hit her too. And I recognized her from the television. I recognized her right away, the day they put her picture up and said she was missing. I'm good with faces, always have been. And I know about responsibility. About civic duty.

"I didn't even call them. I went straight to the police station, straight to Fort Townsend, and they treated me well, brought me into a room in the back and even offered me tea. And one of the officers was writing down what I was saying, about Keith and the girl, at least until the tea came, and the other policeman looked at me and said to the officer talking to me, 'You know you're interviewing the-lady-who-cried-wolf.' He said it real quiet, but I heard it when he said it, as plain as that. And there was more, but I couldn't hear everything he said.

"And then the questions changed, went flat like he was going through the motions. They went away to, 'How can you be so sure?' and 'How dark was it?' and 'Were you wearing your glasses?' and 'Thank you very much.' And he wasn't even writing anything down anymore."

Edythe stopped. Next to her, Mrs. Tinden was murmuring quietly, the felt sheets pulled right up over her mouth so that only her eyes were showing.

"That hurt, I'll tell you. That certainly hurt. A law-abiding person is supposed to do their duty, and when they do, they don't expect to be treated like some kind of joke." Edythe gathered herself up and, without even realizing she was doing it, sat up straight in the bed so that her back was a perfect vertical line. "I certainly have called the police before, I'll admit that. I called them when there were teenagers chasing a girl down the street—it looked horrible. And when the drag racers were tearing up and down. But the police never got there fast enough. And when there was what looked like a man outside the O'Reillys' looking in the windows one night after dark, doing I don't know what. Casing the joint, isn't that what they call it?"

There was no response from her roommates.

"It's not my fault if they're not fast enough, finishing their coffee and doughnuts, if everything is over and done with before they get around to getting there. But it all counts against you, I can tell you that from experience. Everything always counts against you, even when you're the one trying to do good."

Out in the hall, an orderly pushing a woman in a wheelchair stopped. The woman looked in the door at Edythe hungrily, her mouth moving gummily, collapsed, clearly without teeth. Everyone stares here, Edythe thought. Everyone. Outside, the fog was coming in over the land, catching and spreading over the hilltops like a fungus. Edythe thought that it wouldn't take long to reach the hospital, to cover everything right up in grey.

"I tried to tell Evelyn about her husband, believe me I did. It's one of my greatest regrets. I know it was the right thing to do, and I tried and tried. I must have gone across to her house a dozen times when I saw her out there in the yard. But every time I got across the street, no matter how hard I tried to steel myself for it first, her eyes just stopped me." Edythe shuddered slightly at the memory. "Everyone thinks she's so standoffish, but it's not that. It's that she can see right through your skin, like she knows everything already, like she's choosing which things she knows and which ones she wants to ignore. You don't know what she's like, how she just stops you with those eyes. I tried. You can't blame me for that."

There was noise in the hallway again. A small woman in scrubs came into the room with lunch trays, setting them on tables next to each bed and then turning quickly away. Edythe looked at her tray: a black-spotted banana, a cup of tea, devilled ham sandwiches and a plastic bowl that looked like it might contain soup. She felt the outside of the bowl: it was hot.

Edythe was cautiously opening the lid when Mrs. Walters spoke for the first time, sitting up straight in her bed, her eyes bright and bead-black as she stared out over her oxygen hose. "Excuse me," Mrs. Walters said loudly to the woman with the trays, who was already almost out the door. "I have to see your face. I won't eat any of it if I can't see who's bringing it to me."

That's a good idea, Edythe thought. That's a very, very good idea.

103
McKay Street

LEN MENCHINTON

AUGUST 27, 2005

THE YEAR before her daughter brought her to the hospital, Edythe was gardening and carefully watching Len Menchinton on his deck.

He didn't even see her. Instead, he was remembering how once, while he was under contract as security at a home supply store, he had used one single look to catch a shoplifter on the way out the door. One look to freeze him in his tracks, a guy who had so much merchandise stuffed into his trousers that he couldn't even bend his knees to sit in the one folding chair in the holding room where they were waiting for the police.

As Len watched, the man undid his belt and pulled a long carpenter's level up out of each pant leg, and then started emptying fistfuls of drill bits and small power tool attachments out of his pants pockets and from somewhere inside his shirt. Len didn't ask the man how he had gotten into the locked display cases for the small things, or how he expected to walk out of the store with his knees locked straight and a sharply defined rectangle behind each inseam. It was hundreds of dollars' worth of hardware and tools, so much that there was absolutely no way the guy would have been able to shuffle his way out the front door without getting caught. Len didn't even begin to ask why, didn't even care why. But the man started answering anyway.

"My wife has problems, she's sick, and . . ." It was a long story, including words like "congenital condition" and "difficult childbirth" and "expensive drug regimes."

But Len wasn't in a mood for listening. "This isn't about your wife," he said. "This has goddamn nothing to do with your wife. Not now. She's not the one stuffing tools down your pants. You are."

Then Len Menchinton did something he hadn't ever done with a shoplifter before, the kind of thing that the rules say you're never supposed to do, because suspects might try to kill themselves or eat the evidence or something, the kind of thing that "exposes the store to liability," and God knows, you're never supposed to do that. Len got up and went out into the hall outside the holding room and closed the door, cutting off the suspect in mid-sentence. And he stood there, suddenly wishing he could have that cigarette that he hadn't wanted in years, wishing the cops would just show up and take the guy away so he wouldn't have to listen to him for even one more minute.

Outside the room, Len noticed for the first time how barren the walls looked in the back hall of the building supply store, all painted a creamy yellow with dents and scuff marks as high as his waist along both sides, but without a single picture or poster, without any decoration at all. And he thought about how desolate those bare walls made the place, even with the steady noise of the shoppers so close outside, a noise that migrated right through the thin walls.

He remembered whole rows of shoplifters then, like a highlight reel on the sports channel. The woman with a purse full of cassette tapes who started crying the moment he spoke to her and, as far as he knew, never stopped. Even in court she cried. The guy who had just piled a cart full of kitchen cabinet doors and went right out through the front of the store like he had paid for everything already, nine hundred dollars of heavy new oak still in the plastic shop wrap.

The regulars, like Bart Dolimont. He must have caught Dolimont ten times by now, and he was never any trouble at all. Dolimont would hold his arms out and say, "You got me, sheriff," as soon as Len came around the corner and spotted him with something, and he would be all smiles and chatter waiting for the police, like he couldn't wait to be arrested. Len knew that Dolimont would always have something big under his jacket, something worth at least $150, so that the charges were always for theft instead of shoplifting, the kind of things that always carried the promise of jail time.

And Len would never have to testify when Bart was in court, because he would plead guilty at the first opportunity anyway, usually clearing off a whole raft of theft and burglary charges at the same time, a weary judge adding up the consecutive and concurrent sentences in a tangle of numbers and dates. Dolimont made no sense to Len at all, the man being led quietly, compliantly away in cuffs, calling back over his shoulder, "See you next time, sheriff," like it didn't matter whether he'd been caught with whatever he was stealing or whether he had gotten away with it.

What a contrast with Ron Collins, just a kid when Len grabbed him trying to get out of the mall with a fistful of cheap girls' jewellery—Ron Collins, a little stick of a thing then, but Len would never forget those eyes, the way they turned black as ink when Len turned him around, like his eyes were all pupil and nothing else. Len remembered thinking that it was like looking at some kind of primal thing, like looking at someone who was capable of absolutely anything. And the way the kid had fought, Len thought. Fought like a cornered animal, even though Len had forty extra pounds on him, easy. If he hadn't been a young offender, if he'd been a bigger guy then, there could have been real injuries and assault charges, instead of a slap on the wrist from the damned youth court judge, Paddock, who felt sorry for them all and was always sending them home to Mommy, saying, "I hope you've learned your lesson," so they could come back to the store the very next day and try to lift something else. They'd come back all sneering—catch them again and it would just be, "See you again tomorrow, old man," already certain of their imminent release.

Len suddenly wanted to be far away from the store, far away from the shoplifters and the shoppers and all of their particular needs. Len wanted to be fishing on a big, noisy, fast river, watching trout rise and sip at his fly, the small fly caught there on the edge of some big foaming eddy. He wanted to be in a wilderness cabin where one of the jobs was making sure the wood stove never, ever went out. Len wanted to be fucking Ingrid in a motel where the only features worth remembering were their bodies, slick with sweat, and the white plain of the bed with all the blankets stripped off and thrown into rippled, unconsidered topography on the floor. And he wanted Ingrid to be the one who started it all.

And Len wanted Vernie too. But he kept that thought small and quiet, like a whisper.

Len found himself inspecting Vernie's bras one Saturday afternoon, well into summer, when the sun was hard and brassy and yellow. He had his chair turned slightly by then, so that instead of taking in the length of his own yard as he usually did, he was now looking across the fences on the left-hand side of his house, a view-plane across wedges of Vernie's yard and then Mr. Nostrand's and even the yard after that, where a family with small children had set up a hard plastic play castle that the kids ignored unless it was raining and they needed to duck under it for shelter.

And all at once, there they were: two creamy white brassieres with big soft cups, and two others, lacy, filigreed almost, made with the kind of flimsy yet deliberate construction that made them impossibly difficult to figure out, Len thought, like you'd need an engineering degree to decide where all the seams went, what they did and why.

You wouldn't think that Vernie was big like that upstairs, Len thought. Sure, she was a good-looking woman, he'd certainly have had to be blind not to notice that. But the size of the bras, especially the red one, suggested that she was hiding it well.

He hadn't been watching when she'd hung them out, but had come outside with a beer and a newspaper instead, looking for classified ads for flea markets. Sometimes, he'd found, you could get a pretty good idea about what was going to go missing by what was already being sold new on the flea market tables. Razor blades were always a favourite: small but expensive, flat and easy to hide. Lipstick. Eyeshadow. Pockets full of the high-priced things you could move again real quick. But Len found that the lure of the flea markets faded fast once he was looking at the clothesline again.

The summer heat was pelting down on him, the air humid like it rarely is in St. John's, and Len could imagine that there was no way anything would ever really dry on a clothesline, and he could imagine exactly how the damp fabric would feel to his hands, the way the damp would smell if he held it up against the smooth, shallow dip in his upper lip, right there under his nose. To his amazement, the smell was there in his head, damp cloth caught up there as distinctively as if it were a critical, sharp, memorable smell like dark chocolate or burnt cedar.

A week later, across Forest Road at the small convenience store, he ran into Vernie with an armful of packaged hamburger buns and plastic sleeves of potato chips, the bags held up with one arm in front of her chest as if she knew something about what he was thinking, a case of beer dangling at the end of her free arm. She was ahead of him at the short linoleum counter, and they'd waited together as the clerk counted out Vernie's change and put the groceries into bags.

"Hi, Vernie," he'd said quietly, almost shyly.

She had smiled back at him. "Hi, Len."

"Having a barbecue?"

"Reg's having some of the guys over from work. Last-minute thing."

And then she smiled at him again, and Len was absolutely sure every scrap of laundry would be taken in before Reg and his guests arrived to take up the whole deck with their loud voices and big attitudes. Laundry that she clearly had no problem hanging out there right in front of Len.

And after she had picked up the groceries and the glass door closed behind her, Len watched her walking away, watched her ass and wondered, "Which pair of underwear is she wearing today?" and he mentally tried out pairs of underwear he remembered from the line on her departing rear end. Then he felt a fleeting sheer of shame, like for a moment he'd been caught on a ladder outside her bedroom window, watching Vernie get changed in what she thought was privacy.

The clerk had to say "Sir?" three times before Len finally paid enough attention to get his change.

Sunday, and Reg's party had gone late. Ingrid and Len had been awake for hours in their darkened bedroom, listening to the steady grumble of voices from their neighbours' deck, the occasional burst of raucous laughter. Len hadn't heard Vernie's voice on the deck at all, not even once, but he was left with a strange feeling that she was lingering there just the same, that she probably kept coming out to check with the guys to see if anyone needed more beer, hovering like a wandering moth just outside the yellow pool of backyard light.

He lay on his back in his bed and stared at the ceiling, imagining Vernie moving around through the rooms in the house next door by herself, everyone else still out on the deck, thinking that if it were just the two of them, she'd never be left on the fringes of anything ever again. That she'd find a place just within his arms' reach, a comfortable place where she would always want to be. And then he reached for Ingrid, but that wouldn't work either. By then, beside him, Ingrid was sleeping, breathing evenly through her nose with a dry, regular and familiar rasp, and Len felt as if she were really tens of thousands of distant miles away.

In the morning, Len and Ingrid got up late, both exhausted from the night before. Len hadn't slept at first. Ingrid had woken up early, lying as still as she could beside him to keep from waking him. The fractured night left Ingrid cranky, and Len broke the carafe from the coffee machine on the edge of the stainless steel sink while he was trying to fill the coffee pot with cold water.

After it happened, he just walked away from the broken glass, which was piled in uneven shards all around the circle of the drain, and headed out onto the empty deck in his bathrobe and bare feet instead. Behind him, Len thought he heard Ingrid head up the stairs and back to bed. And even though he hadn't heard her, Len saw that

Vernie had already been outside, and that her laundry line was full.

The wind, a steady breeze, was bringing the laundry close to his side of the fence, all of it fluttering like small, desperate flags. The largest pieces were big, fluffy chocolate-coloured towels, snapping and slapping in the brisk wind, trousers bending and straightening at the knees as if unable to make up their minds just where it was they wanted to go.

And underwear. Of course there was underwear, bras tangling and writhing around themselves in the wind, and panties rising and falling, rising and falling, as they first caught, and then slipped, the steady southerly wind.

Before he even really thought about it, Len was reaching out, standing tiptoed on the deck and stretching his body out over the fence so that he could feel the tops of the fence palings pressing hard into his stomach just above his waist. He was stretching so far that he could even feel the effort of it in the joints of his fingers, as if those fingers were reaching until their bones were beginning to separate from their hinge-and-socket seats.

Everything is possible, Len was thinking, every kind of need and every kind of behaviour.

Everything is explainable, given the right kind of circumstances.

It all made sense, no matter how impossible it might seem.

And it was like Vernie was right there on the other side of the fence, too, looking back at him, reaching over towards him, pulling him in.

Okay, he had to admit, that was only imagination. Just the same, he could already feel the fabric in his hands, and it occurred to him that he knew just exactly what it was like when your hand closed around something that you wanted, something that wasn't yours, but something that you were going to go ahead and take anyway.

"Hey."

Len heard a small, distant voice, a voice as sharp and definite as a pinprick.

"Hey, Len, you heard me. I know you did."

And down at the end of the yard, Len saw a face peering over the fence.

He walked to the edge of the yard, feeling the recently cut grass sharp on the skin underneath his toes, and looked across through the Taylors' and the Ryans' yards.

"I always knew you were a pervert," Mrs. Purchase hissed, her face partially obscured by the shifting maple leaves. "I could always tell, just by looking at you."

And her words sounded bright and sharp and alive, like she was relishing the very opportunity to say them out loud, just like she had been waiting for years to say exactly that. But that was before the rest.

"And what do you think Ingrid is going to say about this? Because she really should know, Len. Because it wouldn't really be right if she didn't."

Len could hear the towels up above him still snapping in the wind, and he could imagine seeing the edges of them curling and darting back.

Mrs. Purchase was safely hunkered down behind the fence, her right hand with the trowel held up slightly, the small shovel's tip pointed towards him and then pointed towards the sky. "I couldn't live with myself if I didn't say anything about this," Mrs. Purchase said, and Len heard something like triumph in her voice.

It was a triumph he recognized, the same tone he himself had used handing shoplifters over to the tired-looking police officers. "The good guys win. Got another one," Len had gotten used to saying, like there was someone somewhere who was keeping score of every soul-destroying small tragedy.

Got another one.

Then another one.

Len didn't answer Mrs. Purchase. He didn't speak at all. Instead, he turned and started slowly up the much longer lawn, the deck out ahead of him like the ramparts of a huge and unassailable fort.

Next door, Vernie's panties flew like battle pennants.

Everyone thinks they can get away with stuff, Len thought resignedly, and then they go ahead and blurt it all out anyway. But he told himself he'd be different. He'd watch his mouth and even his thoughts.

And Mrs. Purchase didn't have anything on him anyway, nothing more than a bit of poison to drip into Ingrid's ear, and all he really had to do was to convince Ingrid that the old woman was confused or senile or bitter. Senile—that was the best bet, the most believable, he thought, and just keep it simple.

But then the truth was burbling up inside him like he was about to vomit words, and Len thought it was the most unexpected feeling he had ever had. It was as if a seam might open right down the front of his stomach, a confession spilling out all over the yard in coils like alphabet soup, and he realized he might truly burst with the effort of keeping it all in.

And then, with a sinking feeling, he knew. Whether Mrs. Purchase went ahead and told Ingrid about Vernie's laundry or not, Len suddenly realized with a clear sense of horror that he almost certainly would.

Her Majesty's
Penitentiary, St. John's

RON COLLINS

JULY 17, 2006

RON COLLINS was still in prison, and it had already been five months since he had dropped the shovel in the snow and walked away. But for the first time, his lawyer talked like that was going to change.

His lawyer talked about the fact that Keith O'Reilly had died like he was talking about some kind of game—about how, with O'Reilly dead, there was really only Liz's testimony left. That "if we want to roll the dice, we can concentrate on her character, now that O'Reilly is out of the picture." Red Rover, Red Rover, let Liz come over, Ron thought bitterly. And then he thought about what the lawyer was suggesting, thought about Liz on the stand and his lawyer calculating and savage and trying to take her story all apart like a cat with a mouse. And it just didn't seem right.

His lawyer, talking on about how there was a clear path out of it now that they could work towards discrediting just one witness, now that there was just one piece of real testimony. Testimony from someone who was little more than a girl, and about as believable as if they'd brought some shifty homeless kid in to testify. That's exactly what he'd said, "some shifty little homeless kid." And even that was just plain wrong.

And he'd gone on to say that now, for the first time, there was a slim chance that Ron might walk after all. His lawyer was sure they could tear Liz down to nothing in the preliminary hearing, and it would all end right there.

And Ron said no.

He almost felt bad about it for a moment, because it was the first time his lawyer had seemed even the least bit hopeful. Ron knew he was supposed to be reassured by the lawyer's new-found excitement, but somehow it felt like the worst possible combination. Now it was just him and Liz and the solid, careful police testimony about physical evidence. Liz on one side with them, him on the other—and all he had were the things that, if he ever decided to go ahead and say them, wouldn't make sense to anyone else anyway. And the lawyer deflated right in front of him, looking like he'd lost all interest.

"You could just plead out, plead guilty and hope for a reduced sentence," his lawyer said flatly. It was as if he was thinking about how it wouldn't be as much fun to sell that to the press out on the stone steps in front of the court, the camera lights bright on his face. "You haven't been in that much trouble before. They'd probably take that into account. And maybe we could get them to knock it down to manslaughter. Maybe."

Surrounded by bare walls, Ron listened as the words just kept flowing out of his lawyer. He was wearing a different suit every single time Ron saw him, and sometimes the lawyer had to look at his notes to be absolutely certain he was getting Ron's name right. The lawyer, who was being paid by Legal Aid, was clearly frustrated.

His was the first name on the list that the police had handed Ron after they brought him in. He'd called the guy more because he thought he was supposed to than anything else. "Do you want a lawyer?" the cops kept asking him. "You can call a lawyer." So eventually he did.

Ron thought the lawyer always had a look about him like he felt this might be the case that would shift him up into bigger things, a cannonball shot out of a cannon, blasted into the big time of criminal law, the kind of thing that might make him the first choice of anyone dragged to the lock-up, that he'd be running with the drug guys and the operators, called all the time by the newspapers for quotes. Ron also thought it was almost as if suddenly the lawyer had other reasons to be involved in the case, just like everyone else seemed to have.

It had taken him months in prison to figure it out, but once the answer came to him, it stuck—that everyone wanted something extra. All the time. It didn't matter what, as long as there was something out there for them to take. And sometimes it made Ron want to haul the drunk driver out of his bed in the middle of the night and start pounding on him too, just because there was no rhyme or reason to any of it.

"Your choice," Ron's lawyer said. "Your funeral." Finishing up, shutting his briefcase with a snap and closing the clasps. It was leather, Ron noticed, a smooth buff brown that looked expensive. Everything about his lawyer looked expensive—but everything looked a little worn as well, as if the lawyer had once lived much better times. Times he'd managed to misplace somewhere but could still remember particularly well.

And that night, back in the prison, Ron had the same old familiar dream: he felt the slick slide of the shovel handle slipping out of his hand, the prickle of the snowflakes on the backs on his hands and the nape of his neck, and in his dream he turned his face up, feeling the snowflakes all over his face like cold little stars until his skin was completely covered.

He woke up, as always, because he could hear Liz laughing, and even after he woke up, there was a hint of that laugh, thin like mist in the air, caught like familiar music in his ears. For a moment he thought about how it could have been, and for the first time ever Ron thought back and tried to figure out if there was some particular place he could have done something differently, if there was a place where he could have decided to make another choice, to go in a different direction. But he was still partially asleep, and later the only way he would have been able to explain it was that everything he remembered stretched back behind him like a single set of railway tracks, seamless, and there were no other tracks in sight.

That same night, three cells down the range from Ron, another inmate slipped a coffee mug inside a sock and swung it against the side of his cellmate's head. The mug broke on the first swing, its handle splintering out and through the fabric, but the beating continued for another ten minutes. When the guards found out, they locked down the whole prison and everyone spent twenty-three hours a day in their cells.

It was a rhythm that was completely separate from anything outside the walls, Ron thought, and like almost everything else in prison, an order that made sense only when you were living right there inside it. But inside it, there was a clear-cut, straightforward order that you could depend on.

When the prison settled down again, Ron's drunk-driving roommate was gone, the guards signing out all of the conditional-sentence prisoners as soon as they signed in, and the whole range took on a feeling of suppressed, pressurized menace.

And then Bart Dolimont was moved into Ron's cell.

Small in stature and covered head to toe with fine red hair that was little more than fuzz, Bart was from farther downtown, from a harder downtown than McKay Street. And when he first got to the cell, he was in plaster from ankle to hip, the result of trying to pull rank on a new cellmate who'd knocked him unconscious and then propped Dolimont's leg on the edge of the bed and jumped on it with his full weight, breaking bones in three different places and leading Dolimont to describe to the guards, in detail, how he'd accidentally slipped and fallen off the toilet while he was trying to kill a particularly irritating bluebottle fly.

"My mistake," Dolimont said, shrugging his shoulders as he told Ron what had really happened. "Really. Shoulda known better. Been in here long enough to know the ground rules, after all. Ground rules are simple, once you got 'em figured. Step outside 'em and you get what's comin' to ya."

Bart Dolimont was unlike any prisoner Ronnie had ever met—and after almost six months he was beginning to think he'd seen every single type with only the occasional variation. He'd seen the tough cases rubbing the tears off their faces after only a few minutes on the telephone with their mothers, and he'd seen the sadistic ones who couldn't wait for someone to look afraid so that they could give them another reason for fear. Ronnie had seen criers and fighters, and even the quiet ones who just balled themselves up in a corner of their cells and waited for the days and months and years to run out, concentrating on their own interiors. The ones who smiled cruelly and drew their fists back to hit someone again, revelling in the opportunity. The ones who treated the whole thing like a dream they'd wake up from, and walk away from forever.

But Dolimont was like none of them. For him, the whole day was a pattern he'd come to expect, the rules that everyone else chafed about simply a necessary and expected order.

"Sunny day today," Dolimont would say, looking up through their small window of steel mesh glass as if the weather outside mattered, as if it meant something. He was like that with everything, from showers to linen change, as if the rules didn't weigh on him as much as they helped him move through his day.

At first, the only thought that Ronnie could muster was that he'd really like to punch Bart in the face—that he'd like to pin the other man down and pound him for his absurd hopefulness, to lift the man's head up and then ram it down onto the cement floor over and over again and yell at him, "You can't get out of here, you can't do anything, you're just another stupid rat in a cage." But it only took him a couple of days to realize it wouldn't matter what he did, short of killing the man.

Dolimont knew exactly how long he'd be in jail, how long he had left in his sentence, and he knew exactly how much he'd have to do to get himself right back inside again. And none of it mattered any more than the cell door sliding open before breakfast.

"I'm thirty-four, and this is my fifteenth year here. Sentenced seventeen times, guilty pleas every single time, never anything bad enough to get more than two years and serve federal time, the kind you have to serve out of the province at a big pen on the mainland," Dolimont said to Ron. "My scheduled release date is the seventeenth of November, and if I do get out then, I imagine I'll be back in by the twenty-fifth."

While Ronnie paced, Bart slept. When Ronnie pounded on the wall in frustration, Bart decided which book he'd like to read next, enjoying the pick even if it was something he'd read before. "Back part of it's really good," he'd say. "Can't wait to get there."

While every single man in the prison seemed to be twitching with incipient rage and you could feel the anger in the place growing like someone had turned up an invisible thermostat, Bart talked about what the supper menu would be for the next week. "As long as there's gravy, ya gotta admit there's a reason to live," he said.

"Doesn't it ever get to you?" Ronnie said. "Isn't there anything else you want to do?"

"And what exactly would I want to be doing?" Bart asked. "Working on someone else's yard till I'm beat for minimum wage? Driving truck? Filling potholes somewhere while the rain comes pounding down and gets me soaking wet? Sounds like a ton of fun, hey?"

Then Ronnie wanted to beat the other man all over again just for his stupid simplicity, but when he lifted his fist, it fell right back down by his side again all by itself.

And Dolimont laughed, but not in a bitter way. Not in an insulting way, either. Dolimont laughed because he thought it was funny, and because, watching Ron's hand fall, he understood.

And Ronnie was angry and frustrated and confused, and at the same time he liked Dolimont just a little bit more.

32
McKay Street

VINCENT O'REILLY

JANUARY 12, 1991

ONE SATURDAY in January 1991, nine-year-old Vincent heard his father and Glenn moving around the small workshop on the side of the house, and he imagined that his father was putting tools back in their familiar places. But before he was close enough to hear it, he could imagine the sound of the heater fan's steady whine, the thick red heat that came out through the grill into the room almost like the elements inside were throwing hot liquid into the air.

Vincent had been outside in the falling snow, and there was still melting snow left on one of his boots by the front door. One boot was standing up, the other toppled over on its side. It was coming down heavy this time, sound-catching, noise-bending snow, the kind of snow that made the low foghorn positioned on the outer edge of the harbour seem to move all around him, calling first from one direction, then from another. He and Murray and Twig had gotten into a snowball fight, and then had chased a cat and pelted heavy wet snowballs at it, missing every time but driving the cat into a streaking frenzy to escape. Vincent had seen Mr. Coughlin's truck across the street, the only vehicle on that side of the road that wasn't buried in a thick blanket of snow, the hood of the truck still clean and steaming as the bunched flakes landed on it.

Vincent snuck into the kitchen in his damp sock feet, hearing the two men's voices in the back room, a deep, uneven grumble at first, like some primitive and noisy piece of machinery working its way through a lengthy and slow-moving job. Vincent told himself that he was a spy quietly approaching German sentries, and then he got close enough for the sound to separate out into two distinct voices, one clear, the other muffled, sentences broken up by the smaller clattering sounds of the workshop under their hands.

"Your choice, isn't it?" Glenn Coughlin said.

From where he was, Vincent couldn't make out what his father said in response, the words in an undertone and indistinct from the far end of the shop. Vincent imagined that his father was facing the street, his back to the room as he talked. Every now and then a car went by on the street, the sound of its engine riding right up over his father's voice and then fading away again as it drove out of earshot. He couldn't hear the tires at all, but the drone of his father's voice was steady. It was an unbroken stream of words, falling in pitch at the end, like his father was telling a long story with a particularly sad ending. Vincent couldn't make out any of the individual words.

"Things happen," Glenn said clearly.

Things happen, Vincent thought. Then he said it out loud. But he said it very, very quietly so the Germans wouldn't hear him, testing out the way the words felt in his mouth. "Things happen." He liked the way it sounded, the way it rolled off his tongue like the full stop of a period at the end of a sentence. Mr. Coughlin was like that. He just made a decision and went ahead and did it, not changing his mind and wrestling through different choices over and over again. Vincent wished his father was more like Glenn, more willing to just charge out and do something, instead of thinking of so many reasons to stay in the workshop and do nothing at all.

On the other side of the doorway, there was a long pause in the conversation. "Your choice," Glenn said again, the words sounding as if they had been accompanied by a heavy shrug of the man's shoulders.

Vincent could hear Glenn's words clearly. He had gotten close enough to the workshop that he could even hear things as quiet as the big man noisily swallowing. He could hear the dry whisper of the empty beer bottle sliding back into the cardboard case.

Vincent imagined exactly where they would have to be in the workshop for their voices to sound like that: his father at the far end, standing, and Mr. Coughlin on the four-legged stool, right next to the door but with his back to the kitchen and the rest of the house. It was quiet outside, and equally still inside, and on Vincent's side of the house he could hear only the tick of the electric heaters cooling. Vincent thought, if he listened hard enough, he might even be able to hear the simple, gentle sound of the snow coming down.

Then his father began pulling down boxes in the workshop, cardboard rectangles that uttered muffled metal jangles and bangs, and every time, his father dropped the boxes that last short inch or so to the top of the wooden workbench. Vincent knew that meant his father was angry, that he was working out something he hadn't put into words yet—something like, "Damn it, Vincent, you come home when you're told to come home, and no excuses."

Vincent could picture the boxes slamming down perfectly, as perfectly as the way his mother set the table in the kitchen: three forks, three knives, three plates. Three of everything, laid out in the same order every single time, his mother travelling counter-clockwise around the table without ever realizing she never went in the other direction. Sometimes, though, four of everything, if Mr. Coughlin announced he had decided to stay and eat.

The boxes came down from the shelves in the same way, as if his father were searching for some critical thought right there in the sheer process of it. Then Vincent heard his father's voice clearly, as if he had turned to face Coughlin down the length of the workshop.

"Enough is enough. I don't know how long you think I'm supposed to just put up with this. Damn ship's probably been cut up or sunk years ago, and you're still bringing it up," Keith O'Reilly said, his voice unusually hard and brassy, hard enough that Vincent looked over his shoulder, planning his retreat. "You're in here all the time, rooting around at God knows what. For all I know, you took it. I don't know, for a little insurance or something, just to keep the goddamn leash around my neck. All I know is that it's gone, and you're the only one who could know anything about it, right?"

"I didn't even know you had it. Didn't even know it existed. And that was a fucking stupid thing to do, too," Glenn said. "Beside, in this fucking mess, it could be anywhere. You might have just lost it."

"Bullshit. You know, I don't think you should keep coming around here anymore. I think, by now, we must be square. But if you're going to do something about it, you go right the fuck ahead," Keith said. "If you're looking to rat me out after all this time, you can just go right ahead."

The angry words startled Vincent, as did the long silence afterwards, and he moved slowly backwards, sure the door would burst open any second. And then he heard the distant scrape of the snowplow, and he turned and ran out of the kitchen to the front window, watching for the big green truck. Almost as good as the fire trucks coming to Mrs. Purchase's house all over again. The fire trucks were always stopping there and leaving after a few minutes, after another round of checking whatever she was afraid of this time. The firemen knew Mrs. Purchase well enough that they always waved when the big trucks were pulling away. If it was Mr. Collins driving the plow, and if he saw Vincent looking out the front window, Vincent knew that he would give the air horn chain a short tug for him.

He was already running for the living room in his sock feet, so he didn't hear Glenn's stool being pushed back, or the boxes being swept off the workbench and onto the floor as the two men grappled with each other, throwing awkward fists at each other's faces. Then more serious fighting. A bottle broke, but neither man spoke, except for sharp noises when a fist hit home.

What Vincent did hear was the snowplow slowing down and taking the corner at the top of McKay Street, heard it nose into the sidewalk to spill the snow off the plow in a huge mound and then lift the blade and back up. When the blade dropped to the pavement again, it rang like a great funeral bell, and Vincent heard the truck's engine rev up and muscle the plow into the snow and down the street towards his house. Vincent shut his eyes tight and concentrated on the sound of the plow, imagining himself in the big front seat, heading away. Just away.

Later, from the living room, he watched Glenn Coughlin head out to his truck, fumble with the keys for a moment, and then turn around and look back at the front of the workshop, his arm in the air, middle finger extended.

"You'll need something again, O'Reilly. You know you will—you'll get in over your head before you know it. You always do," the big man shouted towards the house. "You'll need something again, but don't even think about calling me."

111
McKay Street

BRENDAN HAYDEN

AUGUST 6, 2006

BRENDAN read about the skeleton a hunter found in an Ontario provincial park in 1968, nothing more than bones, the remains of a man believed to be Eastern European, with the oddity of an extra rib on his right side and a looped and knotted rope tangled through the collection of small bones from his wrists and hands. The suggestion, the police said on the web page, was that he might have been tied up when he died.

The police had gotten someone to sculpt a face out of clay based on the bone structure beneath, and the clay face stared out of the computer monitor at Brendan as blankly as Brendan stared back at it. At him. At it. Brendan couldn't make up his mind about which it was. Glass eyes, flat and even and empty like any photograph—mirrors of the soul they may be, Brendan thought, but you can't take a believable photograph of a mirror either.

He tried to limit his searches so that he didn't spend much time on the website when he was at work, but small things were so compelling. One corpse, found in the shallows of Lake Ontario, was wearing only a pair of pants, the only distinctive feature some blurry writing in black ink on the inside of the waistband. It had remained unidentified for long enough that the inventory of the corpse's pockets—ten dollars in all and a fistful of small change, every penny accounted for—listed two two-dollar bills, two one-dollar bills. It was a man's body—the corpse's pockets, his pockets: Brendan kept having to remind himself that the corpse was a person, not simply an "it." Brendan couldn't remember the last time he'd seen a one-dollar bill, but he could remember the light green of the paper, and the way it would soften from frequent touch on the oldest bills until they were almost like worn fabric.

Looking at the website was easier at work. At home, in front of the computer in the dark of the front room upstairs, the faces were altogether too haunting—sometimes they'd come back to him late at night or when he woke up in the darkness, that strange, plasticine rigidity they sported around their mouths sharp in front of his eyes. They hung in his memory, faces caught exactly at the point of death like bugs in amber, except this amber had a short half-life, the faces bending and turning with rigor mortis and the inevitable workings of decay.

Brendan read about bodies in water, expanding his research, read about how they might sink for a while but that they'd always rise as the biology in their insides blew them up like fleshy inflatable rafts, pressurized flesh pressing out between the buttons and against the zippers of their clothing. Brendan went to work, went home, divided his life completely between the two. He looked out the window. Took notes. He read impassively about bloat and even about the havoc wreaked on bodies by the ocean, about the way saltwater shrimp could strip away exposed flesh in an afternoon, so that the only parts of a body that would hold together were the parts inside the clothes, like the straw inside a scarecrow—feet inside long rubber boots or sneakers: hands inside fireball-orange rubber fisherman's gloves, the rest of the body long since disjointed and washed away in scattered pieces.

A newspaper article about a coroner's career stuck in his mind, the coroner complaining that it took seven years to have a missing fisherman declared dead so that his family could have a funeral and make claims on things like insurance policies.

"That's a hell of a long time for closure, isn't it?" the coroner had said.

"If an arm washes up with a ten-dollar wristwatch on it anywhere in this province, maybe twenty thousand of that same watch on the market at the same time," the coroner went on, "then I've got six or eight women in here insisting that they're absolutely sure it's their husband's watch, and they're ready to swear an affidavit on it. Pretty much anything to let them move on, to close that door. It's simpler for them to lie than to try and just wait for a truth that's never going to come."

Women seeking any body whatsoever: bodies on a public website seeking any owner whatsoever. It made Brendan think it would be possible to run some kind of macabre matchmaking agency: "Need a body? Find a body." It wouldn't be that hard to do, either, he thought.

Many of the drowning victims on the website didn't even have photographs. Brendan shuddered and decided he could imagine why. Anyone with the brass to do it could probably claim one of those lost souls, haul it home in an airline casket and bury it good and deep before anyone got around to asking the tough questions.

Other bodies would be more difficult.

There were always full-face photos for the bodies found in Toronto subway stations—slurred, smeared faces that looked as if, when death had come, gravity had immediately taken on a new role, one of trying to work up a successful disguise. An expression of gravity—Brendan tucked that thought away, a bad joke he didn't want to admit he'd made, even to himself.

And each individual body was a small but crucial story all by itself.

Witnesses had seen one man walking purposefully out across the ice, had watched him fall through and not even try to swim. By the time rescuers reached him, the man had died in the cold water, his only identification a worn leather bracelet on his left wrist. Lit brightly for the photograph, the bracelet was now stretched flat, and you could see the faint black tracery of some sort of pattern that might have been pressed into the leather and stained dark when the bracelet had been brand new.

Outside the house, the winter wind was blowing again. Brendan looked outside, looked at the matte black of the trees flat against the sky, the street lights bouncing off the low clouds, the houses across the backyard cut into simple planes of light and shadow.

And then he was thinking about Albert Carter's dark blue house, hearing the wind outside and thinking it had been the same kind of February night a couple of years earlier when the fire trucks had shrieked up the street to the address where Carter's house had simply collapsed, like a tooth missing in an otherwise healthy jaw, its roofline shrugged down like a dropped shoulder, splintered clapboard blown right off the front of the house and into the street as if there'd been some kind of quiet explosion inside.

The firefighters had inched into and through the house, slipping jacks and wooden cribbing up under sagging beams until they found Carter, crushed in his own kitchen beneath the weight of a packed second-floor bedroom, and in his mind's eye Brendan imagined that it must have looked like something out of *The Wizard of Oz*, Mr. Carter's legs sticking out all haphazardly from underneath a wardrobe and a bed and the ruckled-up carpet from the room above.

Word on the street was that the inside of the house was even more bizarre than people had expected, even for Mr. Carter: the workers who finished the demolition the collapse had started talked about rooms with their doors nailed shut, about beams sawn through and glass bottles filled with gasoline lined up along shelves on the verge of toppling into the deep V that had been the very middle of the house.

"Only luck the whole place didn't explode," Chris Wheeler had said.

Wheeler had been hired on as a casual labourer by the company that was cleaning up the remains of the house, and walling up the neighbour's row house that Carter's place had pressed against on one side. Wheeler had been hired simply because he had strong arms and a strong back, and because he was standing across the street and watching when the crew arrived, a work crew short of hands, as always. And as he talked to Brendan about the state of Mr. Carter's house, the group of other workmen shook their heads slowly, as if every one of them could see what a time bomb the place had become.

"It should've caved in years ago," Wheeler said. "He had tons of paper upstairs, tons of it. He must have kept every letter he ever got. And there were piles and piles of notebooks all over the place—took me half a day just to pitch them all out into the Dumpster." Brendan wasn't sure how much of what Wheeler was saying he should believe.

He turned away from the front window and went back to the computer screen, to a man found in a subway station by the cleaners after the line finally shut down, a man found wearing four T-shirts, and with one index finger deformed by an old injury. There were carefully posed photographs of the finger that were obviously taken well after death, the hand wrinkled and wet-looking, with a sheet tucked cleanly under and around the wrist so that it all looked like some bizarre kind of trophy.

Then he opened the file for a body "found in a sewer on Lansdowne Avenue."

"Lighter, package Rothman's Mild, $11.57 in change, chewing gum and TTC tokens," read the man's pocket contents. Brendan wondered if there really was any way to end up in a sewer by accident, and he had a nightmare about that later, a simple nightmare where it was dark out and he was up to his waist in water, looking up at a street light through the closed metal grate of a storm drain.

How could so many people just be lost, he thought, lost without anyone really looking for them? There were teenaged girls described as "probable homicides," other bodies "presumably involved with gangs" with garishly tattooed torsos that should be easily enough remembered by anyone who had ever touched that colourful skin. But how could you lose a nineteen-year-old daughter and not keep looking for her forever? Brendan thought. So much different from a nineteen-year-old son, and then he stopped and wondered why.

And finally, one night, Brendan found Case #2006026.

That just could be Larry, Brendan thought, squinting to look past the cheap glasses frames, trying to find a familiar order in the twisted features in the photograph. The mouth gaping open, lips bent downwards in an unnatural curve, but that could just be the result of the last few moments of life, and the rough-and-tumble of post-mortem. He had been found out past the end of the King Street subway platform, in behind the thin rungs of the Employees Only gate. In late January, when the cold wind would be whistling down the tunnels and sapping the heat right out of him, even worse because under him was only heat-sucking concrete, Brendan thought.

It really could be him. It really could.

And it wasn't hard to believe at all.

And that had Brendan thinking about the pictures in an entirely different way. What had Larry been thinking about, Brendan wondered, just then, when he died?

What sort of thoughts had been circling around in his head? Was he wondering whether things might have turned out differently? Was he thinking about who was to blame for where he ended up? Or was he more concerned about how cold he was, and how sleepy the cold was making him?

Brendan looked at the telephone, sitting in a pool of light under the lamp. There was a 1-800 number on the web page you could call if you had "any information as to the identity of the deceased." The file number was repeated at the bottom of the page as well, so that no matter where you were on the web page, the number would be right in front of you, ready to read over the phone, impossible for you to lose your place in the filing cabinet of the dead.

But then . . . But then there would be police officers, Brendan thought. Police officers and questions and more questions, and maybe even tests.

Fingerprints.

Dental records. DNA.

Brendan moved the mouse back and forth across the screen, looking at the face, at the white sheet pulled up right to the man's neck, a sheet that looked as if it was carefully hiding whatever horrors were going on beneath it.

That could definitely be Larry.

He looked at the picture again, tried to imagine the face on the screen involved in some normal action, like talking on the phone.

Or smiling.

Or even just breathing.

Not only could that be Larry, Brendan thought, it had to be Larry.

And that would make it all simpler.

He clicked the website closed.

No need for all that, he thought.

Larry was dead, just dead, and that was the end of that.

And any secrets Larry thought he was lugging around with him, well, that was all just dust now too.

2
McKay Street

ROBERT PATTEN

JUNE 30, 2006

NO, I'M NOT TIRED. Just crippled. Remember?

It just seems like it's never going to end—every sunny day the same.

Here he comes again, around the corner with his little jogging shorts flapping like a flag. Does he think I like being out here, with some thin white hospital blanket with blue stripes tucked tight in around my knees like I'm the kind of formally made bed that drill sergeants bounce quarters off of?

I can look down and see the tips of my toes sticking out from under the blanket, right there, in some kind of pure white specialized elasticized socks that are supposed to help keep my blood from pooling down there and pulling the skin of my feet tight like sausages— and does he think there's anything to like about that at all? Like there's one single scrap of good in it anywhere?

Because there isn't.

"You should be glad you're still alive," people were fond of telling me at first, back when there used to be plenty of visitors in my room, visitors who mixed those easy words with the strange sort of compliment, "You're one tough guy—other people would have been killed outright."

Like I don't ever wish for that.

How much simpler would that have been, to have just died out there? I'll tell you: two simple paragraphs in the newspaper, and then forgotten. It would have been plenty simpler.

But enough blubbering.

It was bad enough that the nurses had us on the clock, trundling us out to the exact same place every single day, but it was even worse that he was like clockwork too, two-fifteen every single damn day, the clockwork goddamn Energizer Bunny, always running smoothly, always lifting one hand for that short little half-checked saucy wave.

Two-fifteen, time to wave to crippled Robert, hop-skip-jump and buddy was on his merry way. I could have broken his fucking wrist for every single wave. Once, I would have been able to do just that. Now I can't even pull my stupid white-socked feet back in under the blanket so no one can see they're so damned clean that it's obvious my feet haven't touched the floor since someone else bent down to put those socks on.

He probably just lives around here somewhere, trundling by the Miller Centre as part of his regular run around the lake. Quidi Vidi Lake is just down below us somewhere, walking trails and sports fields, not that I've seen any of that recently. It's probably just his regular running route, and it's not like it's anything he's trying to do to get under my skin or anything.

But he does. Get under my skin, I mean. And that's not the worst of it.

Four times now—and I've counted, believe me, I've counted every single time—he's gone by here with his wife or girlfriend, whatever the hell she is, not too much more than half his age and drop-dead gorgeous, long straight brown hair right down over her shoulders on its way to her ass, long-armed and long-legged, and you can tell by the way she moves just how limber she is. I know it's not polite to say about anyone, but she's the kind of woman you can't help but look at and wonder what she'd be like in bed. And they've got the stroller and the baby with them, both of them with their hands together on the stroller's handle, if that isn't enough to make you goddamn sick. And I'm pretty sure I knew her for years back on McKay Street, back when she was a neighbour from well down the street and her name was Jillian George. And she could always be counted on to be looking over your shoulder at the bar to see if there was a better-off guy coming in the door behind you. I guess in the end there was, all things considered. Seems to have done all right for herself, running around with him. You can tell she's got it all worked out.

I can almost imagine what his life is like. I can even hear him saying it. "I'm working the hours I want to now, no more rat race. I've checked out, just doing a little consulting work on the side, two days a week at the business school."

Right.

No long, tiring drives heading out behind the wheel to Goobies or Clarenville or Gander to make sure that everyone has the kind of stock and promotional material they're expecting. No daily grind, putting on a smile for every one of the hundreds of store owners whose mouths pull down every time they see you pulling onto their lot, clearly thinking, "No customer here, just someone else selling me something." And I can't be buying bottled water at every single store, just to make them feel better about it. Christ, I bought all that water, I'd be pissing my life away. Literally.

He's probably a lawyer who chucked it all in at fifty to live the better life, new wife, new kid, new focus away from court and clients. Sold his share of the law practice, just doing a little commission work for the government since he's been pitching a few bucks into the right political kitty all these years. Working himself back into the kind of shape he was in when he was in college and playing varsity something. Got his time down below what he could run when he was thirty.

And what a sweet deal that must be, starting all over with all the mistakes smoothed right over, with plenty of cash and plenty of spare time to be thoughtful, chockablock with all the brand new good intentions you didn't have a chance to have the first time around.

And what do I get to do? Not even have the good intentions. No starting over here.

If I ever do get back on the road, I'll just be flogging potato chips again and counting the long, slow days, the endless unrolling pavement on the way to an underpaid retirement. Hell, I can't even reach the wheelchair brakes and release them, even if I'd like to just let them go so I could just goddamn well roll straight out into the speeding, merciful traffic.

How fair is this? I want to yell at the guy. You get the girl, I want to shout, you get the girl and the life and I get the goddamn moose.

118A Cavendish Street, Victoria, B.C.

FAITH MONAHAN

JUNE 15, 2006

FAITH hung up the phone, thinking about Vincent and the idea of moving across the country to a cold place she'd never been, to a neighbourhood that Vincent had always talked about as if he were trying to explain the detailed inner workings of a circus freak show. And she was trying hard to imagine what Vincent's face looked like without giving in and going to look at a photograph.

It was like a secret proof, something she wouldn't tell anyone else. If she could just remember his face all by herself, just draw it up there in her memory, she told herself that it had to be real. If she was able to just hold it right there in her head, then she really did love him. And he must really love her.

Half the time, she hated that little game, and hated herself for playing it. The rest of the time, she clung to it desperately, like it was a talisman that kept her safe. It had been over a month since he had gone back east after his parents died on the same day.

When it happened, their boss, Mr. Latham, had been fine with Vincent going—"Go ahead, sort it out, bud, take as long as you need"—

but Faith knew Latham's patience was fading fast now. It was heading for August, the height of the landscaping season, when everything was growing like mad and had to be raked or clipped or cut, and they were already shorthanded because Larry Hayden, Larry-who-had-replaced-Vincent, had put a stone rake right through his foot, up through the bottom of the sneakers he wasn't supposed to be wearing on the job in the first place. She had told Hayden about the workboots when he'd been hired on, that he would need to have a pair, steel toes and instep, and he'd said he'd get some as soon as he had his first cheque, that he travelled light and didn't have that kind of money yet.

She also told Larry that he was only going to be kept on until Vincent came back, and he'd had an answer for that too. "I knew a Vincent once," he'd said, thoughtful. "Friend of my brother's."

He said he didn't mind short-term work, either. "It's good to keep moving," he said. "Sometimes staying somewhere familiar is as much a prison as the real thing, even without the bars. You could ask my brother Brendan about that." He looked out the window in the office, as if gathering in that the trees and open air were still there. "History's a great thing, but it likes to bite you on the ass." Then he looked at her. "Sorry, miss." The way he said it reminded her of Vincent.

Larry was quite happy to be guaranteed only a few weeks' work, even though the foreman liked him, even though the foreman said he always worked hard right through the day, right up until the day he stepped on the rake. Faith liked Larry's face every time she saw it, the way it was always smooth and untroubled, as if any kind of pain simply swept right over him without actually touching his skin.

Larry told Faith that, when the rake had gone into his foot, he'd felt the individual tines scraping along the bones of his foot like chalk on a blackboard. "Like a sound, but really a feeling instead," he'd said.

The doctors had spent hours cleaning the five separate puncture wounds, washing the holes and talking about "anaerobic bacteria" and infection and "necrosis" while Larry leaned back on the smooth white plain of the hospital bed, leaving long stains of dust and sweat behind him like he had created some kind of rank amateur Shroud of Turin.

Larry told her the doctors had said "the only way it could have been worse is if you'd let someone bite you." They'd told him there were more bacteria in the human mouth, "but only a few more than you'd find in good old Saanich topsoil."

And she'd had to go in and tell Mr. Latham they were short of workers all over again, that Larry had a doctor's note for three weeks and he'd really be gone for every bit that long. Larry had already told her he was going to get in his camper and go up the coast, and she could just hold his insurance stubs until he was back working because there'd be no one to take them out of the mailbox while he was gone anyway.

"Your boyfriend say when he was going to be coming back?" Latham asked when she told him about Larry, peering out over a wasteland of invoices and other scraps of paper on his desk with his sad-sack face drawn up all in long flat planes.

"Not yet." When he heard the way her sentence fell off at the end like a small wave breaking over itself before it could reach the shore, Frank Latham almost regretted asking.

Almost. "Well," Latham said, "when you're talking to him, tell him we sure could use him here."

Back in the apartment, Faith slid the phone onto the counter and went into the living room to look at the photograph again anyway— "just a refresher," she told herself, and wondered just when it was that she'd gotten superstitious.

She was relieved, too: she approached every ring of the phone with palpable dread now, afraid that it would be Vincent calling to say that he had changed his mind about everything, that they were good together but . . . And every time she hung up, it was like she'd been given a reprieve, however short.

The living room of their apartment was small and close, underfurnished and underdecorated, as if they were still in the process of trying to frame themselves up as a couple. Outside the big curtainless window, Faith watched a crow glide by and waited to see another, caught up in what Vincent always said about crows: "One for sorrow, two for joy." She was startled at how that had burrowed into her confidence so quickly, too. It had gone so far in that if she saw one crow or even a raven, she wouldn't stop looking until she'd found another, no matter how long the search took. Like the photograph: Sometimes it occurred to her that, unable to believe her good fortune in meeting Vince, she'd decided it must have been some kind of unwitting magic instead. And if it really was magic, then there were spells that had to be renewed and maintained every single day, charms that had to be handled and trusted, at least if she wanted to have any hope of it lasting. Maybe that was love, she thought. Maybe it was always doubting your good fortune, hunting for something to anchor what was otherwise only blind luck.

They'd deliberately chosen to get the new apartment together, both of them giving up their individual spaces. It took longer than just moving into either one of their apartments would have done, but they did it anyway. Both of the places they gave up were fine, but they'd agreed it would be better to start fresh. "That way," Vincent had joked, "you won't be looking up at the ceiling and thinking about some other guy when you're sleeping with me."

But there was a serious tone underneath the statement. It was like they were both getting rid of excess, leftover memories, agreeing to find a way for both of them to start in a place where the only memories they had were ones that they shared. This seemed especially important to Vincent: he treated moving like a formal, ordered process, a dignified clearing-the-decks of the past. Just taking care of things that had to be done.

Faith liked that about Vincent: he had a curious, old-world formality about him, the only landscaper she'd ever met who would make the other workers stop swearing when they were all at the office and she was getting coffee in the kitchenette. And that was before they were even a couple, back when the effort singled him out in front of the other workers and gained him nothing, just gave them something to tease him about. And tease him they did, ruthlessly.

But Vince hadn't seemed to mind. Later, she'd learned that he had an ingrained need to feel that he was doing the right thing. It was a need that could be more than a little difficult. She knew that when she looked at him and his face was set a certain way, his chin pushed out and square, he was going to go ahead with something he didn't particularly want to do but could see no way of honestly avoiding. She could hear it in his voice, too. It didn't matter if she tried to find a way to talk him sideways away from it—hard as nails, he would stick his chin out and do whatever it was, even if it cost him dearly.

She heard that solemn note over the phone when he called her from his parents' house too. Faith knew that he was caught tight between what he wanted to do and what he thought he should do, and she wanted to scream over the telephone at him that it didn't matter anymore what his parents would have wanted, that they were both dead and couldn't care less what he did with the house or the yard or the workshop or any of it. That responsibilities get buried too. That with them both gone, his only obligations to the place were the ones inside his own head.

Faith knew all about that: she'd spent most of her life trying to live up to the expectations of her own parents, parents who had been crushed by what they saw as the failures of her older sisters. She'd promised herself she'd never disappoint them the same way, until one morning she woke up and felt relief on her skin like a bursting boil, felt the easing that came with the knowledge that whatever she did or didn't do, it would be her own world that felt the effect. And only her own world. Still, she kept up appearances, the good girl for her parents, even though she occasionally felt keenly the schism between reality and perception.

She hadn't said anything to Vincent about his concern over the phone, even though for months his parents' feeling about the house had become a joke between them. She didn't say anything because she knew how deep a family's grain could really go.

"A house is something," Vince would intone, making his voice deep, trying to sound like his father. She'd start to laugh at that point, already shaking next to him on the bed. "A house is something solid, Vincent, something worthwhile. It means you've made a mark, it means you've actually done something. Put down roots. Made a life."

And then they'd laugh out loud like fools, both of them sure that Keith O'Reilly had been completely wrong, that the thing they had between them was far more important than anything someone could build out of wood and paint and glass.

But that didn't mean she wasn't afraid now. Lately, over the long-distance phone lines, the humour had somehow gone out of everything, and Faith wondered just what it was in the distance between them that had made them suddenly so serious. Almost formal.

"I don't know what to do," he'd say, his voice hollow over the phone so that she imagined the sound wasn't coming through wires but instead through a long pipe stretching right across the country, losing energy with every kink and bend and turn. "There's so much here," he'd say. "So much that only I remember. And if I clean it out, it's all just going to be gone. What's it mean if the only place there's anything left is inside my head?"

Faith didn't know what to tell him. She'd heard every single word as he'd said it, but the only thing she could think to tell him was that the strawberries were all gone now in the small garden they kept behind the apartment, and that there were going to be raspberries soon, their green berries now whitish yellow and hard but changing fast towards softer pink and then red. Somehow, those facts seemed crucially important. They felt like they might burst right out of her, and at the same time they seemed foolish and pathetic and unnecessary.

She thought it was important for Vincent to know that the honeysuckle was in blossom, and that the smell of it came in the windows at night, like it was the sweet, thick smell of dark itself, and that he could probably remember something of that smell if he just put his mind to it.

She was sure that somewhere in her reaction was the answer to his question, that if she could somehow formulate it into words, he'd understand. At the same time, Faith was terrified it wouldn't make any sense to him at all.

117
McKay Street

HELEN COLLINS

FEBRUARY 11, 2006

THERE WAS so much to bear, Helen thought. Just so much to bear.

She could tell they knew just by the way people looked at her. She could tell what they were thinking: Helen Collins, whose husband's in prison. Helen Collins, whose husband was a thief.

She could feel it even if they didn't say it, feel it burrowing into her back as if their eyes shot out burning beams that could read it right off her skin, and she wanted to go up and throw it right back at them.

"I haven't done anything," she wanted to shout in their faces. "It wasn't me that did it."

She did say it out loud once, when the smooth-faced little jerk from the bank asked her how many months she expected the bank to let her skip the mortgage payments before she "got back on her feet."

"It's not *my* feet," Helen said. And then, "I'm as much a victim in this as anyone else."

"Well-ll," the banker said, drawing the word out into two long syllables. "Well-ll, either way, I can only hold off head office for so long.

There are rul-es." That last word stretched out overlong and broken into two as if to give it more weight.

The banker, Bud Whalen, was younger than Ronnie, Helen thought, and he had an irritating way of looking as if he was only half paying attention. They were in a street-level office on Water Street, and the man's eyes kept flicking towards the window every time someone walked by, looking away right in the middle of his sentences so she wasn't even sure that he was listening to her.

She couldn't stand the way he had his hair all pricked up in short points with some kind of gel, tight and dark oily points that only served to show off the white of his scalp and the fact that his hair was starting to thin all across the top of his head. She couldn't imagine it was a hairstyle he would have picked if he knew how it looked to everyone else. The sort of thing that he thought looked good but only because he saw his hair as the dark line that capped his face.

"I'd make that payment right now if it wasn't for Tony. There's the fine to be paid, and restitution for the city, but I'm doing the very best I can. I pay what I can, and still they're talking about garnishing the account. If you let them." She smiled at him then, trying to make it seem unexpected and unplanned. She put everything into it, opening her eyes wide as if she were simply amazed by this guy, this Bud Whalen, Account Manager, making herself look as if she thought he was the most amazing Bud Whalen she had seen in her entire life.

But it was no use. When she looked at him, Whalen was looking out the window again, his eyes distant and locked on a woman on the other side of the street. It was a big window, sealed glass, and Whalen could get no closer to that woman, that small, short-skirted blonde in the dark blue wool coat, than he could to a fish through the side of an aquarium.

Dyed blond, Helen thought. You can always tell. Men just take it for granted, trust it's real, never look past the obvious. Jump for the bait, mouths open.

Without even thinking, she put a hand up to the side of her own head, checking her hair, unwilling to believe that he wasn't going to eventually look back at her. Forget it, Bud, she thought, she'll look right past the likes of you.

"Either way," Whalen said, "you're going to have to find a way to come up with a payment soon."

"I intend to," Helen said, standing up and doing her best to sweep out of the office. That's the way she wanted it to look, as if she was sweeping out of the office, as if none of it meant anything to her at all.

And she managed it, at least until she was back out on the street in the cold, where the resolve went out of her fast, like air from a mortally wounded tire. Then it was just the street again, the street and the faces and the long cold walk along Water Street and back up the hill.

At the house, with the front door barely closed, Helen heard the mailman, heard the flat slap of the mailbox closing, his voice answering a question from someone down the street. Just more bills, she thought, more bills that Tony should be taking care of. Helen couldn't help thinking that it would have been much better if Tony had just died. It would have been so much easier to take, so much easier to explain. "So sorry for your loss, Helen," people would have said, sober, and she could have made out like she was bearing up under an almost impossible burden.

So many things would have been better than this. It would have been better if he'd just left her before the police came, so she could have been the righteous jilted spouse. Or better still, if he'd never been caught at all.

The house was quiet, only the occasional ticking sound, beams settling, the gentle, muffled ping of cooling or heating metal somewhere upstairs. And then she heard it, heard it again from upstairs, those two deep, indrawn, familiar choking breaths, and then, even though she knew she was imagining it, the heavy sound of someone falling headlong to the floor in the upstairs hall.

She would always remember Tony running up the stairs, two, three steps at a time, his feet loud on the stair treads, then him shouting back down to her, "Call the ambulance." She had taken the stairs far more slowly, urgency combined with dread. She could remember thinking that she was trapped between what she had to do and what she was afraid she would see. And maybe even a little afraid of what she hoped to see.

Finally, in the hallway before the ambulance crew got there, there were those damned eyes that would never do what they were supposed to do and just close, so that her father lay there flat on the floor as if inspecting the ceiling and being surprised by whatever he saw there.

Even after he was dead, she still heard him. Every single day. "Watch every penny," his voice would say, "so dollars take care of themselves." "Penny wise, pound foolish." "If wishes were horses, beggars would ride."

It had been a mistake ever to move in with her father, Helen thought, even though Tony jumped at the chance. He had jumped at the chance to get a house without a mortgage, practically fell over trying to ingratiate himself with the old man, and he kept telling her it was the solution to all of their problems. What she couldn't tell Tony was that she had been looking to get away when she'd married him, that he was her hope for something new because he was a guy with a good job and a chance to move somewhere far away from Mike Mirren and every single one of his sayings for every single thing that had happened or could happen. She couldn't tell Tony that she'd wound him in carefully, deliberately, making sure at every moment that he didn't feel the hook.

The thing was, Tony had been so perfect in the beginning that she felt like she'd won the lottery. She'd told her friends that he was a real gentleman, but it was much more than that. Tender and kind, he had a way of holding her loose in his arms like she was a child on his hip. That sounded wrong, saying it like that, but what she meant was that she really felt like part of a whole when he was holding her, as if they were the kind of pair the ministers always talked about: "till death do you part" sounded so overwrought until you actually believed it.

And she had believed she was free of Mike Mirren.

"A leopard can't change his spots," her father would bark.

But he never said anything about the apple not falling far from the tree—that was a sentence he couldn't seem to find among his collection of truisms and chin-pulling wisdom.

When her mother first went into the hospital, before the endlessly long stay in the nursing home but when it was just the two of them in the house, he'd cornered her in the backyard and said darkly, "I don't even know if you're really my daughter."

He'd said it to her sharply, dismissively, and she always remembered that it was late spring, the tiny purple trumpets falling from the lilacs in back like confetti from a forgotten wedding.

He'd been looking down at his fingernails when he started saying it, ripping away at a ragged piece of his cuticle so that the raw trench started to ooze blood. And then he counted it out, piece by piece, finger by finger, as if there were some great calculating scorecard he was checking that only he had access to. "You don't look like me, you don't act like me. You're not like me. And on top of it, you've got no goddamn common sense at all. And you should have, if you're really mine."

After that, there was nothing she could do, standing there, the light purple flowers settling on her shoulders as the wind shifted and shook the bushes behind her. The back fence leaned in the whole time, as if listening, strips of ragged white paint always close to falling free, and Helen remembered thinking it was just as well that the fence could hear, that it was just as well if everyone overheard all of it, determining then, in that moment, to be anything but this hard old man's daughter. And to hell with him anyway.

Then Tony had taken her outside and away, and for five years it had been absolutely perfect. First Ronnie was born and then he was two and then four, a serious, smooth little face, and when Tony was working nights, she and Ronnie would sit up and wait for the snowplow to go by, and though it wasn't his route, Tony would find a way to cut down their street, and he'd yank on the air horns even though everyone on the street would call in and complain. And she and Ronnie would wave like mad things at the darkened snowplow cab, the blue light on the roof lighting up the front bedroom in the apartment and all of Ronnie's toys.

And then her mother had to go and die, moving from inconsequential to invisible to interred, and Mike Mirren got all caught up in lonely, suddenly realizing what he should have noticed a decade before, and he and Tony worked out a deal without Tony ever coming to talk to her about it.

Tony came home and told her they'd got a house, and the surprise was that it was "a house you already know really well." When she found out what that meant, Helen didn't know whether to be furious or distraught—and when Tony tried to hold her, tried to console her without even understanding what the problem was, she fended him off the same way she had fended off a dozen high school boys in her teens, cutting sideways out of his reach as easily as if they were trains on separate and diverging tracks.

To end up living with her father, to have to listen to him lecturing Ronnie in those same clipped sentences, was almost more than she could bear. Over and over again, she wanted to gather Ronnie up and take the boy as far away from the bitter old man as she possibly could. And every time, she couldn't get Tony to agree to go.

"He's poisoning Ronnie," she told Tony late at night with the lights off in their room, whispering to keep her father from hearing from the room next door, imagining his body pressed up along the wall, his ear tight to the plaster and trying to discern every distant and bottled word, like he could suck the sound right through the wall.

"He's trying to do the same kind of thing he always tried with me," she whispered. "Telling him the fat cats will always take him for whatever he's worth, that he's always got to watch out for the ones with money because they're the worst, that they're the ones who will find a way to take it all, even if it's a penny at a time. Who are these fat cats supposed to be, anyway? Has he got any idea at all what it is he's talking about?"

But Tony had been unwilling to listen. "The boy's like anyone else," he said. "He's not going to take anything your father says to heart." He stopped. "And you're making the old man out to be far worse than he really is."

Helen already knew that wasn't true, knew it from the way Ronnie looked at his grandfather, knew it from the way Ronnie dogged the old man's steps when her father headed out to the store for the newspaper, a daily newspaper he couldn't do without but whose every story made him curse.

It broke her heart, but she felt powerless. Every time she moved towards him, every time she said anything about it, Ronnie stared at her as if she were something completely foreign to him. Over and over again, Helen wanted to walk up to her father and slap him across the face, tell him he had no right, but every time she found herself in the same room with him, she felt completely powerless.

"We shouldn't have moved here," she said one weekend, watching Ronnie through the window in the kitchen as he and the old man worked around the backyard, out next to the lilacs and the stunted Japanese maple that Mike Mirren had always treated better than any-one in his family.

"Your father offered, and what were we going to say?" Tony said. "Were we supposed to say that we liked living in someone else's base-ment apartment?"

"We could have told him that we were saving for a house."

"Saving what? It's not like we were actually putting anything away. My cheque's all spent by the time the next one comes. Even now, liv-ing here, we're not putting anything away, and we don't even have to pay rent. We couldn't move now if we wanted to."

"But I do want to," Helen said.

Tony let his breath out in a heavy, angry rush and turned around, his back to her like some huge, unclimbable cliff face. "You've got to let this go," he said. "We don't have a choice."

As time went on, she was sure she sometimes caught Ronnie look-ing at her with something dark like hate in his eyes, and before she could speak to him, he'd dart back out of sight and disappear.

Ronnie had a way of simply vanishing—not a sound, not a motion, he'd just be gone. And with every month, he seemed more distant. It wasn't so much that he got in trouble as that trouble seemed to appear all around him. Sometimes she'd hear from neighbours that something serious had happened, but when she asked them about it, their eyes would hood and darken and look away, like they'd realized they'd already said too much. And she couldn't catch him red-handed at anything. If she asked, he'd just look steadily at her, his eyes big and black in the middle like they were sucking the light in. She thought he had to realize that he was doing it, had to know that his stare was unsettling.

"Some people are just born to take," he would say mysteriously, the words awkward coming out of a boy's mouth, and she realized that, somewhere along the line, he'd learned to speak with her father's voice.

Years after that, Helen still found herself trying to make sense out of the scraps of him she got to hear. Shortly before he moved out and into an apartment with that Liz, she'd heard him on the telephone in the downstairs hall, his voice different, the way it went when he was around the small group of other teens he ran with. Helen couldn't really put her finger on it—it was as if he pitched his voice lower when he was talking to them, as if the speed and cadence of his sentences changed, so that the words had an entirely different weight than they did when it was just the two of them together. Like he was someone else, someone she didn't know at all.

"We let him have it good," she heard Ronnie saying into the phone in the hall. "Beat him well enough that he'd know he wasn't welcome here, right?" He stopped and listened for a moment. "Naw, he didn't recognize us. Cops haven't been around, have they? Jest a fight after the bars closed, some loudmouth comin' home and lipping off, that's all they'll think it was. Jillian won't talk either, not if she and her crowd's going to stay around here an' keep all their windows."

She wanted to confront him about what she had just heard, but Helen realized then that she was scared—scared of her own son, scared of the way she knew he'd look at her. No little boy left in there, she thought. No little boy at all—and, for those last few weeks before he left, it was like having a stranger in the house, a total stranger who looked like Ronnie but wasn't him at all.

Thinking about it again, she shuddered, and even though it was snowing, she knew she couldn't stay in the house all evening, not with the weight of it hanging over her.

After her father died, they'd pulled up carpets and junked the old furniture. Tony had even redone the kitchen, putting new doors on all the cabinets—but every time she opened one up and looked inside, it was like her father's voice was coming out of it and right straight into her ears.

The walk to the bar—familiar steps regularly taken, and the bar itself so familiar, so separate, that she couldn't help but feel a weight lift. Same old stool, same lights, same pool table. Same video lottery machine every time, and the same game, too, picking numbers for a keno draw that came the moment her numbers were picked. Up at the bar, Mitt Jones and that guy with the white hair, then the required couple of lawyers still dressed in their suits for work but talking too loud, the pints of beer catching up with them. All we need now, Helen thought, is that slut Jillian George with her latest toy in tow, some professional something-or-other all cow-eyed for her until she loses interest and ditches him too.

It doesn't matter, she thought. None of it matters. It doesn't even matter that there is no escape here, no real escape at all. At least it let her think differently, let her move as if she had changed her life like changing the channels on a television.

Not that it was always an easy refuge. She'd been pinned up against the wall once, downstairs by the bathroom, by a sailor who said his name was Vlado, a big man with a watch cap and a scar through one eyebrow, whom she'd been politely friendly with for a short conversation, and she remembered thinking then, fleetingly, her back against the flat wallboard, that it was pretty much like the rest of her life, one big boozy man or another pushing her up against a wall somewhere and trying to force his tongue into her mouth.

But she'd never said it out loud. In fact, she thought, she'd never had anyone to say it to.

Back in the bar, and she was still doing her best to escape her father with every dollar she played. "Watch every penny. . ." She could hear him saying it, and she pressed the buttons on the machine viciously, as if the buttons could feel her rage.

Up at the bar, Mitt Jones was smiling at her, and Helen smiled back while tamping down the thought that his breath couldn't help but smell like rotting gums. Mitt was still smiling at her, his lips wide enough that she could see the browning gaps between each of his teeth.

Take that, Bud Whalen, she thought, I can still push the buttons. But the thought didn't give her the kind of relief she was hoping for. And she knew she'd keep playing the machine until the bar closed or the money ran out, unwilling to go back home to his turf, and to the damned body on the carpet upstairs, to all that guilt.

Damn him, she thought. Damn Tony. Damn him for taking me back to that house and leaving me alone in there with the ghost of the old man.

Twenty more dollars went into the machine, smoothly.

When she looked in her purse and saw that the bills had run out, she was neither surprised nor particularly upset. She had lost: she had won. Something in there between them both. Resigned, she thought. I just feel resigned.

Mitt smiled as she stood up and she smiled back anyway, just for form, even though there wasn't an ounce of energy left in her that felt like smiling. Helen closed her purse, gathered up her coat and headed back out into the snow. It was falling heavier now, wheeling around her so that she could never really get away from it, the wind picking at one side of her face, wrapping around her back for a gust or two and then pounding straight at her face again. The sidewalks were already filled to overflowing, the snow there knee-deep and hard to push through, so she walked out in the street, staying in the tracks left by scattered passing cars. Whenever there was a break between the row houses, the wind struck her so hard that she'd stagger slightly, and she imagined that the row of footsteps behind her must look like the uneven wobble of a drunk—except for the fact that they'd be filled in almost as fast as she was making them. Three drinks in, she thought, so it's only the wind.

Not a fit night, she thought, and she knew Ronnie would probably be busier than most nights, more pizzas to deliver to those unwilling to risk the snow and looking for an easy way out.

When she got home, throwing the last of her cigarette down into the snow, she saw that there was a police car next to the curb in front of the house. She knew it was waiting for her, knew it by the white cloud of exhaust that puffed out of the tailpipe before being snatched away by the wind. There were no tire tracks left behind the back wheels: the snow had filled them right in. Every now and then, the windshield wipers would flick once across the glass, as if they were too tired to do anything more. The car sat warm, melting and shedding the snow, waiting there like it was alive.

She walked to the side of the police car and the window rolled slowly down, a small breath of warm air escaping and touching her face for just an instant.

"Tony?" she asked.

"No," said the policeman, and she recognized Reg Dunne unfolding himself from behind the wheel and reaching a hand forwards to open the car door. "Not Tony. This time, it's Ronnie. And it's serious."

58
McKay Street

JILLIAN GEORGE

OCTOBER 7, 2005

THE WORST of it wasn't that they'd attacked her, that Ronnie had held her hands and ripped her shirt open, or that he'd had his hands all over her in an awful combination of anger and some perverse kind of intimacy.

More than two years had passed, and there were still parts of it she could pull up out of her memory completely intact, as if it were starting all over again. The physical parts came back to her first, but they weren't the worst of it.

His hand hard over her mouth, even though she wouldn't have screamed anyway. Because screaming wouldn't work. His other hand tearing at the front of her pants. Then the way he'd stopped and stepped back, smiling and out of breath. She'd been sure that Ronnie was going to rape her, she'd even started steeling herself for the pain there in the alley—and then it was like he didn't need to, like the whole thing was a violent show. Leaving her with the implication, the reality that it could happen, almost any time he liked.

She tried to think of her entire body like it was a collection of ever-dying, shedding cells, so that every single part of her he had touched had long since been replaced by new, fresh skin and tissue. That worked sometimes. Most of the time, though, it felt too easy.

And the worst of it wasn't that she saw them in the neighbour-hood all the time, either, those same people who had stood lookout, who'd looked away and done nothing while Ronnie was attacking her. It wasn't Twig Chaulk or his brother, neither of whom even made eye contact with her anymore.

Worst of all were the houses, she decided.

It was the houses, the whole neighbourhood, that she couldn't stand anymore. The generations of it. The way it was all piled up there, stuffed with history that couldn't be undone—the way it cared about no one and nothing, eyes closed, back turned. Like nothing that happened could make any difference at all, like it was all just another useless coat of paint.

She had to get away from here, she thought—and not just get away for weeks, either. Get away entirely. Forever. Somehow.

She'd been thinking about it for months, about the small universe of McKay Street, the way it all just seemed to repeat itself. Like they were all the same people, all destined to live out the same behaviour. She knew that three generations of her family had lived there in the same house at number 58—that three generations had made their way among the same small circle of friends and acquaintances, knitting children and grandchildren into the fabric of a small and definable world. It was one thing to be proud of it, she had thought, and another thing entirely to be stuck in it like a long-dead spider caught in amber. And she knew for certain that she had to be the one to get out, and soon. She just didn't know how.

There were leaves in the street now, she saw, brown, brittle maple leaves from down by number 35 where three big maples filled a side yard. The wind had blown the leaves up and down the street, all along the curbs, like they were everyone's responsibility. And they would be, she thought: everyone would clean up the ones in front of their own doorstep, or else watch them break down into black mush through the freeze and thaw of winter. One person's trees, everybody else's job.

Jillian was in front of her father's house, a house she expected to live in until the point when everything would change. She thought about that every day: the point when everything would change. When home wouldn't be this blue two-storey row house with fake black shutters on either side of the small vinyl windows. The windows had been bigger once, but her father and brothers had taken out the old single-pane ones with their vertical-sliding sashes and had replaced them all with energy-efficient two-pane versions that slid side to side. A big part of the windows' cost had been covered by the electric company, mouthing saving electricity while expecting the same big cheque every month. The whole winter after they'd finished the job, her father would walk over to the thermostat and tap it proudly with his index finger, as if lecturing it on the fact that he'd found a way to keep its errant behaviour under strict control. Never realizing, she thought, that it was the only thing he really controlled.

Her two brothers were selling drugs for a living now, buying bigger and ever more expensive cars that looked out of place on the street and took up too much of the available parking. Jillian was waiting for someone in the family—anyone—to ask either of them where they were getting all that money. No one ever did, and she wasn't sure if that made everything better or whether the tacit acceptance just dragged the whole family in, complicit.

Not that she could talk about it: Jillian was painfully aware that she was a twenty-three-year-old woman living in the only bedroom she'd ever had, a bedroom now dressed up like a cheap apartment so she could pretend she'd found some kind of independence. There was the small white bar fridge she'd bought that ran with a steady and reassuring whirr at night, a dressing table and mirror so that she didn't have to stand in the shared bathroom to do her face and hair, even a Yale lock on the door that her father had installed without her asking.

She remembered watching him screw the lock onto the door, the tip of his tongue through his lips, as if he were making something as involved as the world she was looking for with something as simple as a twenty-four-dollar brass lock. The way he had handed her the key as if it were the key to the city or something.

"There," he'd said, almost with finality, as though he expected she could live inside those small four walls forever, behind the one vinyl sliding window that no prisoner would ever be small enough to crawl through and make an escape. "Now it's like you own it. You want to paint it purple, you want to put up wallpaper, you want to never make your bed again as long as you live, it's all your choice."

Jillian always made her bed anyway. She hung up the black slacks and the uniform shirt they had her wear at the coffee bar four blocks away, where she was a "barista" now instead of serving staff. It was a job she neither liked nor despised, but one she knew would never be enough to get her out of her room and away.

And every time she looked at the lock, she wondered if her father had missed the point entirely. Missed it like he missed the fact that Matt and Carl were moving ecstasy on George Street, missed it like he had obviously missed the fact that they had to have their stash somewhere in the house. Probably the basement, she thought, given the number of times they made their way up and down the narrow basement stairs before they went out in the evenings.

And Jillian wondered how he missed the fact that no matter how much you wanted things to stay the way they always were, the good parts changed and slipped away while the bad parts were marked down all over the place, underneath the edges of everything, like they were written with permanent ink and a stranger's looping, unfamiliar script. Like they were just waiting there for you to turn something over and trip over them all over again.

And sometimes she wondered if perhaps her father knew all those things, and had just deliberately chosen to ignore them for a more comfortable security.

Jillian turned and walked away from the front of the house, ticking each place off on her fingers as she went. The houses of boys she'd slept with, the houses of boys who told their friends she'd slept with them even though she hadn't. The houses of girls who had promised to be "friends forever," and then weren't friends, and then got friendly again just in time to get married or move away. And every single one of the houses was packed tight with information she wished she didn't know. How much better it would be, she thought, to walk by them as "a green one and a white one and, look, another green one," and not have to think of them as Mrs. Purchase's house or the O'Reillys' or "the house where I kissed someone who we made fun of because he left our school to take French immersion." And he's now happily married in Ottawa with a federal job, as far away as if he sprouted wings and took flight.

The leaves caught in the wind and swirled around her feet as she passed the houses that had belonged to the lucky ones who sold off high and moved away, and the ones where new people had moved in and were trying to import their own rules, never realizing until too late that they didn't have an irresistible force to throw against the immovable mountain that was McKay Street. The other ones, too, the ones that just sat there like no single thing would ever change, older every day and more decrepit, just waiting to crumble away into dust.

Sam Newhook hadn't even spoken to her afterwards. Like it was somehow her fault or something. Like she was to blame.

She'd seen him from a distance, half a block away, a couple of days after it happened, his face all ballooned out and coloured like a California plum. His eyes were blackened as if he were wearing a mask, but he'd hurried away from her and in through his front door, closing it quickly behind him. His house had since been bought by a couple who both worked at the same bank branch and who ticked rhythmically down the street every Saturday morning on his-and-hers, expensive-looking mountain bikes. His bike was bright orange, hers bright yellow, and both of them looked complete with helmets and spandex bicycling suits, black with rich blue stripes up the sides, like they belonged to the same cycling team and were just waiting to burst out and win their event. He always rode behind her, single file, as if he liked looking at her ass, or else, Jillian thought, she couldn't be trusted to do anything right and he had to keep a constant eye on her.

Jillian had never spoken to them, even though they took individual gloved hands off their handlebars and waved any time they passed someone they recognized from the neighbourhood.

She had heard somewhere that Sam had changed jobs too, changed everything like he had just changed his shirt, or, lizard-like, had given up on his entire skin and just sloughed it off. She imagined it hanging in a closet somewhere, a glassy, clear sleeve that was the shape of his whole body, complete down to the silly, empty little pocket where his penis would have been when his skin was still attached. And she envied him his ability to shed his skin, if he actually did have it, wondering offhandedly if the problem was that her skin just went too deep for the same skill ever to work for her.

She was still wondering about that when she turned the corner at the very end of McKay Street. She didn't see the jogger with the short grey hair and the quick smile until he ran right into her, and with the force of the collision, they both fell.

2
McKay Street

ROBERT PATTEN

JUNE 30, 2006

SIX MONTHS to the day after the accident, and the hospital switches me to "life skills."

It sounds a lot better than it actually is. What it really means is "Cope, buddy," but they don't come right out and say it that way.

A different wing of the hospital, a different schedule, and I'm not outside with the same crowd anymore. And on the last day I'm there, I don't even know I'm moving yet, and Evelyn looks over at me with that strange glassy look she's had the whole time she's been in here, that glassy look where her eyes seem to be looking right through you, and she says "Go, Vince" to me as clear as a bell. And then she mutters something about taking a chance when it's offered, and then she's asleep. She looks more like herself than ever when she's sleeping.

Then they take me in for a meeting with the doctor, and he tells me that they're "not seeing the kind of progress" they'd like to see, and I'm not sure if they think I'm letting them down by not trying hard enough or if they're the ones who have decided to give up. Either way, it's like I've finally capped out on rehab, reached a point where any improvement is so slight that it's just not worth their continued effort, so they've changed the channel and now I have to start getting used to working with the little I have.

They've stopped with the parallel bars and started showing me how to wrestle a wheelchair up over the curb with no one there to help me, so I guess I know where I'm headed, no rocket science there. No one's talking about me fighting my way back anymore—they're not talking about rehabilitation, they're talking mediation, and there's a counsellor who comes in with a notebook and a serious level stare to ask me how I feel—or no, not how I feel, but "How do you *really* feel?"

And what the fuck does he think the answer is going to be? Does he want "I'm at peace with myself"? Does he actually expect me to say that, even though I'll never again get a chance to do the things I love, and I lost them all without even knowing I was doing them for the last time?

Right.

For most of the day, "life skills" is stupid stuff like how many minutes it takes to boil an egg and how to reach the burner controls while you're always sitting down, how to plan a healthy menu, the right place to call to register for a trip on the wheelchair bus, and, eventually, even how to drive.

I like that part: how to drive. It's different, sure, but a lot of it is just the same. Apparently, the government or the insurance company is going to buy me a van, and instead of climbing into the front door and just slamming it behind me, I'll get to go through an incredible number of contortions to drag my way into the driver's seat from the wheelchair lift, and then I'll get to go on from there.

I was still learning the mechanics of getting into a driver's seat when they had an instructor come out to show me the new rig, to teach me the controls and show me where everything is. But it's not going to be like driving. I mean, it'll be just exactly like driving, except that it won't be the whole thing.

There's not going to be any more stopping out near Avondale, no scrambling down the rough bank of gravel and stone to see just where it is the river goes. No casting to see if there are any quick trout around, the kind of trout that slash up through the surface real fast and strike hard as soon as something lands on the water. I always had my fishing rod in the rig; some light-fingers has taken off with it long ago, no doubt.

It's amazing where the rivers go, you know. Some of them follow surface fault lines in rock in lines as straight as a die, so you can draw them on the map with a ruler and follow them through the country-side without ever having to make a turn. Others meander, always toppling into the lowest ground, nosing around from here to there, sometimes wide and shallow, other times deep and fast, doubling back in oxbows and flat, stupid corners that make no sense at all. Some of them fill in evenly with weeds from both sides; others sprout pond lilies and duckweed; and still others run over great hidden topographies of silt and decayed wood, so that every single footstep you take across them is bound to be changing some creature's entire universe permanently.

One thing I never imagined is that I would end up missing the gravel and rock on the edge of the road, the garbage and broken-off car parts and empty cigarette packs that you have to step over to get wher-ever it is you're really going. That I would actually miss all the crap that people throw out their car windows and then promptly forget.

But I do.

I imagine that even driving's going to end up being something of a curse, not because of what it brings within reach, but because of everything it will so clearly put just out of reach. King Tantalus and all that.

King Tantalus. That's mythology I read in high school, when it didn't really matter, when it didn't really make sense, especially when absolutely everything in the world seemed like it was always within reach, as handy as an apple right there in front of me, on a low branch. You never think for a moment that someone's just waiting to pull it all away.

Don't get me wrong: it will be wonderful to put some distance between myself and the Miller Centre, to get out on the highway with the windows down, even if I'm still going to need someone else's help to do something as simple as taking off my pants. And learning about the van was less about learning to drive than it was about learning where everything was. Seriously, if you can drive a dirt bike, this van would be no trouble at all; the worst part would be that your feet wouldn't have anything to do. But my feet don't seem to mind that. They're both off in their own little world. Bastards.

The accelerator was a hand control, like the throttle on a motorcycle, and I've ridden enough of them. A big knob set in the steering wheel so I could turn it easily, even without the strength to hold on tight, and another hand control for the brake. Easy as pie: it wouldn't be like the old days, holding the steering wheel with my knees while I lit my smoke or used both hands to twist open a stubborn bottle of pop, but it'd do. I'd manage. Heck, there's not much I can't learn to manage. And there's lots of room for sample boxes of potato chips in a van.

They've given me a driving instructor. A driving instructor! For me, who's never put less than 140,000 kilometres a year on the company rig, driving cars right into the ground because they just couldn't take the sort of driving it takes to service a region as big as the ones I always had. And the driving instructor, some pimply youngster, says to me, "Just put it in drive and ease the throttle open, and we'll head out and go around a few blocks while you get used to it." Very much in charge, a kid not much older than some pairs of socks I have back at home.

I tell him, flat out, "It's not like I goddamned well don't know how to drive or anything. I've been driving my whole goddamn life."

That shut him up, Mr. Driving Teacher, so that he's just sitting there in the passenger seat, sitting and staring, like me, and waiting. Wondering if I've actually got the strength and interest to reach over and pop him one in the mouth. There in the lot, and we were still waiting, the engine running and the brake still on, and I know that out behind me the brake lights had to be staring bright ruby red, and the nurses in the lobby are probably craning out through the windows wondering just what it is we're waiting for, anyway.

They're probably wondering and worrying why it is that we don't beetle away with that hesitant start-stop gait of every new driver, thinking about how I'm going to mess up their routine because the schedule says I'm supposed to be safely out and on the road for one-and-a-half-hours-and-we-don't-have-to-worry-about-Bob. One and a half hours when Robert can be someone else's problem. Check mark in the small square box.

And I bet the driving instructor is wondering exactly the same thing, wondering just how long we're going to be sitting there before he finally has to open the door and get out, if for no other reason than to get the nurses to bundle me back out into the waiting chair because I'm being so unexpectedly difficult.

The only difference is that I know exactly what it is I'm waiting for. The clock on the dash says 2:14, and the twin dots between the numbers flash on and off with every single second as it ticks away. And even though I can't see him yet, I'm sure that somehow, over the noise of the engine, I can hear his feet coming, happy, carefree, stringy-muscled feet.

Go ahead. Wave.

Just wave, stringy man. Just wave at me. I dare you. And at the same time, I don't have to dare you, because I'm certain you will wave. And I'll be down the Miller Centre's driveway flat out, the little knob cranked right over, and I'll be moving faster than those stringy old legs can carry you as you do your best to run away.

I'm sure you'll be surprised.

Because no one ever, *ever*, expects to meet their moose.

188A
McKay Street

LIZ RHODES

FEBRUARY 11, 2006

MAYBE one day they'd have a house.

Just a small place, Liz thought, no bigger than the apartment they already had, but a real house just the same.

Maybe a place with two bedrooms and a real kitchen, instead of a narrow slot with a fridge and stove stuffed into it like peas in a pod. Maybe a washer and dryer that weren't six blocks away at the laundromat. A living room with a long window looking out over the street—irises all along the front of the foundation, jumping up purple and tissue-thin for a few weeks every summer, and afterwards, even just the satisfying green swords of leaves, the kind of plants you have because you're going to be settled somewhere for years.

She thought about it absently, the tip of her finger running through the condensation on the side window of the car. February, and another night of delivering pizzas in the snow.

Ronnie was at the top of a long flight of stairs, and there was a woman silhouetted in the door frame, giving him money for a pizza. The woman was probably looking at him and wondering what he was like, this guy who was all whipcord and tendon and long, lean muscle, wondering at the way he looked like a ball of barely restrained energy, the way he was bursting with here-you-go and let's-get-started. Perhaps the woman was wondering what Ronnie would be like in bed, whether he'd be as good as he looked like he could be, Liz thought. And wouldn't you like to know. She smiled.

Maybe they could have a place with a backyard, maybe a big long backyard like some downtown houses had, long and unexpected and hidden from view, somewhere where she and Ron could have a dog. Not a big dog, and not one of those stupid purse-sized things either, she thought. A real dog with a wet black nose, the kind of dog that scratched at the back door when it wanted to go out in the yard and then turned and looked at you with big, round, sad eyes. The kind of house where you could actually have a couple of kids and then eventually just be happy being old.

And she could do that with Ron, she thought. With just a bit of luck. Luck and care.

But everything was just so complicated with Ron. Sure, he was tough, but he also could be more tender than anyone she'd ever met. Lying naked in their apartment, he'd trace his finger down the inside of her arm and it was like he was almost going to burst into tears, he was so happy with just that.

And sure, he'd gotten into trouble before, but Liz knew she could change him. Just seeing him smile, the scar on his lip turning the smile into something far more self-conscious than an ordinary smile . . . she knew it would work, if they just caught a few breaks, if things just went their way a few times, just a few crucial times in a row.

The car was cold and the windows were all fogging up again, new, fine condensation filling in the lines she'd made a few minutes before, the small drops filling in and dropping a curtain over everything outside. It made the world outside the car seem almost ominous, Liz thought, as if the houses were leaning in closer, their windows more black and staring, because of the way their edges were smeared. Funny. Nothing really changes, and at the same time, everything does.

Soon Ronnie would be reaching across with his whole sleeve to wipe the windshield, and then he'd be rolling the window down to grab hold of the windshield wiper at the very top of its arc, lifting it off the glass and letting it slap back down to break off the clotted ice and snow. It was like clockwork, she thought, every stormy winter night the same thing, the car always full of the smell of soggy carpet and steam-wet cardboard from the pizza boxes, and every single night was going to go on being the same, even if the addresses were different. And then they were stopped again, Ronnie already out the door with the pizza in its insulated bag, the car idling rough so that it felt to Liz like it might just up and stop at any moment.

Stop-go, stop-go, the snowy nights even worse, pell-mell forwards through the tunnel of the falling snowflakes, and she knew well the way the snow could hypnotize you, the way it could grab you if you stared right at it and let your eyes gently unfocus, letting the snow have its way with you.

Next was 35 McKay Street, jumbo always, half pepperoni and extra cheese, the other half feta and tomatoes. And Liz knew all of that was for show, knew that 35 McKay would just end up eating the whole thing himself. Because there was never anyone else there.

Ronnie was already pulling over to the curb, and Liz was thinking, why does a guy like that get to have a whole house to himself? A big house like that, and obviously only one guy in the whole place. He's got to be in there all on his own, because who the hell would get hooked up with a guy like that anyway?

She'd seen him before, knew he was the architect. He was a big, soft guy, carrying enough extra weight that his face seemed somehow indistinct, like a landscape where all the identifying parts had been softened by distance. She'd watched him from the car, full of front-seat judgment every time his door opened. He kept his hands out in front of him, too, busy, she thought, and she was sure that when he opened the door this time, he'd be doing it again. He always did. She'd noticed it before, noticed that it made him seem sort of old-womanly, those two white, pudgy hands working over each other as if they were trying to stay out of trouble. She almost laughed at a sudden thought—that maybe the hands were just unable to keep themselves from getting all worked up about pizza.

It had already been a long night, she thought. Every night was a long night.

It was the kind of business where you don't even begin to make any money until it's late, and the money you might make is all tied up in someone else's hands, the worst part of it being that it was goodwill cash, late nights and booze bringing out the goodwill like absolutely nothing else. Some nights, everyone would tip. Other nights, no one.

On good nights, Ronnie would be humming early, and it was like the world was absolutely perfect, like the moon was rolling out completely full every single time. On the bad ones, he'd be complaining about gas prices in the first hour, banging the dash with his fist for emphasis. Then someone would cut him off and he'd forget all about pizza, running right up against the other driver's back bumper, headlights on high beam, sticking to the other car like glue, daring them to stop so that he could pile out of the car and try to haul them right out their side window, throwing fists before they even had a chance to ask him what his problem was.

Liz hoped for a good night, hoped for the kind of night when everything went like clockwork, when the pizzas were ready and the customers were civilized and the night ended early with a pocketful of tips and a slow fall towards warm sleep just after three in the morning.

And 35 McKay was right there in the door before they'd even stopped, like he'd been listening for their car the whole time. As if his entire fucking snowy world depended on a still-hot pizza in the back seat of a piece-of-shit delivery car.

Huddled against the cold, up against the side door of the car with the vinyl hard and unyielding against the point of her shoulder, Liz thought about their apartment, imagined that she was in bed, listening to Ronnie snore, the shallow, simple breaths that she could listen to for hours. In and out, in and out, Liz not sleeping but perfectly content to be awake, every single thing in her world set in its perfect order, in its perfect place. And she thought about getting out of bed and taking the box out of the closet while Ronnie slept, about opening the lid and going over all the treasures, handling each one and remembering where it had come from and how it had ended up with her.

And she imagined that Ronnie wouldn't wake up, that he wouldn't wake up because then she would have to explain. And Liz wasn't sure that she could.

She couldn't remember exactly when it had started. It was like one day her hands just did what they were meant to do. At parties in the summer, Liz suddenly found it impossible to keep her hands off things. In one house it was a grey soapstone walrus, just a small sculpture with one of its short tusks splintered anyway, and she had wrapped it up in her jacket almost without thinking. Once, a yellow-handled paring knife, absolutely nothing special about it except that it had been on a cutting board, cutting lime slices to perch on the edge of margarita glasses at a Mexican-night party.

If she'd been asked why, Liz might have said that it was like trying to capture a piece of wherever they were, a way to save a part of some particularly good time. Like a totem—like some proof they belonged there, in a particular spot all their own, that they would someday be back, and that everything would be wonderful all over again.

The next time, a small art deco jewellery box, empty—she didn't take things because they were valuable. They weren't even things that she really wanted for any reason. And all of it went into the shoebox, so much now that it was hard to get the lid back on.

She wasn't worried even about getting caught. Liz thought about it, and wondered sometimes if it was because she hoped she *would* get caught, hoped she would be forced to explain, the process of explaining making it all clear to her as well. As long as it wasn't to Ronnie. She was afraid that she'd get the blank stare, that cold look he saved for anything he couldn't bother understanding.

But, she thought, he was so good at the things that made sense to him. She could remember having sex with Ronnie on the floor in a bathroom at someone's house, and when he'd turned to unlock the door, she'd snatched the hand soaps from the dish on the sink, mostly because they were shaped like little shells: a pale blue whorled snail, a yellow-brown flat scallop. She didn't even like the smell of them, but that didn't matter.

She had slid both of them into her pocket, and later, sharply aware of how they had taken on the warmth of her body, she had held them in her hands for a few moments before putting them into the box as well. The smell bothered her for months whenever she opened the box, but any annoyance went away as soon as she could see the smooth curves of them and could imagine them as they had been, lying in the dish next to a stranger's sink.

That would be the thing to have, she thought: a small, light blue dish just to hold seashell-shaped soaps. What was wrong with wanting a bathroom where the sink didn't have a rust stain tonguing its way down towards the drain—one where the faucets and sink were brand new and clean?

When Ronnie wasn't around, she'd sometimes take the box out and line up every single thing on the edge of the bed. The box was packed tight, a worn washcloth folded over the top of the items before she closed the box lid up and slid it back into the bottom of the closet. She'd written *Sewing Stuff* on the top of the lid in big square letters with Magic Marker, thinking these words would be as likely as anything else to keep Ronnie from ever looking inside—although she couldn't help but wonder what he would think if he ever did open the box and saw her collection of oddities.

There was a big brass button she'd found at Ronnie's parents' house the first time she'd ever been there, and a single paper bill from Trinidad and Tobago—she'd worked that out from under the Plexiglas bar top downtown, prying it a bit closer to the edge every time the bartender turned his back, Ronnie tied up and laughing with a bunch of his friends when it was supposed to have been only the two of them, out on a formal date. But there were guys there from Ronnie's neighbourhood, and they came over like they owned Ronnie and owned the bar too, slapping each other on the back and seeing who could knock back his drinks the fastest. By the end of the night, the damp bill was folded up in her purse and no one was the wiser for it.

There was a blue felt baby mitten she'd taken from a woman at the grocery store. Well, not so much taken as picked up and kept when it had fallen. The baby was in a cart at the checkout, and the woman was unloading groceries and looking the other way. The baby had regarded Liz with an overly serious look, eyes studying and not blinking, its feet poked out at her, legs ending in knitted bags, and Liz was going to give the mitten back, was actually bending down to pick it up and hand it over, but then tucked it in her pocket instead.

On the walk home, Liz put the mitten under her nose and was amazed that it smelled so strongly of baby—like powder, and also something sour and spoiled. After a day in the box, though, it just smelled like the soap.

There was a spare key to the first apartment she and Ronnie had rented, and a battered toy car she had found in the garden before the landlord told them that the backyard was "technically" only for the downstairs tenants, because they had the deck up top, and Liz shouldn't be down there "poking around." They hadn't lasted long there: hardwood and sun, the ad had said, but it didn't say anything about the mice, or about the way the wind blew in all around the useless storm windows and ate up more heat than they could afford to keep paying for.

There was a shell, two earrings Liz had grabbed in a flash from a bar counter, and the lid from a sugar bowl that was shaped like a cow. Somewhere in a house in Conception Bay South where a woman had tried to pick Ronnie up, smiling all night and pushing her chest out at him, there was the rest of the sugar bowl, the black and white chest and legs and the startlingly pink udder, but Liz had the top of the smiling cow, and when she put it on the bed, it was like the animal was swimming deep in the bedclothes, the comforter almost up to its neck. There was a glass wine stopper, a lavender sachet from another bathroom, and a wedding ring that someone had been silly enough to take off and leave on her dresser for the evening. Liz had seen it when she and Ronnie were putting their coats on the bed, and every time she picked it up, Liz thought to herself that if she had a wedding ring, it would never leave her finger, not even if she was going into surgery. Sometimes she'd stop for a second when the ring came out of the box and think about its owner tearing the room apart in the search for it, desperate. Serves you right, Liz thought every time. Serves you damn right. And that was one thing she never felt bad about taking, not even for an instant.

Ronnie was coming back to the car. She rolled down the window and he tipped a small avalanche of coins into her cupped hands. Why does it have to be coins when the guy's got so much money? She didn't say it, though, the coins warm in her hands in the damp cold of the car. Why not bills and keep-the-change? And just why does he get so much money in the first place? Why does he deserve it?

The fact is, Liz thought, he doesn't deserve it, and one hand closed over some of the coins. She slid that hand into her pocket. Then Ronnie was back in the car, dropping onto the seat heavy beside her. And Liz watched the man at 35 McKay as he closed the door, staring right at him, trying to catch his eye to let him know that he didn't deserve it at all, that it wasn't right.

She thought he saw her at the last moment, caught her eye and snapped the last few inches of space between the door and frame shut fast. Because he knows, she thought, he knows it somewhere inside that big doughy body, and he feels guilty about it, too. She felt the stack of coins through the denim of her jeans, the tips of her fingers tracing the edges: eight loonies all touching each other, overlapping in her pocket, as warm now as her own skin.

They were only at the pizza shop for a few minutes before Ronnie was storming back to the car. He was out in front of her before she could even stand up from the booth, and from behind, she could see that his hands were already clenched into fists. Past the four small red tables with the cracked tops, past the front window with its incongruous see-through cityscape stencilled on the glass.

Outside, even though they had really only just gotten in the door, their feet made brand new slashes in the deep fresh snow, and Liz noticed that the street lights were surrounded by globes of light reflecting off the falling snowflakes. The heavily falling snow was eating up all the sound, so that everything moved through a breath-holding hush, each movement seeming that much more sharp and deliberate.

"We're going back to see that fucker," Ronnie said as she caught up with him and got into her side of the car. Liz couldn't help but notice that, just like every other time, just like every single time all night long, the car was already cold, so cold after the heat of the pizzeria, where the big oven hunched against the wall, so squat and square and hot that it seemed as if it should be glowing.

"Why?" she asked, settling against the already-cold seat.

"Bastard shorted us," Ronnie said. "Thinks he can get away with it, too."

Liz almost told him then—but she didn't. The words were right there, she could feel them, tripping to get out and explain. It was, she thought, almost as if the words got stuck, as though they got held up on the fact that if she told him, she'd have to tell him all the rest too. She'd have to tell him about all the other things, and in the process she would have to try to figure out how to tell him *why*, when she wasn't completely sure herself. To tell him it wasn't about soap and mittens and rings at all, that it was about *them*, about what it was that they deserved together, and also about what they would never have, no matter how hard they tried. That it was a box packed full of proofs, and that all it really proved was failure—and it was, all at once, as clear to her as that. Clear and sharp and all at once there, and Liz knew that there was no way to say it and have it make any sense at all.

So she didn't say anything, and the car swung wide on every corner, and Liz was afraid they'd hit someone else coming the other way because Ronnie was driving so fast and dangerously. And there was a little part of her that hoped they would crash, that hoped in one great smack everything would be taken out of their hands.

It was as if, once set in motion, everything had no choice but to end up at its logical end. It was as if she had no voice, and also as if she could not lift her arms, as if the door handle was right there in front of her but she was incapable of understanding even something as simple as how a door handle worked. Everything unfolding in a simple, direct, unstoppable order.

The car slithered sideways onto McKay Street, slid in close and struck the curb under the snow at 35—and it seemed to Liz that Ronnie was out of the car and at the front door before the car was even at a full stop, and she couldn't decide if everything was moving incredibly fast or if she was in some kind of suspended slow motion.

And Ronnie started punching the man at 35 McKay, and it was angry and fast and definite, and the man's pudgy hands danced up in front of his face as if he were trying to ward off a cloud of particularly persistent flies. Ronnie's fists went right through the pudgy hands, and then the man was lying on his side in the snow.

She saw Ronnie pick up the shovel and raise it in the air, but still her hands stayed in her lap. She looked through the circle she'd wiped clear on the side window and watched the shovel rise and fall, and then rise and fall again. And the only thing she could think, as strange as it seemed, was, "I've lost control of my face."

Liz couldn't even feel her face, couldn't imagine what it looked like, except that blood was surging all around her body, and for the first time since fall she felt warm inside the car, like the heater had burst into life unexpectedly. Then Ronnie was back inside the car and they were speeding away—and caught in Liz's throat was something that felt like a bubble of laughter, a bubble she had to swallow hard to hold in. It felt like laughter, urgent—but she knew it wasn't.

Later, but before the police came, Liz took the loonies from 35 McKay Street out of her pocket and put them on the foot of the bed, and then went to the closet to get the box.

32
McKay Street

VINCENT O'REILLY

JULY 14, 2006

VINCE got the shovel out of the shed and, holding on to the handle, tried to shake the same set of thoughts he had every time he touched anything in the house: the thought that the last time there was someone holding the shovel handle, it had been his father, and he was still alive.

Sometimes, that thought alone was almost paralyzing. He'd open the drawer in the kitchen and find himself just standing there, staring at the spoons, trying to figure out which one he could pick without covering up some important message from his past, every single one of them overlaid with fading fingerprints, prints that could never be re-created or replaced.

It seemed wrong to move anything. It seemed impossible even to stay in the house with the weight of all that hanging over him. The clothes in the closets, the things that should be packed up and sold or given away: he couldn't get away from the fact that every single thing in the house had its own particular weight and importance, far beyond the actual heft and shape of the physical space it inhabited.

He felt like he had been made curator by default in an obscure museum that never attracted any visitors, but where he was the only one who knew the history of each of the exhibits. It was a feeling that came at him from all directions.

Sometimes it seemed to him that the natural thing was to just take over the house and move right in, a custodian for someone else's vanished life, and in the next moment he'd be wondering how anyone could handle inheriting the family house and all the memories that crowded around inside it, that stuffed it so damned full. Then he wanted to pack the whole house up and be rid of it, to be out from under the burden of responsibility for protecting someone else's entire world—and, in a strange way, part of his world too.

He went out the door of the workshop with the shovel in one hand, the jewellery box in the other, safe at least in that particular project, and headed around towards the path to the backyard. He waved to Mrs. Purchase as he went. She was standing on the sidewalk across the street, staring at him as if either trying to figure out what he was doing or else just trying to establish who he was. Some things didn't change: Mrs. Purchase, always eager to mind everyone else's business, he thought. Mrs. Purchase, who was, he imagined, keeping her own collection of what-has-been and what-is-already-done.

The sun had burned the last traces of the morning fog out of the air, but the grass was still wet underfoot. Vincent could feel the dampness soaking in through the canvas sides of his sneakers as he walked next to the house, and when he looked behind, he saw his footprints as dark flattened spots, the rest of the wet grass still standing and pearled with the heavy dew.

He buried the box because he couldn't figure what else to do with it. The backyard was heavy, dark soil, a patch of ground his parents had cared for over the years, building it up and fertilizing it and spreading pesticides like water until everything was treated into its place, grass where grass should be and flowers in their even, bordered beds—and it seemed as good a place as any to put a thing that could only ever be his mother's, a thing that he couldn't look at without immediately thinking of her.

Vincent dug and hit solid rock almost immediately, and then moved over and dug another hole, until finally he had a narrow trench a little more than two feet down, the soil layered in thin, different-coloured stripes like the undisturbed layers of some archaeological dig. Then he dropped the shovel and picked the box up from where he had left it on the grass.

In front of him, a smooth bank of grey bedrock cleaved up from underground, growing out into a ledge and then a narrow cliff. His parents had placed a small trellis there, and he knew what shade of soft pink the roses would be when they eventually came out, and how, three summers out of four, the damp would rot the tips of the flowers, a brown stain stalling the buds before they had a chance to open. The way peonies swelled and then surrendered, giving in to mildew just as it seemed they were about to flower.

When he opened the jewellery box one last time, the music sounded tinkly and far more tinny than it had inside the house. Vincent stirred through the jewellery with his index finger for a moment and lifted the opal brooch, remembering his mother's words about bad luck and his father's brief crestfallen look—a look that had been erased by a stony stare. His mother had then been forced to jolly Keith O'Reilly along by pretending she was more grateful than she really was. Faith would love it, he thought, and it would be as if, by moving it across the country, he had changed the whole sense of it, and it could start fresh in the way it had been intended.

Underneath the brooch as he picked it up, the brief blue flash of the cover of a slender notebook, and for a moment he thought about hooking the book up through the pile of tangled jewellery to see what was written inside. Something important enough to be tucked in with his mother's treasures. Instead, he closed the box sharply. The music stopped in mid-verse. Then Vincent simply dropped it straight down into the hole, nudging it squarely into place with the blade of the shovel, and began to fill the hole in again.

When he put the shovel back in the workshop, he looked around at the rows of boxes and the tools hanging from hooks and leaning against the wall, and then he turned off the light decisively, turned it off as if he knew for certain then that he would never be coming back, that there was only the quick hard work of emptying the place and nothing more. It would be a job for a thick skin—what to keep, what to give away, what to throw away—and he knew that each decision would have to be made in a way that brooked no question, that would be right simply because it was a decision made.

And how do you do that? Vincent thought. How do you take the whole place apart, every marked-up wooden spatula, the butter dish they'd always used even though it had been set too close to the stove element and one corner was melted and ruined? How do you go through and deconstruct it all without tearing down every single memory too?

Two-by-fours and plaster, Vincent thought all at once, and the thought stopped him cold. Remembering how these simple walls had spent so much time hemming him in. And how frightening it would be simply to surrender all that hard-earned freedom and fall right straight back into that grasp again.

Vincent picked up the phone and called Twig Chaulk, even though he wasn't Twig anymore. Now he was just Terry, a smiling, much fuller face on real estate signs all over the city—and pretty much the only realtor's mug you would see anywhere in the neighbourhood. If anything sold on McKay, Terry Chaulk usually sold it.

"Hey, Twig, it's Vincent. Listen, let's just go ahead and sell. And I want it listed 'as is.'"

"What do you mean?" On the other end of the phone, Twig sounded as if he was taken aback. They had talked about pulling out the bathroom vanity and putting in something newer, sprucing the place up a bit, maybe making a couple of thousand dollars more on the sale.

"I mean just the way it is. Every bit of it. If you want to leave the stuff there, fine. If you want it all stripped, then hire Wheeler or someone to come in and haul it all out."

Twig sounded incredulous. "Vincent—wait a minute, now. You're pretty much just throwing money away, doing that."

"I don't care. Donate everything to charity. I'm not taking it all apart. I'm going out the door now, and I want the last memory I have of the place to be just the way it is."

Twig fussed for a few minutes on the phone but realized quickly that he wasn't going to change Vincent's mind. "I'll make a few calls," he said.

"I'll leave my keys in the mailbox," Vincent said.

He felt the smooth oval face of the brooch through the fabric of his jeans with a fingertip as he walked through the kitchen, picking the house keys up off the counter with one long, even sweep of his arm. Knowing as he did it that even his habit of locking the door made him someone very different from the couple who had lived in this house for so long.

109
McKay Street

KEVIN RYAN AND
MARY PURCHASE

AUGUST 11, 2006

THE HOUSE was empty now except for the bedroom Mary had grown up in. Everything else was in cardboard boxes, or else was ready to be there, the whole house just one seriously full trunk load of the car away from having been emptied out completely.

Two towels in the bathroom, always the same pair. A face cloth draped on the edge of the sink. Two toothbrushes standing together in a hard white plastic cup.

In the kitchen, one last open box, flaps yawning, a box that they kept putting things into and then taking them out of again whenever they needed to make a meal. One step forwards, two steps back, Kevin thought hopefully, stirring scrambled eggs, watching the steam rise as the eggs went from flat and opaque to mounded and wet.

The rest of the rooms were empty. The runner was still on the stairs, but the front room was stripped right down to the hardwood floor, the fireplace with its round screen staring out across the room like an open mouth, the coiled-up cable from the television left behind like a sleeping snake. They had made love there once, late at night and urgent, Mary's back flat against the wall as groups of passersby passed the front room, their conversations on the sidewalk louder than Kevin's and Mary's breathing. It seemed to Kevin that they had made love in every room, as if they were marking their terrain, as if Mary was intent on overwriting almost every memory of the place with something new and treasured.

There were no curtains left downstairs, so all the rooms were flat and ringing with echoes whenever either Kevin or Mary walked through them. The basement was so wide open and empty that even light bulbs seemed like an unnecessary luxury—and at the same time, to both of them, the house seemed filled to bursting.

No curtains upstairs either. The realtor had said the curtains that had been there were in such poor shape—raddled with claw marks from the cats—that it would be better if they weren't there at all, if all that was left was bare windows and imagination. Only the ceiling lights were left there, harsh and staring in the empty rooms, and they only turned them on for absolute emergencies.

The realtor was a slight, blond, angry-looking woman with a strange way of holding her face, as if she were constantly smelling something that had just begun to go bad. Every time the woman left, Mary would worry again about whether the house smelled like cats, and whether the smell of the now-departed animals would keep it from selling. And then she'd realize that it didn't matter.

Inside the room that Mary had slept in as a girl, she and Kevin often simply forgot there was anything like an outdoors. It was as if the house, the street and even the whole city had closed in tight around them outside the plaster so that there was really just that single room, and for wonderful, full periods of time there was nothing else they needed beyond those four walls. Neither of them had expected it could happen, and both of them, when they were apart, wondered cautiously if it was really something they could trust.

Outside, the For Sale sign shook against the front of the house in the slightest of winds, smacking the house with flat plastic slaps, the sign sometimes almost vibrating in its eagerness. Mary and Kevin took to leaving the windows open so that the summer air swept through the house on its own schedule, while they both moved silently in the near darkness—a darkness where they believed all things could be explained simply with touch.

Days went by and Mary kept turning down offers for the house, stalling the sale as if there was an unwritten, undiscussed agreement between them that everything, all of it, could only last in the strange, otherworldly hiatus of a house without contents, without curtains, with only one room that still held anything familiar.

That room, with its old posters of forgotten teen stars and the thin, light blue bedspread with a rainbow sewn onto it, was more like a time capsule than anything else. It was all as foreign to Kevin as if he had taken some drug that let him age while staying caught in some out-of-the-way spot in the past. A single bed that Mary knew well from when she was a girl growing up. White-painted louvred doors in front of the closet, and an impossibly small dressing table—also white—with an oval mirror.

Sometimes they talked, but they didn't talk in any depth, and they didn't fool around with framing up and building a future outside the walls they were already comfortably and immediately inside. If they had, they might have had to point out that they were grown-ups and past all that eagerness, that they weren't the right age to be building castles or charting voyages. So they talked bare practicalities instead, like when they had to get to work and when the girls were likely to be home, and whether either of the girls would even notice, during one of the few times that their lives and Kevin's would normally intersect, that he wasn't there.

Mostly they didn't have to talk, because the feel of their skin touching was always sharp, the single note of a tuning-fork vibration. Once, he stood behind her as she fried eggs, both standing naked in the small kitchen, and he felt the room full of the sun and the warm shape of her, and it was like the shape he could draw in the air with his hands thereafter held everything important.

The real estate agent—for the first time anyone on the street could remember, not Twig Chaulk—was growing more and more frustrated, her mouth turned more sharply down every time Mary saw her, the offers still climbing but no one ever offering enough.

Kevin would look out for Mary's car, parked by the curb, from the second-floor window at the front of his house. Then he'd make his way down the street close up against the fronts of the houses that pressed tight to the sidewalk, as if he could make himself invisible, or at least insignificant, but succeeding only at appearing guilty. He would look around, trying to seem careless but with his head darting back and forth too quickly, and he saw only the flat, uncaring fronts of the houses, imagining that was all there was to McKay Street, and that all over the street, no one knew.

But all over the street, they knew. They knew and they talked.

Sometimes, after Mary was asleep, Kevin would walk around in his skin, the slap of his bare feet echoing through the empty house, the tips of his fingers trailing loose along the walls like a cat's whiskers, sensing more than they actually felt directly, wondering about the tingle of them together, the shivering wonder, and knowing also that he would be caught dead the moment Cathy came home from her latest Ottawa trip. She'd come home and just see the colour of his skin, his whole body overlaid with the tan of what they'd done, all of it there like some fine and obvious tattoo. He wouldn't be able to lie, he knew. Not to her. She'd rip right through any lies like thin paper, well attuned and used to every single hint and scent a liar might give off.

He knew he wouldn't even bother to try.

And then Kevin realized, hairs standing up all over his body as a fugitive summer breeze curled through the windows and down the stairs, that he just didn't care. He stood there at the foot of the stairs in the falling cool air, feeling the sudden recognition running through his blood headily, like the knowledge was a new and unfamiliar drug. It was sharp and bright inside him when he went back to bed. Mary was still sleeping, and she pushed her naked back up against his chest without fully waking.

Later, they lay together while the house ticked and settled in the summer warmth, a long quiet morning stretching out as if it wouldn't end.

Then Mary, her voice muffled because her face was next to the skin of his arm, her breath warm on his skin: "This can't last," she said, her voice flat, an arm thrown across his chest. Saying the words as if she thought that simply by speaking them, they could agree to set an end point that neither of them actually wanted. "It can't last this way."

Kevin was quiet for a moment, his eyes searching for any sign of the ceiling in the half gloom above them, the sunlight bright and playing through the leaves so that it cast shadows against the far wall. Kevin, suddenly feeling the dangerous tremble of the possible, the toppling towards decision.

"So what can?" he said.

117
McKay Street

HELEN COLLINS

OCTOBER 3, 2006

HELEN COLLINS stood in front of the mirror and wondered what kind of makeup would say Loving Mother Who Tried Everything, or if she should even try.

Ron's court date had been set for months, and she had planned on being there for almost as long. She hadn't been to the prison, to visit either Ronnie or Tony. She'd been as far as the big heavy walls and the front entrance with the metal doors and the Plexiglas panels, but she hadn't been able to get through the doors. The outside of the squat building was painted a dull grey, and the uniforms of the guards were grey too, except the guards had black piping running down the sides of their uniform trousers.

Every time she got near the building, she started imagining that if she went in, they would have to search her for contraband. Then they would have their hands on her body, as if they were accusing her of something, accusing her of being involved. The warning was on the website, and on the sign out front as well: "Visitors should be prepared for physical search." It made her think of the snap of latex gloves around guards' wrists, and it wouldn't have mattered if the hands involved were male or female.

As soon as she got close to the building, it made her shiver. She didn't want any of them touching her, any of it sticking to her at all. So she had waited for the court date instead, thinking about it over and over again, and when she did, she imagined sweeping into the room while the news media and the courtroom spectators all stopped to stare at her, as if her entrance alone could bring the whole procedure to a halt.

When she got to Courtroom Number One in the Newfoundland Supreme Court, she realized that the place was designed to dwarf ordinary people, to dwarf even her. In the huge courtroom, the actors were always going to be smaller than the set. Long, dark, heavy wood benches like church pews, and at the front, a great upwards-rushing wooden frieze with the judge's chair at the centre of it like a throne, and Helen had hardly gotten settled when a judge came into the room in black robes and wearing a red sash, and he had the exact effect she had wanted for herself: everyone stopped what they were doing and turned towards him, and behind her the chatter of the other people in the court faltered and fell away. The whole room was redolent of wet wool and the autumn beginnings of cold weather and the close, wet touch of steam heat, pipes hissing gently in the sudden quiet.

The reporters were at the front of the court, huddled together on a side bench close enough to hear the proceedings, and not one of them was paying her even the slightest attention.

And then Ronnie: two white-shirted sheriff's officers brought him in a side door, and they stood for a moment in the open doorway, taking off his handcuffs and leg shackles before they brought him into the court, so that he walked in looking like a free man. Like everyone was supposed to wipe that first image out of their minds, him standing there in cuffs and leg chains, like that was supposed to be possible, Helen thought.

He was wearing his high school graduation suit—Helen had expected that, because Ronnie's lawyer had come looking for a suit a few days earlier, any suit at all—but she hadn't foreseen how much it would look like yesterday's clothing on him. Too short at the cuffs and ankles now, the fabric shiny and looking overused, or at least over-ironed. A new white shirt with a collar that was far too large for his neck, but even the extra room didn't stop him from pulling at the collar with his index finger to make it sit more comfortably.

"We don't see the trial running more than a few days," the lawyer had said to her when he came to pick up the suit bag.

Standing by Helen's front door, three short grey concrete steps away from the street, he told her that he expected Ronnie would plead guilty now, that even if they tried to get Keith O'Reilly's police statement thrown out because he couldn't be cross-examined, the police had more than enough circumstantial evidence to convict Ronnie. And then, he told her, there was Liz. Liz's testimony would seal it all—but, the lawyer said, Ron had told him to leave Liz absolutely alone.

"There's really enough to convict just in the blood-spatter evidence," the lawyer said, not noticing the way Helen pulled away from the door as he said it. "But I might have been able to go after that girl, at least throw some doubts on her credibility with the right jury."

She couldn't shake the incongruity of it: the lawyer standing with the wrinkled plastic suit bag over his shoulder, one finger through the metal-and-plastic clothes hanger, while behind him, everything was going on exactly as it was supposed to. Cars were drifting around the corner, their turn signals staying on just long enough as their drivers swung the wheels back onto the straightaway, two arbitrary ticks after the turn and then stopping. Leaves were falling and then rushing along the curb on the wind. Helen could imagine Mrs. Purchase standing out there, staring after the mailman as if she couldn't believe he hadn't stopped to leave something in her mailbox. Mrs. Purchase, her mind coming apart for all these years, Helen thought, so much so that her husband had eventually packed up and left on the highway bus for Montreal with a girl in tow who used to wait tables downtown. A girl he'd been spending money on for years and years, so obvious about it that just about everyone knew. Everyone but Mrs. Purchase.

Helen had heard that they'd shifted Mrs. Purchase off to a hospital or a home or something, somewhere where she couldn't be minding everyone else's business. That her house was going up for sale soon.

And on the front steps, the lawyer was staring at Helen, his eyes hard and direct on her face, as if he had asked her a pointed question she hadn't gotten around to answering yet. And for the life of her she couldn't remember the last thing he had said, so she left him there, stepping backwards, closing the door in his face so that he stood out front, bewildered by all of them, before turning and walking back to his car.

I won't ever stop remembering Ronnie in that suit, she thought, the courtroom all around her. She wouldn't stop remembering the way it failed to make him look formal and serious and suited to the place. Instead, it made him look outside the proceedings, as if he had been thrown into them completely by accident and was only now waking up in someone else's clothes to find out exactly where he really was.

If the idea was to make him fit the surroundings, she thought, then it's gone wrong. All wrong, and she was far too late to ever come close to fixing it. Because it would be over before she found the nerve to stand up and yell at them that they had to stop, that this wasn't Ronnie in front of them at all, that they should be looking at the pictures she had from when he was five years old.

"Look!" she wanted to yell. "Just look at the pictures from Bellevue Beach, when he looked like any other boy with a bucket in the sand." The baseball picture where his pants were too big, where he was trying so hard to look like a professional ballplayer, the bat in his hands held up over his shoulder. She was almost ready to burst with it, wanting to tell them how little of Ronnie they were seeing in the prisoner's box, that they were getting ready to make a decision based on one little part of him, one instant of time that wasn't really Ronnie at all. That they were looking at one single frame of a much longer film, and that they hadn't even heard about her father yet, and how he poisoned everyone he came in contact with. That they couldn't possibly understand why it wasn't Ronnie's fault—they knew only one small inch of him, yet they were ready to judge him based on that.

And in front of her, the court was busy unfolding like any piece of judicial choreography ever does, everyone dancing forwards along a straight line that they seemed to understand and expect. Only she and Ronnie were strangers to it.

That wasn't right, because Ronnie was supposed to be the most important part, she thought—wasn't he?

"The Queen versus Ronald Michael Collins, in the murder of Dennis Conners, murder in the second degree."

The judge was asking for something, and from below him a court clerk passed up a slim file with bright numbers on a tab, a whole line of them in a row, like Ronnie was just one case out of thousands.

"Can we deal with this now, then?" the judge said, pushing his reading glasses down his nose and staring over the top of them at the lawyers. "Or should we be looking at setting dates?"

Ronnie's lawyer up on his feet, clad in a black gown like a polyester crow, his hands tucked behind his back, elbows out like wings. "I think we can go ahead now, your Honour."

Next to him, the lawyer for the prosecution simply nodded, his legs crossed, not even bothering to find his feet.

"All right, then. Ronald Collins—how do you plead?"

"Guilty," Ronnie said.

Helen felt her breath catch, her ribs lock, all air stopping its movement. *Wait*, she thought. Thought it so clearly that it was as if the word should be right up there over her head in big square silver capital letters. Then, *Waitwaitwaitwait* and *Stop*. But she didn't say a word out loud, and nothing stopped.

188A
McKay Street

RON COLLINS

OCTOBER 3, 2006

RONNIE said the word "Guilty" and it felt far easier than he had thought it would. At the same time, he couldn't help but feel that the whole courtroom had changed, like the air pressure had changed, the way a room sometimes feels when the topic of conversation takes a sudden and unexpected turn. But for Ron himself, it felt like one more step along a straight line that stretched back to the very first things he could even remember.

And Ron was strangely concerned that Liz wasn't in the courtroom. He hadn't missed that, hadn't got that wrong, even though he had been steeling himself for weeks for the idea that she wouldn't be there. He had hoped to see her in the courtroom, wanted her to know that he was saving her from what his lawyer would have done to her, to know that he believed even if she didn't.

His eyes had swept the courtroom as they had taken the cuffs off, and he was certain she wasn't there. He'd expected her and he hadn't expected her, and it hit him hard. He wanted to look her in the eyes, just to see if there was still a way that messages could pass between them without words.

He saw his mother, though, front and centre—all alone in one of the front benches, looking like she had simply settled into place, dropped out of the heavens in absolutely perfect form.

"You will be remanded in custody until a sentencing hearing on the fifteenth of December," the judge said, but Ronnie wasn't really listening to the judge anymore, and the fact was, he didn't really care. The guards would be sure to have him there on time, stuffed in the van in his court suit with the leg irons on, and he wouldn't so much as have to look at a clock or a calendar unless he decided that was something he wanted to do. That's the way Bart would think about it, Ron thought, and the idea of it made him smile.

Out in the hall, the guards put both the cuffs and the leg shackles on. "You're officially dangerous now," one guard said.

Across the hall, Ron saw Len Menchinton sitting outside another courtroom. He was wearing a suit and looked uncomfortable too. "Witness or defendant?" Ron called over to him, smiling.

"Witness. It gets to Supreme Court when the thefts get real big," Len said.

"Could be worse," Ron said, holding up his wrists like he wanted to shake Len's hand, the chains noisy. "How's Ingrid?"

"Not bad, Ron. Not bad." Then Len watched as Ron was led away, thinking there was something about Ron Collins all of a sudden that he couldn't quite put his finger on. And Len was used to being able to put his finger on things.

Back in his cell, Ronnie saw Bart Dolimont stretched out flat on the lower bunk, his leg in the cast with his foot up on the pillow, reading a book.

"What'cha get?" Dolimont asked.

"Don't know. Sentencing's postponed for two months. Don't care."

"That's the spirit. At least you know who you are. In here, you're just another lifer." Bart Dolimont smiled. "They'll send you to Dorchester after the sentencing, but that's okay. That's the rules. If any sentence is for anything more than two years, it's federal time, and that means the pen in Dorchester, New Brunswick. And whatever you get, you know it's gotta be federal time."

Bart swung his legs down off the bed slowly, the one in the cast first, letting it settle to the floor before bringing his other foot down. "Some ways, maybe it's nicer here, closer to home. But the rules there are pretty much the same anywhere. And you know what they say—a change is as good as a rest." Dolimont stopped for a moment, thoughtful. "Besides," he continued, "maybe I could get sent up there too. I got me an ace in the hole, Ronnie, an ace in the hole. A little federal time, it might hit the spot for a guy like me, getting older." He looked at the back of his hand as if he were trying to read the rings on a piece of wood. "They catch you stealing stuff, they always expect you to run, and I can't even be bothered to run anymore, Ronnie boy. If I stay here, I'll end up being the only thief trying to get out of the mall behind a walker."

Dolimont started to stand, and Ron reached over and grabbed his hand, pulling the man up.

"You know the routine," Dolimont said. "It's lunchtime. And Thursday's chips and gravy day anyway."

Outside, there was shouting somewhere on the range, but it didn't have anything to do with him. And then it hit Ronnie right square between the eyes, as forcefully as if Bart had reached over and belted him one: None of it had anything to do with him anymore. For once, he'd have no history at all, except for whatever his sentence turned out to be—no past, no relatives, no neighbours shaking their heads. Ronnie realized it the way someone realizes that they're falling into a hole, understanding the fall before they hit bottom but long after there's anything they can do about it.

Then, for the first time since he'd dropped the shovel handle next to Dennis Conners's body, Ron Collins started to laugh—really laugh, his stomach lurching until the muscles hurt with the effort—and he laughed until tears ran down his face, until Bart Dolimont struggled over to him and started to pound him on the back, convinced that Ronnie either had started choking or else had lost his mind entirely.

32
McKay Street

GLENN COUGHLIN

AUGUST 14, 1980

"**KEITH'S** not here, Glenn. He's got an extra shift tonight. I thought that if anyone knew that, you would have," Evelyn said.

Glenn Coughlin had come boiling straight in through the door like he owned the place, like always. Glenn Coughlin, smelling like grease and welding rods. Smelling like Keith's smell. But different, too. Glenn Coughlin closing the door behind him, checking the lock. Thumb and forefinger turning the never-closed lock with a quiet snick. Glenn in his forties then, big and square and strong.

The windows were all open, the curtains touched now and then with the slight breeze darting in, but mostly they were hanging straight down.

The air still. Ten-thirty and airlessly hot, St. John's houses not designed for heat, flat black tar roofs, the people under them never really getting around to expecting the heat until it was piled all over them like extra blankets they couldn't shed.

Evelyn was standing in the doorway to the living room, the television lighting the room behind her with moving blues and greens. Hands up in front of her breasts, sheltering already. Wearing a skirt that hung just below her knees. Wishing now that she was wearing something else.

"I know, Ev," Glenn said. "Keith's on the double, working on some Russian boat with hull damage. They hit something in the night in open ocean, no one on watch to see anything. They sank it, probably, and they don't even know what it was."

He stopped talking. Smiled. Not a nice smile, Evelyn thought.

"I know all that," he said. He looked at his fingernails for a moment, as if hunting down some particularly stubborn dirt under the hard rims. "I also know whatever they hit was painted red. And I know Keith's down welding in the bow tubes, that he's got another three hours of work down there if there's a minute of it, packed in tight enough that he can barely lift his arms up, the fans sucking the torch smoke out. But I wasn't looking for him, was I?"

Glenn's hand smelled of cigarette smoke when it was up next to the side of her face, and Evelyn turned her chin away in shock at the close familiarity of his touch. He had crossed the distance between them in a single motion, one long step. His other hand was set now in the curve in the small of her back.

"How'd you get stuck with Keith, anyway?" Glenn said, close enough to the side of her face that she could feel the heat of his exhaled breath. "He's just a little man, Ev, thinks he's somethin' special, bigger than he really is."

"You shouldn't be here, Glenn," Evelyn said.

She said the words even though she recognized that they sounded flat the moment they came out of her mouth, flat and resigned, as if they were really only the things she felt she was supposed to say and didn't have the strength or conviction to carry off properly.

The things you're supposed to say to keep up appearances. The things you say for form. She knew she was supposed to throw them out there, and she knew already that Glenn was going to ignore them.

She also knew that everything was going to unfold the way she realized it would the moment she saw him coming through the door. That he was bigger and stronger than her, and that everything she did now was a matter of hedging bets, of making the best out of the worst.

Falling, and it was already too late to do anything about it.

She ran through all the options in seconds—all the big things she could do, the fighting back, the screaming (and with the windows open, they'd hear her all over the neighbourhood, sure they would). Evelyn thought about it all, and then thought better of all of it, too.

Everything would get so complicated—that was her first thought. She would think about that later, wonder why the first thing she thought about was that resisting would create all kinds of complications she wasn't ready to deal with. That it could be fast and uncomfortable and awful, but that then it would be done.

She thought about it being done, and she thought about it more as he muscled her back against the wall like he was moving a mannequin into position in a store window. And she let her arms hang down at her sides as if she couldn't move them at all.

Glenn was pushing up her skirt, eager and fast, his other hand undoing his pants, pushing her back hard against the wall, driving a bit of her breath out through her lips like a sigh. And the only thing she could find to think about was how to make the whole thing smaller and farther away from her, crumpling it up small like a sheet of old tinfoil.

Glenn was breathing hard, his mouth next to her ear, his hips thrusting against her. His breath sounding angry—his hands rough and scraping, reaching under her clothes, tearing fabric away from her when it didn't slide fast enough.

"You like it, don't you? You want it. You know it. You all high and mighty. Looking down your nose at everyone. Looking down your nose at me," he said, his hands clenching behind her, pulling her hard against him.

Evelyn tried to remember if she'd ever said anything of the kind, tried to make sense of whatever it was he was talking about, all the time feeling somehow that she was really in another room, watching everything from a distance, from out in the trees.

Except for the pain of his rough hands on her skin. The feeling of him. The way it felt like her own skin was pulling away from his, revolted.

It was, at least, quick. She felt the wet on the insides of her thighs, and he was leaning into her, still and breathing heavily. Thinking that it was almost over, and that then there would be the soft of him, he would shrink inside her and his need would too, and then there might even be apologies, even if he didn't get around to actually saying them.

Her clothes were rumpled up against her skin and damp, and she realized that she was breathing heavily too, physically aroused and hating herself for her body's response, a sharp pinprick of disgust poking at her from inside.

The weight of him leaning against her. Making her stomach roil like she was going to throw up.

Outside, the world was continuing, oblivious.

"You'd better get going," she said, feeling as if she were dismissing a guest who'd foolishly stayed too long, freeing herself from the drape of his arms. At the same time, feeling all at once different. "You wouldn't want to be here when Keith gets home." Saying it made her a little bolder and she kept going. "You wouldn't want me to have to explain just what it is you're doing here."

But she realized that she'd let her voice drop a note with the last word, giving the sentence a declining pitch in its last few words, realized the failing strength of her voice, from the definite to the tentative. And she knew as well that he had heard the change.

"What do ya mean?" Glenn said. "That he's going to find out? That what? That you're going ta tell Keith 'bout this?" Glenn laughed then, the laugh turning into a smoky, rich cough.

Glenn pulled away from her, and she felt her body almost sag reflexively towards him as he moved away.

"You go right ahead," Glenn said. Pants back up to his hips, zipper being zipped, door unlocked again, snicker-snack, the door yawning open. Glenn away from her and moving into the rectangle of the door frame and somehow changing, going back to being all too familiar, everyday Glenn, time itself turning suddenly into single frames, every movement fragmenting as she watched.

"You go ahead. Go ahead and tell him. Hey, maybe he knows already. Maybe he can guess. And maybe he owes me anyway, so even if you do tell him, he'll just keep quiet. Up to you."

Evelyn, unable to shed the thought that something critical had changed, that she was different. Her balance completely gone, her hands turned backwards and pressed hard against the wall behind her, desperate for the familiar support.

When Glenn left, when the door was closed and the room was once again just the room, she let her breath come out in a long gasping rush that turned into a shuddering sob, staggered into the bathroom, where she found she was bleeding. There were long, deep scratches, scarlet, on the backs of her thighs, scratches that she'd have to find some way to hide from Keith.

And by the next morning she began to wonder if there was something else she'd have to keep hidden from him, at least until she was far enough along to go down to the doctor and get a test done. A test for something she wondered if she knew already.

Her Majesty's
Penitentiary

BART DOLIMONT

OCTOBER 4, 2006

THE COPS come in when Dolimont asks for them, both leaving their guns at the guardhouse desk at the front of the prison. The two of them come up together, Ballard and another one, and Ballard's known Bart Dolimont for almost as long as anyone on the force. Ronnie's pleaded guilty, and Bart can't help how much he likes the kid, so it's time, he thinks, to play the last card.

"So what have you got for us that's so damned important this time, Bart?"

Inspector Ballard looks at home sitting at the small table, his legs thrown out wide, one hand up on the flat wood top, fingers tapping. Notebook thrown open, pen lying beside it, cap still on and waiting. Ballard's partner edges in tight to the table, eager, Bart Dolimont staring silent at him until he leans back too.

"This better not be a waste of our time, or we might come up with a real good reason to tell the guys to put you into segregation," Ballard says.

"Something to get off my chest," Dolimont says, and starts talking.

Then he tells them where to find the purse. Sketches in how it happened: "I panicked. Wasn't supposed to be like that. I thought she was going to scream." He's careful—not too much detail, not enough to trip himself up. Keep it simple. Shrug when the questions are too detailed. Nothing for them to hang him up with.

"So where's the body?" Ballard asks. His expression says he's unconvinced.

"There's a lot of ocean," Bart says. Leaves it at that. "Told you I did it. Enough for you, isn't it?"

Afterwards, "I don't get you as a murderer," Ballard says. "Lots of little stuff, sure. Any kind of robbery, absolutely. But murder? I just don't see it. And you would have been—what? Nineteen?"

Dolimont shrugs. "I was more of a hothead then. You know what kids are like. Go and check it out if you don't believe me. Purse is in a footlocker in the crawl space under my mom's old place, just like I told you. You know I've been in here for months, no chance to set anything up. I'm getting older, gentlemen. Just want to clear my conscience."

Ballard unconvinced, staring steadily across the table.

"You don't want to solve this one, don't want it off the books, then fine by me," Bart says. "But you know you do, and this is your only chance. You got the purse, got a confession, and you know I'm going to plead guilty, first chance I get. Slam dunk for you."

Ballard doesn't move, hasn't taken the cap off his pen.

"You might want to write it up so I can sign it, or take me someplace where you can record it all," Bart says, chiding. "What's a guy got to do to get you guys to take a confession?"

Later, Ronnie looks at him in amazement when Dolimont tells him that they'll end up serving time in the same prison, probably, because it's murder, at maximum security in Dorchester. Then Ron says just three words: "But you're innocent."

"Innocent? Don't know about that. We're just talking guilty and not guilty here," Bart says. "I think I'm guilty enough."

Victoria Airport,
British Columbia

VINCENT O'REILLY,
FAITH MONAHAN

JULY 17, 2006

FAITH was at the airport early, well before the flight was supposed to get in, drinking black coffee and watching two sparrows that somehow managed to live inside the great glass arch, flying from seat to seat, picking up crumbs left by people eating pastries with their coffee.

The roof rose so high that when she looked at it, her breath caught in her throat, and she couldn't decide whether it was wonder at the great sweep of the dome, or whether she was afraid someone somewhere had done something wrong, and that at any moment, the whole thing might come crashing down on top of her, the wrong pieces all coming together at once.

Out on the apron, she had watched a small plane roll up and stop, and now it was sitting, one propeller still turning, as a pair of slow-moving grounds crew slid fat chocks under the wheels and rolled the stairs up to the door. Out behind the airplane, the land was brilliant green bushes and leaves bursting out in a frenzy, an uncontrolled orgy of plants.

Soon, she thought, the passengers will start to file out—and it will be time for practice, a dry run, just looking at them and trying to decide which one looks the most like him. That, and the simple game of looking at the passengers and trying to decide just what each one does for a living, whether there is someone coming to meet them, whether they're expecting laughter or tears. But mostly trying to decide if any of them reminds her enough of Vincent to bring his face back into sharp relief in her head.

Faith looked at each one of them in turn. At the last minute she had resisted the urge to bring his picture along, still in the frame, so that she could take one last look when the plane did arrive, like cheat notes at an exam that she would then stuff back into her purse before he got out through the security doors.

Just one careful look, she thought. I could really use it now, just to be absolutely sure.

And she wasn't sure why she felt she had to. After all, she knew every inch of him, how he looked, how he smelled, how he felt to the touch—and she was absolutely sure that he would be as obviously Vincent as anyone could possibly be. But all through the drive to the airport, alone in the taxi as the driver chattered on and on about his children, Faith staring out the window at the wall of lush green on the side of the road, she wondered if, somehow, she had just managed to make it all up in her head. If, instead of being the Vincent she remembered, this would be someone else entirely, and she'd realize as soon as they spoke that she had spent the last few months fooling herself, making it all out to be something much bigger than it actually was. By the time she had reached the airport, she wondered again if he was going to tell her that he was moving out, that it had all been some kind of giant mistake.

And then his plane came swooping in, a silver dart against the distant white-topped mountains at first, then a plane, and then Vincent coming down the stairs, and she was absolutely certain the second she saw him.

When she told him about her fears later, when they were lying in the dark, naked, Vincent laughed quietly and said, "I guess Faith wasn't enough. You should have had a little Hope in there too." Then he laughed again. "Who knows? Maybe soon you will, now."

And she hit him in the ribs, gently, the same old reaction for the same old joke, and he laughed a long, deflating laugh, and stared up at the ceiling for a long time, his eyes not even blinking.

"You all right?" she asked.

"It's not ever the way you remember it, going back," Vincent said. "Nothing is. You think you've got it all down cold, think that you know where every single piece fits, and then someone turns around and gives you a new piece you didn't expect, and it just doesn't fit anywhere at all. And you start all over again, building it up and half afraid it's all a house of cards anyway."

They were quiet for a minute.

"Maybe it's better if it's just you and me," Vincent said, his arms wrapped tight around her back, talking softly into the hair by her right ear. She bent into him, loving the warmth of his skin against hers, and almost missed the rest.

"It's better if we just start from scratch. All new. Otherwise, it gets too crowded."

35
McKay Street

DENNIS CONNERS

FEBRUARY 11, 2006

FUCKED. That was the way Dennis thought about the entire day. It was fucked from beginning to end. And there was no other way to describe it.

He'd been in early for a meeting where—clearly—no one liked anything he had suggested, where they all just looked on impassively when he'd taken the drawings out of their big blue cardboard tubes and unrolled them on the conference room table.

He should have known he was in trouble when the drawings started to roll up on themselves again and no one even moved to help him hold them down. He'd built a ramshackle construction of staplers and tape dispensers on every corner, and the diagrams had finally stayed flat, but Dennis could tell that they had decided to hate the concept, that no one was even trying to see what he had designed. It was as if they had gotten together ahead of time and agreed between themselves that they would reject them on principle. "Builds some character"—isn't that what coaches say when someone smacks you in the face? Dennis thought. It was in the way they all had their hands up around their faces, and also the fact that no one would look at him. Like they'd all simultaneously developed an allergy to meeting his gaze.

Ted, who owned the firm, had given him a dismissive pat on the shoulder at the end of his presentation, a pat that felt like "Good try, but it just doesn't measure up," and no one else in the room had even been able to get a word out. He was sure there was a simple reason why they'd disliked the work, but no one would give him a hint about what it might be. Only a simple plan for a gazebo, a glassed-in octagon, but the whole room had seemed to give off a gas that said, "You're not good enough."

So Dennis had gone to the food court for a club sandwich and fries at ten-thirty in the morning, a double side of gravy, and the woman at the counter smiled when he passed her a ten. That's the first smile I've seen today, Dennis thought, eating the sandwich without even enjoying it, the rough surface of the toast carving up the roof of his mouth. And the gravy didn't do anything to lift the gloom, the food court empty enough that every sound was a brittle plastic slap.

Dennis wondered how he had ever ended up in St. John's, except he knew perfectly well: he'd answered a newspaper ad looking for "an associate for a mid-sized architectural practice," and more than anything else, he'd fallen in love with the building the firm was in. It was all old timber work inside, a redone warehouse, and he'd liked the way the beams had been sandblasted clear of paint so that you could see every join and angle, so that the whole inside of the building seemed as easily put together as a tree house but with massive beams almost a foot across on each face. It was brand new, released from all old, a combination that you couldn't build from the ground up now if you set out to do exactly that, he thought.

But the work he had ended up doing, once he got the job, was nowhere near as enthralling. It was a job, Dennis thought, and that was about the best face he could put on it. It was a job, and it paid the bills, even if it wasn't anything close to what he had thought it would be.

In his mind, moving to a small east coast city was supposed to have been his entry into something like Frank Lloyd Wright and big glass triangles, purpose-built brilliant houses with rooms that made customers weak. He was supposed to bring a whole new world to people who had never seen anything like that before. At least, that's what he'd thought. Every job was supposed to be something dramatically new: a challenge, something that would require Dennis to turn his mind on edge or sideways, and think about moving in a different direction to solve a difficult problem. Architecture had always been like that in school: there had been plenty of time spent on the basics, but there were always the big projects to look forward to, the conceptual work that was all about angles and air and light, the solutions for clients with plenty of money and enough guts to want something clearly different.

He hadn't expected to wind up calculating the load on two-by-six supports for someone else's designs, hadn't planned on being given work drawing up small extensions and glassed-in sunrooms while the other architects with the firm designed houses with timber-framed great rooms and office complexes with centre courts large enough for fully grown trees. Dennis had been involved, all right: they'd let him calculate the likely weight of the tree and the size of floor joists they'd need under it, and he'd spent enough of his time building scale models of buildings. But when it came time to meet with the clients, Dennis was almost always outside the boardroom, sent off to work on the sort of small project that kept steady money coming in for the firm. "There are the occasional projects that build the franchise, and then there are the Wal-Mart customers who keep the doors open and the cash register filling up," Ted told him. And Dennis was sure that he was the one who spent the most time working in the Wal-Mart end of the practice.

"Pay your dues, Dennis," they were fond of saying, and they would always say it with a smile, as if it was some rite of passage that he was supposed to just put up with. "Some projects build reputation, others build cash flow, and you're on the cash-flow beat right now."

Other people did the designs while he filled in the dimensions on the beams in load-bearing walls and non-load-bearing walls— fine, even notations with hard-lead pencils, every word and number underlined with a careful stroke perfectly made with the help of a plastic straightedge, and that was supposed to be enough to keep him content.

Dennis couldn't help thinking that he hadn't come all the way from Toronto for a job filling in everybody else's blanks. Back at home, though, he had a secret.

Upstairs in the front room at 35 McKay Street, he'd converted an entire bedroom into a drawing room. Curtains, a drawing table, a tall stool. He'd wanted it spartan, bare, so that nothing would be able to get in the way of his ideas, and he'd even taken up the carpet. Expensive carpet, "Berber," the realtor had said reverentially, muttering the word like it was a religious chant when Dennis was looking at the house, but he didn't care. He didn't even want it. He'd rolled it up awkwardly, the nail strips along the edges tearing at his fingers, and the carpet and underlay were down in the basement now, the plywood subfloor slowly darkening from exposure to sunlight. At one end of the room, twin front windows, just a little too tall for the balance of the space, he thought; at the other, a fireplace, never used, completely filled with a white-painted metal cover. One ceiling light in the middle of a patterned plaster circle above him, and his gooseneck lamp craning in over the drawing table like it was someone familiar looking over his shoulder while he worked.

A portfolio, a few rolled-up pieces of work from university in their rigid cardboard tubes, and his idea. He'd had an idea, a real idea, a unique idea, and there wasn't any way he was going to give it up. If he took it to work, someone else would be sure to take credit for thinking of it first. So he kept it at home, tinkering and fine-tuning.

Laid out on the drawing table he'd bought for school was a design for a house that delicately crossed the line between traditional and modern, the kind of design that he was sure could catch on and leave a real mark. He called it the Hiding House, and the first kernel of the idea had come to him in the middle of the night, as he looked out the window at the dark windows of row houses across the street, at their constant, repeating, connected rooflines, rooflines that seemed to suggest that each house was both different and yet so similar as to be able to vanish among its compatriots.

The front of the Hiding House would be like a St. John's row house, he thought, and that was the beauty of it. Unassuming and square, it would be the kind of house even a burglar wouldn't find interesting. The idea was that the whole outside would seem nondescript as a matter of course: the windows spaced so that there were three across the front on the second floor, while there was a door on the left front corner of the ground floor and then two windows on the right. The idea was that it was two-dimensional and absolutely flat—the kind of expression, he thought, that you put on for an absolute stranger. A house like a grade-school child would draw. No—a house drawn by a grade-school student trying to blend into a new school, offering up no sharp edges, nothing distinct. No particular personality, no character at all on the facade—and that was it, he thought. *Facade* was the perfect word, because absolutely none of it would be true.

Inside, it would be completely different, the whole thing designed to let in light from odd and unexpected angles. Slanted skylights that bled light down through the flat roof, corresponding gaps down through the second floor to the first, the kitchen on the back all glass and opened up all the way to the second storey. He'd been working on it for months, toying with how the light would travel through the house as the sun moved. Inside, the idea was that the house would have everything—high-tech bathroom and kitchen, energy efficient to a T—but none of it would be revealed to someone just walking by. It was supposed to look like the kind of house you wouldn't even want to see the inside of, until you did. The kind of place you look at and wonder if you'd bother to go to an open house there—and once inside, Dennis thought, a house you'd never, ever want to leave.

He spent nights working on it, and showed his work to no one, convinced it could be his ticket to a new job and a new city. Early on, he'd called a former professor, the architect he trusted most, and told him breathlessly about the idea. There had been a long pause on the other end of the phone.

"It's a great idea, Dennis," the professor had said. "But—"

"But what?"

"But it's an idea that's more about you than it is about the people you want to be selling it to. Most people want to stand out, want to be noticed. They want it to be obvious."

"But it's about discovering things, about how you go inside and learn a bit more with every corner you go around," Dennis argued. "It unfolds, and just gets better."

"It's brilliant, Dennis. But selling it is harder. Some people like it all laid out right in front of them, so they can show off to people they wouldn't even open the door to."

Dennis had stewed over that conversation for two nights, the lights left off in his upstairs drawing room, the pencils all in their careful rows, sharpened, all their points aligned and aimed in the same direction.

And then he had started working again. Slowly at first, but with the project gathering speed again. It has to be my ticket away from this, Dennis thought. It's a good, clean, conceptual idea, ready to deliver, and it's mine—and even if no one wants to buy any of them, it's the kind of project I can take with me, the kind of thing that shows creativity and initiative.

Standing upstairs by the drawing table, Dennis looked out the front windows at the falling snow. The wind was coming up, he thought, and that meant the old house would shake again. On nights when the house was shaking, Dennis couldn't sleep, caught up in what he called his architect's X-ray vision. He could imagine the beams inside the walls working against themselves, corners and angles rocking gently back and forth across each other, each little rock and shiver pulling nails a little further out of floor plates and sills, and it didn't matter to Dennis how long the house had been standing there, the only thing he kept coming up with was that one day, or one night, it wouldn't be standing anymore. It doesn't matter how many times you escape disaster by luck, Dennis thought. Every single time, every corner, is a new flip of the coin.

He looked at the Hiding House again, the final drawings almost done, each line perfect, and knew for certain that he was making exactly the right flip of the coin. He'd seen an ad in the *Globe and Mail* for a new firm in Montreal looking for residential designers with a difference, and he had that difference.

Then the pizza guy's car was pulling up outside in the snow, and Dennis was coming down the stairs with a fistful of loonies and quarters. He'd looked in his wallet, already knowing he was out of bills because the head partner at the firm had been in with yet another box of fundraising chocolate-covered almonds. They always taste like wax, Dennis remembered thinking, but he'd bought every single box anyway, forty-five dollars' worth of almonds out stiffening in the trunk of his car, because he'd thought the boss would have to remember an employee who bought up fifteen boxes of charity almonds. It had to be good enough for a reference, Dennis had thought, even if it wasn't good enough to get him out of the grunt-work gulag. Remember me, Mr. Piper? I bought every single box of your daughter's school-trip almonds. All of her Girl Guide cookies. The packages of seeds for garden annuals that never even sprouted, let alone bloomed. Tickets on draws that never ended up having the winners announced, contests never heard of again once you'd written your name and telephone number on tickets from the big roll, as if the contests simply disappeared into thin air without anyone noticing.

He loved to imagine their faces when he told them he had another job—a promotion to partner with a company that really counted—loved to think what it would be like when they opened *Architectural Digest* and saw the Hiding House all laid out there in front of them with his name on the cover. They'd know that they had missed their chance to be part of something really, really big.

He reached for the door as the pizza guy came around the front of the car, practising holding his face in a serious, steady stare, still thinking about the kind of face he'd like to see staring back at himself from the magazine.

Dennis Conners, serious senior architect. The Hiding Face of the Hiding House.

That would show them, better even than his fantasy of switching the load sizes on beams somewhere in one of their projects so that one of their precious institutional creations came toppling down. Piper and Associates having to explain that all that work, all the heavy lifting, had been done by some faceless junior fresh out of school. It was easy enough to do: just move a decimal place on the load for a big beam, like it was an honest mistake. It wasn't like anyone was checking his math or anything. Chances are they were too stupid to ever figure out what happened.

They were too busy talking up the clients for that—and Dennis thought he'd be long gone before anything gave way under the right snow load, a big wall of glass smacking down into a mall. Piper and Associates could figure out for themselves just how they were going to pay for the lawsuits, running around trying to figure out what had happened and where, who did what wrong and when. Or maybe they would figure it out and be too embarrassed to let on.

He opened the door and gave the pizza guy the money, a big handful of change, and suddenly he was nervous and trying not to drop any of the coins in the snow, trying to smile at the guy.

"Gotta pay you in coin," he said. "All I've got. It's twenty-one dollars, right? Here's twenty-six."

The pizza guy always made him nervous—Dennis couldn't help it. Maybe it was the way the guy kept staring at him, steady, straight at his eyes, as if it was some kind of dare or something. Like he was trying to look right straight inside his head, rummaging around in his thoughts. Not blinking at all. It made Dennis think: wouldn't your eyeballs dry out if you didn't blink?

Now the guy was smiling at him, *smiling*, but in a way that somehow didn't look pleasant at all. "Pizza guys, we all like change."

Back in the living room, with the pizza box open and the steam rising from the hot cheese, Dennis couldn't shake how relieved he was that the door was safely closed and the deadbolt knocked home.

Sitting on the floor, he could hear the wind rising outside, buffeting hard against the front of the house like it was trying to get in. There are plenty of things I won't miss about this city, Dennis thought, and the wind is certainly one of them. Then he thought about finishing his resumé on the computer, and rolling up all of the designs, making copies on the large-format copier at work without telling anyone. All the work he did, they certainly owed him a few copies, didn't they?

It felt like he hadn't even gotten settled away to eat when the door-bell rang again. Dennis, annoyed, was thinking only that the pizza would get cold as he headed into the hall to open the door.

32
McKay Street

EVELYN O'REILLY

MAY 28, 2006

THE HARDEST PART is the words. You really have no idea how hard that is. Not having the words, or at least not being able to get them out.

Not that I was ever much of a talker—I let Keith do that. I always thought it was important to him to always be the one out in front. More important for him than for me.

For a while after the stroke, I wasn't even really putting anything together—it was all just like flashes, like things fluttering out there on the very edge of making sense. I can remember a little snatch of time that lit up in my memory like the sun breaking through clouds: Keith was fishing on a river up in North Harbour, and it was summertime, the river all little triangles of silver in the light. I was sitting on a stretch of fine red sand, leaning back, propped up on my hands, and I could feel the heat coming up into the palms of my hands and the backs of my legs. It was just an instant, really, before the clouds came back together in my head, but the sort of thing you could hang on to, like a life raft, while everybody is so busy trying to fill in the blanks for you, talking away at you like it's really important that every single thing gets explained. They don't realize that it's embarrassing to be told things, over and over again, about a life you can't remember. Like letting the side down, repeatedly.

My father used to say that: "You're letting the side down." He must have said that a hundred times when I decided marrying Keith was more important than either finishing an English degree or starting teacher's college. I stopped hoping to be a poet someday, and started with the hands-on everyday regularity of running a house and planning for babies, even if there was only ever going to be one—Vincent. Vincent, who came so terribly late, who didn't come until I was almost forty, and by then we'd given up, really, because it looked like it was never going to happen. The doctor had wanted Keith to get tested, but Keith said no. It's still hard that it hurts me so much. Keith said there wasn't anything wrong with him, that if there was anything wrong, it was wrong with me. He could decide it just like that, end of story. He said he wasn't going to—I could never say this out loud—that he wasn't going to "jerk off in a cup just to prove some retarded doctor wrong."

Then, after Glenn, it was Vincent. And Keith was proud as could be, and he actually said to me, "See? Nothing wrong with me at all." And I couldn't say anything, couldn't say anything at all.

But at least out of all that we got Vincent.

Vincent, who moved away.

Vincent, who made absolutely the right choice even if I never get to see him now. My father would have loved Vincent, but he came so late my father was long dead.

My father—it's always a marvel to me that some things just pop up out of the fog. He had a moustache, a big walrus moustache, but I think I'm the only one who found that moustache special.

I sometimes remember telling Keith that something was wrong with me just before the stroke, because I knew that something was happening. I know my own body, I wanted to tell him, know it far better than you can ever even begin to imagine, old man. Know each little twinge, from minor to magic. And I knew something was wrong.

There was something about the way things looked, as if when I turned suddenly to one side, my eyes couldn't figure out how to catch up and everything went almost two-dimensional, the whole world in flat planes. And at the same time, I had the most amazing feeling in my fingertips, almost like a buzzing that swelled and faded. I told Keith I was sure something was wrong, and he told me it was all in my head.

All in my head. Funny—he was right about that, just not the way he meant it. There was the wall of dark then, everything breaking up into shards. They tell me I fell in the kitchen and Keith found me, and that in the ambulance they told him not to expect much.

Things got clearer and clearer in the weeks afterwards, and the sharpest thought, the clearest recollection, that I have of anything is that one morning it was a hospital bed that I was lying in, the bed linens crisp and hard and institutional, a little rough under my fingertips the way the big washers make things. And then it was words and sentences in my head, and an order came back. Sort of. Because it's an order that doesn't always stay with me. Worse: it's an order without any way to get the words out, all of them in there and stuck fast, like they're piling up behind a dam that will never, ever break.

That's bad enough—but there's the fact that everyone is always assuming something, too. "You must be cold, Evelyn," they'll say, and then it's someone feeling so damned good about themselves just because they're putting a blanket across my legs. And it's easier to go along with it than to fight, but that doesn't keep you from getting angry, especially if you're not cold at all.

I mean, you'd like to say, "If I wanted a blanket, I'd let you know, wouldn't I?" But that's just it. I won't say it. Because I can't.

I'm resigned to the fact that I won't talk again, but I'm less comfortable with the fact that I can hardly walk either. That I take a few steps and often fall, loose and boneless like I was made of rags. One whole side of my body is like baggage that I just drag along beside me. Keith always coming to help me to the bathroom, to help me into bed.

I can imagine him talking bluntly to someone about it, the way he used to talk to Glenn, saying, "I didn't sign up for this," and "Seventy years old, and this is what I have to look forward to for the next ten years?" Out there somewhere in the house when he's pretty sure I can't hear him.

Hear him? I can barely hear anything over the television, and I can't get organized enough to change the channel or turn the darned thing off.

I go around the house in my head now, and I think that I remember more about it than I ever did before the stroke. I remember more because I have to think so carefully about all of it. It's like exercise, really, like moving your muscles, like a test where no one ever gives you your marks, where no one ever gets around to grading your paper. I mean, I can draw the whole bedroom in my head as clear as that, every single thing in its place, and not only do I not have to check, the fact is that I couldn't if I wanted to. So I guess I'm right every time.

The bedspread, folded back. The comforter folded at the foot of the bed. I try to see how many pieces of it I can hold in my head, like it's my job to tote them all up every time, to keep them safe in a way that nothing in my head ever feels safe.

But I do know where every single thing is—what's on the dresser, what's in the top drawer—and if I think about it, I can move them all around, as if they were levitating and moving to new spots under my command. And when something moves, I know it, even if Keith always told me I'm just a stubborn old woman. He still says that to me—I think he likes the fact that I can't talk back when he does.

I was worried at first. I don't know why. I was worried that he'd go through everything, sort it all out his way, that Keith would not be Keith anymore after all. That instead of being like a framer, he'd somehow have turned into a finish carpenter—a detail guy. That he'd look in the jewellery box and read the diary and then he'd know. If he didn't know already. But I don't think he does. I don't know why I thought Keith would ever get around to sorting out anything in the house—anything outside his workshop, anyway. Rough and ready when I married him, and rough and ready now. Stunned as an ox, and blind to things that are right there in front of his face. And that's not always a bad thing.

I like to think he didn't know about it at all, that he still doesn't know. But then there's Vincent. I'm terrified it will wind up in Vincent's hands, that he will read it and that it will change everything. That it will do damage far beyond anything I can imagine. And I can't do anything about it.

It was a stupid idea. The worst idea I ever had. And I can't do anything about it now.

I thought at first it would be best for Vincent to know where things began, even if it would be hard. I didn't want him going and looking up Glenn or anything like that. I don't know if anyone can look up Glenn, really. After he left the yard, Keith heard that he had bought one of those silver Airstream trailers with his retirement package and had headed out for the southern United States. No one's said anything about him for years.

So I wrote it all down—how Glenn had come to the house, how I got pregnant right afterwards, how in the end I wouldn't have changed any of it for the world because I ended up with Vincent. You get ideas like that sometimes—great big full-of-yourself ideas that you're going to set everything right, that you're some kind of guardian of truth, that you're doing the right thing because you're only going to say it like it is. Like you're in white robes with a great big shiny sword. I mean, there has to be a boxful of sayings like "The truth hurts" and things like that, but all of them circle around the idea that people are supposed to be told the truth, no matter how painful it might be for them to hear it, no matter how much damage it does. It deserves to get told, because it's the truth.

I'm not so sure about that now. And I don't know why I ever was.

I know exactly where the diary is. Calling it a diary is a little too fancy, really. Just a notebook. Blue. One of those little lined notebooks that you might put grocery lists in.

You never think anything's going to happen to you. That's the problem. I mean, you do in the long run—you know you'll get sick eventually and die. But you never think anything's going to happen to you *today*. So you don't get things in order, don't write up a list of where you do your banking or what you want done with your body after you die; there will always be time for that later. I could have moved that notebook a thousand times—I could have torn it up any one of the times when my brain was clear and I realized, as I often did, what a bad idea it really was. When I wasn't thinking about how important it was because it was the truth. But I never got it done, and then there was the stroke.

Since then, I've tried three times that I can remember clearly, getting up out of the chair by myself the hardest part, and I've wound up on my face on the carpet every single time, never even made it into the bedroom. Stuck just lying there, staring up close at the little tufts of carpeting until Keith came in and found me. What scares me most is that I might get halfway—that I might actually have it in my hand when I fall, and that Keith will come in and find me with it, find it thrown out in front of me where it's fallen from my hand, with me able to look right at it and still not able to reach it. And that there will be no way I can stop him from reading it.

Keith's been outside a long time now. Painting trim, I think that's what he said he was going to be doing. He had his overalls on when he went out to the back room. He's always at something, as if keeping his hands busy enough will make him forget anything else that might be missing in his life. He'll come in—he cycles like a little anxious moon, orbiting in and out all day long just to make sure I'm still breathing.

Sometimes it's like my memory is as sharp as if I'm looking at the ground through binoculars, everything fine and textured, as if I could reach over and feel it with my fingers, memorable as the rasp of sandstone. Every little thing in perfect pitch and balance. When I was a girl, I had a record my father gave me, called "Music for Glass Harmonica," and I played it over and over, the kind of haunting notes that make you think of fog or something just as ethereal. It's the strangest kind of instrument, really—it can be as simple as crystal wineglasses filled with different amounts of water, and you rub your finger around the rims and each one makes its own particular note. I wonder if people aren't like that too. You see something, hear something else about it, see something else, and all of it gets put together into one unique package in your memory. And then that's the only way you can tell it. And only you can tell it, too.

I like that idea. Me and Helen Collins and even that Carter man who never came out of his house—we're all some sort of breakable crystal, each of us a glass filled to a certain point, and that's the note we sing, because we can't sing anything else. Not one of us the same, each one changing every day.

And breakable, too. Just look at me. I'm filled to just the right level, almost to the top, and I can't squeeze out a single note now. But every bit of music is still right here.

The television can be on, chattering away with one game show or another, the room almost dark, and I can be miles away, caught up in a summer from years ago, hearing the water rushing over rocks in a river, the ragged line of the treetops against the sky. Out on the juniper barrens under August sun, the air thick with the smell of the hundreds of plants you're crushing under your feet, each smell distinct and different and combining into a complex wonder so that you could just stand there for hours, just smelling it all and trying to hold it in your head, impossible to completely remember until you get a chance to smell it again.

I've seen a thousand bog flowers, each one different and special, and I'd sometimes think that there were actually so many that it would be impossible to come up with a combination of colour and shape and size and scent that didn't already exist, if you had the time to seek it out.

He'll tell you he has a heart of gold, Keith will, that he's always the first one to lend a hand. He probably believes it, too—but it's not really as simple as that. Maybe he did once, but I doubt it. He's certainly been good to me since the stroke, but whether that's anything more than a simple sense of duty, I'll never know.

He told me about the man across the street, told me in short, bare sentences as if he was trying to make sure I wasn't too upset by it all, but stuck here, it all unfolded in my head like a storybook, all of the description gone so that I had to think of it as played out by stick figures, unless he stopped long enough for me to make up my own details. And he told me that he would have done something, even if he was an old man taking off after someone much younger, except he had to be sure he would be able to care for me, and I tried to look at him as if I believed him. The truth is that he hasn't ever picked a fight that he didn't already know he would win. He'll take any kind of abuse when he knows he's outmanned. But that's a cruel thing for me to think. There's none of us out there without our own faults.

I have a clear picture of Keith hefting his old knapsack out of the trunk of the car in by the Four-Mile, an economy of movement that showed he'd done it all hundreds of times, his fishing rod already in his other hand, a hat pulled down tight so the bill covered his face. We even used to call it a rucksack then, that knapsack, made of heavy canvas that turned dark green when it got wet, and it fit there in the middle of his back like it belonged. And we'd have sandwiches in waxed paper, sandwiches I had made, crispy bacon and thin-sliced onion and butter on thick bread, and a fire for the kettle and Keith's hatchet. A bottle of rum for a belt back there in the woods.

And we'd be miles into the woods and he'd be tucking the bottle back into the knapsack and he'd look at me out of the corners of his eyes—inspecting, feral, hungry—the sort of look you recognize if you've ever seen it before. He'd kiss me then, sloppily wet and smelling rich and plummy, his clothes still full of the stale sharp of woodsmoke, and we'd duck back into the trees again, all hands and mouths and shedding clothes. The great musk of the peat and the moss rising up thick all around us so that it was like it wasn't just Keith and me there on the ground, but a great moist, hot world all around us, all hunger and desire and marvellous need. It didn't even matter to me that it was so quick.

But that was only half of it. Sometimes he'd be by the side of the river drinking thirsty great slugs of rum straight out of the bottle, his head tilted back so that I could see his Adam's apple shifting up and down with each swallow, and he'd turn a kind of mean that I don't think anyone but me ever really saw. He could pull the back of his hand across his mouth afterwards in a way that made me know he wanted to slap me with that same hand, and alone and outweighed up there in the woods, there wasn't a whole lot I could do about it except pay for whatever sin he'd decided I'd committed this time.

It was a sharp contrast, the sudden slap of flesh on flesh while all around us the world was holding its breath, and once I found myself lying face down on a small rocky beach, blood dripping slowly out of my nose, looking at the ground while an ant slowly foraged in among the river sand, and I remember thinking that there was nothing the ant would be able to do if the river rose even a few inches—a great wide watershed up there above us so that all the rivers in the basin could rise startlingly quickly—nothing the ant could do but struggle and be buoyed along by it all, and hope that it would eventually find its little feet on shore again.

The funny thing was that I always thought it had nothing to do with me at all, when he hit me, that it was really about every other single thing in the world, and it was like I was just the canvas he happened to have in front of him. I suppose it's really like that for everyone— nothing that special about me. It didn't stop, it didn't ever stop. I kept it away from Vincent as much as I could, but I think he always knew. At least, he knew something. Children are like that: they can feel the currents in a room the way eagles find thermals—their wings just happen to be in the right place, and they rise and fall accordingly. But the obvious parts, when Keith's mood went jet-black—it was like bad weather coming, even if Keith didn't realize it, and I'd try to steer it right into me when I knew the clouds were about to split, and sometimes I paid dearly for that.

Part of my job, part of my choice, I guess.

Once, we hit a dog on a dirt road heading home and we didn't even stop, a small, sandy-coloured, short-haired dog, and we left it there trying to haul itself off the road, dragging its back end like its spine had been broken. And Keith was furious, and kept talking about the dog when we pulled around the bottom of the Eight Mile pond where the beaver dam used to be, the car going too fast in the loose gravel. How it was the dog's fault for straying onto the road, the owner's fault for letting it go around untied, the highroads department for letting the alders grow in too close on the shoulders.

And "Sometimes you just get what's coming to you," and he said it through clenched teeth, because we were just above the Cataracts bridge then and sliding sideways on loose gravel towards the guardrail. He pulled the car back under control then, the old Chev we'd had for years, and we rattled across the battered concrete bridge deck, and he looked across at me for a moment as if, if he'd had a gun with him, he would have had no problem at all pressing the barrel up next to my ear and pulling the trigger.

Like staring into a shark's eye, that's the way I think about it now. Big and black and unblinking. And I still shiver. And I wonder just exactly what he knows, and when he knew it.

Some days, my memory just isn't so good. To be honest, I still wander, and sometimes things get in the wrong order in my head, so that Vincent is a little boy and then he's all grown up, like it happened in minutes, and I get distracted and lost. I think children come out as opposites of their parents—forced to be big where their parents are small, allowed to be small in the parts where their parents are too large. At least, that's the way I think about Vincent.

Sometimes, still, the words go away inside my head, and it's like I'm grabbing at unfamiliar shapes looming all around me in the dark.

Right now, I wish I could rub my hands together, just wring them to make the blood flow a little more quickly, to stop the endless buzzing. Like bees in my fingertips and there's something so familiar about that, so familiar that I should be able to figure it out—so strange and yet so familiar. Like I should remember something important about it. But it's all like fighting your way through spiderwebs, so much work just to put some order to the simplest things.

When Keith comes in, maybe we can get all of the fishing gear, jump into the car and just go. I should probably be getting ready now, get changed. I can see the closet, his clothes on the left, mine on the right, and I know exactly what I'd wear.

The little bright leaves must be out on the alders by now, the fish sharp and fast and hungry now that there are bugs around again. Out above North Harbour—there are three or four big rivers out there, the kind where there's enough water for big fish but you can still cross them in hip waders. The partridgeberries will be flowering white confetti, and there will be all those fine smells that you forget going through the winter, when the most familiar smell is the heat coming on in the radiators and sending the burning fine dust back up into the air. There's no smell like the wet smell of spring—the fullness of it, the complicated roundness of it.

Keith would say I'm just getting carried away by it all, that it's just a smell, even though I know he'd be lying about that, because I'll never forget the way he came in our first winter together and held his cloth gloves under my nose so I could smell the fir sap.

"There," he said. "There. Now you know you've smelled it, and part of you will never be able to forget." And that's in him too, the wonderful piece, and it's all part of the same man. Part and parcel.

We'll find a place there where I can sit and he can fish, and we might stay there until the sun angles down behind the hills and it all starts to feel like long sleeves of dark are running down along the arms of the valley, so that we're in evening already while the high ground is still lit bright with the sun.

And sometimes it's like something inside my head is blossoming somehow, like my head is filling up and warm. Pressure, not unpleasant or painful, but clearly there. Reminds me of waking up and finding Keith's hand weighted and warm in the middle of my back.

And sometimes I can't even think of the right words, as if they are all right there and yet don't make sense.

Sometimes things rush right at me, the way I imagine a subway train must sound, pushing all that wind and noise out in front of it. Lights seem to flicker. Or is it me? There's also a claustrophobia.

Maybe that's not the right word. There's a feeling I get, as if the world is going to come in and find me here, even that a person is going to come in here to rob the place, and I'll be unable to get out of this chair. I'll be unable to do anything, unable to stop it, unable to make a sound—and I don't even know just what it is that they'll do. Not even that they'll hurt me—I think I'm long beyond that now. I think it's that they'll look at me and know that they can safely ignore me, that then they'll go through the drawers and rob the place, knowing that I can hardly tell anyone what happened. Then everything will only be there in my head—all my little treasures gone, except for in my memory.

And if anyone has learned you can't trust that, no matter how hard you try, it's me.

There.

What was that noise? Was that Keith? I don't think so.

I don't think we should let Glenn come over anymore. I know he's your friend, I just don't think he should have the run of the place, all right? The man scares me, especially when I'm alone.

Someone in the kitchen?

I hate this, the way it runs in over me, like lying unable to move on the beach long enough for the tide to finally catch you. You know it's coming, you can even imagine the cold of the water, just then when it first touches your toes.

My breath is running away from me, and everything is like a weight. Like a . . .

Lights flickering or . . .

Is the dog barking?

I've never liked dogs.

Keith wanted one once—to hunt in the fall, he said.

A big sad-eyed beagle, the kind of dog that just eats and lies around and smells wet. Shedding and drooling and messing up everything. Waddling off to the back door when it has to go out, whining to come back in, and who would be opening the door every time?

I said no, and Keith just nodded, but I knew that somewhere in there he was adding it up, saving it, keeping a tally, another legitimate reason for those dark stares of his that clearly had to be hate.

Those stares, the ones that shake you, that make you feel small, make you want to admit to anything, just so they will stop. I think it happens with everyone you know really, really well—that sharp flash, that window into their real insides. Marks you up—changes your timbre. Silly word—*timbre*. Where did that come from?

Keith?

I wonder if he's coming in.

Coming in now. Heavy words, those: coming-in-now.

Keith, please come in now. I can never find that little light switch when I want to, can't make my fingers close around it, can't let him know out there in the shop. It's too far.

I can't reach.

I can't lift my hand.

Come in now.

Can it really be dark already?

Acknowledgements

This book is far better—and in fact even exists—because of the help and support of a number of people.

Leslie Vryenhoek, my consort and editor, devoted a considerable amount of her own valuable writing time to both editing and hearing endlessly about this book. My friend Pam Frampton also gave her editing time unstintingly.

Philip and Peter Wangersky—and Raquel Bracken—who put up with me commandeering the main computer in the house and the kitchen that computer lives in.

Publisher Patrick Crean and Senior Editor Janice Zawerbny at Thomas Allen Publishers, who saw this book from its very beginnings, drawn on a sheet of scrap paper in a Toronto restaurant, and never let their doubts show.

The Newfoundland and Labrador Arts Council and the Canada Council for the Arts, who provided much-needed financial assistance—even though it is not, actually, the book of short stories they were promised. That collection is complete, and will be next.

My employers, the St. John's Telegram and Transcontinental Media, who have been endlessly flexible with time.

Thanks to all. I hope, in the end, it's worth the investment.